SIMON451

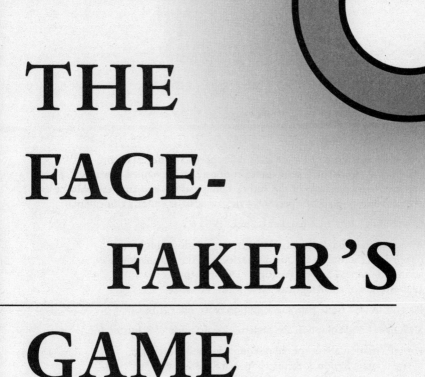

# THE FACE-FAKER'S GAME

*Chandler J. Birch*

SIMON451

New York  London  Toronto  Sydney  New Delhi

 **SIMON451**

An imprint of Simon & Schuster, Inc.
1230 Avenue of the Americas
New York, NY 10020

First Simon451 trade paperback edition November 2016

SIMON451 and colophon are trademarks of Simon & Schuster, Inc.

For information about special discounts for bulk purchases,
please contact Simon & Schuster Special Sales at 1-866-506-1949
or business@simonandschuster.com

The Simon & Schuster Speakers Bureau can bring authors to your live event.
For more information or to book an event, contact the Simon & Schuster
Speakers Bureau at 1-866-248-3049 or visit our website at www.simonspeakers.com.

Interior design by Lewelin Polanco

Manufactured in the United States of America

10 9 8 7 6 5 4 3 2 1

Library of Congress Cataloging-in-Publication Data

Names: Birch, Chandler J. author.
Title: The facefaker's game / Chandler J. Birch.
Description: First Simon451 trade paperback edition. |
New York : Simon451, 2016.
Identifiers: LCCN 2016019143 (print) | LCCN 2016027291 (ebook) |
ISBN 9781501147753 (pbk.) | ISBN 9781501111990 (E-Book)
Classification: LCC PS3602.I57 F33 2016 (print) |
LCC PS3602.I57 (ebook) | DDC 813/.6—dc23
LC record available at https://lccn.loc.gov/2016019143

ISBN 978-1-5011-4775-3
ISBN 978-1-5011-1199-0 (ebook)

To Kelsey, who fights and cares and does what's hard.
And to Mom and Dad, who believed.

# Contents

# *Prologue: A Bold Sort of Lie*

**N**IGHT had come, and the fog came with it: a thick fog that clutched and grasped at things, and would crawl down your throat and sit heavy in your belly if you let it. Lampposts presided over every street corner in this neighborhood of Teranis, though they did little good. The dark, rather than being pushed back, flowed around the gaslights like a vast river around stubborn stones. The fog swarmed up the poles and enveloped the lamps, and their pale yellow glow seemed bottled within a cage of pure glass.

A man stood beneath one of the lampposts, unperturbed by the fog and the dark and the clinging cold. He was dressed neatly, in a long black greatcoat and a tall hat, and he held a silver-handled cane. The features of his face were indistinct, blotted out by the fog and, perhaps, by something else as well, something difficult to put one's finger on. There was a sort of slipperiness to him, as if most of him could be changed at a moment's notice, and those parts that couldn't be were not important anyway.

Only two things about him were clear: his eyes, which were bright as candles, and his hands, which were gloved in black. The third finger of his right hand was missing.

He was standing quite patiently, and had been doing so for a quarter of an hour without shifting from where he stood. If someone had been watching him, they would have been impressed at how well he kept himself still, and at how little he minded being kept waiting—for he had exactly the air of a man who was being kept waiting.

In fact, someone *was* watching him, and she *was* impressed with his stillness. She had been creeping around him in a wide circle ever since he arrived, and she was beginning to wonder if, perhaps, he really had come alone. That would be convenient and more than a little unnerving, since it was entirely unprecedented. Promises, in her experience, were just a bold sort of lie.

Twenty minutes had passed since the man's arrival when she finally gave up. If he *was* a trap, and she felt more than a little certain that he was, then she wasn't clever enough to spring it safely. And if he *wasn't* a trap, then she had found something quite rare indeed.

She came up to him. At last, he moved.

"Good evening, young lady," he said pleasantly, as if they were meeting at the party of a mutual friend and he was delighted to make her acquaintance.

"Evening," she said cautiously, peering closer at him. It was odd, up this close, how his features registered in her memory; and she found herself trying to memorize the details of his face. The shape of his nose, the color of his eyes, the lines around his mouth. But then she blinked, and she could not remember any of it. When her eyes flicked open again, the face was entirely unfamiliar.

"You will exhaust yourself trying to do that," he said softly.

"Who are you?" Her hand had moved to her side. There was a pistol in the pocket of her coat, a small one that she touched rarely.

"A friend," he said.

"I know my friends' names," she said, and chided herself for being too aggressive.

He didn't seem affronted. "Perhaps it would be better to think of me, then, as someone sympathetic to your cause."

She pulled her hand away from the pistol, searching his face again without meaning to. He was like the hollow place left by a lost tooth.

"I have money."

"Please," the man said, lifting a hand. "Keep it. I have no need of money. I give this freely . . ." He peered at her. She tried to read the emotion on his face, but the slipperiness kept her from finding anything at all. "Although now that I meet you, I wonder if, perhaps, I could impose."

She tensed. This part of the conversation had a familiar rhythm to it. "What is it you want?" she asked, preparing to walk away. Or run, if she needed.

"A lock of your hair," he said. She thought he sounded like he was smiling.

The woman frowned, feeling perturbed in a way she couldn't fully articulate. She wrestled the feeling down, knowing immediately that such a reaction was silly. This was a trifle.

She ran her hands through her hair and offered him the strands that came loose. Individually they were almost colorless, bleached by the fog and the dark, but twined together they became pale red, like a line of distant fire.

He took them and, almost reverently, slipped them into the pocket of his greatcoat. He leaned forward on his cane and said, "You will find the proof in his bedside table. In the second drawer, beneath a hidden panel. Do not presume to touch the thing, or it will go poorly for you." He stood straight again, looking at her impassively. "That is all you need to know, I am sure, to reduce his little kingdom to ashes."

She looked at his face, trying one last time to see it for what it really was. "Any particular reason I should believe you?"

"None I am willing to admit." He strode into the fog, and in a moment it had blotted him out entirely, as if he had never been there at all.

# PART 1

*Ashes*

# 1 Cunning

**A**SHES was cheating, and he was pretty sure the man sitting across from him was going to figure it out soon.

"Hurry along," Ashes prodded. "Figure I've started growing whiskers waiting on you. These cobbles're cold, eh?"

The thick-faced man across from him grunted, glaring at Ashes before looking back at the cards in his hand. He was a massive individual, with biceps bigger than Ashes's thighs and a ferocious mustache. He had the look of a surly bear, and wits to match.

"Y'need some help? They've got numbers on, but by the seems of you, numbers weren't a favorite subject." Ashes flashed a vicious smile, but his eyes flicked left and right, looking for exits. The alleyway where they sat was secluded enough, but all it took was one overcurious copper wandering in and wondering if Ashes was as illegal as he looked. Going for a third hand of Rob the Moon had been imprudent, but the man kept demanding double or nothing, and Ashes couldn't stand to pass up a mark who begged to lose more money.

Besides, no one had ever called Ashes prudent.

"Something got you in a hurry?" the man grumbled, eyes still darting between the cards on the ground and those in his hand. "I didn't think bastards had much in the way of schedules."

"I dun't figure what me schedule's got to do with the price of whores in Yson," Ashes snapped. "Maybe I've an invitation to tea with the Queens so's I can woo their princess, or a powerful need to move me bowels sometime before me balls drop. Care to move along a mite?"

Ashes could have sworn the man let out a low growl. It would have been amusing except for his size. Ashes developed a sudden, acute awareness of how well his own skull would fit inside the man's palm.

"Fine," the man said, slapping a card against the cobbles. "Face of Judgment, red. Unless you've some manner of magic up your sleeve, I've just won."

Ashes smirked. "Funny you ought to say that." He laid his card down atop the man's, moving with exaggerated carefulness. The Face of Cunning in black. "I've got all manner of magics up me sleeves, by the seems." Ashes spread his hands and screwed his face into mock amazement. "Would you look at it—that'll be thirty pence to me, I think? I'm a generous sort, so I figure I'll count 'em. Wouldn't want you taking off your shoes just to count some bastard's money."

The man's eyes bulged at the sight of Ashes's card. "That's impossible," he muttered, looking at Ashes's face, at the cards, and finally at his own hand. "That's . . ." He looked again, intently now. Ashes imagined he could hear gears twisting in his head, creaking a protest at being called on to move.

"*Impossible*, eh, I heard you. Care to skip to where you open up that purse of yours and acquaint me with my—?"

Ashes didn't even have time to take a breath before the fellow's hand caught him in the throat. A moment later the wall smashed into Ashes's head. His feet were off the ground, and the world had gone woozy and red.

"You *cheated* me," the man said. His voice went up just a little, making it sound almost like a question.

"I'm sure I dunno wha—guh—"

"You gods-damned little *liar!*"

"Now, now," Ashes gasped out, scrabbling with one hand at the man's arm. His efforts there proved fruitless. "Mustn't—get—rowdy—" His feet were level with the man's crotch; Ashes aimed a desperate kick. The man redirected it deftly, tilting his hips to throw Ashes's aim and slamming the boy against the wall again for good measure. Ashes's vision started cartwheeling.

"I ought to kill you," the brute snarled.

"Seeing as I won, maybe y'ought to *pay* me, yeh streperous miser," Ashes spat, and was rewarded with another universe-shattering choke. Something in the back of his mind muttered that this had been a poor plan.

"I'll not throw you to the sewers. Consider yourself paid." The man drove his fist into Ashes's belly, crushing out what little air the boy had left. The brute released his grip, letting Ashes fall in a heap on the cobbles. He heard, as though from far away, the man's footsteps exiting the alleyway.

Ashes coughed a bloody trail of spittle. He grimaced, blinked twice. His vision had gone swimmy, and his thoughts seemed wrapped in muck, but there would be time to catalogue his wounds later. He set grimly to picking up the cards, making certain that all fifty-seven were accounted for and hoping his counting was not impeded by the ringing in his skull.

His head spun of its own accord once or twice more, and his knees smarted abominably, but even so, when Ashes stood and wobbled toward the alley's end, he did so with a faint smile. He tapped the waistband of his trousers, making certain the brute's wallet hadn't fallen out. Still there, and it was fat enough to make Ashes's grin even wider.

He'd chosen a good mark: smart enough to recognize cheating, eventually, and too stupid to notice Ashes's hand inside his jacket. It had cost some bruises, certainly, but nothing came for free.

The boy paused before he exited, forcing his head to stop spinning. Stumbling through Lyonshire like a drunk was a sure way to get himself noticed, and *noticed* would be bad with a Denizen's wallet tucked in his pants and no iron name on his person. He tugged his ratty collar up against his neck, hiding what he could of the livid hand-marks on his throat. He shifted his posture, his face, his attitude, and in the blink of an eye he seemed almost an entirely different person. An apprentice running errands for his master, perhaps, or one of Lyonshire-Low's "accidental" children lost on the way home.

But certainly, *certainly* not one of Burroughside's sneak-thieving gutter-rats. No, sir, not him. He was totally drab; that was the key. Invisibility was just being what people saw every day.

With his pretending fixed firmly in his mind, Ashes stepped onto Argent Street. The crowd was much thinner than he'd expected: there were only a couple dozen people in eyeshot. How long had he been in that alley? He checked the sky, and cursed inwardly as he marked the sun. Dusk was an hour away, maybe less. That wasn't anything *like* enough time.

He sprinted down Argent Street, darting around gawking shoppers and pushy merchants. Sure-footed and confident, he slipped around the lowlier Denizens—anyone who looked dreary enough to work in a factory, or whose clothing only cost a week's wages instead of a month's—and whenever he spotted colorful tentlike dresses or long coattails, he slowed to a respectful walk, gave the wealthy Denizen a five-foot berth, and kept his eyes down. He drew stares once or twice, but no cries of alarm and no calls for police. That was all he needed.

At Strave Avenue he crossed to Wending Road, slithered through the gaps in the fence around Harrod Park, then leapt onto the back of a south-going carriage, and managed to go undetected for fully two minutes before the driver cracked his whip at Ashes's fingers.

In merely fifteen minutes, he crossed out of Lyonshire's posh territory and into Lyonshire-Low. He let out a relaxed breath as he crossed the border. Here there were no coppers prowling the streets, no Denizens to irritate, and—significantly—no Burroughsiders watching him as he scuttled behind a building and began to count his day's take.

*Twenty-six . . . twenty-seven . . . Face of Cunning.* He counted again.

The second count came out the same, and he had to keep himself from shouting with triumph. Twenty-eight crescents. Bless the man who'd made money from paper! Denizens carried whole fortunes now and didn't even notice when the weight disappeared!

He forced himself to calm down, but it was hard. This would buy him time and food, and he could always do with more of both. He tugged five of the notes out and placed them strategically about his person, then stuffed the wallet through a carefully torn stitch under the arm of his too-large coat. Nestled there, it would be invisible even to Burroughside's numerous and talented pickpockets. He was liked well enough in Burroughside, but a lumin and eight would tempt anybody, and secrecy guarded better than a sharp knife.

## 2     *Kindness*

**B**ARRISTER'S coffee-house stood, technically, in Lyonshire, which was to say that it stood on the right side of the district boundary for police to come if Barrister called for them. Even so, Barrister saw few upstanding Denizens in the course of his business day. His clientele were dirty folks who walked in with oversized clothes and undersized moral compunctions, who could only afford cheap stuff and were unlikely to complain (and might, in fact, celebrate their good fortune) if they found stray rat tails in their soup.

The coffee-house was nearly empty when Ashes entered. Some of its occupants he recognized: Slippery Rafe and Iames the Fool muttering in hushed tones in a corner, and Quentin Cobb at the bar, and grizzly old Owan Meek sucking down alcohol that smelled strong enough to melt iron. None acknowledged Ashes except Barrister, whose eyes flicked to him at the sound of the door opening; immediately the man's mouth went thin.

"You'd better have something better for me than that long face, boy," he said, pointing a dirty mug at him, "or you're wasting your breath and my time."

Ashes pulled out a crescent and placed it on the bar. "Not properly religious of you, Barry. Where's your Ivorish charity?"

"Buried somewhere underneath my Ivorish greed, more than likely." Barrister cocked an eyebrow at the crescent. "Besides, if that's real enough to pay for your food, you've got more than your fair share of charity for today. Your benefactor know you have that?"

Ashes smirked. "By now? Eh, I reckon he does."

"He give you that red necklace as well?"

Ashes tugged his collar up to hide the bruises. "Generous bloke."

Barrister picked up the crescent-note, testing its texture with his fingers. "You spending all this at once?"

Ashes nodded. "Chicken and bread. Put the change on something that'll keep."

Barrister nodded and disappeared into the back of the coffeehouse. He came out a minute later with a loaf of bread, into which a dry breast of chicken had been stuffed, and hearty goods wrapped in newspaper. Ashes picked up the food almost before it was out of Barrister's hands, tore a bite out of the bread, and reveled in it. Not more than two days old, he'd bet anything. It was glorious—far better than the scraps he'd survived on since he left his old crew. It felt as if he were tasting real food for the first time.

He was so absorbed that he didn't turn when the door banged open again. He would have continued in blissful ignorance if not for Barrister.

"Make certain your boy's careful with that door, Saintly," the man said sternly. "I've only the one."

The back of Ashes's neck tingled. He swallowed his last bite too quickly, slipped the food inside his coat, and slid off the stool, keeping his eyes down—

"So sorry about that, Mr. Barrister, sir," came the reply. It was a smooth voice, full of smiling. "He'll not do it again, sir, I'm certain of it." A pause for breath, and then, in tones of delight: "Surely that won't be you sneaking away from me, aha, Ashes?"

The bottom dropped out of Ashes's stomach. There wasn't any point in pretending, and he couldn't run while Saintly's boys were standing at the door. He bottled his fear and curled his lips into something faintly resembling a smile before he turned.

Saintly Francis was one of Burroughside's great mysteries. The district was littered with the diseased and dying, and folk who had lost limbs or eyes or noses to the Gleaming Law. Many younger children were strategically mutilated, the better to beg from sympathetic Denizens. Saintly, though, was as beautiful a boy as could be found in Teranis, with dark, curly hair and wide eyes that oozed innocence. Somewhere near fifteen, he was a couple years older than Ashes, and the crewleader of the Broken Boys, one of Burroughside's most fearsome gangs. Right now, he was smiling, and that made Ashes's guts twist.

"What a fancy thing, aha, seeing you here," Saintly said, approaching. The room seemed to reorient as he walked, making certain that its center was always right where he stood. Ashes could feel people glancing in their direction, eyes drawn by Saintly's irrepressible gravity. "How've you been?"

Ashes looked at the door, at the three boys Saintly had brought. They'd want food; if he left now, he could get away while they were eating. "Bit busy, Saints. Probably ought to run."

"Nonsense!" Saintly slapped him on the shoulder, and his hand stayed there. "Been so long, Ashes. Surely we ought to catch up. It's been months. Too long, Ashes." Their eyes met. The look in Saintly's face was catlike, predatory.

Ashes smiled, and it came out braver than he felt. "I'm afraid it's like to stay too long." He stepped out from under Saintly's hand. "I've got business—"

"So've I, mate." Saintly slid in front of him. His eyes were dark now, his voice low enough that not even Barrister would hear it. "We're due for a conversation about monsters, you and me. Why don't we take a walk? Chat about things?"

*Where nobody else'll see* hung unspoken on the end of his sentence. Ashes felt his hands start quivering and couldn't force them to stop.

"I don't think he wants to do that, Francis," someone said. Saintly and Ashes both jerked, as if woken from sleep. Iames the Fool had Saintly by the shoulder; Slippery Rafe stood beside him. Both were staring fixedly at Saintly. Rafe's fists were loosely curled.

For a fragile moment, Ashes feared Saintly would make a fight of it. It was four against three, in Saintly's favor, but Iames and Rafe were both sixteen and wiry. They belonged to the Motleys—Iames, in fact, was its crewleader—and Motleys were not known for fighting fair. They could use anything as weaponry, and both were in grasping distance of Saintly's arms . . .

Ashes imagined he saw the same thoughts go through Saintly's head, quick as winking, and just like that his eyes were clear again. "Aha, hello, Iames," he said. "Rafe. Such a pleasure to be acquainting with you again. You can take your hands off, lads, aha." He turned and grinned at them. "Just wanted for a bit of catching up, you know." He looked at Ashes, his stare glassy and calm. "We'll have to talk some other time."

He swept out of the shop without another word. Barrister followed the boy with his eyes, then scoffed as the door closed. "Without even buying anything. By the Faces . . ."

"Bastard," Iames muttered. "You all right, Ashes? He didn't gut you or nothing while our eyes was away?"

"Neh," Ashes said, watching the Broken Boys as they made their way back toward Burroughside. He edged toward the door. Now was the time to leave, while Saintly was still worried about the Motleys at his back. He could circle around Barrister's, take the long way home—

Iames put a hand on Ashes's shoulder and looked him in the eyes. "You shouldn't be going out there," he said sincerely. "Give it a while. Rafe and I'll leave in a bit. We can walk with you, keep the whorestain away."

Slippery Rafe nodded. "We've got an open space with the Motleys, if you need somewhere to doss."

Ashes smiled weakly and shook his head. "Thanks. I got a place already. Best be getting to it." He was not the sort of person to belong to a crew, not these days.

"You can't dodge Saintly forever," Iames whispered. "Mark me."

"Don't need to dodge him forever," Ashes muttered. "Just till solstice."

Iames frowned as he processed the implication, then frowned deeper when he understood. "Don't count on the Tithe. I've seen kids like you hope for it, and it never turns well. You're too young for the Lass. If she's your best hope, you're better off in the sewers."

Ashes gave a low laugh to hide his shuddering. "Me best hope ain't Bonnie the Lass, Iames. It's me."

He hurried outside, walking the opposite direction from Saintly and his Broken Boys. He could take a circuitous route back home, and even Saintly wouldn't be mad enough to follow him after dark. Even so, he didn't breathe easy until he felt sure that none of the Broken Boys had followed him.

The shift from Lyonshire-Low to Burroughside was not a subtle one. The cobbled streets ended as if they'd been chopped off with an axe, and then sewn awkwardly together with streets composed mostly of mud and excrement and broken rocks. One moment his shoes were on worked stone, and the next they sank into a thin but perpetual veneer of stinking muck. He could smell the shift in the air, too, as all the pleasant scents of a thriving district were subsumed by the odors of a dying one: vomit blended with cheap beer, stale waste, and rot nearly as old as the street itself.

Burroughside. Home, or what passed for it.

He picked his way more carefully through these streets, on guard against Broken Boys and other crews. Seeing Saintly had rattled him more than he would care to admit. Hardly a year ago, they had been friends. Before Saintly put a red smile across Mari's throat and took the Broken Boys for himself.

Mari had never seen it coming, but Ashes should have. He'd been Saintly's shadow for months before Saintly put the knife to their crewleader. Saintly had been nervous and cagey in the days leading up to it, enough that Ashes should have sensed something off. Ashes had told no one, and Mari paid for his stupidity.

A familiar, muttering voice pulled him away from the dark thoughts. Around the corner he found Ben Roamer, hugging himself and whispering urgently to a blank wall. Ben was one of a paltry few Burroughsiders who could honestly claim to be older than fifty—though it was almost always guesswork, as birthdays, to the gutter-rats, were profoundly useless. His beard was equal parts dirt and hair and perpetually flecked with spittle. He was also mad as a boiled owl.

Ashes made to walk around the man, but Ben must have heard him. The old fellow spun on his heel, and his eyes locked on Ashes. "Eshes," he muttered. "Know ennethin bout kitchin' kits?"

"Ho, Ben," Ashes said. The tension in his body began to dissipate. In truth, Roamer did not make him half as nervous as some Burroughsiders; mad as he was, the old man had been harmless as long as Ashes had known him. "What's on?"

"Wanna kitch a kit," he said urgently. "Gots to kitch a kit. Know ennethin bout kitchin' kits?"

"Can't say as I've caught many. Probably the trick is just being faster than them, right?"

Ben shook his head and spat on the ground. "Kent do that. Kent do that. Kits is too—too—" He stabbed angrily at his temple. "Kent kitch 'em that way. Too *sneaky*."

"Sorry to hear that, Ben." Ashes grinned uneasily, preparing to step around the old man. Ben seemed a little more off-balance than usual today.

"Piddlin' thinks from all of you," Ben murmured furiously, and threw up his hands. "She ent help much et all, neither. How your sort goen' to survive, ye kent kitch kits?"

"She? She who?"

Ben jerked his head toward the lump of mud on the ground, and it stirred. Ashes's eyes widened. It was a girl, young and small and frail, with lank hair hanging in her face. She was trembling—a cold breeze had brushed through, and the girl's shift looked thinner than skin.

"Face of Kindness, Ben!" Ashes said, dropping to his knees next to the girl. "Yammering about catching cats! How long has she been here?" He put one hand near her face, wary in case she tried to attack. The girl didn't move, didn't stir—didn't recognize his presence at all.

"Gots to kitch a kit," Ben said under his breath, turning away from them both. "Gots to kitch a kit."

Ashes pushed the hair out of the girl's face and whispered a curse. Her eyes were blank as slate, and dark.

A *rasa*. Had to be.

"Can you talk?" he asked in a low voice. "You've got— D'you have a name? I'm Ashes. Can you talk?"

There was a spark behind her eyes at the words, though it seemed distant and dim. Her cheeks were terribly pale, but her hair wasn't near as matted as he would have expected. She hadn't been here long, then—this might be her first night in Teranis, even. He pulled a bit of bread out of his coat, held it in front of her mouth. Her head tilted forward mechanically, and she took it from his hand with her teeth.

She could move, at least, and there was a bit of life inside her. Ashes looked at the sky. Violet and crimson coated the western clouds, but the sun itself wasn't visible any longer. The Ravagers would be out soon. Did this girl even know what they were?

The girl trembled again, an all-over shake that couldn't have been just from cold. "Let's call you Jennie," Ashes whispered. "Jennie Trembly. How's that?" Naming her was practically a reflex. *Rasa* needed names; it gave their minds something to hold on to.

"Y'know how you kitch a kit?"

"Go home, Ben," Ashes said. "Dark's coming. Y'hear me? *Dark's coming.* There'll be Ravagers soon. Find somewhere safe."

"Gots to be *clever*," Ben said, stabbing a finger at his temple again. "Gots to *think* like 'em. Give 'em a clever trap."

Ashes took the girl by the shoulders, guiding her gently to her feet. "Whatever you say." He wrapped his coat around the girl, taking care not to move too quickly. She would spook easily. "Go *home*, Ben."

"Clever traps," Ben said again, but he turned west, presumably toward whatever stretch of covered space he called home. "Make 'em hard to get to, is all. Hard to get to the trap, they'll climb up jessa get inside it. Straightaway. *Straight*away."

The girl followed Ashes's lead, moving clumsily on bare feet. She walked as if she had forgotten how to do it. And, Ashes thought, it was very possible she had.

"You'll be all right," he said. "You'll be all right. We'll get you somewhere safe."

● ● ●

*Evening was settling on* Teranis like scattered rain by the time he made it to Batty Annie's house. It came in droplets first, dripping into the pools of shadow until they were swollen near to bursting. Finally, the dams burst, and the shadows connected and spread until they filled every corner. Not twenty minutes after sunset, the streets were soaked in black, looking as if they had always been dark, and only pretended to be lit during the day.

Ashes's throat tightened as he pounded on Batty Annie's door. He shivered, half because of the chill he felt without his coat and half because of how quickly it had gotten dark. He'd expected the evening gray to last just a little longer, and he'd expected the girl to move just a little faster. Both expectations had turned out to be wrong, and now all he could do was hope he'd be quick enough.

He slammed his fist against the door again and shouted, "Open the bloody door!"

Half a moment later the door was open, and Batty Annie was glaring imperiously down at him.

"What the *hell* do you want, facefaker?"

It was said that a witch lived at the end of every street in Teranis; if that was so, then Batty Annie was the witch of Bells Street. She was older than anyone Ashes had ever met or seen or even heard of, and sometimes he could swear she creaked when she walked. He didn't know if she could summon bolts of flame and shadow, but she lived in Burroughside without paying a slim penny to Mr. Ragged, and that counted for a lot.

Ashes presented the girl for Annie's inspection. "Her, ma'am," he said quickly, throwing glances over his shoulder. "She needs a place to stay. I found her—"

Annie's bony fingers snatched Ashes's chin, forcing him to look her full in the face. It was like meeting the eyes of a tiger. "She carrying your seed, boy? She gonna be heavy with your get come Festivale?"

"What? No!" Ashes felt the blood drain out of his face. "No. Nothing like that."

She stared at him fiercely, then released her grip. "You're telling the truth. Rare for one of yours."

"I don't lie to folks that's smarter than me."

"Oh, I'll just bet you don't."

"Please, Annie—I found her out near Barrister's. She can't speak a word, she dun't know her name, barely moves when you give her food—she's *rasa*. I'm sure of it."

"You would be." Annie's gaze had shifted now to the girl, and she bent to give a more detailed inspection. "Eh. Empty as a corn-husk, her. How long's she been in the city?"

"Not long, I think."

"Any name?"

"She dun't remember. Or if she does she dun't remember how to speak it. She's Jennie Trembly for the moment."

Annie's hard stare seemed to grow even harder. "And what would you have me do with her?"

Ashes paled. "I—I thought you might take her in. You've done that before, sometimes. Haven't you? I'd heard that Hennah Verston took up with you after—"

"I'm no charity-house, boy, nor'm I a church," she said. "If this girl's to stay, and if she's to stay *alive*, then I'll need somebody to pay her way. There's nothing that comes free."

Ashes looked at her helplessly. "How much?"

"Six crescents for the night," she said flatly. "And you'll be sleeping in separate rooms and *you* will be out by morning."

Ashes shook his head. "Just for her, Annie, and I want her safe a good long while."

"You some kind of stupid, boy?" Annie eyed him. "Ravagers won't care naught for that tongue of yours."

"Hence I got no time to barter," Ashes snapped. "Just for her."

"Sun's down—"

"Just. Her."

"A lumin and three, then," she said.

Everything left in the Ivorish man's wallet, not counting the notes Ashes had hidden. Nearly everything he'd earned today. He'd need to go out and beg or thieve tomorrow if he was to make enough for his tax, and he would need to do it away from Lyonshire.

He looked at the girl, pallid and frail and helpless. She was as bad a *rasa* as he'd ever seen: no memory of her name, of where she came from. And no one to take care of her. He knew that feeling far better than most—three years ago, he hadn't been so different.

He took the coat off her shoulders and pulled out the Denizen's wallet.

"It's all in there," he said.

Annie smiled a cold smile as she took his money. "It's been a pleasure doing business with you, boy." She tugged the *rasa* girl gently past her door. "I'll be sure to keep her safe."

"One other thing," Ashes said, speaking before he could think better of the idea. The old woman glared at him, as if shocked that he would dare speak further. "Don't let Mr. Ragged know she's here. He'd sell her off to the Silken, or someone. Just—just don't let that happen."

She regarded him with a chilly blankness that made his insides squirm. "If I do?"

"Nothing I can do to punish you, Annie, even if I wanted to try," Ashes said honestly. "But I'm the one as brought her here, and I'm the one paying her dues to you. Once she's walking and she knows her words and her name, you find some place for her. Far away from Mr. Ragged. That's all I'm asking."

Annie huffed. "Compelling," she said, with not one ounce of sincerity. "But you've done a good thing tonight, boy, so I'll let you in on my secret." She leaned toward him and whispered, "I wouldn't sell that child to Mr. Ragged for all the money in the world, sure as the drift of the moon. I don't sell that Ivorish-addled jackass *anything*. Nor'm I going to tell him the girl's here. That's because I do what I do." She lowered her face so her frightening eyes were on the same level as his. "And *no one else* tells me what I do."

Ashes swallowed and nodded. "Yes'm," he said, shrugging into his coat.

"Along with you," she said, turning smartly and retreating into the house. "Faces help you, if they can."

Ashes nodded fervently and turned to go, but the *rasa* girl caught his arm. Her eyes, brighter than before, were fixed on him. She reached inside the pocket of her shift and pulled out the tattered remains of a handkerchief, blue as an evening sky. Wordlessly, she took his hand and looped the cloth around his wrist. She tied it solemnly, brow furrowed in deep concentration.

He peered at her, looking for some explanation. "Thanks," he said.

She said nothing, but her eyes had turned bright and lively.

Annie pulled the girl past the threshold. "Along with you, then," the old woman said, closing the door.

The moon was coming up. *Time to be gone*, he thought.

He ran.

# 3 Monsters

NIGHT came. In the districts near the river, it came with fog. In Burroughside it brought silence.

The streets were deserted, picked clean of everything valuable. There were no police to coarsen the quiet with their footsteps and no young lovers to sweeten it with whispers. There were no scurrying thieves out in the dark; the second-story boys had long since departed for other districts, and would not return until well after sunup. Burroughside had all the stillness and pallor of a corpse.

It was only playing dead, of course. Its silence was an intentional, held-breath quiet. Behind tightly fastened doors, beneath false floorboards, nestled in hideaways too high to reach, the gutter-folk clutched whatever weapons they could find and waited for morning. Very few of them slept. Folk said you were safe behind a threshold, but no one was stupid enough to trust that.

An outsider might be tempted to think the makeshift blades

were defenses, and would not notice how few of the gutter-folk carried cudgels or coshes. An outsider would not think how the broken-glass knives might be used if there were no hope for survival.

The moon had hardly risen when the howls began.

● ● ●

*Ashes froze and felt* his guts turn to water. A prayer to the Face of Cunning tumbled out of his mouth, and another one to the Face of Kindness followed, for all the good it would do. The Faces had no power over Ravagers.

The howl had come from the south. That might have given him hope, but an answering cry rang out from the north, and another from the east.

Still fifteen minutes from home at least. He could try his luck banging on doors, but there wasn't a Burroughsider living who'd open their door after nightfall. No hiding places nearby, either.

He could feel his heartbeat in his ears.

More Ravager cries broke out, coming from every direction, wild and hungry. Hunting howls.

Ashes's hands started to shake, and he clenched his fists to stop them. Fear would do him no good here. He slipped off the main road and slid inside the scattered patches of deep darkness, and tried not to think what would happen if they found him.

He kept moving toward home, careful and slow now, stepping where the mud wouldn't suck on his shoes and his skin wouldn't flash in the moonlight. He had to be silent now. Silent and invisible.

Sloshing footsteps from down the street. He pressed himself against a wall and held his breath.

Three figures loped into sight, backs hunched, heads thrust forward. Their naked skin was striped with scars, mottled with rust-colored blood.

He caught their scent, foul and rotted, on the wind; his stomach twisted.

The Ravagers would have looked human, almost. Their *shape* was human; one even looked female. But their eyes were wide and bloodshot; they moved like wolves. Raw red sores dotted their bodies. One let his mouth hang open, revealing something glittery inside—his teeth had been replaced with shards of glass.

Ashes heard a rumbling growl. Another Ravager appeared at the other end of the street, twice the size of the others, powerfully built, chest crisscrossed with puckered scars. Blood dribbled from his mouth, staining his patchwork beard. He looked vicious and formidable until he moved, and Ashes saw he was favoring one leg.

The other Ravagers saw it, too. There was not a moment of hesitation; all three dashed forward. The large Ravager stumbled backward, tried to run, but they were too quick. The female caught his leg in her teeth and jerked her head, ripping a bite out of his calf.

The other two landed on him together. They underestimated the brute; he grasped one by the arm and flung it headfirst into a wall, so hard Ashes heard its skull crack. The brute grasped for the next, but not quickly enough. The glass-toothed male grabbed the brute's head with both hands and wrenched it savagely to one side. Ashes flinched, though the snap was almost inaudible.

The feeding took far longer than the fight. Wet, sloppy noises filled the street as the Ravagers disemboweled their kill, piece by piece by piece. The third pack member lay still by the wall, blood pooling around him, until the other two finished with the brute, and moved to their former comrade.

Minutes crawled by. Finally the noises stopped. Sated, the two Ravagers clambered to their full height and retreated back the way they'd come.

Ashes's muscles ached. He let out a breath.

The glass-toothed Ravager stopped, turned. His nose flared. Ashes pulled his coat tighter, suddenly aware of the meat hidden in it.

The female stopped to watch as the male crept nearer to Ashes. The male's lips curled back over ruined teeth.

Ashes didn't dare move; the Ravager would hear him. So he held perfectly still and pretended with all his might that he was invisible. He closed his eyes, not wanting the whites of them to give him away.

He heard another step. The Ravager's stench filled his nose, a stink of rancid meat and infection. Ashes scrunched his eyes tighter. *I'm not here.*

Every muscle in his body clenched. A warm, foul wind brushed across his face.

There was a scream in the distance, wordless but human. Ashes heard the Ravager grunt, then hurried footsteps. When Ashes opened his eyes, the monsters were gone.

When his knees were not shaking, he continued creeping toward home. He had gone half a mile before the screams stopped.

●●●

*The Fortress was a* slipshod building. Five stories tall and slender as a maiden, it looked ready to fall over if it could ever find a reason. It shook in high winds, couldn't keep out rain or snow, and was cold as a witch's heart. Someday he would leave it, or it would crumble to ruins while he was asleep. For now it was home.

He had named it the Fortress to be funny, and realized sometime afterward that no one larger than him could possibly enter. The building's innards were mostly burned away except for one floor at the very top, which could only be reached by the rickety iron staircase welded to the outside wall. The staircase didn't touch the ground, but a ladder hung from the bottom of it, nearly ten feet off the surface, and there was a window just below to serve as a jumping-off point.

Ashes glanced left and right, wary in case a Ravager tried to creep up on him. He saw nothing, and so took a running start and jumped, first to the window and then the ladder, catching its lowest rung with the tips of his fingers. Pushing against the wall with his feet, he worked his way up, and made the top in a matter of moments. He caught his breath there, pulling the ladder onto the staircase to prevent followers.

He ascended the stairs, and near the top he got on his belly and crawled through a slim gap in the wall. The fit was uncomfortably tight. On the other side was another flight of stairs, this one missing its bottom half. The top half still held weight, though it regularly made vague threats to collapse on itself.

The room on the highest floor was small, and latticed by shafts of moonlight that slipped through the empty places where brick and mortar ought to have been. It was made even smaller by the eclectic junk inside: rags and bits of string, bottles with the ends broken off, castoff Ivory handkerchiefs too wretched to be sold to the ragmen, and—strangest of all—nearly two dozen books. Books of all sizes and types, on all subjects, some with original covers and others swaddled in cloth to keep the paper dry and sorted. Each and all were stacked with precise care, largest to smallest, in five short towers. Not one corner was out of place.

Barely one Burroughsider in twenty could read. Even those who had their letters weren't likely to own books, not for very long: paper made good kindling in wintertime. A collection this size, so rigorously tended, would have drawn a great deal of notice.

"Blimey," he said softly. "Blimey?"

There was a soft rustling, and a silhouetted head appeared behind the farthest tower of books. Its hair stuck out at odd angles, making the head seem misshapen and lumpy—or, rather, more misshapen and lumpy than it already was.

"Ashes!" the boy exclaimed, and scurried out from behind the books. "You're alive!"

The streaks of moonlight revealed him in greater detail: slender-shouldered, shorter than Ashes. Probably younger, too, but it was difficult to be certain of anything where Blimey's face was concerned. It had the usual details—nose, eyes, mouth—and they were all in their standard positions, but they didn't seem to belong on a face, and certainly not all together.

His nose was large and crooked, as if it had broken and never quite healed. The whites of his eyes were slightly yellowed, his irises mismatched: one blue and the other green. A long, pink scar stretched from his mouth to one oversized ear, reigning over a spiderweb of white scars scattered across his face. A noticeable lump marred his temple, though it lay buried beneath unkempt hair.

"Got you supper," Ashes said, producing the chicken-stuffed bread from his coat. "Bread and meat today. Sorry I'm so late."

Blimey didn't seem to notice the food. "I heard howls—"

"Weren't nothing," Ashes said, contorting his lips into a confident smile. "Got caught up doing things, is all. They can't catch me. I'm too quick."

Blimey's mouth thinned, just a little, but he took the half-loaf that Ashes offered. "What were you doing?"

"Had a bit of a run-in with a copper," Ashes said, keeping his voice perfectly level.

The blood drained out of Blimey's face. "Why? Did he ask— What did you do?"

Ashes shrugged. "Nowt he could prove."

The lie, though necessary, niggled at him. Blimey claimed he was *rasa*, and that he'd received his unusual name from the first person he met in Teranis. But something about the claim had always seemed off to Ashes; Blimey *knew* things. Things about Teranis, about Ivories, about Yson's exports and Boreas's colleges and the countries outside the city. He could read and do sums.

A real *rasa* was lucky to remember their own name.

Ashes had never pressed him about it. Everyone had the right to their secrets. Besides, whatever secret Blimey was keeping, it had to be terrible indeed if he would rather be *rasa*.

Blimey eyed him skeptically. "A copper held you up and you *didn't* get tossed in the Basty?"

"I'm a quick talker." His confident smile came more naturally this time. "You know me. Here, now, I brought you something."

"Apart from supper and mendacities about pliable policemen?" Blimey asked innocently.

"What's mendacities?"

Blimey blinked. "Stories."

"Men*da*cities." The word had a unique shape, a fancy-sounding sneer inside it. Ashes could put that to good use. "That's Ivorish?"

"Lyonshire and Yson, mostly."

Ashes mouthed it to himself a few more times, getting a feel for where it could fit in his sentences. "You got more words for me?"

A grin twisted onto Blimey's face as he hefted his book. Of everything Ashes had ever scrounged, bought, or stolen, this was Blimey's prize possession. Within it were more words than either of the boys could readily count, each followed by detailed definitions. Blimey spent much of his time sifting through it, memorizing new Ivorish words to teach to Ashes. On days when Blimey tired of new words, which were rare indeed, he read from a slimmer book Ashes had found outside a window in Glades. In it were all the rules for proper Ivorish speaking. They were far more numerous than Ashes could have guessed; the print was tiny. Blimey had read through it a dozen times.

"I used one of yours today," Ashes said proudly. "*Streperous*. For being loud and nasty, right?"

One corner of Blimey's mouth turned down. "*Ob*streperous?"

"Right, yeah. That one."

"You said it 'streperous'?"

"So what if I did?"

"It's nothing. It's just wrong, is all. Probably whoever heard you say it thought you were stupid, though."

Ashes prickled. "I ain't stupid," he said.

"Say it in Ivorish, Ashes. We have to practice."

He blew out a breath. "I *am not* stupid."

"There you are. And I know you're not stupid. Just—if you muck it, somebody *will* notice. And the coppers won't take kindly to you twice."

He was right. The Ivorish language was a world unto itself, nowhere near as easy as imitating accents. It was complicated by the legions of arbitrary rules that Denizens, apparently, understood from the womb. Speaking it properly was like walking through Boreas Gutters on a moonless night: the roads were never where they ought to be, and a single misstep could be ruinous. In its own way, pretending to be Ivorish was near as perilous as sewer-scouring.

He had to be perfect. At the end of the year, Bonnie the Lass—queen of Teranis crime—would come to Burroughside to take her Tithe from Mr. Ragged, and Ashes would catch her eye. He had to. Winter was approaching, and if things didn't change soon, he and Blimey would starve or freeze to death.

"Sorry. S'been a . . . long day." He realized he was rubbing his neck, and dropped his hand. It was, fortunately, too dark for Blimey to see the bruises. "What're your other words?"

Blimey's gargoyle-smile returned, and he began to recite them, referring only occasionally to the book in his lap. Ashes paid dutiful attention, memorizing what he could and keeping himself from looking bored or tired. Finding new words was all Blimey had; he hadn't set foot outside the Fortress in almost a year. Yet another necessary sacrifice, because, as far as Mr. Ragged knew, Blimey was dead. Ragged would be displeased to learn otherwise.

He reached the end of his list and beamed at Ashes. "Do you like them?"

"I do," Ashes said, patching the smile on again.

"Which was your favorite?"

Ashes chewed his tongue before saying, carefully, "Pussymouse."

Blimey stared for several seconds before he said, "Pu—pusillanimous, Ashes. Pusillanimous. Cowardly."

"That one," Ashes said. "I like it. Good word to call people when you're insulting them and wanna show you're smarter, innit?"

Blimey beamed. "It is good for that."

"Good words, Blimey." He smiled winningly. "You'll get us out of here yet."

He stretched out on the cold floor and closed his eyes. Faces, he was ready to sleep.

He heard Blimey fidgeting. Ashes propped himself up on his elbows. "What's it?"

"You said you had something for me," Blimey said.

"Oh! You're quite right I do," Ashes said. He undid the tatty handkerchief around his wrist. "I thought you might could use it for keeping some of your books together. Some were falling apart, you said."

Blimey took the handkerchief with unmasked delight. "This'll be right helpful, Ashes. Thank you. Where'd you get it?"

"A princess gave me it," Ashes replied smoothly. "Leastwise I figure she's a princess, visiting from someplace. She didn't know the city to save her life, and some foul old man kept babbling at her, so I pulled her away and pointed her off toward Balal. She gave me that to show her gratitude."

Blimey's mouth quirked. "A princess's favor, eh?"

"I figure as much," Ashes said, sensing Blimey's skepticism. "Or might've been she were a witch in training. Maybe."

"Witches don't need any training," he said. "They've got magics from their first breath, Ashes. Everyone knows that."

Ashes smiled weakly. Blimey's books had given him a somewhat skewed idea of how much everyone knew. "A princess, then."

"Wish I could've seen her."

Ashes's stomach clenched as if he were hanging over a chasm. "Better that you stay here, mate," Ashes said. "I need you here."

"Maybe you could talk again," Blimey said. "With—him."

Ashes held his breath. As far as Blimey knew, Mr. Ragged had agreed to repeal the price on Blimey's head on the condition that he never be seen in Burroughside again. Ashes let Blimey go on believing it; better that than the messy truth of how Ashes had convinced Ragged that Blimey was dead. The details would only give him nightmares.

"I can't convince him no further," Ashes said firmly. "You got to stay here until we find some other place, Blimes. Somewhere safe." He grinned weakly.

Blimey nodded reluctantly. "If you say so."

"I say so," Ashes said. "Reckon we ought to get some sleep?"

Blimey nodded and climbed into the nest of rags he used for a bed. "Tell me a story?" he asked.

"Oh, Blimey, I'm tired—"

"Just a short one! Please?"

Ashes grinned. "Eh, all right." He lay on his back and stared at the ceiling, burrowing in his memory for one of the stories Mari had told around their fire. "What about—?"

"Clever Tyru!" Blimey interjected.

"Why him?"

"I read some about him today," Blimey said proudly. "In my books."

"Do you know how he tricked his way into being an Ivory?" Ashes asked. "He snuck inside one of the great revels—"

"*Everyone* knows that one."

"What about when he used his Glamours to convince King Cathar he was the Face of Marvels?"

"You told me that last week."

Ashes sat up. "Sounds as *you* ought to tell me one, since you know so many."

Blimey didn't even bother to look apologetic. "Something new," he said. "Come on, then."

"All right," Ashes said. He remembered another now—he wasn't sure it was a Tyru story, but it would serve. "Here, then. So Clever Tyru—you already know, sure, that Clever Tyru's true love was Lady Claer Elimorne, and Lady Claer loved him back. Only, her father was a greedy man, and he wanted to marry Claer off to some vile Ivory lord 'cause he was rich. Now Tyru, of course, he'd mastered Glamours, and so he stitched together a cloak for himself that'd make him look like a true-blooded Ivory . . ."

Blimey had always been an excellent audience. He grinned when Tyru bested Lady Claer's suitors at swordplay, and laughed when the cruel chamberlain was Glamoured to look like a pig, and looked appropriately frightened when, near the end, Tyru ran afoul of a man with eyes like the moon—an Iron Knight. The Knight destroyed Tyru's illusions and threw him in a dungeon. Blimey didn't calm down entirely until after Tyru tricked his way out of his cell and escaped with Lady Claer to live happily ever after.

Blimey was asleep mere minutes after Ashes finished the story, but Ashes, despite the exhaustion in his bones, lay awake for an hour or more. Iames's warning circled his brain over and over. *Don't count on the Tithe . . . If the Lass is your best hope, you're better off in the sewers.*

Ashes had to prove him wrong. He and Blimey couldn't fall in with a crew; it would only be a matter of time before Mr. Ragged found out Blimey was still alive, and came for both of them. They needed to get out of Burroughside permanently, sometime before the winter air froze them to death or the Fortress fell to pieces or Saintly came calling . . .

Sleep crept up on him slowly, burying him in a half-awake limbo where his worries melted together.

*It was Taxing Day, and everyone he begged from was the bear-faced Denizen, who beat him for his money. But Ashes had nothing, so the man killed him and threw his body in the sewers, and the sewer-beasts tore his corpse to bits.*

*His remains seeped into the river. Ragged found them, only Ragged was Saintly, because Saintly killed Ragged just like he killed Mari, and now he ruled Burroughside. Blimey had snuck out to look for magic princesses, but he found Saintly instead, and now Blimey was screaming—*

*Ashes could do nothing but watch.*

# 4

# Marvels

I**T** was three hours past dawn, and, gradually, Yson was waking. Its first yawns and stretches were the Denizens who did not belong to it, who stumbled drunkenly toward their homes. Many were hungover; all were poorer than they had been last night. Victims of Yson's Invisible Tax: the punishment for entering Yson's borders with more money than sense.

Not long after them came the Ysonne, who *did* belong, and they came full of smiles and charm. They gave no sign they had drunk last night, or indeed that they had ever touched drink. They laughed easily, and their eyes were sharp.

Ashes stood near a street corner a mile south of the Savoir Theatre, waiting. When the streets were filled, he sat on the corner and produced three cards from his coat, setting them facedown on the street.

There was almost a palpable shift in the air as the Denizens noticed him. Ysonne could smell games of chance at fifty paces.

They were doubly attuned to games that favored them—and gambling against a dirty runtling dressed in a tattered, man-sized coat favored them by a long way. Ysonne cheated at cards before they could walk.

He waited until there was a crowd before he looked up, wary for passing coppers or overzealous priests. He saw only Denizens: three well-to-do women, intrigued but not eager, whispering to one another. A dark-haired, shabby man with narrowed eyes, holding himself away from the rest of the group—clearly uninterested. A husband and wife, Ivory-blooded, removed from the crowd even though they were standing in it.

*Come on, now. Who wants to give me some money?*

At last one met his eyes: a bespectacled gentleman with a shrewd look about him and expensive clothes. Ashes nodded toward the cards before him.

"You looks like a most estute individual, milord," Ashes said brightly, mangling his speech with a Lyonshire-Low accent. "Care to play a bit?"

"I don't," said the man, though Ashes saw a gleam in his eye.

"Oh, c'mon now, sir. Don't you be a spoilsport. The people want to see a good show, don't they? Here." Ashes dropped a coin on the ground, a shiny copper ha'penny. "I'll make it interesting."

The man let out a harsh laugh, turning to leave.

"You coward, then, sir?" Ashes smiled as the gentleman glared.

"I ought to call for an officer," he snapped.

"Ah, but where's the fun in that, sir? C'mon. Just a couple games."

The small crowd looked expectantly at the man, who swore softly and sat in front of Ashes. He dug in a pocket and pulled out a half-crescent note.

"My buy-in," he said.

Ashes grinned. "Right generous of you, milord. You familiar?" He gathered up all three of the cards in one hand and displayed them. "Face a' Cunning, Marvels, Kindness. I'm going to mix 'em up, fast as ennything, and likely I'll try to confuse you some with me swift fingers and clever banter. Your job, milord, is you find Her Ladyship." He tapped one finger on the Face of Kindness, a minimalist portrait of a woman who was neither old nor young and wore a crown of twining leaves. The other two Faces were black.

"I know the game," the man snapped. "Begin your little ruse, child. I have better things to do."

Ashes smiled. He bobbed his head as he separated the cards: the two black in his left hand, the Face of Kindness in his right. He bent forward and began the shuffle. "D'you know, sir, 'bout the story of the barber and the magwitch?" Ashes's hands moved with calm deliberation, as if dancing to slow music. "If'n you don't mind, I'm going to tell it so's to entertain me crowd here." His hands moved swifter now. He threw a Cheater's Toss, mostly to honor the man's expectations. "Once upon a time, not so terrible far from here, there's a barber. Kindly sort of bloke, just the nicest chap you ever did meet." He bit his cheek; he was playing up the accent too much. "Quick as a fox with his razors, too. No sooner you set down, *fwip*, you're all shaved up, and not a cut to be seen. Him and his razors, they were unioned, like. He kept 'em shiny and bright, and he always spoke about 'em like his own sons and daughters. Ah, sir, if you'd just point out for us where Her Ladyship is?"

The man tapped one card disdainfully. Ashes flipped it, revealing the laughing portrait of the Face of Cunning.

"Shame, sir," Ashes said, snatching up the first half-crescent. "Double or naught?"

The man slammed down another half-crescent and bent forward, peering suspiciously at Ashes's hands. Ashes tried not to smile too broadly as he began swapping cards.

Anywhere but Yson, Ashes would have needed a partner to play this particular game. Enticing a mark took careful work; they

needed to feel confident the game was straight, or at the very least
that they were clever enough to swindle a swindler.

In Yson, *everyone* thought he could swindle a swindler. The
danger was that they were usually right.

"So this barber," Ashes continued, "one day, he sees a witch
coming down his way. Only he doesn't do the usual things we
do—there's no swearing, 'cos he weren't that type of man, and
anyway this was back before everybody was scared of witches.
No, our barber, right away he gets out his biggest smile and he
welcomes her to his little shop. 'My lady!' he says, 'Why, it's such
a pleasure to be making your acquaintance!' Ah, speaking of,
sir . . . ?"

The man pointed, and Ashes flipped over a card. This, too, was
the Face of Cunning. The man yanked out another half-crescent
and smashed it against the street before Ashes could say anything.

"Again."

"Your wish, sir. Anyway, this witch, she says, 'Oh, sir, you've
got to help me! It's my boy, me only son, and he's got something
a-stickin' on his face!' That'll be a beard, sir, in case you didn't
know. Dun't look as yours has come in just yet. No shame, sir,
some folk got too much woman in 'em." This drew an uncomfortable laugh from the onlookers; the man himself was too focused
to notice.

"Anyways, her witchiness goes on, 'If you get that horrid thing
off his face, I'll repay you whatever way I can. If you wishes, I'll
even bring your razors to life.' Now, that barber had never heard
such a generous offer in his life, and so he follows missus witch to
her home. He finds the— Ah, sir?"

The man flipped the card himself and let out a triumphant
crowing sound. "Ha! There she is! Her Ladyship, the Face of Kindness!"

"It's a fair cop, sir," Ashes said, not quite succeeding in keeping the doubt from flickering across his face. His Tosses had been

clean, but the Ysonne man had spotted Her Ladyship anyway. "Care to try again? I've still got one of your notes."

"I bet both," the man said, grinning savagely at Ashes as he pulled out one more half-crescent. "And this as well."

"As you say, sir." That was odd. The man didn't need more of a buy-in—

"One other thing," the man said, holding up a finger. "You lose, and I'll have the pleasure of handing you to the police."

Ashes swallowed, then delivered his most winning smile. "Your wish, sir."

His heart crashed against his chest as he picked up the cards. He forced himself to breathe slowly, to focus. *Quick and fearless.*

"So, our brave barber, he finds the witch-lady's son all convalessin' and such in his bed, and he pulls out his razors to go and slice up his beard. Only, see, soon as he comes close up on the boy he realizes something ain't right. For starters, it's no beard on his face. And for seconders, laddie looks sick to death. His face is the color of spoilt milk, and he's got eyes wide as me fist, and they're iron-gray all the way through.

" 'This ain't a beard,' says the barber.

" 'No,' says the witch. 'He's a deathly enchantment on him. You must take it off.' So he pulls out his first razor, his best one, and he sets to working." Ashes swept up the cards and threw a Cheater's Toss; then another one, and another, and another. "He puts his blade up against the lad's ear, and he wiggles round, trying to find where the enchantment starts, but nothing doing. He tries again at the boy's forehead, still nothing. Last of all he goes to the neck.

" 'This is dangerous,' he says to the witch. 'If I slip . . .'

"And Her Ladyship says, 'Then he will die, and so will you. Don't slip.' So he makes the first cut."

Ashes stopped, glancing around. The crowd had nearly doubled in size. The man across from him was staring fixedly at the cards, fingers curled to fists. One eye twitched, just a little. "Your turn, sir. Where's the Lady?"

"I'm thinking," said the man. "Finish your story."

"Story's all finished, sir," Ashes said. "Nothing more to it."

"It's a buggery story, then. There's no proper ending."

"I wouldn't know, sir. Found her yet?"

"Bah!" The man pointed. "She's under there. Show me her face."

Ashes's stomach dropped. Instinctively he glanced around, seeking exits. The man saw him looking, and tensed, preparing to grab him. There was nothing for it. Ashes turned the card over—and felt, as he did so, something liquid run down his arm.

The awestruck expression of the Face of Marvels looked back at him. Ashes's eyes widened, but he recovered almost instantly.

"Shame, sir," he said coolly. "The Faces favor me today, looks like."

"Hmph," said the man, staggering to his feet. "You're a clever blighter, boy. I could have sworn . . . gah." He fixed Ashes in a steady glare. "Take your money, then, beggar."

Ashes smiled nervously and swept up the coins as the man left. Not a moment later, Ashes jumped to his feet as well.

"What a 'garious individual he is," Ashes said, searching for a break in the crowd. He darted toward the first one he saw. "Thankee, folks, for being such a grand audience. You're credits to your kind, and all that. S'been a pleasure to entertain."

He ducked away. He didn't know Yson half as well as he knew Burroughside or Lyonshire, but it wouldn't take too much effort to make himself lost here.

When he felt sure no one had followed him, he huddled against a wall, pulled the cards out, and swore. All three of them were black: two bore the Face of Marvels.

"What the *hell* are you doing in there?" Ashes muttered.

He rubbed his thumb against them, trying to understand the

trick. But there was no difference, except that one of the Marvels looked strangely blurred. He scratched it with a fingernail and shook it like it was wet, but nothing changed.

He murmured another curse, and just then the Face of Marvels dissipated, like water thrown against a furnace. The Face of Kindness reappeared beneath his fingertips.

"Furies and Kindness," he said aloud, and threw the card on the ground as quickly as if it had caught fire.

A Glamour—an illusion, the arcane work of an Artificer. Somebody had put magic on his cards.

It made him distinctly uncomfortable, not just because he knew for certain now that he'd mucked the trick. Some illusionist had interfered with his cards. But why?

His instinct screamed at him to quit Yson for the day, perhaps try to convince Mr. Ragged that begging had been slim and throw himself on what little mercy the man had—but no. He needed more. He couldn't risk losing Ragged's protection; it was the only thing keeping Saintly away. He had to keep going, and he had to be perfect this time.

*There won't be another second chance*, he thought.

Well, then, he wouldn't slip.

● ● ●

*Some three hours before* sunset, Ashes's pockets were heavier by four crescents and eight—enough for Ragged's tax, and food for him and Blimey besides. He'd earned a pair of bruises on his ribcage to match his reddened neck but, apart from that, fared quite well.

Altogether he felt more comfortable with Yson. It was tricky and conniving, but it favored the clever. And it was big enough to get lost in for a while. So long as he kept a wary eye out for past marks, he could do well for himself for a while. And after that, if Lyonshire was still too dangerous, he could try his hand in

Ubärsid, or the Boreas Gutters. His safe places were thinning far too fast.

Still, he and Blimey were safe for tonight. That would do.

His thoughts were interrupted by a sudden sense that some-one was watching him. He tensed, and found the watcher almost immediately, sitting on a bench not far from him. A youngish man with an open face and wide eyes, which were trained on Ashes. He looked vaguely familiar.

"Evening," the man said, tilting his head. "You're that card player. I saw you, earlier." He grinned. "You made a gentleman very angry."

"Lots of folks get angry at Find the Lady," Ashes said warily. He kept his distance. The man could be some sort of trap—someone to slow him while another fetched the coppers. He didn't intend to be caught off his guard.

"You're quite good," the man said. His smile widened in what Ashes guessed was supposed to be a disarming way. "Care to play me?"

Ashes took a step back. "Don't particular care to, sir, I'm afraid," he said. "Places to be, and what—"

"I can make it worth your while," the man said, producing a thick gold coin from his pocket.

Ashes sucked in an involuntary breath. He'd not seen a true crown in person before. It was worth everything he had in his pocket five times over.

*Trap.*

"Beat me," said the man, "and it's yours. And if you lose, then nothing. We go our own ways."

*Definitely a trap. Get along.*

But they were still in the open. Ashes could dash off at the first sign of trouble. And if he won, he and Blimey could eat like kings for weeks, and have enough left over to pay Mr. Ragged's tax for a good while. Enough time for Ashes's face to fade out of

Lyonshire's collective memory, perhaps, or for him to search out new ways to impress the Lass at New Year's . . .

"D'you know, goodly gentleman-sir," he said carefully, slipping back into his routine, "I reckon it'd be criminal of me to deny a man wanting to see some magic at work. We'll need to be quick, though. Owing as I've some things left to do today." He glanced significantly at the sky.

"Best of three games, then," said the man, eyeing Ashes sharply. "I'll not take long."

"Deal."

Ashes slid the three cards out of his pocket and sat before the bench. He showed them to the man all at once. "You know the game, sir?"

The man's grin was unnervingly calm as he nodded. Ashes resisted the fluttering sense of danger in his belly and began.

"Did you ever hear the story, milord, about the magwitch and the—?"

"I have," the man said. "I watched you tell it several hours ago. Tell me, what were the barber's razors made of?"

"Metal, milord, I'd assume," Ashes said, flashing a smile to hide his growing unease. "Probably steel."

"Somehow I doubt it," the man replied, rubbing his chin. "What's your name?"

Ashes Tossed, throwing Cunning instead of Kindness. "Francis," he lied smoothly.

"Odd name for a street magician."

"Odd-name-for-a-street-magician is me surname, sir."

"Well, my name is Jacob Rehl." The man wasn't watching the cards. His eyes were on Ashes.

"S'a pleasure, sir." Ashes stopped rearranging the cards. Something here was *very* wrong. "Where's Her Ladyship?"

Jacob looked at the cards as though he were surprised they were there and pointed carelessly to the card on his left. "Is she there?"

Ashes gave an uneasy grin as he flipped over the Face of Marvels. "Apologies, sir. Looks as though—looks as though the Faces favor me today."

"For the moment," Jacob said with another lazy smile. Ashes shivered as he gathered the cards, threw out a Cheater's Toss, and began again. "I have a question for you, Francis Odd. Earlier today you swindled a man who would have had you carted off to prison. Probably beaten you senseless, too. Why keep playing?"

Ashes shook his head a little, trying to clear out the fog within it. "The bloke in the spectacles? 'Cos I could win." He swept the cards again, threw a Cheater's Toss and, just because he knew he could, a perfect Cacklewitch, swapping all three cards in a single motion. Even if the man had been watching Ashes's fingers, he would have no way to know where Kindness had gone.

"You like winning. Being the best."

"Dun't everybody, sir?"

"Did you think of the risk?"

"Don't tend to."

"You shouldn't have won," the man said softly. "I was watching your cards. He picked the Face of Kindness and you made it *not* the Face of Kindness. How?"

Ashes forced a laugh and shrugged. "Just a bit of presty-dation, goodly gentleman-sir. *Legerdemain* to you folks out here."

"They're not my folk, and no, it wasn't. You can't lie to a liar, Francis Odd."

"Mister Rehl," Ashes said, looking him in the eye, "that's all I *ever* do. Where's the Lady?"

"Under the left." Jacob didn't even look down.

"Wrong," Ashes said. "Marvels."

"Prove it."

Ashes flipped over the card, and felt something brush against his skin.

The Face of Kindness stared up from the card, red as flame. Ashes looked from the card to the man, and to the card again. It was a perfect representation, but Ashes had kept track of the cards. Hadn't he?

"You're cheating," Ashes said. "Somehow. You're cheating."

"Prove it." Jacob's eyes were bright.

"Look. Here's the *real* Face of—" But it was the Face of Marvels, awestruck and beatific, that looked back at him when he turned the card over.

Ashes stared at the man, eyes narrowed. "How are you doing this?"

"Me? I'm not doing anything. Maybe you shouldn't have thrown Cacklewitch. Notoriously difficult trick, that one. Are you sure you didn't simply muck it?"

His jaw bulged. "You're doing something to it, ain't you? You're a— You're some kind of Glamourist. A Fisher."

"So what if I am?" Jacob fixed him in a cool stare. "The crown is still at stake. You may walk away, or you may try one final time. I'm not even going to call the police if I lose."

"Course you won't. You *can't* lose." Ashes snatched up his cards and leapt to his feet. "I don't got to stick around for this. You think it's fun just mucking with me, well, bugger off. I've places to be."

Jacob didn't stand. He met Ashes's eyes. "Very well. Yes, I'm an Artificer. Yes, I cheated. Play one more. I'll conjure nothing on your cards."

"Swear to it."

"By my face and on my name," the man said immediately, "I, Jacob Rehl, shall conjure no image, effect no magic, and cause no change to occur on, within, or to any of the items you hold, by any power available to me. Should I break my word, may all misfortune and calamity fall upon me and mine. May I ache with untold pains. May I fail in all my endeavors. May my flesh rot on my bones and my spirit wander eternal." He finished by blowing out a long breath, then looking at Ashes. "Good enough? Your cards have their faces back."

Ashes still didn't trust him, but he had only lost a few minutes. He still had time, and he could still have that coin. "Good enough." He held the cards out. "You ready?"

"Exceptionally," Jacob said. "But be warned, lad. I am a better liar than you."

Ashes didn't respond except to throw the first card down. Jacob's eyes were fixed now on Ashes's hands, which were swift and unerring. After a day's worth of practice, his fingers knew the dance intimately. He kept his mind bent on the Face of Kindness, imagining that she was faceup, staring at him. So long as he could see her like this, he would never lose her.

He glanced at Jacob's eyes. They were following the Face of Kindness, too.

*He knows the game*, Ashes thought. *He's keeping track and he's not even trying.*

Ashes increased his speed, shifting cards as fast as he could without losing control. They seemed to blur, though he could still see Kindness, watching him like a worried mother.

Ashes stole a look at Jacob once again. The man's eyes hadn't left Kindness.

*Bugger that*, Ashes decided. So the man knew the game—what of it? It wasn't just about the tricks.

Ashes's hands sped up. He threw the cards recklessly, barely keeping them from flying out of his hands. They were nearly a blur between his fingers. For several moments he kept track of the Face of Kindness, until the motions were too fast even for him. When finally he stopped shuffling, he could not have found Her Ladyship any better than someone else could have.

He looked at Jacob Rehl and felt his heart beating faster.

"Where's the Lady?"

Jacob pointed. Ashes took the card by its corner and flipped it up. He let out a long, relieved breath.

"Cunning," Jacob muttered. "How about that."

"Sorry, milord," Ashes said. "Looks like the Faces favor me today." He glanced skyward. "And I'm afraid that's all I'm going to have the time for. Mr. Rehl, it has been a real pleasure taking your money." He snatched up the coin. "This even real?"

"Oh, it's quite real," Jacob said. He gave Ashes a strange look, curious and calculating. "You did . . . very well."

"Uh-huh. G'bye, Mr. Rehl."

Jacob nodded, and Ashes felt the man's eyes watching as he left.

5

**D**EEP in Burroughside was a house.

This was unusual. Burroughside did not have houses; mostly, Burroughside had ruins. The few buildings still standing were creaky, riddled with holes, on the verge of falling over or falling in; they were filled with rats and desperate people. This house had no rats, and it consumed desperate people like food.

It had only one door, made of a dark and heavy iron, which one approached by way of three stone steps. Beyond this was a rough courtyard that had rocks rather than grass, and the rocks were discolored by old blood, souvenirs of the public fights that happened in the yard every month. Further on was a high fence, which surrounded the house. At the top of the fence were barbed wires, and thorny vines, and needles that glistened when the light wormed far enough inward to find them. These were tipped with a cruel poison, the sort that set fire to the bones and turned the guts to ice on its way to making the heart burst.

Inside, the house was well appointed, with lush carpets and new-looking furniture. The chairs could swallow a grown man whole. None of the paint was allowed to peel or chip, and along the central hallway of the house were numerous portraits of dour-looking old men. Apart from their embittered expressions, they had nothing in common.

The right sort of people would see it for what it was: a crude but passable imitation of an Ivory manor. The iron door, the style of furniture, the strange artwork in the hall, even the high fence— these were the hallmarks of Teranis's ruling class. The house was far too small, of course, and the fence too obviously patchwork. But the resemblance was there all the same: this was an Ivorish house, but made of castoffs and rubbish.

They would notice something else, if they stayed long enough: something quite different from the homes they were used to, something they couldn't quite articulate until they left. In every room— nearly hidden by the paint, nearly covered by the carpet—sunken into the skin of the house, was a perpetual, barely noticeable hint of smoke.

This was Ragged House.

● ● ●

*No one could enter* Ragged House without permission. This was what Mr. Ragged wanted Burroughside to believe, and because they believed it, it was true.

The girl on the roof did not believe it, and so it was not true.

● ● ●

*The bell on Ragged* House's fence made a shrill and ugly sound when Ashes rang it. He had a strong suspicion Ragged wanted it to do just that. Ashes couldn't imagine what sort of craftsman specialized in bells that made people want to tear their ears off, but Ragged had certainly found him.

He shifted his weight from foot to foot while he waited. No one else was around, but the Broken Boys roosted just around the corner from Ragged House. If they passed by while he was just standing here . . . he rang it again, louder this time.

The door opened, and Carapace, Ragged's butler, *proceeded* from it. Proceeding was how Carapace moved. He did not walk, or run, or stumble. He moved like a priest, with grand, slow steps. Carapace was a deliberate man. From his tightly trimmed eyebrows to his polished cuff links to his perfectly bald head, each detail seemed the result of a decision that had taken hours. Even his overlong nose and pale gray eyes seemed to have been selected consciously.

The only thing that didn't seem to be under Carapace's control was his scent. Ashes always caught a whiff of something spoiled in the man's breath, like old milk.

Carapace opened the gate wide. Ashes held out a bundle of money notes—his entire take for the day, save the golden coin he'd won from Jacob the liar. That was hidden carefully away, buried in the dirt underneath a loose stone in an alleyway, for fear that other Burroughsiders would be desperate enough to rob him. It wasn't unheard of; people got desperate on Taxing Day. "My tax for the week."

The butler didn't look at the money. "Milord wishes to see you."

Ashes was too experienced a card player to let his surprise show through on his face, but his heart juddered against his ribs. What could Ragged want with him? If he had found out about Blimey—but no, he couldn't have found out about Blimey. Even so, Ashes's skin was crawling the way it did when a copper walked by.

"It's getting dark, Carapace, and I've places to—"

He didn't even glimpse Carapace's spindly arm moving, but somehow Ashes's wrist was caught in the man's hand. The grip was viselike, fingers digging down to the bone.

*Furies.* "What's he need me for?" Ashes said, as if nothing out of the ordinary had happened.

"I am not privy to his reasons," Carapace said.

Ashes frowned, not at all comforted, but he had no other move. He stepped inside the gate.

Carapace led him wordlessly into the house. Ashes had been within it only once before, less than a year ago. He remembered bits and pieces: the Bärsi carpets, the eerie men staring at him out of their portrait prisons, the smell of smoke. He wondered if Ragged had tried to root it out and failed, or if he kept it that way to unnerve everyone who entered.

Carapace opened the great oaken door to Mr. Ragged's office. Ashes hesitated, just for a moment, wrestling down an instinct to sprint away. Everything in him was screaming that he mustn't enter that room. But Carapace's eye was trained on him, and he had seen how quick the man was. He took a deep breath, steeling himself.

The first thing he noticed was the soft sound beneath his feet. He looked down, confused, and saw that the floor was covered in faded yellow newspaper. The second thing he noticed was that he was not Mr. Ragged's only guest—Iames the Fool sat before Mr. Ragged's great oaken desk. Saintly stood to one side of him, looking like a guilty cat. The look alone would have been enough to make Ashes nervous, if he were not already.

Last of all he saw Mr. Ragged.

The Beggar Lord had a potent and not at all pleasant reputation; visitors often expected someone ancient and scarred, with a grizzled beard and three missing teeth and a chin that curled slightly upward. But Mr. Ragged looked unremarkable. No older than thirty, with chestnut-colored hair and dark eyes, he could have been fresh from one of the Boreas colleges, or from an apprenticeship with some Lyonshire merchant. His suit was pressed and his silk top hat, which he wore even when indoors, always looked new.

Carapace bowed as they entered, grabbing Ashes by the shoulder to make him do likewise. Ashes found himself distinctly aware of how exposed his neck was, and swallowed. But if Ragged planned to kill him, he wouldn't need Ashes to present his neck.

"You may go, Carapace," Ragged said. His voice did not quite fit his looks. Too raw, too coarse and throaty. Like every word pained him. "Shut the door."

Ashes straightened; his insides were crawling. Why had Mr. Ragged called in Saintly and the Fool? It couldn't be anything good. Saintly's eyes were filled with smug satisfaction.

Mr. Ragged gestured Ashes to the chair beside Iames. "Do sit," he said. It was not a request, and Ashes obeyed, keeping his questions to himself and his face carefully still.

"Francis has told me an interesting story," Mr. Ragged said. "About the pair of you."

Ashes and Iames exchanged a look. Iames said, "We've done nothing wrong, sir."

"Not at all, not at all," Mr. Ragged said. "No, I am not searching for blame. I am interested in facts—context, perhaps. I understand there was something of a disagreement between you and Francis, Ashes?"

Ashes didn't let his nervousness show. "Something of one."

"And Iames came to your aid, I understand," Mr. Ragged said evenly. "Helping to enforce my laws. Maintaining the peace. Would you say you are allies? Friends?"

Ashes and Iames exchanged another bewildered look.

"All due respect, sir," Ashes said, "but why're we here?"

"Is that a yes?"

"Sure," Iames said. Mr. Ragged looked at Ashes, who nodded.

"Francis has brought an opportunity to my attention," Mr. Ragged said. "I've— You see, I have found myself becoming somewhat bored with Burroughside lately. There's very little excitement in it, you see, compared to when I took it over. And Francis has given me an idea." Ragged inclined his head in Saintly's direction. "Try not to make a mess."

*A mess?*

Ashes heard a sickening, metallic sound, and he turned. Saintly stood behind Iames, and his expression was horrid—gleeful and cruel. Iames's face had gone rigid, and Ashes wondered why until he saw the raw gash opening under Iames's chin, and the wet, red blade in Saintly's hand.

Iames fell forward out of the chair, landing with a *thunk* on the floor.

Ashes stared. He heard, as if from far away, the sound of Iames's blood gurgling in his throat, and thought that he must go to him, and try to stop the bleeding. That was what he ought to do. But he couldn't move.

Iames's blood spread across the newspapers, staining the yellowed pages red.

An image flickered behind Ashes's eyes, just for a moment: Mari's still, cold body on the ground, her face frozen permanently in shock. Ashes's breath caught.

The blood reached Ashes's feet. He couldn't move. Iames's body shook all over, and then he was still.

"Terribly foul business," Mr. Ragged said. "Leave us, Francis. Send Carapace in to clean this up."

"Of course, milord," Saintly said. He leered at Ashes as he left, his eyes dancing as if he'd just played a particularly clever joke.

Ashes's mind felt viscous, as if he were thinking through wet clay. His tongue was heavy and awkward. He could focus on nothing but the red pool spreading across the floor. It occurred to him that Mr. Ragged cared very much about his carpets, to have covered them for this . . .

After some time, he heard Mr. Ragged's voice saying, "Listen." Ashes looked up. There was a red veneer over his vision. He kept seeing Mari staring at him, eyes wide, blood trickling down her forehead. Iames's body was gone, though the blood still soaked the papers.

"Are you paying attention?" Mr. Ragged asked. Ashes nodded. "Good. Listen carefully to me, boy. You have my permission to seek justice."

Ashes stared at him. He didn't speak.

"Are you understanding, Ashes? You may kill Francis."

"Why?"

"He has killed your friend," Mr. Ragged said, giving him a patient look. "Not for the first time, either, if I understand correctly. I am giving you permission to punish him for it."

"Iames paid his tax," Ashes said numbly.

"Immaterial, at this stage," Mr. Ragged said. "He was more valuable to me this way." He tapped his fingers together, thoughtful. "My father bred dogs, you know, as guard animals. Savage creatures if you know how to train them. And you must keep them savage. Make them fight, make them kill to eat. Or they become worse than useless."

Ashes saw it, then: the pieces fit together rather neatly. Mr. Ragged hadn't brought him here as a punishment or to remind him who was in charge—not primarily, anyway. Mr. Ragged had wanted him to watch Saintly kill Iames. *Would you say you are allies? Friends?*

"You want me to fight him," Ashes said. "As—what, a training exercise? Keep his teeth sharp?"

"I would prefer you think of it as an opportunity to impress me," Mr. Ragged said. "I have dozens of whoresons living here.

Perhaps hundreds. Some of them could kill Francis. None of them can frighten him." He nodded respectfully toward Ashes. "You do. That interests me."

"What if I don't want to do it?"

Mr. Ragged smiled in what was probably supposed to be a charming, indulgent way. It looked predatory. "Francis will be receiving a similar liberty in three days. By that point, I suspect it will no longer be your decision."

Ashes ground his teeth together. "You're a rank bastard," he said.

Mr. Ragged's smile vanished and his eyes went perilously dark. "Show proper respect, boy, or I will rip your tongue out and feed it to you." The dark expression passed as quickly as it had come. Mr. Ragged leaned back. "You may leave, now."

Just then there was a loud thump upstairs, followed by a high, agonized scream. Mr. Ragged's eyes darted upward. His face shifted almost imperceptibly, just enough to reveal an expression of shock and uncertainty.

The scream cut off. There was a sound of shattering glass, and Ragged looked, briefly, frightened. Ashes memorized the look; the sight of Mr. Ragged afraid would keep him warm for weeks.

"*Leave*, boy," Mr. Ragged commanded. He rose imperiously and strode out the door without another word.

Ashes obeyed without a second thought. He was out of the office quickly as anything; his head was already spinning with fear and dashed-together plans. He had three days—probably not even that; he couldn't count on Mr. Ragged's word.

He and Blimey needed to be out of Burroughside by morning.

They could doss somewhere in Boreas, maybe a cheap Ysonne inn if the innkeeper cared more about the weight of Ashes's coin than the absence of his iron name. That solution wouldn't last more than a pair of weeks even if they were terribly lucky, but what choice did he have? The Lass didn't take any Burroughsiders but for her Tithe, and that was months away. Far, far too long—he had been a fool to think he could count on surviving until then.

He was halfway to the gate when he heard Ragged scream something, but he was in too much of a hurry to feel curious. Something like a thunder-crack erupted behind him as he slipped out the gate. He ran.

Sundown had come and leached the color from Teranis. Everything was silhouettes. Ashes thought of the Ravagers, felt his heart slam against his chest. They wouldn't come out for some time, but—were those footsteps he heard?

Then came wild whoops, shouts, garbled words. Not Ravagers: they sounded young. Other Burroughsiders, out this close to dark?

No time to worry about it. He hurried to the alley where he'd hidden the coin and dropped to his knees, scrabbling in the dirt. He shifted several stones, felt muck between his fingers. The shadows in the alleyway had deepened; he couldn't see nearly well enough.

His heart stuck in his throat. He hadn't buried it *this* deep—had he missed it? Had someone stolen it?

His breath caught just as he felt something cool brush his finger. He yanked the coin out of the mud and leapt to his feet, dashed from the alley—

Something crashed into him and wrapped arms around his neck and bore him to the ground. He landed hard on the street. Breath burst out of him. Instinctually he scrabbled in the muck for something to fight with. His fingers wrapped around a heavy broken stone and he rolled to his feet. *Quick and fearless*, he thought. He had to hit first or it was over, he'd never win in a fair fight—

He saw his opponent and froze: it was a girl, slender and wide-eyed, crouched against the opposite wall. She had deathly pale skin and a horrid wound in her belly, which she was trying and failing to stopper with her hand. Bright lines of red seeped between her fingers every moment.

"Furies and Kindness," Ashes muttered, and dropped the rock.

The girl's eyes fixed on him. She said, "Please . . ."

More shouts behind him. The girl shuddered, and without thinking any further Ashes pulled her into the alley.

"Who are you?" he demanded in a low voice. "What happened?"

The girl gave him a withering look. "Got shot," she said curtly. "Please. Need your help."

"Why? Who *are* you?"

"No'n important," she snarled. *"Please."*

"What—?"

More shouts. Ashes let her rest against the wall and peeked around the corner. He could see three older boys approaching, carefully checking corners and hideaways as they moved. It was too dim, and they were too far away, for him to make out their features, but even at this distance he recognized Saintly's prowling walk.

"Ragged's," the girl said, nodding toward the mouth of the alley. "They're after me."

"Furies and Kindness," he said.

"Got to—catch my breath," she said. "Need help."

Ashes peeked around the corner again. Saintly's group had swollen to six boys now.

"Please," the girl said.

"I don't think—"

"I can repay you," the girl said, wincing. "Please. *Please.*"

"I—"

"I work with Bonnie the Lass," the girl said.

Ashes blinked. He regretted it immediately—no self-respecting card player let their surprise show, and now the girl could see what the words meant to him. Work *with* the Lass—not *for*. If she was the sort of person who could think of the Beggar Queen of Teranis as an equal, helping her would be more than worth his time.

If there was a chance she was telling the truth, he didn't dare pass it up.

He pulled his coat off. "Take that," he said. "Get as far back as you can and cover up your face. *Go*."

She disappeared in the darkness behind the alley. Ashes watched her go, then took out the gold coin, kissed it, and got on his knees.

He heard footsteps approaching, and loudly scrabbled in the dirt, then stood quickly and brushed himself off. He turned just as Saintly came around the corner, eyes dark. Ashes clutched the coin tightly and hid it behind his back.

"Ashes," Saintly said, smiling darkly. "What might you be doing down that alleyway just now, I wonder."

"No business of yours, Saintly," Ashes said.

"Blubbing, were you?" Saintly sneered. "Weeping over the Fool? Scared that he won't protect you now he's rotting on Ragged's fence?"

Rage boiled fierce and hot in Ashes's chest. "Make sure you mention how proud you are to Rafe," Ashes said. "I'll bet he comes up with all manner of inventive ways to get around Ragged's fondness for you."

"He can try," Saintly said. "You're looking rather, aha, nervous, Ashes. Something you're hiding from me?"

Ashes didn't twitch—it would have been too obvious—but he did let his grip around the coin tighten. "What're you doing out here anyway?"

"Looking for somebody, mate," Saintly said calmly. He jerked a thumb over his shoulder at a pair of Broken Boys checking an alley across the street. "Ragged's got work he needs done."

"Perhaps you ought get to it, then," Ashes said.

Saintly drew his knife. "I'm getting to it just fine," he said. "Tell me. Somebody come by this way? Bleeding out her belly? She'd stick in your memory, I reckon."

"Nobody here for you, Saintly," Ashes said.

Saintly met his eyes and grinned. "You're lying to me." Saintly took a slow step forward. "I suspect Ragged wouldn't be fussed if I had to kill you. In the, aha, course of my duty, you see."

"I don't—"

Saintly grabbed him by the throat and shoved him against the wall, pressing the knife against Ashes's neck. Ashes yelped as Jacob's coin flew from his hand, landing heavily in the mud.

Saintly glanced at it and grinned. "Aww, Ashes," he said. "*There's a handy secret.*"

"Oi—"

"This'll buy me all manner of pleasant things," Saintly said, picking up the coin without taking his eyes off Ashes. "Bet this buys something lovely and warm from the Silken."

"Saintly!" someone called.

Saintly winked at Ashes and twirled the knife. "Enjoy your night, Ashes. I look forward to the next time we see each other." He gave a wide smile full of satisfaction, and he left.

Ashes ground his teeth convincingly until Saintly had gone. He checked the street, and it was empty. "You can come out now."

The girl's face emerged from the darkness deep in the alley. She had gotten even paler. Ashes hurried to her and helped her stand.

"Thanks," she said, offering him his coat back.

"Keep it," Ashes said. He helped her toward the street. "We got to find shelter for you before dark."

She shook her head. "Need to be back tonight," she said. "Can you get me to the Boreas border?"

"Eh," he said, feeling his stomach jump. He'd have to doss in one of the hideaway holes rather than return to the Fortress; Blimey would worry, but it wouldn't be the first time Ashes had been gone all night.

"So you really work for the Lass," Ashes said.

"Don't bandy it about," she said. "But yes."

"Why's Ragged got his boys after you?"

The girl's mouth drew into a thin line.

"C'mon, then," Ashes said. "Least you can do, now I'm out a gold crown saving your life."

"It's not saved yet," she muttered.

"Don't talk like that." Ashes kept his voice firm and confident. The worst thing the girl could do now was give up. "You've made it this long, haven't you? Wound like that would've killed you by now if it meant to."

The girl grimaced. "How fortunate am I to have been saved by a honest-to-Faces doctor. Which of the colleges took you on so young?"

"Ha bloody ha," Ashes said. "Keep on making jokes, miss. That'll do you fine."

They walked on a little farther, and finally the girl said, "I was trying to steal from Mr. Ragged. Got in under the fence, there's a weak spot beneath the bars. I climbed up to his room."

"What were you trying to steal?"

"His Glamour." The girl shuddered.

Ashes's eyes widened. "Mr. Ragged has—?"

"That's all I'm saying on it," she said sharply. "And I'll thank you not to ask me any more. You're more than repaid for your coin."

Ashes frowned, but decided not to press her for more detail. "I heard you scream."

"Trap," she said. "Should've known better."

"Why's Bonnie want it?"

Her jaw clenched. "Who was the boy?"

"Saintly Francis," Ashes replied. "A more dangerous bastard you're not like to meet."

The girl laughed low in her throat. "I've met a lot."

"Not like Saintly, you haven't," Ashes said.

Darkness had claimed the streets by the time they reached the border of Boreas. "Will you be all right from here?" Ashes asked.

"I know my way about," she said, taking her arm off Ashes's shoulders and wincing as she put her weight on her leg. Ashes couldn't be certain, but it seemed that some of her color had come back since they'd been walking. That was good. "Thanks."

"Don't mention it," Ashes said, and paused. "Er—well, actually, do mention it. To the Lass, if you can. Might come a night I show up on your doorstep begging for help."

The girl smiled weakly. "Take care."

She limped into the Boreas fog, disappearing in mere moments. Ashes watched her go, feeling vaguely worried. She seemed well enough, but how far could she get without anyone to help her? He felt he ought to have taken her all the way to the Lass's hideout, but knew the girl wouldn't have let him come.

He didn't have time to worry over her anyway. There were police in Boreas who'd be only too pleased to throw him in the Basty for daring to walk about after dark without an iron name. He turned and made swiftly for the bolthole in Lowrens Street.

He reached it just as the howls began. The entrance to the hole was smaller than he remembered, barely large enough for him to fit, and the space within was so cramped he'd have to hug his knees all night long.

Ashes mulled the girl's words as he crawled inside the bolthole. Did she really work for Bonnie the Lass, or had it just been a ploy to get his help? He couldn't help but admire the strategy in that. Burroughsiders' love for Bonnie bordered on worship. Very few would have neglected an opportunity to help one of the Lass's agents.

But even if she did serve Bonnie, would the girl feel any duty to return Ashes's favor? He'd saved her life, but gratitude was unreliable. He had no bargaining power, no leverage.

If the girl had been lying about who she worked for, or—worse—felt no loyalty to him, and he and Blimey arrived to beg shelter from the Lass, what would happen? Would Bonnie kill them? Dismiss them? Tie them up and send them back to Ragged?

Ashes couldn't stand the thought of wagering Blimey's freedom on the honesty and goodwill of an admitted thief. No, he needed a trump card . . .

The Ravager howls began outside, but Ashes could hardly hear them. An idea had burgeoned in his head, something audacious and absurd. He needed a trump card—and apparently one was lying around in Mr. Ragged's bedroom, just waiting to be stolen.

# Folly

**6**

THE closest thing Burroughside had to a holiday was Bruise-maker Eve, though it differed significantly from Ivorish holidays. Firstly, it occurred more often: each month, an hour before sundown on New Moon's Night. Instead of commemoration, its primary purpose was to pit two combatants—occasionally lone fighters, but more usually crews—against one another in brutal, but rarely lethal, combat. Thus, rather than the exchange of tokens, terms, and trinkets of affection, it involved the pounding of skulls against stones, knuckles against teeth, and knees against groins.

It was universally agreed that this holiday fit Burroughside the way a knife fits a wound.

● ● ●

*Sixteen boys stood in* the bloodstained courtyard of Ragged House. Eight belonged to John Flint's Kidney-Punchers, a crew of thugs who cornered people in alleys and broke bones until money fell out; the rest came from Charle Find-alone's Hangmen, wiry second-story boys who specialized in picking window-locks, slithering down chimneys, and scaling buildings. Their profession favored the small; the tallest of Charle's fighters wasn't eye-level with even one of the Kidney-Punchers.

Outside Ragged's vicious fence, Burroughside had gathered in force: the spectacle of Bruisemaker Eve drew them irresistibly. Something about seeing teeth punched in—occasionally, if you were lucky, teeth belonging to someone who'd bullied, spat on, or stolen from you—struck a deep chord in the Burroughsider heart. Many had been victim to Flint's Kidney-Punchers once or twice; they jeered boisterously, though very few were bold enough to fling more than uncouth names.

Behind Ragged House, dressed in the darkest clothes he could find, Ashes crept toward the back of the fence. His step was quick and quiet, though the Bruisemaker audience would have buried the sound even if he had shouted. Dirt and mud were smeared on his cheeks, darkening his skin enough that he wouldn't stand out in the twilight.

Ragged's fence looked just as imposing in the back as it had in the front. The wire and poisoned needles twined at the top. The bars were too close together even for Ashes to squeeze through. Fortunately, if the girl had been telling the truth, Ashes wouldn't have to worry about either of those details. He was more concerned with the ground.

The crowd outside the courtyard roared, presumably in response to Mr. Ragged stepping onto the porch. This, like the spitting and the jeering, was traditional; no one dared stay silent when Mr. Ragged arrived. Ashes tensed at the explosion of sound, but kept searching. The gap *had* to be here somewhere.

The crowd quieted as Ragged addressed them. Ashes couldn't hear his words, but he knew the thrust of what was said. *"I keep*

*you safe from the police and Denizens and the Gleaming Law, because
I'm just so bloody kind. And all I ask in return is a few of your coins to
make certain the place still runs, and all the right bribes get to all the right
places. Remember that, will you? My tax may hurt, but it's only here to
help you."*

"So long as I doesn't get too bored," Ashes thought bitterly.

He kept searching for the weak spot under the fence. He had
reasoned, after he returned to the Fortress that morning, that the
girl's entry point had to be here in the back; Carapace would have
seen her sneaking in if she'd gone through the front yard. He recognized there was a possibility that Mr. Ragged's servants had
found the gap and repaired it since last night, and if they had, he
was right back where he started. But it had only been a day; Ashes
had to hope that wasn't enough time to find the breach *and* fix it.
There were, after all, so many places it could be—which, of course,
might be just as much a problem for him as it had been for Ragged.

The ground shifted beneath his feet. He bent and tested the
ground; one of the stones was loose, just enough to give him a few
extra inches of space.

He shifted the stone and lay on his back, squirming beneath the
poles. They dug into his stomach, doubtless leaving bruises behind,
but their ends were neither sharp nor tipped with poison, and for
that he was grateful. He wriggled halfway through, and with a
great push he slithered inside. He stayed crouched as he pulled
the broken stone back to its former resting place, then sprinted to
the side of the house and flattened himself against it. He heard no
cries of alarm or recognition, only assorted shouts from the Bruisemaker Eve contestants.

Ashes breathed deeply, willing his heart not to pound too hard.
He wouldn't be capable of much at all if he couldn't think straight.

The girl had said she'd climbed to Ragged's room, hadn't she?
Ashes looked up and his gut twisted. Mr. Ragged's bedroom was
on the second floor, near the back. Now that he looked, he could

just see a series of bricks jutting out of the corner of the house, forming tenuous handholds. The path ended several feet away from a window—enough to jump, but not easily.

*Quick and fearless*, he thought, and leapt for the first brick. His fingers grasped at it, catching it just enough for him to swing another hand on. He pressed his feet against the wall and scrambled upward, catching the next handhold with his full palm. By the third handhold he had a feeling for the motion he needed, and swung quickly, boosting himself with his momentum.

He tried to time his movement with the roar of the crowd, figuring they'd be less likely to spot him if they were focused on Charle and Flint. It sounded as if the Hangmen were giving at least as much as they got. Good—the longer they could make a fight of it, the more time Ashes had to—

His fingers missed the last brick.

He clutched his previous handhold tightly just in time, and found himself dangling from it with his stomach in his throat. It took him several hasty breaths before he found enough composure to place his off-hand on the wall and force his body into a better position. Heartbeat still thudding in the sides of his head, he waited.

The crowd had gone strangely quiet. Had he taken too long? Bruisemaker fights rarely lasted more than fifteen minutes. Desperately, he lunged for the last handhold, getting a firm grip just as he heard a Burroughsider's voice around the corner: "Take him, Charle!"

This was followed by a brief silence, and then a roar—of indignation or pride, Ashes couldn't tell.

He gulped a deep breath, knowing he had precious little time. The gap between him and the windowsill made his head spin: it looked to be nearly three feet. Not an intimidating gap—unless you were two stories up.

*Quick and fearless*, he reminded himself again, and jumped.

The empty air welcomed him. For a moment—it seemed long

enough for him to take a breath—he seemed to hang there, supported by nothing, as if his body had forgotten how to fall.

The windowsill reared up in front of him. One hand snatched at it clumsily and missed—

His other hand latched on like the jaws of a predator. He swung from the sill madly, bashed his knee against the wall, and then got his second hand on the sill. He forced his torso onto the ledge, and heard Ragged's voice coming from the courtyard, announcing the winner.

*Move!*

He pressed a flat palm against the window, expecting it to be latched. Instead, it swung open with just the slightest *creak*. A noxious stink struck his nose, and he had to force himself not to jerk backward. He reached inside the window and tugged himself forward, forcing his belly over the ledge. A moment later, he spilled face-first onto the floor.

Judging by the smell, he'd fallen into Ragged's lavatory; someone must have forgotten to lock the window while airing the place out. Ashes plugged his nose, pulled the window shut behind him, and made swiftly for the door.

The lavatory connected to a larger, lightless room. He could see the silhouettes of a large, opulent bed, a table beside it, and a wardrobe. To one side was a vanity with a full-body mirror; to the other, a tall dresser. His bare feet squished against a thick carpet. Prickles ran across his skin.

He was standing in Hiram Ragged's bedroom.

He gritted his teeth. No time to stop and gawk. Ragged would end the festivities in minutes and return here shortly thereafter. Ashes needed to *move*.

Glamours were always in clothing, as far as he'd heard, so he made for the wardrobe first. It was large enough to swallow Ashes whole, and when he opened it, his heart sank. There were a dozen different suits inside, and more shoes than Ashes had time to count.

He ran his fingers over the fabric anyway, trying to feel for—what, some sort of tingle? He swore under his breath.

He abandoned the wardrobe and sprinted to the bedside table. The first of its four drawers contained a set of spectacles and many differently colored pocket-watches, none of which seemed particularly magical. The second had a magazine displaying well-dressed Ivorish men in a variety of fashionable outfits. The third was locked, and the fourth filled entirely with paper, each sheet covered in tiny, neatly scribed print.

His heart was thudding terribly fast now. He needed more time.

He jerked at the sound of footsteps coming up the stairs. Quick as winking, he shut the drawer he'd been riffling through and darted inside the wardrobe. He buried himself in the suit jackets and trousers, then pulled the door nearly closed, taking care not to lock himself inside.

Through the crack in the door, Ashes saw light spill in from the hall. Ragged entered, cackling madly.

"Oh, John, John, John. Aren't *you* in trouble."

"He cheated!" John Flint protested. His voice trembled.

"Oh, but he cheated cleverly, my boy, very cleverly indeed. And that's what matters in the end, isn't it? Now, undo those."

"Mr. Ragged, please—"

"*Don't* argue with me, boy," Ragged snarled. "These were always the rules."

"He . . . No, he cheated . . ." Flint was almost sobbing now.

"Don't weep, John. This won't hurt a bit."

● ● ●

*Ashes forced himself to* wait an hour. He counted the seconds. After that, he forced himself to wait another hour. He had no fear of falling asleep; his blood seemed to be pounding hard enough to break through his skin. He wondered if his heartbeat could be heard out-side the wardrobe, and if Ragged knew he was in there and was waiting just outside, sipping tea and smiling.

When he couldn't bear it any longer, he eased the wardrobe door open. The room was blacker than tar, but his eyes were used to it by now. He could just discern Ragged's form sprawled on the bed, motionless. Carapace had come and removed John Flint a long while ago. Mr. Ragged fell asleep only a few minutes later.

And, Ashes noticed, he had not removed his hat until he got into bed.

Ragged had multitudes of suits and shoes and accessories. But there were no hats in the wardrobe, or anywhere Ashes had seen. It seemed more than a little strange that a man who was never seen without his hat would only own one.

Ashes crept closer, the carpet muffling his cautious footfalls. Ragged had set his hat on the bedside table, mere inches away from his reach. It was far too dark for Ashes to see Mr. Ragged's face, but he knew with a cold certainty that it had changed. Noiselessly, he grasped the hat and backed away.

He turned to the vanity and set the hat on his head. Something soft and gossamer-light fell against the skin of his cheeks, like he had walked through a spiderweb. His eyes were just sharp enough to see, even through the dark, that his appearance in the mirror was changed.

He was wearing Mr. Ragged's face. The thought made him want to be sick.

Ashes turned to the sleeping man, and curiosity welled up in him. What did Mr. Ragged *really* look like?

He took a step toward the bed. As if in answer, Ragged snorted, fidgeting uneasily in his sleep. Ashes's heart smashed against his throat. Not the time to satisfy his curiosity. Time to be somewhere different.

He shivered once again as he approached the door. He stood

before it and paused—half out of instinctive caution and half, perhaps, to prove to himself he wasn't scared.

The door opened.

"My Lord?"

A tall man in black and white servant's clothing. A stink vaguely
reminiscent of sour milk, a sense of unease.

*Furies.*

*Carapace.*

# 7 Descent

**A**SHES froze. His heart stamped against his chest mercilessly, as if trying to escape his body. Carapace stood just an arm's-span away from him, shoes brightly gleaming, pants pressed—Furies, did he ever sleep? A tray of varied foods, some sort of late-night snack, rested in his gloved hands.

He couldn't see Carapace's face; instinct had grabbed his neck and forced him not to look upward, screaming that Carapace would recognize him, forgetting entirely that his face was different.

"My Lor—?"

Movement came all at once, erupting out of his gut and surging through him. There was no involvement from his mind; better to leave the thinking part out of this.

He struck the tray of food from the bottom with his fist and fruits and little meats exploded off the platter and something like a pained cry broke out of Carapace's mouth. This was because Ashes's knee had landed squarely between Carapace's legs. Carapace lurched to one side and gasped and Ashes didn't wait another moment. He ran.

Mr. Ragged's frenzied voice behind him. "Get him!"

Ashes's feet struck the stairs. He bounded down them, taking three at a time and jumping the last five, scrambling to his feet—

He slammed against the front door of Ragged House, scrabbled at the doorknob, while Ragged's voice rose in pitch and volume. "Thief! Don't let him get away!"

The knob twisted. Carapace's heavy footsteps on the stairs as Ashes slammed his shoulder against the door—

The courtyard opened up before him and he slammed the door shut and ran wildly. He heard voices behind him, unintelligible, furious.

He crashed against the gate and it swung open and he burst onto the street without slowing a bit. He clutched the silk hat to his head to keep it from falling.

He did not look back but he heard Ragged screaming.

"You can't outrun them!"

The corner came up fast and he took it without slowing at all and his feet went out from under him. He caught himself on one hand and got his balance and took off once again.

Ashes ran flat-out for several minutes before he glanced back. He saw no one behind him. He slowed, sucking down air that burned his throat, and ducked behind a corner and checked again. Still no one.

He'd lost them! Carapace and whoever else Ragged had sent out had been too slow. Ashes would get away free and clear.

A howl split the night air, and was answered by three others, and all at once Ashes realized that no one had been sent after him. Ravagers.

He had never been outdoors this late. It had to be nearly midnight. Every Ravager in Burroughside would be awake, and hungry—and they would have heard Ragged's screaming, and smelled the scent of Ashes's sweat and fear . . .

Could he hide somewhere? No Burroughsider would open the door for him this late, but he knew a bolthole a mile and a half to the north. The question was how many Ravagers stood between him and safety.

No time to wonder. He turned north, and just then a Ravager loped into view at the end of the street.

Ashes froze, but not quickly enough: the Ravager's eyes landed on him and the creature's face split in a grotesque parody of a smile. Slaver dripped from its mouth. Its teeth were discolored but sharp as knives.

The Ravager stood perfectly still. Ashes quivered. It had not stopped out of fear or caution. It was waiting for him to run. It wanted to chase.

Ashes had a lead of nearly thirty feet. Ravagers were inhumanly fast, but that distance had to be significant. His blood was singing with adrenaline—he could run the mile and a half without slowing once, terrified as he was. He just needed to catch his breath.

He heard a noise behind him and turned. Another Ravager stood at the intersection, between him and freedom. The second Ravager's eyes flicked between the prey and the competition. It let out a low, primal sound from deep in its chest.

Ashes tensed. His exit was blocked off, but the Ravagers weren't part of the same pack. They would fight each other first. If it gave him just a few moments . . .

The Ravagers keened and dashed forward.

Ashes faced the nearer one and bent at the knees. The creature was impossibly fast—in a breath it had closed the distance between them. Ashes threw himself to the side, but the Ravager reacted immediately, shifting its direction without visible effort. It crashed into his chest and tackled him to the ground—Ashes felt his leg twist violently to one side, sending a shock of pain from his knee to his hip. He cried out in agony, which only encouraged the Ravager; it let out a wild snarl and sank its teeth into his shoulder and tore out a mouthful of flesh. It reared its head in triumph, spraying hot blood over Ashes's face.

The second Ravager reached them just then and struck Ashes's attacker with the force of a careening carriage. Both monsters fell in a heap to one side, screeching and growling. They struck at each other with their hands crooked like claws, rending skin with each strike.

Ashes rolled to the side and tried to get to his feet, and screamed as his leg gave out beneath him. He fell hard on his belly and looked at the leg. Not broken, but twisted enough that he didn't dare run on it. He needed something else, he looked around desperately—

There was a sewer drain just a few feet from him.

Suicide. He knew it was suicide. The creatures beneath the streets could kill him just as easily as the Ravagers could.

He looked back. The Ravagers were still tangled together, snarling and screeching, but one would win eventually. And Ashes didn't have a chance at outrunning it.

He gritted his teeth and snatched Mr. Ragged's hat off the road and crawled toward the hole as fast as his twisted leg would permit. When he reached it he turned on his belly and let his feet slide through the hole first, wondering as he did whether something would bite off his bottom half before he made it through.

There wasn't time to wonder. One of the Ravagers had trapped the other underneath it, and as Ashes watched it struck a merciless blow to its foe's temple. The other Ravager stopped moving immediately.

*Furies.*

The victorious Ravager keened in satisfaction and looked around for its prize—for Ashes. It found him in a moment, and lunged—just as Ashes gave himself a final push and slid through the gap into the sewer.

The drop couldn't have been more than three feet, but he landed hard enough to send a spike of pain up his twisted leg. He collapsed just as the Ravager's hand shot through the opening and passed through the air over Ashes's head, nearly catching him by the hair. The Ravager snapped and howled in rage, but it was far too large to fit through the gap. It screeched one final time and then pulled its hand out, apparently defeated.

Ashes, meanwhile, reoriented himself to put the sewer wall to his back as quickly as he could. He stared up at the drain as the Ravager stamped its feet furiously above him. When, finally, the creature finished its tantrum, Ashes counted off a full minute before forcing himself to his feet.

Would the Ravager wait for him to come back up? They weren't known for their cleverness, but it didn't take a great deal of strategic skill to wait where prey disappeared. But the alternative . . .

Ashes had heard dozens of stories about the things that lived in the sewers. Serpents with the faces of men on the backs of their flat heads, and enormous lions with flaming breath, and man-shaped hollows in the world that could swallow you up just by touching you. The details changed, except for this: there were monsters under the streets of Teranis, and they knew the scent of blood.

He didn't dare try to climb out the sewer drain; the Ravager might have gone, but if any of its kin wandered by, Ashes would be dead for certain. He wasn't sure he had the strength to pull himself out anyway. And the stories were—were *just* stories.

Weren't they?

● ● ●

*Ashes walked. He held* Mr. Ragged's hat in one hand, and kept the other pressed against the tunnel's curved wall to keep weight off his twisted leg. He followed the trickling path of the water, which would flow unerringly toward the Lethe; if he could only get there, everything would be all right.

Time had passed. Ashes couldn't have guessed how much. An hour? Two? Was it dawn above him? However long it had been, he had not encountered anything monstrous or bloodthirsty, and he counted that a blessing. Still, he found that as the minutes crawled by, he didn't grow more confident.

The darkness didn't help. It was darker beneath the street than any darkness Ashes had ever known. It muffled his ears and made his skin prickle; the dark had *weight*. Even if there had been light, it would have shattered, like a sliver of glass beneath a boot.

And there were sounds. Skittering, hissing things. They sounded like rats, sometimes, a multitude of them. Other times they sounded like serpents in the water, or like footsteps and a whispered impression of music.

He was being a fool. A silly, naive little boy frightened of the dark. But he couldn't even pretend to be fearless here. His belly was tense. His fingers quivered.

There was an eddy in the water at his feet, and he bent to check the bottom of the whirlpool. His fingers brushed against something heavy. He tugged it out of the water, felt over its edges, and frowned. Too smooth to be a bit of broken brick, and he could feel an odd, finger-sized hole in the middle. But it fit well in his palm, and felt heavy enough to hurt someone if he swung it well. Absently, he clutched it.

*There really could be anything down here*, he thought. Something could be standing right in front of him and he would never see it. Sewer-beasts could smell blood, and fear, but Ashes was drowned in the darkness, and he could smell nothing but the cloying stink, and he heard nothing but—

*There!*

He spun and smashed the heavy thing in his fist against the

ground. Instead of striking water or stone, it hit something soft and fleshy. He swung again, and the creature squealed as it died.

Fur underneath his fingers. A rat. Not even a very big one.

He wobbled to his feet, shaking all over. He still heard movement. It seemed louder now. And he heard . . . footsteps?

The faint strains of someone singing reached his ears. He recognized the melody in an instant—or he thought he did, for he realized just as quickly that he couldn't remember any words, or where he had heard the music before. The voice sounded human. Almost.

Ashes shuddered and turned away, moving down another tunnel. The music did not follow him, but it took a long time to fade away.

*Wonder if I'm going mad.*

How unfair it would be to come so close. Stealing a Glamour from the governor of Burroughside was a damn high accomplishment, wasn't it? He could've brought it to the Lass, moved to Boreas, forgotten about Saintly and Ragged forever. He'd come so close.

*Don't think like that,* he told himself. He wasn't mad yet. Just spooked, and who could blame him? He couldn't see, and there were horrid singing things down here, and who was talking?

He blinked and the voice stopped. Him. He'd been muttering to himself without noticing.

"I got to get out of here," he said, knowing that he'd said it aloud. He wouldn't lose his mind down here. Not this way.

He stopped and tapped his shoe against the floor. There was no splash; he'd lost the stream.

"Damn," he said, and something behind him hissed.

*Faces, Blimey, I hope you make it out all right.*

Sharp teeth struck him once, and again, and the dark swallowed up his screams.

# 8 *Deceit*

**T**HE place where Ashes woke did not smell like Burroughside, or the sewer, or anything else he knew. It smelled sharp, and the smell burned, a kind of aggressive, acidic emptiness that forced its way up his nostrils and set fires on the edges of his brain.

The last thing he remembered was teeth—terrible, curved knives, longer than his fingers—sinking into the flesh of his leg, his belly, his shoulder. He'd realized death was coming when the venom reached his bloodstream and his veins caught fire. After that everything was a blur of pain and confusion, and a final burst of bright light.

Now Ashes felt wrung out, but his head was shockingly clear. No more stink of the sewer, no more cloud of pain. The wounds where the creature had bitten him were gone, and even the raw bruises around his neck no longer throbbed. All of that pain was gone, erased completely.

He drew the quite sensible conclusion that he had died.

This air that stank of emptiness, then, was where the Faces kept the newly dead. He'd heard a Facepainter Priest once say that after death, the Faces—all nine, or thirteen, or one hundred seventeen, or however many of them there were—would evaluate you, and if you had honored them, they took you with them into the afterlife.

*I'm fair buggered, then*, Ashes thought, with more calmness than he would have expected. The Face of Marvels and the rest of the pious ones would never have him: he didn't really belong to Teranis, after all. Kindness only took women, and Prudence wouldn't so much as spit on Ashes. His best hope would have been the Face of Cunning, but that was only a faint chance now. Cunning didn't tolerate those who died of their own stupidity, and what had Ashes done if not that? He had hidden in the wardrobe rather than running for the window: a stroke of spectacular idiocy. He had earned this death.

Would the Faces leave him here, then? Ashes hadn't stayed to hear the specifics of damnation. What would the Faces condemn someone to? Eternal boredom? Utter emotionlessness?

His thoughts were interrupted by a detail, something that didn't fit if he really was dead. Why was his back so cold?

His eyes opened. He was in a small room, lying on a table of polished stone, or something equally smooth. There was a harsh white light directly above him, too bright and unwavering to be a candle or a lamp. He sat up and saw to his left a shelf filled with strange metal instruments and glass jars full of clear liquid. To his right he saw a door.

His head spun as he swung his legs off the table, and when his bare feet touched the floor he shivered; the stone was freezing cold. He stood—or he tried to. Immediately his head spun and his legs went numb, forcing him to sit back down. Everything below his waist felt prickly and cold; something had gone quite wrong with his legs.

"What the bloody *hell* is going on?" he said aloud. He still sounded like himself; that was some comfort. But his legs seemed to be conducting a mutiny, and his sense of balance was gone entirely. And—how had he not realized earlier?—his clothes were gone; he was wearing a simple white shift. Ragged's hat and the stone he'd picked up in the sewer had vanished as well.

He set his feet against the floor again, testing his weight slowly. He seemed to have flimsy stilts attached to his waist instead of legs; his knees were rubbery and functionless. Gritting his teeth, he hobbled to the door and tested the knob. It swung open at his touch, revealing a narrow, dimly lit hallway.

He walked toward the source of the light as stealthily as he could, keeping a hand against the wall to support his weight. More strength returned to his limbs with every step. By the time the hall turned its corner, his footfalls were nearly noiseless.

The light was coming from an expansive sitting room. Ashes froze at the entrance, eyeing the inside. Lush carpet, a grand bookcase on one wall, and three lamps that he could see from here. The sharp nothing-smell was gone, replaced by an amalgam of dust and books and cologne.

*Denizen,* he thought immediately. *Maybe Ivory, even.* The thought made him shiver. He wasn't dead—he was trapped in some Denizen's home, nearly naked, with jelly instead of legs and no idea how he'd gotten here.

His head throbbed in time with his pulse. What was going on?

A voice came from the side of the room that Ashes couldn't see. "You ought to come in, I imagine. You'll get very little done out there."

Ashes hesitated. He was helpless and confused in someone's home; he couldn't afford to be incautious. But whoever was speaking had saved him from the sewer. Whatever else was going on, Ashes felt sure about that much.

He hobbled around the corner. His eyes went wide.

Directly across from him was a window that filled most of the wall. Teranis lay beyond it, pulsing with the fog-swamped light of a thousand streetlamps, looking as if the stars had spilled over the brim of the sky and dripped into the city. In the distance was a fiery red glow, a self-contained sunrise in the wrong side of the sky. Even farther away, intermittent strokes of lightning streaked along the horizon, too low to be a storm. Finally, his eyes found the Silver Tower—the center of Teranis, home of the Kindly Ones. It gleamed in the dark, a great sliver of carved moonlight.

Ashes did not realize there was a man standing at the window until the fellow turned around. His clothing was that of a high-ranking Denizen: a silk shirt with more buttons than could possibly be useful, a tapered suit jacket that ended sharply at his waist, and shoes bright as mirrors. He wore a beard on his hawkish face, and his eyes were a fierce, burning green.

Ashes peered at the man for a moment, puzzled. Recognition struck him—he knew the fellow. The Denizen's face had changed since they'd met in Yson, but Ashes knew in his gut that the man standing across from him was the Artificer, Jacob Rehl.

His recognition must have shown in his eyes. The man tilted his head. "*There's* an interesting development," he muttered. "Good evening, Francis Odd."

Ashes eyed the man warily. Had his legs felt more awake, they would have tingled with the instinct to run. "Hullo."

Jacob gestured to a chair. "You may sit, if you like. I doubt you're much for standing just now."

For a moment, Ashes thought of standing just to be contrary. But his legs *were* tired, and it wasn't as if sitting would put him *more* under the Artificer's power. He had no advantages here, no leverage. So he stumbled to the chair and fell into it, exaggerating the effort it took. Getting the Artificer to underestimate him would be something, at least.

Jacob took the chair opposite and busied himself for a moment with his jacket. When he looked up, the false face was gone; his beard had vanished, and his eyes were simple brown. This new man looked profoundly unremarkable, like a farm boy who'd grown up without realizing it. Another illusion? Or the Artificer's true face?

The Artificer fixed Ashes in an even stare. "Listen to me very carefully, lad," he said. "I think you've already sussed that you're in a certain amount of danger. You're in my home, relieved of your effects. No one knows where you are, and even if they did, I deeply doubt they would be in a position to help you. You're tired, probably hungry, and not particularly imposing in a physical sense. Do you understand what I'm saying?"

"That I'm small," Ashes guessed.

"That one of us is *in command* here. And it isn't you."

Ashes ground his teeth. "Did you drug me?"

Confusion flickered across the Artificer's features, then vanished as quickly as it had come. "Ah," he said. "Doubly curious."

"What're you talking about?"

"Nothing of importance to you, I'm afraid," the Artificer said, and he waved a hand. Instantly, the room, the floor, and the Artificer himself vanished, replaced by impenetrable darkness. Ashes jumped and let out a frightened cry before he realized he was gripping the arms of the chair. It hadn't disappeared; the Artificer had blinded him.

The veil of darkness dissipated a moment later, revealing the Artificer lounging comfortably. But his eyes were hard.

"I haven't drugged you," he said. "I trust you understand why I wouldn't need to."

Ashes swallowed and nodded.

"Good lad," the Artificer said. He leaned forward, looking suddenly amicable. "Now, I see no reason we can't both be professional about this. Continue understanding your position and we'll be jolly pals." The smile he gave was brittle as sugar-glass. "Now. Why were you following me?"

Ashes blinked. "I—erm—"

The Artificer held up a hand before Ashes could continue. "I hope you won't feel any need to lie to me," he said. "What loyalty you might have given your employer is, surely, diminished by his willingness to fling you into the sewers."

"Nobody sent me," Ashes said. The Artificer's eyes flashed fierce red and the light in the room seemed to warp around the Artificer's body. Ashes shivered. He knew the display was engineered—entirely fake. But that did not make it less frightening.

"A valiant effort, Francis," he said. "You may tell me the truth now. Mind, if I like your story, I might even let you leave this place."

Ashes paused, thinking furiously. He *hadn't* been sent by anyone. Why was the Artificer so convinced otherwise?

*He's got enemies*, Ashes realized. The sort of enemies who would send a tail after him. But why would it matter if someone followed Jacob into the sewers? It wasn't illegal, just stupid. Why would the Artificer care if someone had seen him down there?

And then Ashes realized that he was focused on the wrong thing. *Why* didn't matter at all. What mattered was the Artificer wanted something, and he thought Ashes had it.

Ashes could work with that.

He met the Artificer's eyes timidly and admitted, "I dunno who he was. He never let me see his face."

Jacob leaned forward, intrigued. "You're certain it was a man?"

"Sounded that way," Ashes said. "His voice was all— It was gravelly, like. And throaty."

Jacob frowned. "Easy enough to fake. How did he keep his face hidden from you?"

Ashes's mind raced, but his mouth was faster. "Magic," he said. "He— There was always a sort of cloak over his face. Like shadows." He cursed inwardly; hiding your face in woven shadow was storybook nonsense. If anyone was likely to know that, it was an Artificer! But the man's eyes betrayed no confusion or skepticism. Perhaps it was not nonsense to this sort of man.

"And how long have you worked for him?"

"Only since the day I met you," Ashes said immediately. "He caught me after I left Yson. Said he needed somebody small and clever and he could pay me whatever I wanted. He never mentioned I'd be going in the sewer."

The Artificer rested his chin on one hand, staring at Ashes calmly. He didn't interrupt, so Ashes continued with a grimace, "He wouldn't even let me bring a light with me. Said I'd be motivated to follow you if I knew I wouldn't survive otherwise."

"And how were you to get in contact with him afterward?"

"He said I had to watch for something, and I'd know what I was looking for when I saw it. And if I saw it, I should go sit in Harrod Park tomorrow and wait for him to find me. And—and he said, erm, that if I betrayed him, or tried to lie so I could get his money, then I'd wish I'd never woken in this city."

Jacob made a noncommittal noise deep in his throat. "What a pleasant fellow."

Ashes nodded timidly and shrank back into his seat, hiding his satisfaction. Harrod Park! That had been a cunning stroke. If the Artificer wanted to tempt his enemy into the open, he would send Ashes to the park and watch for his enemy—and Ashes would slip easily into the crowd, never to be bothered with Jacob Rehl again.

"And what of this?"

Ashes looked up. The Artificer was holding a glass-smooth stone smaller than his palm. The hole in the center jogged Ashes's memory.

"What about it?" he asked.

The Artificer's eyes glinted. "Where did you find it?"

Ashes hesitated. Why would the stone matter to this man? "In a water trap. Thought it might be handy in a fight."

"You needed something to fight with?"

"I lost your light," Ashes said, more smoothly this time. "I was following too far behind and I got turned about, and I wanted something I could fight with."

"Against aetherlings?" His tone was familiar: the same he'd had when he asked why Ashes kept playing cards against the surly man.

"If that's what you want to call them."

The Artificer leaned back in his seat and stared at Ashes. Ashes stared back, keeping his face neutral. Eventually, the Artificer sighed heavily and said, "Bollocks."

"What?"

"Bollocks," Jacob said again. "Tell me, did you go into the sewer on some asinine dare? Or did you simply fall through a grate and strike your head?"

"I—" Ashes paused. "You don't believe me?"

"About your mysterious employer whose face is wreathed in shadow? No. *Stunningly*, I am not convinced by your fairy tale."

"It's true! Every word of it! Come with me to Harrod Park if you don't believe me!"

"I don't think we need to go quite that far." Jacob pocketed the stone and tapped his cheek thoughtfully. "I don't find your story of a mysterious employer particularly compelling—but, fortune of yours, I am having the most damnably difficult time believing that you are a spy."

Ashes froze halfway through another protestation. "Why?"

"Because someone clever enough to beat me at cards is not likely to be an idiot," Jacob said. "And following me into the sewers for a dodgy employer is an idiotic thing to do. What were you really doing down there?"

"I told you," Ashes said. "Nobody sent me."

"Oh, I'm perfectly convinced of that," Jacob replied. "But what drove you down there?"

"I was hiding. From Ravagers."

Jacob let out a single, sharp laugh. "Honest enough, by the seems. You're just the right sort of reckless to try escaping *anoma* in the bloody sewers. *That* I can believe."

Ashes grinned weakly, unsure of what to do next. The Artificer had changed his mood as suddenly and completely as he had changed his face. Gone was the threatening, dangerous man; someone charming, almost jovial, sat in his chair now. Somehow, the shift didn't make Ashes any less nervous.

"Ah, me," Jacob said. He sank back into his chair, mouth twisted in a wry grin. "No need to look so glum, lad. The fact that you're not a spy is exceptionally good news."

"Good news for who?"

"Both of us. It means we're not enemies. It also means I didn't wake a witch in the middle of the night for the sake of a traitor, which puts me in rather a buoyant mood."

Ashes stared at him, confused. "You took me to a witch?"

"I would've taken you to my surgeon and saved myself the expense, but there was more venom in you than blood, and there's naught for that but magic," Jacob said. "The crone's fees are extortionate, but I couldn't afford to lose your information if you *were* sent to follow me."

Ashes held in his awe. Witch-favors were mind-bogglingly expensive; even some of the Ivory Lords couldn't afford them. This Artificer had a secret, and he was willing to pay piles of money just to protect against the possibility that someone had found it out. *What's he hiding?*

"Your legs were the worst of it," Jacob went on. "And the witch couldn't quite make the magic behave, not knowing your true name. Still. Better than the alternative, eh?" The Artificer stood. "Your effects are in the next room. I'd recommend burning the lot, but that'll be your choice, ultimately. The blood'll probably wash out."

Ashes blinked. "You—you're letting me go?"

"I've no reason to delay you," Jacob said. "Quite frankly, I've other things to be getting on with." He gave a wan smile. "I'm afraid I'll have to blindfold you on the way out. Somehow, I doubt it's in my best interest to let you know exactly where I live."

Ashes hesitated. The Artificer would let him get away, free and clear. He could get back to Blimey, and they could find Bonnie the Lass and get out of Burroughside for good.

But he couldn't leave, not yet. Not when such an opportunity had fallen directly into his lap.

The most important part of any grift was getting marks to buy in. The more money they committed, the more determined they became to win it all back—to keep playing even though they were doomed to lose. In truth, most cons were won with the first gambled coin. Getting the rest was a formality.

And Jacob Rehl had wagered hugely on Ashes. First a crown, now a witch-favor. No one wanted to take a loss on a gamble like that.

"Probably it isn't," Ashes said slowly. "But it's not in your best interest to let me leave, either."

The Artificer raised an eyebrow. "Oh?"

"Seems to me you're in a bind," Ashes said. "Whatever you were doing in the sewer, it's not the sort of thing you want getting found out. And you've been doing it a while, or you wouldn't be so worried that someone had sent a tail after you. I bet there're even folk who'd pay a lot of money to find out what it is."

Jacob's eyes darkened and the light around him shuddered, just a little. "You threatening me, lad? In my own home?"

"No, sir," Ashes said. "I want a job."

The Artificer laughed. "Wanting is weakness, lad," he said. "You think I'm in need of a courier?"

Ashes bristled. "No," he said. "Not a courier. But you need somebody who *can* go places. Someone clever and small and hard to notice. Someone who wouldn't be tied back to you, if he got seen."

Jacob eyed him; Ashes couldn't tell if he was amused or intrigued. "And you think you could be of use to me in that regard."

"I figure so, sir."

"I admire your self-esteem," Jacob said drily. "But you can't be older than—what, fourteen?"

"All that means is folk underestimate me," Ashes said. "Means I can go places you can't without being noticed. And you know I'm clever."

Jacob grinned wryly. "I don't hire people for their ability to beat me at cards."

"That's not all I got, sir. You know who Hiram Ragged is?" Ashes asked. "Governor of Burroughside? Rank bastard, got a big fence?"

"I know of him," the man said. "Unsavory fellow."

Ashes drew himself up, assuming a mask of bold confidence. "I broke into his house not five hours ago. Got out free as anything, too."

"To arrive ignominiously in the sewers," Jacob pointed out.

"So I'd be loyal. You saved my life. I wouldn't throw you over. I owe you."

Jacob chuckled again. "It's not quite so simple," he said. "I don't employ people simply for their cleverness, or their loyalty."

"So what do you employ them for?"

Jacob held out his hand. The air around him became dull, and a searingly bright sphere, no bigger than a thumbnail, erupted over his hand. It hurt to look at. Jacob clicked his fingers, and the light vanished.

"What do you think?" the Artificer asked softly.

Ashes watched the display with barely contained awe. Spots swam in front of his eyes. The man had created a miniature sun in

a single breath—he hadn't even strained. Weren't Glamours supposed to take time? That was what Ashes had always heard.

"That's— Well, anybody can learn Artifice," Ashes protested.
"I know letters. I could learn things."

"Anyone can learn Artifice," Jacob said. His voice lowered,
becoming almost reverent. "But it's a rare gift, exceedingly rare,
to be an Artificer. And I've no use for an agent without the cant.
Have you ever snatched raw light from the air? Made your face
look like someone else? Willed the world to be different, and been
obeyed?"

"Not— Well, no," Ashes said. "I don't think so."

"Then I'm afraid I've nothing to offer you, lad," Jacob said. He
rubbed his jaw thoughtfully. "Although . . ."

"Although what?"

The Artificer looked at Ashes with the skeptical, curious look
of someone appraising goods at a market. Ashes felt very small,
being looked at like that. Small and young and foolish.

Then the man walked to the bookcase on the opposite wall and
plunged a hand through one of the books as if it weren't there—
which, Ashes reminded himself, it wasn't.

Jacob pulled something from the hidden space behind the
books; he turned around holding a small box made of glass or,
rather, something that was almost glass. It was frosty blue, and
webbed with thin, lightning-white veins. There were no seams, no
lid or hinges, and it was hollow. Inside was a viscous silver fluid.

Jacob brought it to the table, and as it came closer Ashes could
see that the liquid within was unlike anything he knew. It moved,
constantly and of its own will: expanding and shifting like a cloud
of smog without losing its glossy, smooth texture. With each shift,
it assumed a new, vaguely familiar shape. One moment it had the
face of a woman; then it became a horse and carriage; then the
prow of a ship cresting a wave. For the barest fraction of a second,
it was Ashes's own face.

Jacob set the box on the table, and the instant he removed his hand from the glass, the liquid collapsed onto the bottom of the box. It was perfectly still.

Jacob sat and folded his hands together, eyeing the box warily. "This box was made at least two and a half centuries ago," he said. "It may be twice as old as that. There are not more than fifty like it in the wide world. If you break it, or damage it, or in any way cause it harm, your hands are forfeit. Do you understand me?"

Ashes gulped. He nodded.

"Put your hand on top," the Artificer commanded. "Gently."

Ashes set his palm on the glass. He shivered at the touch; it was much colder than he expected. The silver fluid remained pooled at the bottom, placid except for a single ripple that bloomed in the center.

"Now close your eyes."

Ashes hesitated. The Artificer looked at him.

"I've no intent to harm you," Jacob said. "And your sight wouldn't keep you safer, even if that were the case."

Ashes closed his eyes. It made him feel fidgety and nervous, but he forced himself to stay still.

"Good. Hmm . . . are you an orphan, Francis Odd? Do you remember your parents?" Jacob asked.

Ashes cracked one eye. "What's that got to do with anything?"

"Answer the question. And close both eyes."

"Don't remember them."

"Shame. Emotional connections make it easier."

"What?"

"Where do you live?"

"What?" Ashes said again.

"Your home. Where you sleep. Where is it?"

"Burroughside."

"But what does it look like?"

"No business of yours!"

Jacob laughed. "Very well. Leave that, then. Tell me something about you, Francis Odd."

"I'm starting to think you're off your rook. That count?"

"You give new meaning to the term *ornery*," Jacob said drily.

Ashes thought that sounded like the kind of word Blimey would say, and just as he thought it the glass box sent a current of lightning through his fingers. He snatched back his hand and opened his eyes to see the silver fluid pressed against the top of the box. The liquid fell back down almost immediately, but not before Ashes glimpsed the shape it had taken: Blimey's face.

"Ah," Jacob said. "How intriguing."

"What was that?"

"Evidence. Rather compelling evidence."

"Of what?"

The Artificer did not reply except to look at Ashes. His expression had taken on the opaque blankness experienced card sharps wore when they played each other, when a bluff could be as incriminating as a tell.

"What's it mean?" Ashes asked again.

The Artificer didn't even look as if he'd heard the question. "What's your name, lad?" he asked softly. The man's voice had gone strangely flat, the vocal equivalent of his unreadable face. "Don't lie to me. Pretend the answer to this question is important."

Ashes swallowed. He sensed danger, but he couldn't be sure just what kind, or why it had come now. "Ashes. Sir."

Jacob's eyes widened, a momentary crack in his mask. "My gods. You're *rasa*."

Ashes nodded. "Been in the city three years, or near it. No memory of before that, not even the name I had."

"Why Ashes?"

"I was coated in coal and dust and such, when they found me," he said. "From the factories."

"By my blood and bone," the man said. "Well . . . Ashes . . . one good turn deserves another. You may call me Candlestick Jack." He stood again, looking faintly perturbed. "I think we could reach an arrangement."

Then he walked through the solid wall behind him.

Ashes blinked, and then, reminding himself what the man was, followed.

# 9 Student

**Y**OU'RE not wrong that I'm in the market for certain . . . extralegal services," Jacob—Candlestick Jack—said as Ashes passed through the false wall onto a stairway leading down. "Of the breaking, entering, deceiving, and swindling variety. And there's a very good chance I could make use of you in those, if you're as clever as I take you to be."

At the bottom of the stairs, Jack plucked a key from his pocket and slid it inside a lock that looked far too small to fit it. Even more Glamours; the man took his hidden staircase seriously.

"Why?" Ashes asked. "Two minutes ago you didn't want nothing to do with me."

"They have been two very enlightening minutes," Jack said as he opened the door.

The room beyond gave an impression of great space that was nevertheless filled to the brim. Tall shelves lined the walls, every inch covered with an assortment of knickknacks: multitudes of rings, necklaces, hats, ruffs, scarves, folded capes and robes and jackets, ribbons, large keys, small keys, wood-carvings, pocket-watches, woven baskets, playing cards, bricks, bird feathers, alchemist's bottles, dreamcatcher jars, bright metal gears, and one flintlock pistol. Every item had a neatly written label, though written in some opaque code. Ashes was struck with the impression that he'd stumbled into the largest magpie's nest in the world.

Two tables stood in the center of the room, each covered with curious metal tools and bulging ledgers. The only other furniture was a cabinet at the end of the room, and, in the corner, a grandfather clock big enough for Ashes to sleep inside.

"What do you think?"

Jack was watching his face, evaluating his reaction. "There's a lot of stuff in here," Ashes admitted.

"Anchors," Jack said, walking toward the tables. "At least, that's what any half-decent Artificer would call them. To the uninitiated, everything is Glamours."

"Eh?"

"Anchors," Jack said, and then recited: "Solid objects with the capacity to retain a construct for a period of time. As opposed to Glamours, which haven't existed for centuries."

Ashes frowned. "I don't—"

"I know you don't," Jack said. He plucked one of the ledgers from its pile and began leafing through it absently. "But you will, very soon."

Ashes nodded, distracted by a delicate, expensive-looking vase. A piece of him—a rapidly shrinking piece—wondered how many of these Anchors he could steal, and whether he'd be paid well for it.

"Sir—" he began, but Jack made a cutting motion with one hand.

"No more of that," Jack said. "No 'sir' or 'milord' or 'goodly gentleman.' I'm Jack, and you're Ashes. Let's have a bit of honesty between liars, eh? Down here, certainly."

"I still don't understand what's going on," Ashes admitted.

"I should think you'd understand rather quickly, sharp boy like you," Jack said. He let out a soft "Aha!" and snapped the ledger shut, then whirled toward one of the shelves. "I take it you've already realized that every one of these items is, in one way or another, magical?"

"All of them?"

"Every single one," Jack said. "Some have been done under contract. Some for practice or personal enjoyment. Still others are there in anticipation of when I may need them. Then, of course, comes my apprentice's handiwork, which is . . . voluminous, all things considered." He selected one of the items on a high shelf and turned around, bringing it back to the table. "Any given one costs close to ten crowns to make."

Ashes's eyes widened without his permission. Ten crowns was an almost unthinkable sum. More money than he'd collect in a good year of begging and thieving. And everything in this room was worth that much . . .

"Delightful," Jack said. "You *can* be shocked. That's good—you ought to understand how much money is around you right now. Because if you work for me, and work well, I can make you wealthy enough that you would scorn the very thought of pinching my Anchors. Do you understand?"

Ashes nodded.

"Good. The next thing you should know is that I don't intend to give you easy work." Jack slid the item he'd gotten off the shelf across the table. It was a pocket-watch, polished to a high sheen. "Open it," Jack commanded.

Ashes clicked the clasp. The watch-face within was gorgeously made, constructed of silver and pure white stone. An image sprang from it as the cover moved aside: a woman, no taller than Ashes's thumb, with her hands held over her head in a graceful arch. She stood on tiptoe, one leg outstretched in a balletic pose. The miniature dancer wore a slender purple dress and an expression of concentration. She traveled slowly around the center of the watch-face, revolving on one foot as she did. The detail was astounding. Her hair, dark as a raven wing, had strands that floated away from the rest. Her nose was small in proportion to her face, and turned up just a little. He could even distinguish her dark eyelashes.

"My apprentice brought me this," Jack said, "as an *application* to study here. Synder. You'll meet her. She's smarter than you."

"It's pretty," Ashes said skeptically. "What's it got to do with me?"

Jack's eyes gleamed as he snapped the watch shut and strode to the wall opposite from where they'd entered. He banged on the wall with one fist. "William!" he shouted. "I know you're awake."

"Never," came a reedy voice, "has such knowledge been so brazenly leveraged as blackmail."

"Pull your face out of the sink and come meet our newest woe-begone," Jack commanded, and returned to the table.

A wooden panel in the wall slid to one side. The man who ducked through it was tall, narrow-shouldered, with his mouth turned down in a faint grimace. "It boggles the mind to think how little consideration you give to simple hygiene."

Ashes peered at the newcomer with unabashed rudeness. The man had a papery face, devoid of all color, as if it had been permanently drained of blood. His hair, too, was pure white, and hung to his shoulders. Strangely, though, he looked quite young. Apart from his coloring he seemed no older than Jack. He wore a crisp, well-tailored suit, blue as a moonlit night.

"You can get back to them in a bit," Jack replied. "I figured now would be a good time for you to meet the new fool in our fold."

Ashes shot him a look, but Jack's gaze was fixed on the pale man. Ashes looked at him, too, and found blank blue eyes staring at him.

"He is canted?" William asked.

"Quite," Jack said. "I'd venture he's a Stitcher, though it's early to tell."

William lifted an eyebrow; the motion looked awkward and ungainly on his face, like a heavyset man trying to dance. "You summoned me from my ablutions to inflict a student on me, Weaver? Have I offended you recently? Or am I paying for some past sin?"

"Be nice, Will."

The man placed a hand in front of Ashes; it looked so mechanical that Ashes took fully three seconds to realize it was a handshake. "I surmise it is considered to be a pleasure, child. I am William, called the Wisp."

"Ashes," the boy replied. The man's hand was cool and smooth. It reminded Ashes powerfully of metal, or old, worn wood.

William looked at Jack. "Satisfied?" the pale man asked, and Jack nodded. William said, "I shall take my leave, then," turned sharply around, and returned from where he'd come. Jack chuckled as the man left.

"What just happened?" Ashes asked.

"I thought it would be good to get the shock out of the way as quickly as possible."

"He did seem . . . very strange," Ashes said.

"Hmm? Oh! Ha! No, sorry, for *him*." Jack grinned. "I suppose it's shocking for you as well. So that's good."

"He's an Artificer?"

"Canted from his first breath," Jack said proudly. "Just, it seems, as you are." He gave Ashes a calculating look, one the boy couldn't decipher.

"What are you on about?" Ashes demanded. "What's canted? And why'm I down here? What's going on?"

"So many questions," Jack said, his eyes shining. "*Canted* is an old word, from back before the Queens took over Teranis." Jack met his eyes. "It means 'gifted.' You are down here, my odd young *rasa*, because you are an Artificer. Tip to top."

Ashes frowned. "That can't be right. I've never done any of those things you said—pulling light, and that."

"Some Artificers don't manifest for a long while," Jack said, waving a hand. "And maybe being *rasa* delayed your development a bit. The important thing is, you have it. You're made of the same stuff as the folk who built this city, Ashes. The ones who forged every brick and building out of nothing but their thoughts and their magic. Just as I am. Just as Will and Synder and Juliana are." He held up his hand and dragged his finger through the air. The lamplight spooled around it, leaving behind a jagged shadow, like a tiny rip in the world. "In sum, Ashes, it means I'll take you on. Courier, thief, cardsharp—I'll find some use for someone of your abilities. And I'll do you one better: I'll teach you to use that cant of yours. Stick with me, lad, and I'll make you into someone this city will *fear*." Jack grinned widely. "If you'll have us, of course. Will's scared students off before."

If Ashes had not spent three years learning to keep his face blank, he might have shouted. "I—I think . . ."

"I should mention as well that I'm willing to reimburse you for living arrangements," Jack said carefully. "Five lumin a week should keep you safe from the cold." He thrust out a hand. "Do we have a deal?"

Even Ashes's blank face couldn't withstand it. He grinned and shook the Artificer's hand once, firmly. "Eh. I think we do."

## 10 Safety

IT was perhaps an hour before dawn; the eastern sky was blushing light blue, the fog on the streets receding. Ashes had crossed into Burroughside nearly twenty minutes ago, and heard no howls yet, but that hardly made him feel safe as he hurried toward the Fortress. Older Burroughsiders would swear blind that if you needed to move through the district at night, New Moon's was best for it: the Ravagers roamed only in ones and twos, rather than packs. Still, even a single Ravager would be more than enough against Ashes in his current state. So he kept a sharp eye, trying not to let his mind wander.

Half an hour's cautious travel got him safely to the Fortress. The witch-healing's side effects, compounded now by exhaustion, nearly prevented him from grasping the bottom rung of the ladder. Even when he had hold of it, climbing to the top left him with a stitch in his side. Dull fire seemed to have taken up permanent residence inside his legs.

Ashes had barely twisted the doorknob before it was wrenched from his hands. Blimey stood on the other side, face flooded with relief. "Ashes!" he exclaimed.

"Morning," Ashes said. He didn't bother to hide his grin.

"You're alive! Where've you been?"

"Time for questions later, mate," Ashes said. "Just now, we got to *move*."

Blimey stared at him, confused, and Ashes took him by the shoulders.

"I'll tell you everything," he swore. "Soon as we're safe. We've got to get somewhere else fast."

"Why're we not safe?"

"You trust me, Blimey?" Ashes asked. The boy nodded without a moment's hesitation. "Then wrap your face up. We're leaving."

Blimey's bed quickly shrank as they repurposed the rags into a makeshift mask; Ashes had no intention of letting Blimey's face be seen even in passing. In mere minutes, Blimey's features were entirely obscured except his mismatched eyes; even the strange shape of his head was mostly hidden. His ears still looked lumpy.

"Come on, then," Ashes ordered, but Blimey didn't follow. He turned to his collection of books.

"Blimey," Ashes said wearily, "no."

"I *need* them." Blimey's voice trembled, and so did he.

"We can't carry those down." Ashes tried to be firm, though he hated himself for doing it. "It'll take too much time, and we got to get there fast. Before sunup."

"Are the Ravagers out there?"

"Neh. I checked. Not a one I've seen."

Blimey shook again, looking fit to have a seizure. Ashes's gut twisted. He hated to separate Blimey from all his books. It was all the worse for the fact that he had no reason to leave except a suspicion that Saintly might seek him out here. He and Blimey weren't in explicit danger, not yet, but they would be certainly safer elsewhere.

Ashes sighed. "Blimey, look. I know you hate to leave them, but we can't stick around here. You can pick one, all right? But you got to do it now. We got to *go*."

Blimey let out a small noise, one Ashes hated to hear, and pulled the tome of new words out of the pile, along with a slim volume Ashes didn't recognize. Ashes eyed them both skeptically as Blimey produced a long strip of cloth and fashioned it into a makeshift sack around his books.

"That looks heavy."

"I can't leave it," Blimey said. He sounded steady now. Firm.

"It'll slow us down."

"I'll *not* leave it!"

Ashes could talk him out of it, but not quickly, and they couldn't afford to lose the dark. "All right. Come on."

●  ●  ●

*"You're properly mad, boy,"* Batty Annie said only a moment after she opened her door.

"Miss," Ashes said, "please. I promise we'll be worth your trouble."

"You know what time it is, facefaker?"

"Arse-off o'clock?"

"Precisely that," Annie said. "Exactly bloody that."

"Miss, you know I wouldn't bother you if it weren't an emergency," Ashes said. Her hand was still on the doorknob, prepared to shut the door in his face. "Please. We need someplace to hide, and you're the best I've got. I can pay."

She jerked her head at Blimey's mask. "What's under there?"

Ashes nodded to Blimey, who peeled the cloth upward so Annie could see his face. "Hello, miss," he said, clear but quiet.

The old woman's eyes narrowed; Ashes saw the brief spark of recognition, though Annie dimmed it quickly. She grabbed Ashes by the collar and yanked him forward, so that they were nearly nose to nose. Ashes controlled himself before he let his nose wrinkle. "*This* is what you bring to my door? At five o'clock in the Furied morning?"

"You're the only one I can trust, Annie," Ashes whispered. "No lies. No faking. If Ragged knew he was here, he'd burn Burroughside down to get at him."

"That supposed to compel me to let him houseroom?"

"Yes," Ashes said nervously. "Who else'd take someone in just to thumb their nose at Ragged?"

Annie let his collar go and took a step back. There was a bright, frightening light in her look. "You look like you ought to be dead."

"Ought to be. It didn't take." He held up five lumin, Jack's down payment on his services. "How'll this serve?"

The witchy woman stared at him a moment longer before taking the coin from him. "Follow on."

She led them briskly inside, through a densely packed sitting room and a small kitchen. "You can stay in the room at the bottom. Meals are twice daily, dawn and dusk. You miss them, you find your own." At the end of the hall, she opened a creaking door to a staircase leading down. Blimey glanced at Ashes, then walked quietly into the dark. Ashes paused at the top.

"You found a place for Jennie Trembly yet?" he asked the woman.

"Yes," she said. "And no, I'll not tell you where, owing as it's none of your damned business, boy."

"I don't need to know. But thank you."

"Hold just a moment," she said, snatching his wrist. "Mind me. You're not wrong I enjoy tweaking Ragged's corset. But nor'm I stupid. Seems to me you and your ward've got some semblance of targets on your backs, and I don't intend to burn for you. Come Festivale, you're gone from here."

The new year—only four months away. Ashes put on a charming smile. "Come, now, miss—"

"Gone. From. Here. You heard all those words, facefaker? They made sense to you?"

Ashes gritted his teeth and nodded.

"Good. Keep yourself to yourself and we'll get on famous." She left with a swish of her dress.

The room at the bottom of the stairs was small and dank, lit only by a single candle in an alcove. There was a single bed in the corner, and a shoddy desk, on which Blimey had already placed his two books. Blimey himself sat on the bed, looking pensively at the wall.

Ashes eyed the space. "We'll have to share the bed," he said. "I don't expect I'll use that desk much, that's yours. That's probably the water closet down—"

He stopped when he saw Blimey's face.

"What're you on about?" Ashes asked.

"Do we gotta stay here?"

"No other place," Ashes said firmly. "Batty Annie'll take care of us, Blimes. She's scary and she's strange, but we'll be safe. That's sure."

"Safe from *what*?" Blimey's voice cracked on the last word. His fingers were shaking. "What's going on, Ashes? First you're appearing out of nowhere after you're gone all night. And then we got to leave the Fortress, and leave all the books behind, and now we're— What are we doing? Why're we *here*?"

Ashes hesitated. How much could he tell Blimey? His friend was smart, certainly, but fragile, too. Ashes would *not* inflict nightmares on him. It was bad enough that Ashes dreamed of Saintly's knife every night.

"You just have to trust me," Ashes said. "There's—there's just been some trouble, is all. I figured we ought to lay low a span."

"Is it Ragged?" Blimey asked softly.

"Yes," Ashes said, before he could think better of it.

"He took my pardon back," Blimey said. "Didn't he? He decided he wants me dead again."

The conclusion struck Ashes out of nowhere, but he hid his shock. Where had Blimey come up with that idea?

"I knew he wouldn't leave us," Blimey admitted. "We were lucky he let us be as long as he did."

"I guess we were," Ashes said slowly. "How come you knew?"

"I just did," Blimey said. He seemed to shrink into himself then, retreating behind some wall in his mind. Ashes decided not to press him.

"It's not all bad," Ashes said. "We won't stay here forever. And—I met someone while I were out. An Artificer as wants me to work for him."

Blimey's eyes went wide as wheel hubs. "You speaking true?"

"Eh. I had to convince him some."

"What's he want you for?"

"Dunno yet. Sneak-thieving, probably. Says he'll make me rich. And . . ." He paused. He almost wanted *not* to tell Blimey; what if it was a dream? "And he says he'll teach me how to do what he does. Make Glamours."

Something shifted in Blimey's expression, almost unnoticeable. His eyes were hungry.

"You telling me truly?"

"I am," Ashes said. "Come a day when I'll make Glamours for both of us and we'll walk out of this place like real Ivories, all right? But meantime, we got to stay *here*. I know it's not where you want to be, but it's where you're safe. That's what matters right now."

Blimey looked around the room. He bunched up the blanket in his fists. "I don't . . . I don't have any books."

"I'll bring you some, mate," Ashes said. "We just got to stay safe a while. Till there's nobody coming for us."

## 11 Gutter Justice

THE carriage was pulled by four horses, each so dark it blended into the murk of the Teranis evening. They were massive beasts, glossy and beautiful, impressive even if an observer knew nothing about horses. *Striking*, that was the word. The carriage they pulled was striking, too, painted midnight black with silvery accents on its sides. It eased forward on wheels that made no noise, except for a soft whisper as they traversed the cobbles.

It was an extravagant mode of travel, the sort of carriage someone would buy to send a message. *I'm richer than you. Just look at my horses.*

Its owner sat within, a corpulent man dressed in fine silk and velvet. He wore a goatee, the sort only seen on people with enough money and pride to avoid honest friends. He was balding at the top, but one would never know it: he wore a gold earring specifically meant to make his head look lushly decorated. The ring in his pocket, when he put it on, would transform him even further, making him slender and sleek. He did not wear it in the private confines of his carriage; letting one's Weaving malfunction in public was quite gauche, and he could not afford to be wasteful.

He jerked upright as the carriage stopped. After a moment of waiting, he banged at the front of the carriage.

"Henri!" he shouted. "Why aren't we *moving*?"

He heard a *thunk*, as of something heavy landing on top of his carriage. A chill ran through him, but he was prepared for this. He slid his ring on, and opened the door.

"What is the meaning of this?" he demanded, deciding to take charge of the situation at once. He had built his illusory body to be immediately imposing: the shoulders were broad, the arms rippling with muscle. Its sole use was discouraging a real fight, which he was profoundly unlikely to win.

Five young men dressed in dark colors surrounded his carriage. They looked at him placidly, and did not reply. None of them seemed concerned that an obvious warrior had just exited the carriage.

"I will not ask again," the Artificer snarled, coloring his voice with as much confidence and fury as he could manage.

"Shouldn't be expecting you to, goodly sir," said a young voice from above him. The Artificer jumped and looked up.

Henri, his driver, fell off the roof of the carriage in two pieces, body and head.

"Best of eventides, milord," said the young voice, and a slender boy appeared just next to him. Handsome, he was, with knife-sharp eyes.

"I know your face," the Artificer said in shock. "You're—one of Ragged's boys, aren't you?"

"One of them."

"What are you doing here? I was just on my way to meet—" The Artificer looked around, feeling that cold wash of fear in his belly again. "Why did you kill Henri?"

"Seems to be some corporate espionage going on, sir," the boy said innocently. "Mr. Ragged's a little unsatisfied with how you treat your customers."

"What? I don't understand—"

"You'll have to forgive me, sir, if I'm not jumping at the chance to trust a man who don't wear his own face." The boy gestured, beckoning the other five forward. "Mr. Ragged, aha, sends his best."

*My old friend,*

*I hope sincerely that you still test my letters for hidden Artifice, the way we used to. Otherwise I fear you'll not see this, and reply a recounting of your holiday which, forgive me, I do not presently crave.*

*I daren't write to you of precisely the circumstances which have led to this letter, for though our methods may seem secure, I have come to fear they are not. The potential consequences of such a breach are worrying enough that I must write circumspectly.*

*You will recall the nature of my hobbies, I trust, as well as the need for secrecy that surrounds them. The mere fact of this mention, no doubt, reveals the core of my predicament: I fear someone has discovered them—or, at the very least, set himself on the path to discover them. This alone would make me wary, but it is not all . . .*

*I am penny-dreadfuling, aren't I? Then I shall dispense with these cryptic hints and arrive at the point.*

*On my most recent excursion I encountered a boy, not older than fourteen, whom I had met only once before under unusual circumstances (which I shall detail in a later correspondence or when next we meet; I am confident you will find them as intriguing as I have). I took him immediately for a spy, but upon interrogation he seemed harmless, if frighteningly ambitious (he refused to leave when I released him because he wanted to pursue a position in the company—the audacity! I almost hired him for that alone). I have since revised my opinion; he cannot be harmless. He is <u>canted</u>.*

*You may mock me for a paranoid fool—Will has already made good on the opportunity—but the boy's arrival, combined* with his determination to work for me and his natural affinity for such work, is far too convenient for my taste. Were I to lay a trap for myself, it would look terribly similar to this.

Meantime I have taken him on as student and larcener-for-hire. If indeed he has been sent to gather information about me, at least I shall gather information about him and his potential masters.

And before you chide me, no I do not intend him to find out anything of substance and yes I am being careful—or is the nature of this letter not evidence enough?

Ever your student,
Candlestick Jack

*"Ever your student"? I'm coming home at once.*

# PART 2

*Embers*

12

THE sun rose fierce and red over Teranis. Slate-gray clouds, thick with the promise of rain, hung heavy over the city. In less than an hour, the sun would slip behind them, not to be seen until tomorrow; but for now it hung between clouds and horizon, like a lamp visible through a cracked door.

Candlestick Jack stood under the eave of a building on Redchapel Street, staring eastward. He was half a foot shorter than he had been yesterday, with blond hair, a beard, and wire-rimmed spectacles, but Ashes recognized him immediately. Something about the man stayed constant no matter what face he wore. It wasn't anything Ashes could articulate, not the color or shape of his eyes, or the way he stood, or even the way he moved. But it was there.

"Good morning, lad," the Artificer said as Ashes approached. "I hope you slept well. I need you sharp today."

Ashes stifled a yawn. "Did m'best, sir." He stretched his arms as stealthily as he could. "What're we doing out so early?"

"Embracing the brisk morning air," Jack said brightly. "Dawn is the only decent time of day in this city. Dusk is pretty, but sunrise is a kept promise. We went to sleep, and the world went on spinning."

Ashes rubbed his face. "Poetry this soon in the day, sir? Seems a bit . . . er, keen."

"I've told you there's no need for that." Jack looked at him sternly. "I'm not *sir* to you. That sort of courtesy is just an elaborate lie, and I'll have no lies between us liars."

"If you say so. Jack."

"Better," the Artificer said, starting into a brisk walk. "Though it's unwise to bandy our real names about when we wear false faces. For the morning, I'll be . . . mm, Richard. You'll be Francis. Fair enough?"

Ashes squirmed. "Mite tired of that name."

"Roger, then."

Ashes nodded. "We really just out for early-morning air?"

"Is that not reason enough?" Jack smirked. "There are certain opportunities that come about at this time of day, and this time *only*. I think we should exploit them."

Ashes frowned, confused, but Jack went on too quickly. "Dawn and dusk, Roger. Those times belong to us. Enough light for us to use. Not enough to be caught out in our deceit. Tell me everything you know about Artificers."

Ashes faltered, off-balance at the suddenness of the question. "Erm—they— Sorry, *we* make illusions. Glamours. And they can look like anything but they take a long while to make—or I thought they did."

"Why do we make illusions?"

"You can sell them," Ashes said. "Ivories'll pay to look pretty."

"Why else?"

"Spies. Assassins. Thieves."

"Oh? It seems dangerous to sell illusions to such blatant criminals."

Ashes looked at him in confusion, but Jack's face was impassive. "So you *don't* sell to those folk?"

"Oh, we do," Jack said. "We just do it cautiously. What else do you know?"

"You said our ancestors built the city," Ashes said. "With their magic."

"And they did," Jack confirmed. "I'm afraid I'll have to leave your history lessons to Will, though. Anything else?"

"You stick your Glamours in clothes," Ashes concluded. "Hats and rings and things."

"Well, you are not utterly misinformed," Jack replied. "I'll have to do precious little unteaching. We'll begin with your vocabulary. You and I and my company are Artificers. You will not call us *Fishers*. We are also, very definitively, not Glamourists."

"Don't we make Glamours?" Ashes asked.

"That *would* be something," Jack said, a note of regret in his voice. "But Glamour hasn't been done in this city in ages, I'm afraid. The Vanishers are dead and buried. People still call constructs 'Glamours' because they're idiots."

"What—?"

Jack waved a hand. "It's not a matter to spend time on just now. You can read up on it, if you like. For now, we focus on more practical matters."

Jack glanced over his shoulder, then dragged his fingers through the air. Thin ribbons of light curled around them, leaving shadowy gashes behind. These did not last long; even as Ashes watched, the light around began to seep into the rips, like water flowing into a ravine.

"Canted Artificers come in two kinds. Breeds, if you want to think of it that way. Weavers and Stitchers. I am a Weaver."

He curled his fingers around the light, then opened them to reveal a delicate white bird in his palm. It was perfectly still: it did not breathe or blink or twitch. Ashes watched it hungrily, fascinated.

"Weavers can manipulate light like clay," he said. "Most famously, we make faces, but it's not all we can do." He flicked his fingers, dispelling the image into trails of light that re-formed around his hand, making his skin seem luminous. "It's the most visibly impressive magic, and the most taxing. Gilders practice for decades before they can Weave worth half a damn."

"Gilders?" Ashes asked.

"The men and women who imitate our magic," Jack said. "Anyone can learn to use Artifice if they have the right tools and the mental fortitude it takes to chew bread and walk at the same time. But it takes years, and even the best Gilder can't do what a canted Artificer can. For instance." He snapped his fingers. Thirty feet away, a small sunburst of white light erupted over the street. Ashes's eyes filled with spots, and he had to blink furiously before they faded.

"Raw light belongs to true Weavers," Jack said. "We can gather it, shape it, hold it together with our will. Gilders can't, and Stitchers can only do it with great difficulty."

He produced a glass phial from his jacket. The substance inside was colorless, but split the light like a prism. It cast a seven-colored shadow on the road.

"This is aether," Jack said. "The most valuable substance in the world, if you're an Artificer."

"What's it do?"

"It makes the Artificer's trade possible," Jack said. "Even a strong Weaver can't hold an illusion together for very long—an hour, perhaps, if he had no other concerns. Adding aether to a finished construct lets it retain a shape for days on end. You can distill it with light as well, to make liquid light—as good as the real thing, but more malleable. With the right equipment and a decent supply of liquid light, anyone could be an Artificer. Magic made easy."

An errant thought slipped through Ashes's head. Jack must have anticipated it, because he glanced at Ashes and said plainly,

"One phial of this is worth near fifty crowns. But only if you can find the right buyer and, forgive me, you certainly can't."

Ashes bristled. "I'm not an idiot."

"I'm sure," Jack said, "but that's neither here nor there. The fact is that ninety-nine out of a hundred black market aether dealers are, in fact, spies for the Guild of Artificers. No one outside the Guild is legally allowed to sell aether. It's how they keep Artificers under control—our magic is limited by our aether supply. They're very . . . *determined* where it comes to illegal aether selling. They might feel generous, and only take your fingers, eyes, and tongue—they call it hobbling. Or they won't feel generous, and they'll kill you."

Ashes shuddered. "Right, then."

"No one outside the Guild is allowed to practice Artifice, either," Jack said. "Bear that in mind if you ever feel an urge to show off your gifts."

"What would they—?"

"Fingers. Eyes. Tongue. They feel no need to be diverse in their punishments."

"I can keep a secret."

"Good," Jack said. "Weavers live by three rules, Roger. Rule the first: never touch pure aether with your bare skin. It's poison. Try not to breathe too much either." Jack's mouth made a grim line. "If it gets inside you, it'll burrow into your brain and hollow it out. Your body would survive. The rest of you *wouldn't*. Understood?"

Ashes nodded, feeling a chill creep down his back.

"Rule the second: every face you make *must* be original. Never make something that looks like someone else's true face."

"Why's that?"

"Because it's legally considered Impersonating a Denizen, and the Guild polices it," Jack said. "Fingers, eyes, tongue. Sense a pattern?"

Ashes fingers tingled. Who knew Artifice was so dangerous?

Clever Tyru never had to bother with Guilds. "What's the third rule?"

"Bloody *don't* bloody *touch* bloody *aether*," Jack said. "Remember that one, and you'll do just fine. I'm required to tell you Impersonating is illegal and not worth your effort, but aether's the real peril in our line of work. The Guild is an obstacle."

Something about the way he said it made Ashes peer at him curiously, but Jack didn't seem to notice. "The other sort of Artifice is Stitching."

"That's what I do?" Ashes guessed.

"Near as I can tell," Jack said. "You and Will. We'll have to test you to be certain."

"How—?"

"All in good time, all in good time," Jack said. "Stitching is . . . difficult to explain. Will would say it's a subtle art. It'll be easier just to show you."

Jack checked over his shoulder and, seeing no one, pinched Ashes's nose and *pulled*. Ashes's nose followed him, growing instantly a foot longer.

"What in *Furies*?" Ashes asked, pressing his fingers against his new nose; but it was insubstantial as air, and his fingers passed right through it.

"Relax," Jack said, pulling the nose even further. It shook as it lengthened, then, all at once, it vanished. There were no trails of light this time. "Illusionist, remember?"

"That's Stitching?" Ashes frowned. "I don't understand."

In answer, Jack waved a hand and plucked an illusory glove, fully formed, from the air. "If I put on a glove," he said, "it covers my skin—but there's a gap. An ant, say, could burrow between skin and silk and see that my hand is not, in fact, made of cloth. However." Jack released the glove, letting it float to the ground, dissolving into threads of light as it did. The Artificer rubbed his hands together, and then displayed his palms: they were chalky white and smooth. "Such a problem does not exist if I paint my hands instead. You understand? Weavers put masks on the world. Stitchers treat it like a canvas."

Ashes peered at Jack's hands, confused. "How come you can do it, though? You're a Weaver."

"Any Weaver can Stitch," Jack said. "And any Stitcher can Weave. Not naturally, of course. Your magic needs to be tuned first."

Ashes gave him an eloquently blank stare. Jack laughed.

"You've not learned to dance, have you?" he asked. Ashes shook his head. "You'll have quite a lot to look forward to when my wife finds that out. Then you'll understand—you can't *really* learn to dance unless someone dances with you. Your body learns it faster than your mind. It's the same with Artifice. Your magic knows how to two-step already. It can't waltz unless someone takes it waltzing."

"You're married?"

"Not half as monstrous as I seemed at first, am I?" Jack grinned. "Returning to the important subject, Stitching is about coaxing images into a different shape." He pointed at Ashes's face. "Your body knows its own shape very well. But a Stitcher can convince it to look different. Not *too* different, or your shape bounces back. The stronger the Stitcher, the greater the changes he can manage. Will, for instance, could make your skin a different color, or change the shape of your eyes, or make you look taller." Jack smirked. "I, being a Weaver, could make you look like a damn *sparrow*."

Ashes frowned. "Dun't sound too useful," he mused. "What's the point? If Weaving can do the same thing?"

Jack's eyes shone. "Stitching can do quite a number of things that Weaving can't. For one, a Stitcher can make changes to a construct even after it's solid. No one ever gets a construct perfect on the first try—something will be indistinct, or the wrong color, or blurred. That's when you need a Stitcher."

Jack checked around the corner before he stepped onto the next street, a row of shop fronts that would be bustling in an hour or two but was sparsely inhabited just now. Ashes scanned the early-morning crowd, habitually checking for things to steal. He searched, too, for the person Jack was following—for they *were* following someone. Jack's glance around the corner had tipped him off.

"The other duty of the Stitcher," Jack continued, as if he had done nothing out of the ordinary, "is reconstitution, which is a showy word for collecting the aether out of decaying constructs. Useful skill if you're short of the stuff."

"But . . . that's all?" Ashes asked. He kept the disappointment out of his voice. Mostly.

"Don't be too crestfallen, lad," Jack said. "It's still magic. And Stitching is the only kind of Artifice that can *really* hide you."

Ashes frowned. "How's that?"

"It's—" Jack paused as they crossed onto Oldtown Lane, one of Lyonshire's longest-standing thoroughfares. This street was busier than the last; already, nearly a dozen people milled around, setting up stalls and calling out old, crude jokes to one another. One industrious cart salesman had started peddling fresh fruits. There was even a fine horse-drawn carriage, with the purple-and-scarlet sigil of Lord Edgecombe painted across its doors.

"Hold the thought, lad. Hold this, too." Jack dug a silver ring out of his vest pocket and passed it to Ashes. He tilted his head forward, and Ashes followed his gaze to a man some fifty feet ahead of them. He had the straight back and outthrust chest of someone wealthy and powerful; the effect was only enhanced by the texture of his expensive suit, the gleam of his shoes, and the cut of his hair. He had money to waste.

"Elleander Bloom. A Guild Artificer. You might call him a rival of mine," Jack muttered. "He has a pocket, just here, which he thinks is a secret." Jack gave Ashes a significant look. "Keep on him. Don't be obvious—wait for the right moment." So saying, he ducked down a side street, and was gone.

Ashes frowned. Mari had always insisted on her crew knowing the plan before they tried anything. She'd had contingencies for her contingencies—not that it had done her much good, in the end. Jack seemed to enjoy the thought of his student making up the plan as he went along.

Well, if all Jack's half-baked plans came with magic included, Ashes wouldn't complain. He slipped the ring on, and felt the gossamer-light weight of a new face fall over his skin. He grinned wildly and hurried through the crowd to get close to Elleander Bloom.

Bloom had stopped at the fruit seller's cart. Ashes stopped on the opposite side of the street and pretended to look through a shopwindow, keeping his ears pricked for a signal of Jack's "right moment." He couldn't help but notice the details of his new face in the glass; he looked cleaner and better-groomed than he could remember being, with curly dark hair and bright eyes. He looked practically Ivorish.

"Fine fruits, sir," the seller said behind him. "Picked fresh just this morning."

Bloom said something Ashes couldn't quite make out; he turned and repositioned himself a little closer.

"It's a fine choice, sir," the seller said.

In the window, Ashes saw Bloom begin to walk away, and the seller staring after the man in confusion.

"Sir? You forgot to pay . . ." The man's voice trailed off as Bloom turned to look at him.

"Today," Bloom said, in a slithery, self-satisfied voice, "you may tell your customers that a Guild-licensed Artificer approved of your apples." He adjusted his coat. "I rather think I have over-paid."

The fruit seller had gone pale. "Sir, I—"

"Certainly you would rather have that kindness," Bloom went on flatly, "than receive my displeasure."

The fruit seller wrung his hands, then dropped a little half bow with his head. "Of course not, sir."

"Good day to you, then," said Elleander Bloom. "I will—"

Ashes caught a tiny flare out of the corner of his eye. A moment later came the crack of hooves against cobbles, and a high whinnying scream. He turned and saw the carriage behind him, *far* too close, and its horse rearing on two legs.

"Out of the way, sir!" Ashes cried, throwing himself into Bloom. The Artificer stumbled and fell, graceless and cursing. His apple tumbled out of his hand.

"Idiot boy!" the man shouted, just as the horse's hooves came whistling to the ground. One landed on Bloom's apple like the hammer of a god; the fruit burst in a spray of white mush.

"Don't stop moving now, sir!" Ashes said, clambering to his feet and dashing out of the animal's way. Bloom, wisely, did likewise.

People were screaming. Someone, crying hysterically for the police, dashed past Ashes, and he heard another voice crying for help from the Faces. Ashes shut his mouth and backed away from the chaos; Burroughsiders who stood too close to disaster tended to get blamed for it, and imprisoned or beaten shortly thereafter. Even his new face couldn't overpower the instinct.

"What the devil—?" A heavy-faced copper came sprinting onto the street. He wore Edgecombe's colors on his shoulder and a heavy club on his hip. "Everyone calm down! Whoa, there!" The man hurried to the horse, holding up both hands to calm it.

"Officer!" cried Bloom. Ashes turned, and saw Bloom pointing at him imperiously. "Arrest this vagabond!"

The policeman laid his hands on the horse before he turned to Mr. Bloom. "Sorry, sir?"

"He assaulted me!"

"I saved your life, you tosser!" Ashes snapped.

Bloom's face turned so red it was nearly purple. "Do you hear this vagrant? Do your duty, captain!"

The policeman glanced at Ashes, looking half confused and half apologetic. Something in the back of Ashes's head noted this as fundamentally wrong, and then went silent.

"Best move quickly, officer," Bloom said in dark tones. He looked fit to burst a vein. "Were I to find you still standing here in a moment, rather than taking this ruffian to his due reward, I should think I would be exquisitely displeased."

*He's really rubbish at threats*, Ashes thought. The policeman laid a firm hand on Ashes's shoulder; Ashes wrestled down his instinct to run and put on a contrite face.

Satisfied, Bloom turned to the carriage. "And who owns this beast?" he demanded, gesturing wildly at the horse. The animal in question, which had calmed while Bloom raved, was licking oats off his driver's hand. "I fashion Glamour for Lord Tyr himself! I will see your entrails spread across the—"

Bloom's mouth snapped shut as he saw the seal across the door of the carriage. The fury vanished from his face, and without another word he spun around and left. He plunged a hand inside his pocket as he did so, and his appearance transformed, the wealthy, straight-backed man replaced by a humble Denizen in clothing just respectable enough to be out in public. Even the constructed face was deathly pale. Ashes raised an eyebrow. Apparently Lord Edgecombe didn't only frighten Burroughsiders.

The policeman led him peaceably down a side street, saying nothing. Ashes followed his lead until they were well out of the crowd.

"Handy trick, that," Ashes noted absently when no one else was in earshot.

The copper smirked and undid his collar. The heavyset face dissolved, and Candlestick Jack emerged from underneath it.

"Just how illegal is it for you to impersonate a copper?" Ashes asked.

"That depends," Jack said. "A specific officer? It'd likely cost me my fingers. Wearing a construct that just happens to be the same color as a police uniform, however—probably the Guild would only fine me. Somewhere in the neighborhood of seventy crowns."

"*Furies.*"

"Fairly steep, even for Artificers," Jack admitted. "It would have been quite a deterrent to me, when I was younger."

Ashes frowned. "Where do you get so much money?"

Jack held up a hand. "That, I'm afraid, is not information I share too readily. You're only a free lance, lad, not one of my company. What did you pilfer from our esteemed gentleman's pocket? I do hope it was worth our time."

Ashes pulled two gold rings from his pocket. "Just these. I figure they're Anchors." He rubbed them both with his thumb. There was something buzzing on the inside of the metal, he felt sure of it.

Jack took one and looked around, checking for possible witnesses. "Count of three, then? Three." He slipped the ring on. Ashes did likewise, swapping his silver ring for the gold one.

They looked at each other, and Ashes burst out laughing.

Jack's new face frowned. "Stop your nonsense. How do I look?"

"Gorgeous, boss," Ashes said, putting a hand over his mouth.

Jack—who, currently, looked remarkably like a well-bred, cold-eyed Ivory Lady in a ball gown—glanced in a darkened shopwindow and frowned. "Intriguing." He slid the ring off, looking at it with a calculating expression. "Quite intriguing."

Ashes tried to look at himself, but couldn't see the illusion that lay over him. "What am I?"

"A cheeky little imp. But your construct seems to be my dancing partner." Jack rubbed his chin. "One wonders just who this was for." He pocketed the ring and held out his hand.

Ashes lifted an eyebrow. "Something you need?"

"Ha very ha," Jack said drily. "That construct's much more use to me than it is to you, lad. Hand it over."

"I'm just a free lance," Ashes said flatly. "Way I figure it, this little trinket is mine. You can keep that one, 'cause of you knew where the mark kept his stuff, but—"

"You've got about two seconds to give up your new habit of being an arse," Jack said. "I'll have Will reconstitute those. You get an even cut of the aether we pull out of it—which will, by the way, be substantial. You can stuff quite a lot of Artifice into gold."

Ashes pressed his lips together, and handed Jack the ring.

"Good lad," the Artificer said. "We ought to be moving along. Your lessons aren't over just yet." He glanced at the sky. "Don't bother putting that construct on again. It looks fit to rain."

"Eh?"

"Running water," Jack said, pointing at the sky. "Makes active constructs malfunction. '*River, rain, and iron cold,*' as the songs go. We don't have to worry about the sewers up here, thick as these streets are, but rainstorms are more than enough to muck up a perfectly nice face."

Ashes nodded halfheartedly. His face was carefully composed into a look of sullen anger. It was one he wore often when he wanted to avoid attention, one that belonged on a gutter-rat who'd been put in his place by the powerful, clever Denizen.

More to the point, one that didn't indicate that there had been a phial of pure aether in Elleander Bloom's pocket. There could be a tidy profit on it, if Ashes found the right buyer.

He was, after all, just a free lance.

## 13 Rumors

THE shop was not markedly different from the others on Redchapel Street; it stood three stories high, and its brick face was clean and well tended. The two upper floors protruded beyond the boundary of the first floor by two or three feet, forming small nooks with walls that were mostly windows so that someone could sit within and see the whole of the street at a glance. A sign hung above the door, decorated with an insignia like a lit candle and the words:

**REHL CO.**
**ILLUSIONS AND MARVELS**
**REASONABLY PRICED**
**GUILD-CERTIFIED**

"Posh," Ashes commented.

"Your good opinion means ever so much," Jack replied, glancing anxiously at the darkening sky. "Come along, Roger, you won't be using that door while you work here."

Jack led him around the back of the shop, to a studiously blank stretch of wall. There, he showed Ashes the secret lever concealed at the bottom, which he could trip with his foot if he moved it just right, and which caused a slight squeaking noise to come from the wall. Jack frowned, then walked through the wall.

"Too long since I've oiled the hinges," he muttered.

The secret door opened into the back of the shop. Jack steered Ashes skillfully through the building, expositing on the functions of the arcane tools and the locations of several hidden doors as they went.

The first floor functioned as both storefront and concealed living space. Someone entering through the front door would find a cramped room with a check counter and several shelves, on which could be found a few selected samples of the Rehl Company's handiwork; these were notably shabbier and sparser than the items Ashes had seen in Jack's workshop. Behind this room was a comfortably appointed sitting room with a weathered table and several neatly collected ledgers, where Jack could negotiate commissioned work; as the only room in the building with a fireplace, it doubled as a living room when the shop was closed. It also sported at least one hidden door, which connected to a kitchen and dining room and a small library. Jack admitted baldly that only two of the books in the last room belonged to him; the others were all William's and "dry enough to set a fire in your brain."

From the library they ascended a curving staircase to the second floor, which Ashes recognized quickly: the southerly end was the sitting room with the great window; in the back was the clean room where he'd woken after his misadventure in the sewers. Jack identified it as William's surgery.

"Avoid it at all costs unless you're invited," he warned. "Will's particular about where he puts things; it's more than your life's worth to move anything without permission. And the smell is abominable."

"Why've you got a surgery?"

"For when I need to save foolish young thieves from their poor decisions. Call it a hobby."

The attic Jack showed him next would have been cramped even if it had been empty, and it was decidedly *not* empty. The place could only be described as suffocated; even the air seemed reluctant to move around for fear it would get trapped in a tight corner and die there. This state of paralyzing constriction came as a result of the apparatus in the center of the attic; Jack called it the light distillery. It was constructed primarily of glass and iron, twisted into unlikely shapes and complex curves ending in a glass sphere half full of gold-tinted aether.

"Pity it's so dreary today," Jack said as they exited the garret. "Otherwise we could stay and watch until we got a bit of light in. It's worth seeing once or twice, very pretty."

"Eh?"

"The distillery harvests sunlight." Jack pointed toward the ceiling. "The apparatus treats the light so it can mix with aether, which we can use for constructs."

"You said you don't need liquid light, though," Ashes pointed out.

"I don't," Jack admitted. "But the Guild of Artificers remains blissfully unaware of the fact, and I should like to keep it that way."

They descended to Jack's workshop in the basement, which Jack warned was not to be mentioned or hinted at or even thought about very loudly outside the shop. Despite its vast size, it took very little time to explore: Jack flatly refused to let Ashes inspect every Anchor, as some were fragile, others were for sale, and all were expensive. "I'd rather we not tempt you to old habits," Jack said. "Doubly so when your habits are not particularly old."

The last stop of the tour was Jack's second workshop, which

he referred to acidly as his "cave of necessary evils." It was nestled on the first floor, and exploring it took more time than all the rest combined: Jack insisted on explaining the function and proper handling of every tool he used—or, rather, didn't use. Despite being able to shape light with his bare hands, Jack owned four pairs of Gilder-gloves: heavy, thick things lined with metal, which ostensibly made Artifice available to any dullard with working fingers. He also kept a vast and polished array of alchemical implements for mixing the liquid light he did not need, glass-tipped needles for binding constructs to Anchors, and various eyepieces for use in studying and dissecting constructs. Jack had Ashes try each one on in turn while they studied an old construct fashioned to look like an exotic bird. One lens reduced the bird to multiple streaks of deep red and shocking violet; another made the skin of the construct invisible, so that Ashes could see its fragile and incomplete skeleton; still another let him see thin silvery veins outlined on the construct's outermost layer. Jack identified these as active aether lines, and pointed out how the thickest lines met at the core of the illusion, forming a dense, twisted knot.

After what felt like several hours, they adjourned to the sitting room upstairs. Raindrops clung to the outside of the great window; the world outside was gray and sodden, but the rain had stopped. The city had grown darker, and Ashes noted with some surprise that it was well into the afternoon.

"Beautiful view, isn't it?" Jack asked. "Even in the rain." He sat in his chair and stared thoughtfully at the window. "I've lived here my whole life. Stepped away from time to time, but she always brings you back. There's no place like it."

"Jack?"

The voice came from the hall. Ashes turned to see the newcomer, and the bottom fell out of his stomach.

"Juliana, love," Jack said. "Come in."

Ashes had seen Ivorish women. He had even seen beautiful women. He had not realized until this moment that they had all been imitators, frail shadows. He had not seen beauty or grace yet, because he had not seen *her*.

The lady at the door had smooth and delicate features, as if she had been crafted from glass; chocolate-dark hair, eyes the cool gray of a morning mist. Her skin was full-blooded Ivory; it didn't gleam, like the Lords and Ladies were said to, but it seemed luminous all the same. She wore a faded lilac dress of extraordinarily modest cut, showing barely more than her neck. He had seen nothing so sensual in his entire life.

Ashes realized he was staring, and could not think why he should stop.

"We missed you for tea," the Lady said. She set a hand carefully on Jack's shoulder and pressed her lips softly to his cheek.

"Slipped my mind," Jack said. His eyes flicked at Ashes.

Juliana straightened and followed Jack's gaze. Ashes's head became wobbly and clouded as the woman's eyes found him. His tongue seemed thick in his mouth.

"You didn't tell me we had company," Juliana chided. "You're making poor hosts of us, Jack! Did you offer him lunch?"

"It's all right, ma'am," Ashes said awkwardly. "I—I didn't notice, really."

It was quite true. He could count on one hand the number of times he'd had multiple meals in a day. He knew in a vague sense that Denizens ate more than that, but it was like knowing the sea was "rather large."

"I hope you'll forgive us all the same," she said. She smiled apologetically. "My name is Juliana Rehl."

"Ashes, ma'am."

"Will you stay for supper?"

"I—ahm—" He glanced at Jack. The Artificer was watching him, but Ashes couldn't read anything from the man's stare. Was he supposed to say yes? He ought to get back to Annie's house. Blimey would be wondering where he was. It would be dark soon; Annie was at the edge of Burroughside, so he needn't worry about Ravagers, but the city police didn't take kindly to curfew-breakers with no iron names. And anyway, Ashes wasn't part of Jack's company; he was only here for a little while. There was no sense in getting tied up with these people.

"I *do* insist," she said, still smiling.

"Yeah, all right," he said, before his brain caught up with him.

● ● ●

*Ashes liked to think* he had a good card-player's face. He was difficult to surprise; even when something shocked him, he could mask his expression with admirable quickness.

When he entered the dining room, he caught his breath, and it was all he could do to keep his jaw from falling open.

Supper was a dirty necessity in Burroughside. Typically it was rotted, maggoty, crumbly, torn, or stolen. Even on good nights, Ashes and Blimey had never eaten well. In their vocabulary, a feast was any meal with enough bread for both of them to eat.

This was not a feast. This was a festival of food.

Multiple dishes—a bowl of apples, two loaves of bread, a roast ham, turtle soup, and something green and leafy he didn't recognize—all within reaching distance and filled to bursting. He noticed several plates and, beside them, more silver than a human could possibly use at one meal. Why were there so many forks? The only reasonable conclusion was that they were decorative. Rich folk *loved* to decorate.

The food was arrayed on a long table of dark, rich wood Ashes had never seen before; it was smooth to the touch, soft as cloth. The chairs, which numbered a full dozen, were made of the same stuff. Ashes found himself running his fingers over it.

"My," Jack said, surveying the supper. "She must like you. She's got out the *nice* silver." He looked sidelong at Ashes. "Do me a favor and don't nick any of it, all right?"

Ashes smiled thinly, barely aware of Jack's joke. Could he eat all of this?

They sat; Ashes found himself to Jack's left, directly across from Juliana. William had taken up a solitary position two seats away from the rest of the group; Ashes hadn't noticed him entering, and that had only a little to do with William's quiet nature. A copper lieutenant could have walked into the room and Ashes would have missed it, with his attention split equally between the glorious supper and the Artificer's wife.

His eyes flicked around the table, taking note of everyone's posture and behavior. He decided his best hope here was imitation; Denizens had rules for their language that numbered in the hundreds, so the rules for eating had to be nearly as complex. He straightened his back a little, and folded his hands only half a second after the others.

"Thanks and praise to the Makers for their bounty," Jack intoned. He had closed his eyes, and everyone else had, too, apparently at some private signal. Ashes stared at them, baffled. Prayer? About food?

"Amen," Juliana said.

"Thanks and praise to the Faces for their gifts. For ingenuity, for joy."

"Amen."

"Thanks and praise to the Kindly Ones, the Queens." A shadow crossed Jack's face at these words, and flickered away quickly as it had come.

"Amen."

Jack opened his eyes and caught Ashes staring. Ashes felt he ought to blush, but he was still too confused.

"Right, then," Jack said. "Dig in."

Ashes hesitated, wanting to be sure he wouldn't make a fool of himself. Jack began eating immediately, as vigorously as if he had not eaten in weeks. Juliana was far more composed, using her knife and one of the innumerable forks to carve her food into manageable bites, chewing each one deliberately before she cut away the next. William, just as deliberately, was carving his food into evenly sized squares, and it didn't look like he intended to eat until he'd completed the project.

After several agonizing moments, Ashes tore into his food. He kept himself from looking like a savage, but only just.

"Where is young Synder this evening?" William asked as he sawed a portion of his meat into a perfect square. "I would have expected her to burst through solid walls in her haste to meet your new student."

"Holiday with her parents," Jack replied between bites. "And a bit of time off to work on her passage project. Our genius won't be rejoining us for near a month."

Juliana's mouth tilted downward, just a little; Ashes would have missed it entirely if he hadn't been so focused on her face.

"A month of peace?" William looked up from his cutting. "Perhaps the gods of this city *are* merciful."

Jack scoffed. "I'm sure you'll still feel that way in a week, and decidedly *won't* be trudging through the house humming dirges because no one's given you any half-decent riddles."

William delicately placed a square of meat in his mouth and chewed. Jack smirked.

"What's a passage project?" Ashes asked.

"Guild of Artificer nonsense," Jack said. "A waste of my time and hers, but what can you do?" He paused, taking a sip of his wine. "She's putting together a construct for the Guild to evaluate, to determine whether she can advance to the next level of study. I told her to keep it simple and straightforward, nothing too ostentatious . . ."

William let out a quick breath—Ashes guessed it was what passed for a chuckle by the Wisp's standards. "That certainly seems the sort of advice she would follow."

Jack smirked again. "I almost hope she ignores it. Can you *imagine*? It would be so satisfying to see her shove their whole way of thinking up their pompous"—he glanced at Ashes, and seemed to think very quickly—"noses."

Ashes snorted, barely covering the sound with his hand. Juliana's face went tight for just a moment, and she eyed Jack imperiously.

"In any case," Jack said, as if the air had not abruptly turned tense, "she's out for some time. And I haven't mentioned Ashes to her yet—or anyone, in fact. As far as anyone outside this room is concerned, Ashes does not exist."

William nodded as if this was an entirely expected pronouncement. Juliana looked a little less calm. Her eyes flicked to Ashes; he could have sworn there was concern there, or nervousness, but only for a moment. Her face calmed almost immediately, like she'd put on a mask.

"It's a pity not to exist," Juliana said warmly. "Tell us about yourself, Ashes. Where are you from?"

Ashes glanced at Jack, who tilted his head slightly forward. "Burroughside, ma'am."

"Are you indeed?" she said, with either genuine interest or the best imitation Ashes had ever heard. She gave no sign of distaste or horror. "How long did you live there?"

"Three years," Ashes said. "Ma'am."

"What of before that?" she pressed. "Where did you grow up?"

Ashes blinked. "I'm *rasa*, miss."

Confusion flickered over Juliana's face. Jack leaned toward her and whispered in her ear. She retained her composure—no noise, no look of shock—but Ashes could tell he'd surprised her. Had she never heard of *rasa*?

"And you're studying Artifice?" she continued, as if she hadn't missed a beat.

Ashes hesitated, confused by the question.

The Weaver cut in. "He'll be with us a while." He smiled, looking Juliana in the eye. Something passed between them, a message Ashes couldn't interpret. "Any new and interesting stories from you, William? I thirst for entertainment."

William waited three seconds after he had finished chewing to answer. Ashes made a note of that, in case it was some kind of unspoken requirement. He also noticed that everyone was staring at William as they awaited an answer, and swiftly made one of the bread rolls disappear in his jacket.

"Courtly gossip has struck upon a drought of late," William said carefully. "It seems most of the relevant scandals have run their course."

Jack snorted indelicately. "None of the young lords and ladies making dramatic declarations? No one caught carousing in Yson? They can't go twenty minutes without doing *something*."

"It is a slow season," William replied coolly.

"Come now, William," Juliana teased. "You have something, or you wouldn't be teasing us this way."

William inclined his head. "Lord Edgecombe was absent at Lyonscourt today. It is his third sequential failure to attend."

Jack's eyes narrowed. "That's interesting, given Ashes and I saw his carriage today."

"One of his stewards, no doubt. They're practically heirs. Lord Edgecombe himself has been laid low—my most conservative sources guess he has been ill." William's lips tilted upward. "Syphilis, specifically."

Jack frowned. "With his money? He could afford a witch-favor, even for something that sensitive."

"I deduced the same." William rubbed his chin and met Jack's eyes. "There are fringe theories that he has lost his ring."

Jack nodded calmly, but Ashes sensed the man tense, like

pressing down on a spring. There was a light in his eyes. "Has he petitioned the Queens?"

"Quietly indeed, if he has." William paused in the act of spearing another bite of meat.

Jack grinned at Ashes, whose eyes were traveling between the two men in confused fascination. "I'm afraid we've lost the boy, Will."

William turned to face Ashes. "Lord Edgecombe is one of the High Ivories of Lyonshire."

Ashes nodded. "I know'm." Ashes's encounters with police always ended in bruises, but coppers in Edgecombe's colors were famously brutal; one had to be very stupid or very desperate to try anything untoward in Lyonshire Harcourt. "Why would it matter if he hasn't got a ring?"

"Every High Ivory family has a set of glass rings," Jack explained. "They represent legitimacy. Importance."

"No Ivory is seen in public without one," William said.

"But it's just a ring?"

Jack smirked. "Of course it's not *just* a ring, lad. Folk recognize the High Ivories because they can light up a dank alleyway with their faces. That's Artifice if anything is."

"Glass is quite a powerful Anchor," William added. "It has the lowest rate of construct decay. The only substance that can hold more light is gold."

Juliana's mouth turned down a fraction of an inch, as though she had something to say. She caught Ashes looking at her, and the expression flickered away as cleanly as if it had never been there.

"The final thought," William continued, "is that he is being cautious. You recall his pet Artificer, a Mr. Tremaine? He was immolated on Galway Street two nights ago."

"Sounds as though he was fraternizing with some unsavory people," Jack said. Ashes saw the man's eyes flick toward him, but the look only lasted a moment.

"What's immolated?" Ashes asked.

Juliana spoke in her crisp, clear voice. "I think that will be more than enough talk of that, gentlemen."

Ashes almost protested out of habit, but a look at Juliana's face stilled the instinct. The Lady's expression was streaked with a cold, bottled anger. Her eyes were fixed on Jack.

The Weaver put on an ashamed look and spread his hands. "Milady's quite right, gentlemen. We'll table that discussion for later, I think."

He glanced at Ashes, and the boy could have sworn he winked.

Their conversation lapsed into idler talk. Ashes, uncertain of his place in the hierarchy and wary of annoying his employer, listened more than he spoke, trying instead to understand the people around him.

Denizens, in his experience, did not differ from one another much. On the whole they were proud, sneering folk whose foremost survival skill was calling for police. And a great many things threatened their survival: children with overlarge clothes and soot on their faces were first among them. Ashes's existence in their clean world made them uncomfortable.

Jack was . . . not that way. He laughed easily. He seemed genuinely interested whenever Ashes spoke. And he was clever enough to tease a smile out of Juliana, and even got a faint smirk from William now and then.

Juliana reminded him of the Denizens he'd known, but in the way a tiger can be reminiscent of a tomcat. She was more Ivorish than her husband—more Ivorish than anyone Ashes had ever met, in fact. Refined, poised, perfectly in control of herself. She made Denizens look like children trying out grown-up clothing. Her Ivory blood *fit* her in a way it did not fit other people.

William was simply odd. Alien in every way possible. He spoke when he was spoken to, or when he had a relevant thought, but not otherwise. He did not ask questions or make jokes. The Wisp listened, and watched, and ate when he remembered to.

There was one other strange detail about them, something Ashes couldn't quite put his finger on. He teased at the thought for several minutes when, finally, it struck him: no one was *watching* him. They paid attention to him, certainly, but not in the way he was used to. They were not watching the way he handled the silver. They did not eye him warily when he reached for a biscuit. They gave no sign that his presence at their table worried or unnerved them. He was a guest. He was welcome.

## 14 Bargain

"YOU'RE late, facefaker," Annie growled.

Ashes frowned as he entered Annie's house. He could still feel the delicate weight of Jack's construct over his face. "How'd you know?"

"No one else stupid enough to bang on my door after dark," the woman said flatly. "*You* seem to be making a habit of it."

"I'll put a stop to that, then."

"See that you do," Annie said, and hobbled away. "Take off that damned ring as well. My house, you don't wear nothing but your face on your face. *No* exceptions."

Ashes obeyed, following after Annie at a respectful distance. "There's no supper left," she said.

"Didn't expect any. How's Blimey?"

"Like conversating with a rock," Annie replied. "He's just my kind of dinner party."

Something twisted in Ashes's core. Blimey was many things, but "quiet" only appeared on the list when he was scared or sullen.

"I'll leave him to you," the old woman said, pointing toward the stairs.

"I reckon we've some talking to do first," Ashes said carefully. "Concerning our rent."

"Terms is *fixed*, facefaker," Annie snapped. "You try to sweet-talk me and I'll throw you out in the street 'fore you can say *Please, miss, don't throw me out in the street.*"

"I'm not aiming to sweet-talk you, Annie," Ashes said. He dug in his coat and pulled out a phial of aether that had, until this morning, belonged to Elleander Bloom. "I've got a payment."

Annie's eyes locked onto the phial with the speed and hunger of a predator. Too late, she tried to compose her face. "What'm I supposed to think this is?"

"No sense faking like you don't know," Ashes said. "Let's skip to where we talk about how much it's worth."

"Where the hell'd you come across one of them?"

"I'm a dastardly clever pickpocket, Annie." Ashes gave her his best confident smile. "I could steal out of the Ladies' own skirts, they figured to walk Teranis for a day."

"That's a poor joke," Annie said darkly. "And what're you look-ing to buy with it, pray?"

"More time," Ashes said. "Six months, and you'll thank me for giving you an opportunity to rob me blind."

"Ha!" It was a profoundly humorless laugh, almost a bark. "No. Absolutely not."

"Annie—"

"Not for all the money in Teranis, boy," Annie said firmly. "You and your friend will be out of my home come the new year."

"You can't be serious," Ashes said. "I know Ragged's a danger, but with this—"

"I've more worries than Hiram Ragged on my mind, boy," Annie snapped. "New year. Term's fixed."

Ashes ground his teeth. "Fine. This is my rent until then. And I want better food for Blimey."

"You'll pay me *that* for *meat*?"

"I want him to be happy while we're here," Ashes said. "Give him the best you can. *And* he gets run of your library."

Annie scoffed. "That's a deal. I've no library to speak of."

"Don't play that to me. You got books in here somewhere."

"And what's giving you *that* impression?"

"What d'you do all day, Annie? For trade, I mean."

Annie glared at him and said, with a straight face, "Prostitutin'."

Ashes looked at her. Annie looked back.

"All right," he said. "Fine, if you say. But you do it all from here. You're *always* here, or near enough to always as makes no difference. There's nobody sits around their house all day without they have *something* they like. You seem the sort to read."

"Sometimes I knit."

"And sometimes I shit, but it's not how I spend my days." Ashes locked eyes with her. "Run of your library, Annie. Term's fixed."

Annie's mouth worked for several seconds. Finally, she said, "Very well. Meat for the boy when I can spare it, and he gets run of my books—*one* of them at a time, and if he damages the singlest page, I'll have it out from him in work and weeping. Blood, too, if I feel that way."

"Deal."

Blimey was asleep when he arrived in their room. Quietly, Ashes prepared to bed down, bundling his coat to make a pillow, and felt eyes on him.

"Mornin'," Blimey muttered.

"Still evening, actually, Blimes." Ashes grinned weakly.

"I saved you some supper," Blimey said, reaching under the

thin blanket. He produced a thin crust of bread. It looked hard enough to be used in self-defense in an emergency.

A small lump formed in Ashes's throat. "Aren't you just the very finest," he said.

"It's not much," Blimey said. "There was tripe, too, but I figured Annie wouldn't want me sneaking and my fingers aren't very quick—"

"Don't you worry none, mate." Ashes pulled Juliana's Ivorish food out of his pockets, peeling off the greasy cloth he'd wrapped it in. "Seems we got each other the same present."

Blimey's eyes widened. He snatched the food from Ashes quick as winking, and tore into it fiercely. "Roast beef!" he breathed in wonder. "And *cheese!*"

Ashes looked at him curiously. "You know roast beef?"

"Read about it," Blimey said, very quickly. He ripped a chunk of the meat off and chewed it for several seconds, savoring. "Where'd you *find* this?"

"Nicked it," Ashes said immediately. Everything in him rebelled at the thought of telling Blimey how he'd been feasting with three Denizens while Blimey had eaten supper at Batty Annie's table. "Jack wanted to see if I could get inside some Ivory's servants' quarters. Figures it'll be handy for me."

Blimey nodded, plainly absorbed in his food. "How'd it go?"

"Brilliant, of course," Ashes said. "Walked in and out easy as breathing."

"Did he let you wear a Glamour?"

"Eh," Ashes said. He pulled the ring out of his pocket and slipped it over his finger. The construct settled gently on his face. "Can you say uncle to that?"

"Face of Kindness, that's *brilliant*," Blimey said. "Can I . . . ?"

"Course," Ashes said.

Blimey put the ring on reverently. The Ivorish face formed around his features, obscuring the mismatched details of his natural face beneath a handsome, clean, curly-haired illusion. His expression remained the same, wide-eyed and delighted.

"Did it work? Am I different?"

"Like a proper Ivory lad, mate," Ashes said. A shadow passed over Blimey's face at the words. He handed the ring back, looking faintly perturbed.

"Thanks," he said, not meeting Ashes's eyes. "He let you keep it?"

"He said it'd be useful." Jack had also said that he had no desire to rescue Ashes from the police because he'd been picked up after curfew; police were keen on "troublemakers," and the face in the ring looked as far from troublemaker as you could get without being sainted.

"What about teaching you?" Blimey asked. "He still going to do that?"

"Started already," Ashes said, grinning widely. "I can't do nothing just yet, but give me time."

"That's brilliant as anything." Blimey grinned through a bite of cheese and beef. "You're learning *magic!*"

"Eh." Ashes tried to grin, but the expression faded off his face before it took hold. What good would magic be in four months when Annie threw them out?

They couldn't stay in Burroughside; Ragged would find them. They couldn't live in Lyonshire or Yson or any of the other posh boroughs; leasing a room required an iron name, and only Denizens had those.

He would need a solution, and soon.

"I talked with Annie tonight," Ashes said, eager to get away from thoughts of the future. "She'll let you read her books some, so long as you promise you'll not harm them."

Blimey shuddered. "Course not."

"And I'll try to bring you some later, right? I need you to keep bringing me words." Ashes smiled. "You got anything for me?"

"Oh, erm . . . no," Blimey admitted. "Not tonight."

Ashes nodded as though this were perfectly understandable, though it bothered him more than a little. Blimey never stopped reading. He was more upset than he was letting on. "Well, that's no problem," he said. "Actually, that's brilliant, 'cause I brought a word for you instead."

Blimey perked up.

"You ever heard of *immolated*?" Ashes asked.

Blimey blinked. "That's—oh, erm, it's burned alive, right?" He shut his eyes in concentration. "Eh, that's it. Kill something by burning it."

*Unsavory people* . . .

"Well, bloody and damn, Blimey, I'm impressed," Ashes said quickly. "I thought I'd have you with that one."

"Got to get up earlier than that to pull one over on me," Blimey said proudly.

"Guess I do," Ashes said.

Not long after, Blimey's soft snores indicated that he had fallen asleep. Ashes lay on the floor, staring at the ceiling. He longed to sleep, but it wouldn't come; he couldn't stop thinking.

Ashes had seen someone burned alive once. Two years ago, when he'd been part of Mari's crew. The dominant crew back then called themselves the Bone Collectors. They were more than forty strong, and their leader was a vicious, one-eyed boy named Robb Scars.

Someone had told Ragged the Collectors were planning a coup. So Ragged went to the old warehouse where the Bone Collectors lived, walked past forty gutter-rats who'd been planning to kill him, grabbed Robb Scars by the neck, and returned to Ragged House. Bruisemaker Eve was canceled so that Burroughside could watch the one-eyed boy blacken and char until there was nothing left but sooty bones.

No one had been allowed to leave. Ragged wanted everyone to know what happened when you tried to stab him in the back.

Ashes couldn't be certain, but his gut said Tremaine had made Mr. Ragged's false face. And Jack thought the same, if his look at dinner was anything to go on. Perhaps someone else had wanted Tremaine dead, but it seemed far more likely that Ragged himself was responsible. But why?

Was Ragged *scared*?

Ashes's face had been hidden when he escaped, so Ragged had no way of knowing who had taken his hat, or how they'd known it existed. Naturally, he would assume he'd been betrayed, and Tremaine was the likeliest candidate—Ashes would bet anything that the only person Ragged had trusted with the secret was Carapace. Burning Tremaine was a message to whoever had worked with him: *I'll come for you if you show yourself.* Ragged could have killed the Artificer quietly, but setting fire to him on Galway Street was distinctly *not* quiet. Ragged wanted the thief too frightened to do anything. Too frightened to try blackmail, or pawning, or . . .

Ashes sat up. He looked at Blimey, fast asleep on the bed, and then dug under the desk to find Ragged's hat. He checked his pocket for the Denizen-face ring. He stood.

If Ragged wanted the theft kept quiet, there was no doubt that Ashes's best move was to make it known, preferably to someone Ragged feared. Someone who could use the information against him—perhaps even oust him from Burroughside before the end of the year . . .

Ashes needed to see Bonnie the Lass.

## 15 Barter

THE Lass. Bonnie Ne'er-do-well. Stonejaw's Iron.

They called her the Undercity Queen, too; her castle, the Court of the Lass, was a crumbling warehouse in south Boreas. It hunched over a bend of the River Lethe, and, infrequently, if you stood close enough, you might hear the distinctive, heavy splash and cut-short scream of someone who had unwisely tested Bonnie's temper.

Bonnie's location was no secret. The police knew where to find her; the criminals knew where to find her; even those Ivory Lords whose business interests occasionally ran counter to the finer points of the law knew where to find her. This had yet to cause a problem for the Lass. Though she was often the victim of sordid rumors designed to tarnish her reputation, Bonnie had a comfortable working relationship with the local constabulary. They understood that certain disputes were the sort that should be resolved privately between individuals, without the complications that might arise when the law got involved. And, because they were so understanding, the police of southern Boreas often found themselves the blessed recipients of an anonymous donation of money, and never worried about their families when they left home.

Of such things are kingdoms built.

●●●

*Ashes had never tried* for an audience with the Lass; he didn't even know anyone who had. If the Lass wanted to speak to you, you were brought to her. Circumventing that established tradition was a frightening proposition at best. The Lass was fair, but she didn't suffer fools.

Fortunately, Ashes had an ace up his sleeve.

The door to the Court of the Lass was guarded by two surly men, both of whom looked to have a bit of bull in their ancestry. Ashes decided to keep this observation to himself; it wouldn't do to irritate Bonnie's doormen. He decided to take off the ring before they saw him, as well. The Court was one of the few places where it would be better to look like a scoundrel than an Ivorish ponce.

Ashes got within five feet of the door before one held out a hand and said, "Hold it there."

"Fine evening, innit?" he said with more calmness than he felt. "I'm here to see the Lass."

"She expecting you?"

Ashes smiled winningly. "She'll be pleased to see me."

The second guard eyed him cannily. "Sounds an awful lot like 'no,'" he said.

Ashes grinned again, hoping that he looked nonthreatening. "I've got something she wants," he said. "Something she wants very badly. I ent armed." He spread his hands, letting the hat dangle casually from his fingers.

"You're pissing in the wrong stream, pygmy," said the first. "There's nobody comes through this door without the Lass intends to see him."

"Do I look like I could threaten Bonnie the Lass?"

"You don't look like you could threaten the rats living under your bed," the guard replied. "Dun't change it. You'll get through this door over our corpses."

Ashes bit down on his tongue, but his hand wasn't played yet. "Look, mate, I'm a friend of hers—"

"That's likely," one scoffed. "Except all Bonnie's friends are big enough to hold a pistol without falling sideways."

"A friend of a friend," Ashes corrected. "There's a girl I met, says she works for Bonnie. Bright red hair. Likes to climb into places and get shot. I saved her life."

The guards exchanged a glance. Ashes felt a brief thrill of exaltation—the girl *had* been telling the truth, then. They would have to let him in now, surely.

The man on the left took a step toward Ashes and laid a meaty hand on his shoulder. "Word of advice, pygmy," he said. "If you're going to lie about knowing someone on the inside, pick some'un who *exists*."

His fist connected hard and fast with Ashes's temple. Stars erupted in the boy's eyes. Ashes staggered to the side, and the world tilted violently, and he felt his elbows connect with the street. At some point after that his head struck the stone. Everything spun harder.

"Go con someone stupider," the guard said. "*Don't* let me catch you here again, understand? The People don't con the People."

Ashes's ears were ringing. He fought his way to his feet and clenched his jaw. He brushed the dust off his hat and started to put it on. Then he thought better of it; if the guards saw him use the Glamour, he'd be lucky to keep his head, much less the hat. They'd take the construct from him, pass it off as their own find, and toss him in the river. He needed to speak to Bonnie herself.

"Right, then," he said. "Sorry to have bothered you."

"Sorry to have bothered you, *sir*," the guard corrected.

Ashes scowled and walked away without another word. One of the guards muttered something to his friend; they both laughed harshly. Ashes had the distinct sense that he had just been made into a joke.

*Don't be an idiot*, he told himself. If he turned around now, he would only do something stupid, and both the guards were big enough to turn him inside out. Blimey would be stuck in Batty Annie's basement forever. He kept walking.

That damn girl! He should have known she was lying about working for the Lass. It had been clever of her to manipulate him that way, but the thought gave him no comfort. He'd been played for a fool. Did the Lass even know Ragged *had* a Glamour? Perhaps he ought to sell it to Jack for whatever profit it could bring—except that wouldn't really help, not in the long run. No matter where he and Blimey ran, no matter what faces they put on, they would always be living under Ragged's shadow unless someone removed him. Bonnie had the power to do it; she only needed a reason, and an advantage. If Ragged was so desperate to keep his Glamour a secret, Ashes would bet anything that Bonnie could put the information to good use.

Ashes turned the corner toward Burroughside, and he was so lost in his thoughts he nearly crashed into the man walking the other way. Ashes sidestepped just in time, barely brushing the man's long coat. Nevertheless, it earned him a scowl.

"Insolent creature!" the man snapped. "Watch where you step!"

"Watch where—" Ashes stopped when he saw the man's face. "Er—I mean, I'm sorry, sir."

"What are you staring at?"

"Nothing, sir," Ashes said. "Nothing at all."

The fellow sneered at him, flicked his cloak, and stalked imperiously into the night. Ashes stared after him, feeling a sudden rush of curiosity: what, exactly, was Elleander Bloom doing in the bleak end of Boreas, and why was he wearing the illusory face Ashes had seen that morning?

He thought of returning to Annie's, but discarded the thought. His pulse thundered in his head. He could use a bit of distraction.

Ashes followed Bloom at a safe distance, sticking to the darkness and keeping low to the ground, using the fog as a layer of cover. Bloom, for his part, checked over his shoulder every few moments, as if he could sense Ashes's presence, but he was always obvious about it. Ashes evaded his glances every time.

They entered deeper into Boreas Gutters, a neighborhood Ashes had walked but never really explored. It resembled Burroughside in many ways, though it was better put-together, and every so often Ashes would catch the lamps of the police rather than Ravager howls. The roads grew narrow and restrictive, the buildings looked more and more run-down, and Bloom kept on walking. Finally, he stopped, checked over both shoulders once more, and stepped cautiously into a hushed little building with boarded-up windows and dull light visible through the cracks.

Ashes waited several seconds before he darted toward the building. He crouched beneath the window first, listening intently for voices. He heard nothing and no one. He tried to peek through the boards, but could see nothing but the wall. He grasped the handle of the door.

*Reckless*, he thought, and turned it anyway.

The room beyond was almost entirely empty, except for a wavering candle in the corner and a thin-faced man sitting beside it. He stared at Ashes impassively.

"Hullo," Ashes said.

The man's eyes narrowed. "You police?"

"They turned me down," Ashes said reflexively. "I intimidated the other recruits too much, on account of my size."

The man chuckled. It was a throaty, hoarse noise. "Go on

down, then," he said, tilting his head at the floor. Ashes followed his gaze, but saw nothing except blank wooden slats.

"First time, eh?" the man said. "Don't be nervous. If you need to learn they'll teach you. Go on down," he said again.

Ashes stepped carefully into the center of the room. His foot sank deeply into the floor before it struck something solid. Ashes took another step, and found the next stair. He sank into the floor up to his knees.

The man grinned at him toothily, which was impressive, given that several of his teeth were gone. "Never gets old," he said.

When Ashes's head passed through the illusory floor, he let out an involuntary gasp; the entire world had gone totally dark. For a moment, he was back in the sewers, surrounded by the chitterings and hisses of the beasts below—but he shook his head and forced himself to breathe. He reached the bottom of the staircase and groped blindly until he found a doorknob, and turned it with relief.

The smoke struck his nose instantly, and struck his eyes shortly after that. He coughed, shoved his face into his elbow, and looked around. The room was surprisingly large—as big as Jack's dining room—and filled with beds and cushioned chairs. Nearly a dozen people were scattered throughout; those on the beds looked to be sleeping, while others muttered quietly to each other. Several had pipes in their hands. An opium den.

Ashes spotted Bloom and quickly lost himself among a group of dreamy-eyed smokers. The Artificer was sitting across from someone, a rickety-looking old man with a humped shoulder and fraying, wispy hair. Ashes edged closer to them, trying to catch their conversation.

". . . a rather diseased sense of humor, Selmanhov," Bloom was saying.

"Better a sick one than none at all, sir," replied the old man. His voice was coarse, as tatty as his clothing, and faintly familiar. "It keeps life interesting."

"How much do you have?"

"Six drachms," said the old man. "Selling for a pretty penny, too, eh. My boys suffered dear for this take."

"Funny you should mention your boys," Bloom said, his voice dropping to a low and threatening growl. "I think I must have run into one this very morning."

"I don't take your meaning," Selmanhov said.

"Then you are far more foolish than I thought," Bloom snapped. "You stole from me!"

"I have done no such thing!"

"Lies. I left my home this morning with two laden Anchors and a phial full of aether, and found all of it mysteriously *absent* before noon. Curious, don't you think?"

"Perhaps you are just absentminded," Selmanhov suggested.

"Do not take me for an idiot. Return what is mine, and we may continue our business together. Fail to do so . . ." Bloom tried to let the threat hang in the air.

"I did not steal from you," Selmanhov insisted. "Not I, nor any of mine."

"Do not—"

"I am not some filthy pickpocket!" The man was visibly angry now; a vein pulsed on his temple, and his voice had become tight and strained. His Errasan accent thickened. "My boys and I are not so stupid. Steal from Artificers in broad daylight? Idiocy! Folly! We may just as wisely dance naked before the Guild!"

"Perhaps," Bloom said. "And perhaps, Selmanhov, you ought to consider that preying on your customers leaves you naked before the Guild as well."

"Do not tell me my business," the old man snapped. "If the Guild discovers me, it discovers you, *Elleander*. And I am far more adept at disappearing. Now, have you come to do business, or are we to sit here arguing until dawn about who pisses farthest?"

Bloom scowled. "Very well. I will take the six. How much?"

"Seventy-five," Selmanhov said flatly.

"The poppies have melted your mind. A *full* phial is fifty."

"A full phial comes from the Guild." Selmanhov's grin was full of satisfaction and pride. "And the Guild does not give lightly, does it, especially if you are foolish enough to lose their gifts? My boys risk their necks for every drop. I risk my fingers to sell it. Seventy-five."

"Sixty."

"*Seventy-five*, boy. Do not play this game with me."

Bloom's scowl deepened. He produced a small purse, and even at a distance Ashes could hear the heavy clink it made falling into Selmanhov's hand. The old man tested the weight of the purse for a moment, opened the bag, and bit into one of the coins. He seemed satisfied.

"A pleasure, Elleander," he said. He counted out five crowns from the bag and gave them back to Bloom. "A discount, in exchange for your information. If someone is stealing from my customers, I will put a stop to it. You may rely on it."

Bloom clenched his jaw and took the coins, standing brusquely. "See that you do," he said imperiously, and left the room.

Ashes waited before following him out, not wanting to be caught tailing the man. Selmanhov, too, waited as Bloom left the room. After some time, the old man picked up a short wooden cane and got laboriously to his feet. He stumbled toward the door, and something about his movement struck Ashes strangely. He seemed terribly familiar, but Ashes couldn't place him. He'd never known anyone from the Erras, and the only gray-hair he knew was Ben Roamer. Had he seen Selmanhov somewhere before?

Ashes watched the man closely, determined to understand why he felt so familiar. He took a step closer, trying to peer through the murk and smoke.

Selmanhov reached the door and cast an errant look back at the room, looking faintly suspicious. Ashes ducked closer to the wall and buried himself in the darkness; the old man peered a few moments longer and left.

Ashes's heart pounded. He *did* know Selmanhov. He had been difficult to recognize through the makeup and the false hair, but the man underneath was, unmistakably, Candlestick Jack.

# 16   *Distraction*

WILLIAM'S workroom reeked with a familiar burning, empty stink; Ashes could smell it all the way down the hall. He felt woozy before he reached the doorway.

"You may enter," William said. He was bent intently over the metal table, back turned to the door. Gleaming silver tools, neatly arranged on a black mat, sat to his left. Whatever was in front of him gave off a faint light, like a shrouded lamp.

Ashes stepped inside the surgery, pinching his nose to keep the smell under control. "Jack left a note," he said. "He said to find you."

"I deduced the same from your presence," William said, voice muffled slightly from a mask hanging over his face. "Ergo, your pronouncement is a waste of time, ergo, you should not have said it."

*Well*, Ashes thought. *Won't this be fun.*

The Wisp turned to face him. The mask covered his nose and

mouth with a dark metal snout; wide, clouded-glass lenses made his eyes look bulbous and strange. Something like iron gleamed on the rims. William pulled the snout down so that his mouth was no longer encumbered before he spoke.

"I will not waste time," the Wisp said crisply. "Not on the vagaries of Ivorish courtesy. Not on pretending I am glad to have you as a student. We are both mortal. Sleep alone will rob us of a quarter of our lives. I see no reason to fritter away our shrinking span on something as insipid as liking each other, particularly in the service of what is sure to be a thoroughly abortive attempt at education. Am I understood?"

Ashes paused, taking a moment to understand the man's phrasing. "Yes, sir," he said.

"I will not repeat myself. If your attention lapses, *my* time will not be lost reeducating you."

Ashes didn't hesitate this time. "Yes, sir."

"Approach the table." Ashes did so.

As Ashes came closer, he saw that someone was lying on the table—and realized just as quickly that it wasn't *someone*: it was the illusory woman in the ball gown, the construct he had stolen from Elleander Bloom yesterday. The woman was headless; her face was on the other side of the room, floating serenely above a wooden ball. Ashes suppressed a shiver.

William didn't notice Ashes's discomfort, or if he did it didn't bother him. "Reconstitution is the prime skill of a Stitcher," William intoned. "Weavers are wasteful personalities, as a rule. They use more than they need. Stitchers may recover what has been lost, or renew what has faded. We are not glorified, admired, or sought after. We are crucial."

Ashes nodded. "Right. How come you took the head off?"

William stared at him. After a moment, he blinked, shook himself a little, and said, "Your syntax is abominable."

"Eh?"

"Grammar," William said, "is a fundamental aspect of communication. If you must speak, do so clearly and succinctly."

Ashes's jaw clenched, but he nodded.

"Jacob requested that I separate the face from the construct," William said. "In case it is of use later. The rest is to be reduced to its components, that it may be used now."

"So we're regathering the aether from it?"

"*Reconstituting,*" William replied. He pointed toward a cabinet. "You will find your equipment in there."

The cabinet was filled with arcane-looking tools set in orderly rows. Ashes recognized some from Jack's tour yesterday, but there were many new items as well: crystal bowls stacked inside each other, tongs made of silver, and something that looked like a naked telescope made of a dozen monocles of sequential size. These he ignored, scanning the cabinet quickly to locate one of the strange masks.

He found one on the bottom shelf and put it on. Even cinched as tightly as it could go, it was still loose around his skull, and he had to hold it in place with one hand to keep it from sliding down his nose. The mouthpiece turned his breathing whirry, and the lenses made everything look warped. The brightest light in the room came from the construct, a wavering luster of gold that seemed to speckle the man's masked face.

Ashes approached William's table again, looking intently at the figure lying there. The woman's shape hadn't changed, but he could now see the threads of light that composed it. Most threads were singularly colored, but he spotted several silvery lines that seemed to shift through the spectrum. Aether.

"Inspect the construct," William commanded. "What do you notice?"

"There's a lot of aether in it," Ashes said. "I can't tell how much, though."

"Seven drachms," William confirmed. "Or so I would estimate. Nearly a full phial's worth. What else?"

"It's hollow," Ashes observed. With the mask on, he could see through the voluminous dress to the nothing beneath. It fascinated him; to the naked eye, the construct had looked so lifelike.

"Anything further?"

Ashes shook his head.

"Then we shall begin our task. Grasp the aether."

Ashes blanched, then nodded. He pressed one hand against the construct, pressing his fingers against the lines until he felt resistance. They were thin, incredibly fragile, but *there*. He could touch them . . .

He grasped, but the lines turned wispy as he did, resisting his attempt to shape them. He looked at William, who stared back impassively. "Do not *seize* it," the Wisp said. "We are not Weavers. We do not grope."

Ashes tried again, moving his hand slowly. The light slid over his skin, tickled his fingertips, but he couldn't make it change.

"Bah," William said. "You think like a Weaver, brash and gaudy. Wasteful."

Ashes felt his muscles clench. "How'm I supposed to think?"

"Invisibly," William said. "The best Stitchery is unnoticeable."

Ashes bit back a retort. He dipped his hand in the light again and closed his eyes. He relaxed.

The threads pulsed beneath his touch, like miniature veins. He could feel the way they twined and twisted. He hooked his finger around one thread and pulled it back with deliberate slowness. The thread went taut, and then limp, as it broke away from the rest of the construct, coming free into Ashes's hands.

"Face of Cunning," he swore. "I did it!"

William slid a glass jar across the table. "Adequately done. It belongs in that apparatus there."

William's total disinterest couldn't dull Ashes's triumph. *I'm doing real magic*, he thought, stunned. He was canted. One person in a thousand. Not just a clever gutter-rat, not one of Ragged's playthings. There was power in him, something brilliant and unique. Real magic.

William was staring at him. He looked quizzical, though it was difficult to tell past the cloudy eyepieces embedded in the man's mask. Ashes realized with a start that he hadn't responded yet.

"Thanks, sir," he said.

"There is no need for gratitude," William said. "I am simply making note of a situation. You are not utterly talentless." The Wisp moved briskly back to the construct. "Do not gawk. We have more yet to do."

They worked for what felt like hours, William plucking strings of aether out of the dress with the ease of long practice, and Ashes tugging them carefully, almost fearfully, out of their sockets. Every line of aether released a wisp of light as it was removed, as if letting out a long-held breath.

Ashes felt sweat beading on his forehead before they were halfway finished. By the time they had reconstituted all the remaining aether, Ashes's fingers were sore, and there was a persistent ache in his forehead. The false dress lay flat on the table, deflated. Feathery threads of light eked out of it from every edge.

William pulled his mask off. The Wisp did not look even a little tired; he was simply blank.

"You may ask questions of me now," William said. "If you must."

"Dun't think I have any," Ashes admitted, rubbing his head. "Er—well, actually, there was something Jack said yesterday, about my magic. That I needed to be tuned, or learn how to dance, or—something."

William inclined his head. "The Weaver speaks in metaphor because he cannot stand to state his point outright," he said. "Artificers come in two sorts—"

"Right, eh, I know that," Ashes said. "I was just going to say

I didn't need any tuning to Stitch. So by the seems I'm a—a *real* Stitcher."

William's head tilted. "I beg your pardon?"

"A real Stitcher. Right?"

"Not that," the Wisp said. " 'By the seams'?"

"You not familiar? It means 'by the looks of things.'"

"I am *quite* familiar, child," William said. "I have studied your Ivorish language at greater length and with greater dedication than the vast majority of your scholars. But you misuse the term."

"I don't," Ashes said, bristling. "People say that all the time."

"Then they are *wrong*." There was more passion in that statement than in everything else William had said to him put together. "*By the seams* is a phrase used by Stitchers. It references the seam of a construct, the place where its Weaver's concentration was weakest. If a Stitcher takes a construct 'by the seams,' he has taken control of it, completely enough to dissipate it at a stroke. The term has been in use since the Nine—"

"Furies, Faces, and Kindness above," came the voice of Candlestick Jack. The Weaver appeared in the doorway a moment later, grinning widely. "Your talent for getting in over your head borders on the uncanny, lad. Best not get Will into a talk about language if you have plans for the week." Jack stepped inside the threshold and made a face. "Bloody Furies, Will. What did you do to this room?"

"It needed sanitizing," William said.

"The boy wasn't even bleeding when I got him here!"

"That smell you detect," William said primly, "is the boundary between recovery and sepsis. There is a reason your Lyonshire surgeries only return three patients for every ten they take in."

"So long as you're not sending my students into a coma, you can keep bragging about how successful your surgery is," Jack said, tipping a significant look at Ashes. "The boy looks fit to keel over. How'd he do?"

"I found his performance sufficient," William said. "He succeeded in plucking an aether thread without aid and caused nothing to explode. Altogether, a strict improvement over the last student you foisted upon me."

Jack rolled his eyes. "Rejoice. I'm taking him off your hands." He led Ashes into the hallway. "Didn't turn your ears to lead and make them fall off, did he?" he muttered.

Ashes grinned. "Neh. I figure I could've done without the Ivorish lesson, though."

"You'd never believe it's not his first language, would you?"

"He's not from around here?"

"How *did* you guess?" Jack asked drily. "Was it the accent, or the general impression of his being fundamentally different from all sane humanity?"

Ashes laughed. "The first one, mostly."

"Will's technically a citizen," Jack said. "Foreign parents, but he was born inside city limits and has the iron name to prove it. He's as much a Denizen as I am, so far as the law's concerned."

Jack led him into the parlor with the great window, where Ashes saw with some surprise that it was nearly evening. They passed through the intangible wall, down the stairs, and into the workshop. The Artificer moved quickly to the cabinet at the back of the room.

"I've got a present for you before you head home for the night," he explained as he pulled out a long-handled silver key and unlocked the cabinet. He moved his broad shoulders to hide the inside from view, though not before Ashes caught a glimpse of a dozen phials of liquid light on the top shelf. When Jack turned back to him, he was holding a small stone circle, the same Ashes had found in the sewers.

"This is yours," Jack said.

"What is it?"

Jack gave him a strange look. "It's called an optic, or a seeing-stone," Jack said. "Another tool of the trade, though not one you're likely to find in the average Artificer's lab."

Ashes held the stone to his eye. Through the circle, the workshop was transformed. The shelves shone with gold and silver lights brighter than the lamps. Where there had been blank stretches of wall, now there were doors. Ashes looked at Jack, and saw brilliant lights in the man's coat, as if he were smuggling stars in his pockets.

"Seeing-stones reveal Artifice for what it really is," Jack said. "It makes Weaving disappear, makes Anchors damn near impossible to conceal." He smirked and passed a hand over his face, and his features shifted subtly: his jowls became heavier, his nose short and brutish, his eyes a bright, searing green. Ashes looked at him with the seeing-stone again, and squinted. Through the lens, Jack's face looked the same, except that it shone like a miniature sun. "Doesn't play nicely with Stitching, though."

"What the hell was that?"

"Stitching, lad," Jack said proudly. "It's the only sort of Artifice that can really keep you hidden." He pointed at the seeing-stone in Ashes's hand. "Those are not terribly common, but there are Artificers out there who've got their hands on one. If you'd rather keep your face entirely to yourself, Stitching is the way to do it. It works against Iron Knights, too."

Ashes laughed, but Jack gave him a flat look. "Something funny?" the man asked.

"Iron Knights are a fairy tale," Ashes said.

"Are they really?" Jack said drily. "Bugger and damn, I've wasted so many years devising ways to keep them off my scent. Iron Knights are just as real as we are. Not as powerful as they are in the stories—they can't destroy your Artifice just by touching it.

But they *can* see through it. Their eyes are seeing-stones. They're too single-minded to trick. They're strong enough to rip your head off your shoulders, and humorless enough to do it. You meet a man with moonlight where his eyes should be, mind your manners and be very, very obedient."

Iron Knights were real. Blimey would have a fit.

"Why are you giving it to me?" Ashes asked.

"I don't need an extra," Jack said with a shrug. "And where optics are concerned, finders are very much keepers. They're old, old magic. You found it, it's yours, no matter that you've been an Artificer for hardly two nights."

Ashes pocketed the stone. "Thanks," he said.

"Don't mention it," Jack said. "Besides, I'm not done playing gift-giver yet. Hold out your hand."

Ashes looked at the man skeptically, but obeyed, presenting his palm.

"Make sure you don't close your eyes," Jack said. "You'll miss the exciting part."

Jack held his open hand beneath Ashes's. A ball of light appeared above Ashes's palm and began to spin, and as it spun it grew larger, until it formed a luminous maelstrom. Jack twitched a finger downward, and the light dove into—*through*—Ashes's bare skin. The boy could have sworn he felt something cool and ephemeral rush through him, and wondered how much of it was simple wishing.

"There," Jack said.

"There what?"

"You're a Stitcher," Jack explained. "And I intend to teach you Weaving. Your magic doesn't know how to Weave naturally, so my magic has shown it how." He grinned broadly. "Technically, I only have to touch you and Weave at the same time, but there's no *spectacle* in that."

Ashes looked at his hands. He didn't *feel* any different.

"It'll be some time before you can do anything impressive, of course," Jack said. "Think of it as your muscles needing to bulk up."

"I— Thanks," Ashes said.

"Again, really, don't mention it," Jack said. "To anyone, ever. The Guild would chop off my lovely hands."

Ashes laughed. "Told you already, Jack. I can keep a secret."

Jack grinned at that, but when he met Ashes's eyes it was with a serious, calculating gaze. Ashes kept his face studiously blank, though he wondered if Jack had seen him last night in the opium den. He had been well hidden, but still . . .

"I'm sure you can," Jack said.

# 17 — *Focus*

THE next three weeks passed in a blur. Ashes came to the Rehl Company shop every morning at ten o'clock, entering by the back way when no one was looking. His lessons were many and varied, and every night he returned to Batty Annie's feeling like his brain was swathed in thick cotton.

Mondays, Wednesdays, and Saturdays he spent with William. This practice made sense in theory, since Ashes was theoretically a Stitcher. It took Ashes fewer than three lessons to start wondering if, perhaps, something was wrong with that theory. He was certainly no Weaver; moving raw light felt like trying to pick up a house by his fingertips. But Stitching was, if anything, even harder.

William started every lesson with an exercise to review basic principles: binding Anchors so that illusions appeared when they were touched or breathed on or held horizontally; or finding a construct's seam; or molding an illusion that had solidified. Even the easier exercises took Ashes nearly twenty minutes. William informed him, in his dispassionate way, that none should have taken more than five.

When William was not tonelessly reminding him about basic principles—of which there seemed to be thousands—he was correcting his grammar. "Enunciate." "Yes or no. *Eh* and *neh* are neither charming nor, in fact, words." "*Do you.* Enunciate." Against his will, Ashes felt his command of the language sharpened by pure frustration.

The Wisp's pale face showed emotion only rarely, but Ashes could sense the man's disappointment like a constant stench. His eyes bored into Ashes's fingers when he worked. He guillotined words with his teeth when he reminded Ashes of simple things. He assigned exercises with what would have seemed like vindictive pleasure, if it had come from anyone else; but the Wisp gave no sign he enjoyed seeing Ashes bind and rebind one construct to the same Anchor in eight different ways or peel aether out of outdated illusions. William's cool distaste only angered Ashes more. At least if William were vindictive, Ashes could have hated him guiltlessly.

But, in truth, Ashes was frustrated, too. After three weeks of constant practice, there was no significant improvement in his skill. He was a little faster at reconstituting, and could make minute adjustments to congealed constructs. The only discipline he had any knack for was finding seams, but even that he could only do if he watched it being Woven. The most impressive skill—making illusory changes to the real world—resisted him entirely.

On Tuesdays and Sundays, he studied with Juliana. These days were marginally better, since Jack's wife always brought food to their lessons, and he never tired of looking at her. Even more encouraging, she seemed to enjoy having him around, though it was difficult to be certain that he wasn't simply receiving Ivorish courtesy.

Her subject matter, however, could not have been more hateful.

She taught him drawing, anatomy, and a smattering of alchemy's foundational principles. All three subjects made him want to beat his head through a wall. His fingers, sly enough to tease a neckerchief out of unsuspecting pockets, were utterly confounded by pencils and inks. The other two subjects consisted entirely of memorizing tables upon tables of information, and the occasional use of arithmetic. He had a quick memory, but the sheer volume of material made his head spin. On the occasions when he begged for a respite, she switched to Ivorish customs: courtesies and manners and traditions Ashes would need to know if he ever pretended to be someone of a great rank. Those lessons were even worse.

Thursdays and Fridays belonged to Jack. Initially Ashes had been excited, if wary: he ached to shape light on his fingertips. He would even endure unorthodox teaching methods for it; between their first lesson and the myriad stories he'd heard about trickster teachers, Ashes was willing to bet that Jack would run him through a host of mundane exercises only to reveal that they were all, somehow, fundamentally important to Artifice. Ashes was ready, even eager.

By the second week he realized the stories were full of trash.

Jack's lessons, rather than containing the merest mention of Artifice or light-shaping, mainly involved subjecting Ashes to a series of arcane games. The connection between the exercises and Artifice was tenuous at best; it seemed Jack's sole aim was forcing Ashes to think faster. He would uncover a table full of objects and give Ashes thirty seconds to memorize the arrangement, colors, and shapes of the pieces, and then quiz him on it, often with trick questions about items that hadn't been on the table. He would mention something offhand at the beginning of the lesson, and demand that Ashes repeat it word for word at the end. He told Ashes to read long, complex passages from books while Jack did his best to distract him—by creating flashes of light, or yelling, or insulting Ashes's mother, or throwing whatever he had on hand—and if

Ashes dropped or mispronounced a single word, they started again from the beginning.

Jack's favorite game was having Ashes play pretend. *Pretend you're Lord Trevilian. Pretend you're from Boreas Glades. Pretend you're an Iron Knight. Pretend you're drunk and need to see a medic.* On these occasions he would make minute adjustments to Ashes's posture, speech, voice, expression; frequently he Wove new faces for Ashes to wear while he pretended. Sometimes he asked questions about what Ashes, as someone else, thought about a particular topic, or asked his reasoning behind a given action. On one memorable occasion, he made Ashes play out an argument between a priest and a heretic entirely on his own.

On the third Thursday, after fully five hours of this educational terrorism, Jack handed him a phial of liquid light.

"Do *not* waste it," he said. "We're going to play Distract Me." This was Jack's name for the read-aloud-while-I-throw-things-at-you game.

Ashes eyed the phial carefully. "What's the light for?"

"You're not reading today," Jack said with a slight smile. "Today it's real magic."

The objective was to dole out a tiny measure of the liquid light and keep it in a tight ball. Ashes would change the color of the ball according to Jack's instructions, but *only* if Jack said "The Ladies say" before he called out the color.

With an effort, he made the light hover above his palm while Jack took up position, and at the first "Ladies say," turned the ball blue.

Immediately Jack began his onslaught. In his periphery, Ashes glimpsed brilliant flashes, miniature supernovae that lit the entire workshop in varying shades of purple, blue, red, and green. He was so focused on the ball of light he hardly noticed them, until Jack called "Ladies say violet. Mauve. Silver. Ladies say blue. How did your mother feel about goats? *Very* fondly, judging by your face."

Jack clanged the more durable metal Anchors together, and overturned a table, and threw a Gilder-glove that hit Ashes in the face. "Ladies say green!" He called Ashes a variety of colorful names, then cursed every Face, individually, in wonderfully inventive ways, and shouted so loudly Ashes was sure folk heard it on the road. "Gold! By the way, I've figured out why you stink so. I think you must've been born in a privy. Your mum must've been *very* confused." He gathered light around his hands and flung it in the boy's eyes. "Ladies say white!"

And, when Jack finally stopped, the ball of light still hovered over Ashes's palm, revolving slowly, pale and fragile but as glitteringly white as a diamond. Jack eyed it, and muttered something about how Synder would have done better.

On Friday, Jack gave him another phial of light and told him to make himself a face.

"What kind?" Ashes asked.

"The kind you wouldn't mind being caught in," Jack said. "We're going out tonight, you and I. Something I want you to see."

● ● ●

*Light, Ashes decided, was* ornery. If he remembered correctly, Blimey had said *ornery* meant it behaved like Ashes did with grown-ups, and that was exactly what light was like.

He had been sitting at Jack's worktable for four hours. The first face had come out misshapen and strange, with skin of a mottled color. For fully an hour, he'd tried to Stitch it into something more tenable, and all he'd managed to do was make the skin slightly smoother and the shape less monstrous, which was to say it had boils, pockmarks, and horns instead of boils, pockmarks, horns, and sharp edges. Discouraged, he'd reconstituted the thing and started over.

The second face looked vaguely more human, but still undeniably demonic. On the third face, his attention slipped, and the

Weaving burst with a flash so bright it left trails in his eyes. It took him fully twenty minutes to gather the light back together, and he lost at least a quarter of it.

Noon had nearly arrived. His forehead was damp with sweat, and his fingers ached. His most recent illusion floated in front of him, and if his exhaustion hadn't been evident in his eyes and his body, it was evident in the work. The face was all angles and sharp lines, harsh and frightening; the eyes were too large and the teeth too long for the mouth. It looked to have been carved from obdurate stone by an unskilled, talentless apprentice. Which, he thought, was very nearly accurate.

He let out a heavy breath as he Anchored the face onto a pole in the center of the table, a temporary home to keep the construct from evaporating. Though, looking at it, evaporation might well be the best destiny for this thing.

The magic ought to have come more easily than this. Story heroes always took to their magic innately, didn't they? Jack *had* told him that some people took months and years to do the simplest things, but he'd been talking about Gilders. Ashes was *canted*. It should have been easier than *this*.

He ran his hand through the illusory face, feeling the threads against his fingertips, and prepared to rip the thing apart again: no one, at least, would be able to say he'd given up. He shaped his mind and perspective, preparing to be invisible, and then he heard a footstep behind him.

He jerked backward, and his senseless legs, unpredictable even a month after the witch-healing, overbalanced. He tipped backward and crashed to the floor.

"Oh my goodness!" someone said.

He rolled to his side and forced himself to stand. Fire lit in his cheeks.

The newcomer was an Ivorish girl with a heart-shaped face and eyes sharp enough to cut glass. "Are you all right?" She took three quick strides toward him before he stepped back reflexively. She halted, looking at him with concern.

"M'fine," Ashes said. His blush could have boiled water. "I was just— I, erm. Hullo." He tried to gather the stray pieces of his confidence back together. This was difficult to do while exhausted, embarrassed, and confused.

"I didn't mean to startle you," the girl said. "I do apologize for that. Juliana said you'd be in here."

Ashes swallowed and tried to reorient himself. Something about the girl gave him pause. "Who're you?" he asked, though he felt pretty sure he knew.

"Synder." The girl glanced around Ashes, at the mangled, sharp-featured face he had made. "Previously Jack's only student."

The errant detail clicked. The Ivorish girl was wearing *trousers*. Was that allowed?

"I'm Ashes. S'good to meet you." She didn't look *that* smart. Maybe she just knew lots of big words, the way Blimey did. "Jack's mentioned you a bit."

The girl rolled her eyes. "He does that. He showed you the watch, too, didn't he?"

Ashes nodded.

"Ugh." She flopped indelicately onto the bench, pulling a wearied face. "He does that to everyone, I hope you know. I don't think a single person in the entire Guild *hasn't* seen that thing. He just likes showing off, that's all."

"It was pretty good," Ashes said. He could admit that, at least.

"Thank you," said the girl swiftly, like it was a reflex. "It took much longer to make than I wanted it to. And my cousin helped me through half of it. He was actually the one who thought of rebuilding the watch so the dancer would rotate."

Ashes frowned. "What?"

"My cousin. He was a bit of a—"

"You rebuilt the watch?"

Synder smiled. "Michael did. He thought you could bind something to a rotating gear so it could move on its own. He took it apart, told me what needed to go where, Anchored it for me. All I did was the Weaving." She moved the hair out of her eyes and blew out a breath. "Jack's very fond of telling all his peers about how I don't even have my Stars yet and I'm already more brilliant than half the Guild. I can't *stand* it."

Ashes smirked. "Does he know it weren't your idea?"

"I told him that when I applied. He'd die before he'd admit it to the Guild, though. I don't think he could abide his star student being anything less than perfect."

Ashes peered at her. He'd thought she was nearly sixteen, but now he could tell she was hardly any older than fourteen—perhaps not even that.

The girl nodded toward the ugly face on the table. "Is this your first time?" She gave a reserved smile. "I remember when he had me do it. Are you a Weaver?"

"Neh," Ashes said, feeling an inexplicable wash of shame. "Stitcher." *And not even a half-decent one.*

"Oh!" Synder said, nodding swiftly. "That's brilliant! Everybody needs a Stitcher. I'm *rubbish* at Stitching. Do you want any help with this?"

"What?"

"Help. With making the face." She gestured once again at the lamp. "It can be really difficult if you aren't born with it. Has Jack showed you anything?"

"Don't want no help. I can figure it out myself."

Synder raised her eyebrows. "You're sure?"

Ashes clenched his jaw, recalling William's scathing comments. "I don't need any help."

"If you say so." Synder squirmed on the bench, moving with a weird sort of stiltedness. She wasn't gangling, but she wouldn't be graceful for a few years yet. Her body was still growing into itself, arms and legs longer than they ought to have been. The motion drew Ashes's attention once more to the scandalous attire on her legs.

"You wear trousers," he said, and immediately regretted it. Ivory-blooded folk were tetchy about their clothes; Ivory-blooded women doubly so.

The girl laughed. "I do," she said proudly. She smiled, and there was not the slightest tint of shame about her. "You can imagine what my parents said the first time. I considered keeping a few Anchors with me that could imitate petticoats and all that nonsense, but then I decided, you know what? That's stupid. I like trousers. I wear trousers. I'm going to wear trousers and nobody's going to tell me any different."

"How's that gone for you?"

Synder rolled her eyes. "Poorly, for the most part. You'd be *stunned* at how some people react when they see something they don't understand. *Stunned.*"

Ashes smirked. "I doubt it, miss."

"Don't call me miss. That's silly. You can't be more than a year younger than me."

Ashes shrugged. "Couldn't say."

She looked at him curiously. "I'm fourteen."

"That's nice."

She gave him a *look*, one that made clear how unimpressed she was with his quip. "How old are you?"

"Told you, didn't I? I dunno." Ashes sat as well.

"How can someone *not* know their age? When's your birthday?"

"Haven't one," he replied, curling his fist beneath the lamp. He could almost feel the light, just at the edge of his perceptions, but he hadn't managed even to tug raw light in the last three weeks. "I'm *rasa.* Never really got a birthday."

The girl blushed, looking flustered for the first time. "I'm so sorry. I didn't realize. Is that why you . . . speak the way you do?"

"Burroughside, bred and buttered," Ashes said with a winning smile. He dredged through his memory to find an accent that nearly matched hers. "Of course, it's all just a matter of how you talk, wouldn't you say?" He added the Ivorish trill out of instinct. The girl's eyes lit up. "Sometimes I'm from Lyonshire. Sometimes Boreas. Depends what'll get me the littlest number of troubles. Where're you from?"

"East Lyonshire." She seemed almost apologetic now. "My father's a shopkeeper. Mother keeps his books."

"Oh, aye?" Ashes grimaced as the word smashed against his teeth and abandoned the Lyonshire accent. "She knows rhythm-ticks?" He felt a warm glow in his chest. Blimey would have been proud to see him using that word.

"Mhm. Father's no good at maths—positively abysmal at them, actually. Mother's much better. It's kind of a joke in my family now, because if the world had any sense, Mother would run the shop entirely, and Father would just sit in the study and paint all day."

"Your da's a painter?" Ashes stopped himself from laughing just in time. "That's . . . Don't think I've ever heard that one before."

"He never has time for it. Not with maintaining the shop. But that's what he would do, if he could." The girl dragged her fingers across the table, and Ashes couldn't help noticing the light congealing around them. Jealousy flashed through him. "Probably where I get all my Weaving from, honestly. Mother would never go for something so impractical."

"You been doing it a long time? The Weaving?" Ashes looked at her fingers again, and imitated her under the table. No droplets gathered to his skin.

"A few years. I showed signs of Artifice when I was very young—grabbing light, changing little details of my face, that sort of thing. It took my mother a while to admit it, though. I don't think she could handle the idea of me being so much like Father. They probably wouldn't have let me apply to study with Jack's company if not for my cousin being a Stitcher. We applied together."

"Your cousin studies here?"

Synder's face changed in an instant, like a door being shut. "Not anymore." She hesitated, visibly looking for a change of subject. "Why are you called Ashes?"

"S'my name."

"Jack didn't tell you to go by it?"

"What? No."

"You're *sure*? It seems like the sort of joke he'd like."

"They called me that when they found me," Ashes said. "I was in Lyonshire-Low, where the factories are. Had it over my face and all."

"Like a disguise?" Synder smiled. "That's delightful! Facefaking right from the start. How did Jack find you? I mean, if you're from Burroughside, how are you paying for the apprenticeship?"

Ashes paused. The girl had to know about Jack's—what had the Weaver called them? "Extralegal services"? If she didn't, though, Ashes couldn't confess the secret. Jack would dismiss him on the spot, favors or no favors. "Jack's got me doing odd jobs for him, paying my way."

Her eyes went wide. "You must be an incredible Stitcher to be here on a scholarship," she said.

Ashes blinked, then said, "I guess."

"What did you make for your application?" She seemed to be vibrating with excitement. "It had to be some kind of Anchoring system, didn't it? Jack *loves* clever Anchoring. Or—did you make something very intricate? Most Weavers can't really do fine details, Stitchers are better for that."

Ashes's mind raced. What lie would be plausible here?

He waited half a second too long. The girl looked at him curiously. "You didn't make anything for an application, did you?"

Ashes gave her a sheepish grin, one that he hoped would dampen her curiosity a little. "No. Sorry."

The girl's eyebrows lifted. "You must have something very

special about you. I can't wait to find out what it is." She stood abruptly and thrust out one hand. Uncertainly, he took it. "It's been very nice meeting you, Ashes," she said, giving his hand one firm shake. "I look forward to working together."

"Eh," he replied. "Same to you, I think."

She whirled around and disappeared through one of the walls.

Ashes sat back and exhaled. Jack's genius pupil . . . she seemed sharp, certainly. Ashes didn't know if he would say she was smarter than him, though.

He turned back to his mangled construct and stretched out a hand, willing the shape to change. Nothing occurred.

"Bastard bit of stupid bloody magic," he muttered. He glanced at the wall.

What a strange girl that had been. He'd seen girls wear trousers: Burroughside didn't have much room for propriety. But young Ivorish ladies wouldn't dare. It would be scandalous, which in Ivorish circles was more or less the same thing as plague-ridden.

And she did *seem* clever. He had to give her that.

He stared back at the construct, pursed his lips, and leapt off the bench.

"Oi!" he called, hurrying to the wall where Synder had disappeared. "Oi!"

Her face erupted out of the wall, looking eager. "Yes? Something you need?"

Ashes swallowed. "My faces are bloody awful today. Would you— D'you think you could help me? Maybe?" The stuttering tone of his own voice stunned and annoyed him. This was absurd. He could hold an entire crowd of Ysonne captive with nothing but his voice and charm. Now he felt out of place, like a child wearing his father's clothes.

The girl didn't seem to care about the awkward stammer. "Of course! I'd be delighted."

She moved to the mangled construct with an almost frightening enthusiasm. In half a moment she was bent over it, inspecting it with a critical eye. She passed her fingers through it, made a face, and repeated the motion. Without looking, she snatched a glass lens off the table and held it close to her eye.

"Well," she said after several minutes, "this is . . . not . . . bad . . ."

Ashes gave her a flat look, the twin of the one she'd given him earlier.

"All right," she admitted. "It's actually quite good, if you were trying to make a gargoyle." She smiled broadly. "How quickly can you reconstitute this?"

"Erm—"

"Never mind," she said, flapping her hands in a way very reminiscent of Jack when he was getting impatient. "It'll be faster if we use mine." She slid a phial out of her pocket and set it on the table; Ashes recognized the distinctive shifting hues of liquid light. It moved very slowly, probably from a high aether concentration.

Synder clapped her hands together. "Right! Give me your hand. Your good hand, mind."

Ashes offered his left. She took it in both of hers and placed it beneath the table lamp, then rested her palm underneath his.

"Before we get you making masks for yourself, you need to know how your body works with the light," she said. "Jack's played Distract Me with you already, right?"

Ashes nodded.

"Focus is the Weaver's most important muscle." She closed her eyes, and Ashes felt something on the underside of his hand tugging at him, as if pulled by a sort of gravity. "Focus lets us shape light, keeps our aether from setting too quickly. You'll never make anything if you can't focus."

Ashes nodded again. That made sense.

"Don't imagine a face," Synder said. "That's the first mistake you can make, just thinking *face*. There won't be any proper detail.

You need to develop each portion individually and then put them all together. But *don't* think of it as a face. It's a collection of unique features."

She cracked open one eye. "Close your eyes! How are you supposed to focus on something if you're looking somewhere else?"

Ashes obeyed, and began thinking of details. He tried starting with the nose, but it felt wrong to him. Better, he decided, to begin with the eyes. The girl he'd found running away from Saintly—she'd had brilliant, fierce eyes.

"Hold that first detail in your head," Synder ordered. "Pick another. Eyes, ears, cheekbones, teeth, freckles. Find something *real*, but don't think generically. They're not *big ears*, they're three inches high, and they're thinner than you'd expect, and the right one has a mole on the lobe. Something like that. Detail, detail, detail."

She walked him through each detail, ordering him to hold every one in readiness until he could put them together. After three minutes, he had imagined every one, and he was sweating again.

"Don't open your eyes," she ordered. "Just keep all those details there. *Don't* let them blur together."

He nodded. He was juggling seven different features in his head, forcing them to stay separate and unique, just as he'd imagined them. It felt like having his mind split into pieces.

"All right," Synder said after a second. "Put them together. *Focus* on that image. You can see it, right?"

The face didn't fit together, not quite. But the features were mostly pure, he thought.

Something fell into his hand. The details became fuzzy and blurred, but only briefly. Synder's voice snatched him back.

"Don't think about what you're touching," she ordered. "The *details*. Keep them steady."

The liquid light in his palm roiled. With an effort, he turned his thoughts away, back to the face. He brought all the force of his will against it, forcing it to stay the same.

"Steady," Synder urged. "Very steady, now. Keep holding it right there."

His fingers trembled. Sweat dribbled down his face, slid along his eyebrows like a snail—

The face wobbled, briefly overtaken by the image of a slug. He ground his teeth together and snapped the image back in place.

"Steady," Synder whispered. "Ten more seconds, Ashes, just hold it there."

He felt the light quivering, and dismissed the sensation. There was nothing in the entire universe except the face he held in his mind. He pulled in a breath and held it.

"Done," Synder said. "You can open your eyes now, Ashes."

He opened his eyes. "Furies and Kindness."

In the bowl of his left hand was a lifeless, motionless face, with eyes like chips of precious stones. Its nose was overlong, its cheeks fleshy and dusted with dark freckles. The skin was blotchy, but recognizably Ivorish in complexion. The chin dropped too low and one eyebrow rested higher than the other, and now that he looked closely he noticed a dozen other little flaws: differently sized nostrils, one front tooth that was sharp like a cat's, the left ear smaller than the right.

But the face was *there*. It looked recognizably human, maybe even convincingly so.

"Furies and Kindness," he said again.

"Not a bad job," she said, and sounded honest this time. "I think you could wear that in public and not even need to feel ashamed."

"This is amazing," he said.

"I wouldn't go *that* far, maybe," she said with a grin. "But you've certainly got room to reach amazing."

He bound the face to a thin golden ring and let out a heavy breath. "Faces." He couldn't think of anything else to say.

Synder glanced at the monstrous face Ashes had made earlier, and visibly shuddered. "You might want to reconstitute that, before you make Juliana drop dead of fright," she said, standing. "Plus it'll be handy to have some liquid light with you, in case you run into an emergency. It's good to have in a pinch."

Ashes nodded, trying to make sure he didn't forget anything. His heart was pounding, and he was weary all the way to his bones. He'd need to rest, and maybe eat something, before he and Jack went anywhere.

Synder was leaving again. Ashes felt something tug at him, noticing something absent. Had he forgotten— Oh.

"Synder!" he said, leaping from the bench and following her. She turned, looking vaguely amused. "Um. Thanks." He thrust out his hand. Synder shook it just as firmly as before.

"Of course," she said. "Got to look out for my Stitcher."

He saw something in her eyes before her face closed: something vulnerable and frightened. The image was gone in a flicker, but not quickly enough.

"I've got to get going," Synder said, reclaiming her bright exterior. "Assignment to finish. I'll see you at supper tonight, then." She smiled again, as if no shadow had passed over her face. Ashes returned the smile.

The monstrous face waited for him back on the table. He could let the reconstituting wait; it would take at least half an hour, and his head was buzzing. He Anchored it to an unused wooden ring and put the ring in his pocket, deciding to take care of it later.

He picked the golden ring up off the table, ran his fingers over the metal. He felt the thrum of energy within it, and smiled.

Magic. Real magic.

# 18      *Strategy*

**A**SHES was cheating at cards, and he was becoming increasingly confident that the Wisp sitting across from him was not going to figure it out.

"Prial of Delight." Ashes smiled a wide smile as he laid his cards down, revealing the Faces of Delight, Hope, and Delirium.

William stared. He blinked. He set his cards carefully on the table and said, flatly, "This defies rational sense."

"I'm a lucky bloke."

"He's not wrong," Jack, who was setting the dishes away, chimed in from the next room.

It was just after supper, and Ashes felt simultaneously satisfied and faintly ashamed. Satisfied for the obvious reasons—Juliana's delicious, rich, fattening Ivorish food—and ashamed for the obvious ones, too. Blimey was at Batty Annie's table just now, having eaten something unseemly, and wondering if Ashes was all right. Ashes was trying very hard not to think about that, and playing cards against his Stitching teacher helped him forget that very well indeed. Besides that, he and Jack would be going out tonight, *and* he had told Synder he'd stay for supper. He owed her that much, surely.

Synder came to stand over his shoulder. She stared critically at the cards. "He's not telling the truth, either," she said. "I feel pretty confident I saw five or so copies of the Face of Marvels, Ashes."

"You did not," William asserted with powerful confidence. "My memory is flawless. And Jacob has taught me about using extra cards. It is against the rules."

"I really am just very lucky." Ashes grinned innocently. Synder rolled her eyes.

"There, there, Will," Jack said as he walked through the door. "You're right that he didn't use extra cards." He glanced at the table. "Palming some of them back into the deck, though—that he *has* been doing. What have I told you about letting someone else shuffle the cards?"

"Don't give it away!" Ashes protested.

"He has been cheating?" William looked aghast. More than aghast, personally betrayed, as if the entire world had just let him down. "I did not . . . I did not notice."

"Don't take it too hard," Jack said. "Ashes is quite a good cheater. He beat me at cards, once."

"*And* I wasn't the only one cheating that time."

"Seems you could use a bit of competition." Jack sat at the table, gathered the cards together, and shuffled them with a practiced ease. "Care to play a bit, Syn?"

"Juliana wants me to wash the dishes," Synder said, failing to keep an affronted sniff out of her voice.

"Do them after," Jack said. "Jewel's gone upstairs anyway, she won't notice you slacking for a few minutes. You can bet the dishes away, if you like."

Synder fidgeted uncomfortably. Ashes watched her out of the corner of his eye, fascinated. He'd grown used to Juliana's quiet, exact manner, but Synder wore every thought and decision on her face. He saw the precise moment when her resolve crumbled like a weakened dam.

"One game," she said, and sat. "Just one."

"Fantastic," Jack said. "A quick game of Brag, I think, with the usual bets. Reconstitution, dishes, laundry." William and Synder nodded, Synder rather more skeptically. Jack flashed a smile at Ashes. "You know the rules, lad?"

"I've played Brag before," Ashes said, feeling faintly insulted.

"Not like this, I think," Jack said, flicking a card out of the shuffle and blowing on it. The face of Delight melted away, becoming Marvels, and then Duty. "House rule. You can Stitch or Weave whatever you care to. It's legal." He smirked. "So long as no one catches you."

Synder nodded along. "You have to double the last bet to call for iron," she said. "And if you're wrong then you lose, no matter what they're holding."

A pinched agony came over William's face at her words, the Wisp's equivalent to a look of utter disgust. Jack laughed softly.

"Will's had pretty poor luck with that in the past," Jack said conspiratorially.

"Poor fortune!" William scoffed. "By the bones! Have you any idea the odds that three players would hold a prial at once?"

"Not the faintest," Jack said, dealing three cards to everyone in a series of swift, smooth movements.

"Our master lives and moves with the onus of gods," William said in mournful tones. "We shall live to regret this."

"Oh, come, now, William," Synder said. "He can't *always* win."

● ● ●

*"I recant,"* Synder said. "Every hopeful thing I ever said about this game, I rescind it. I am a false prophet of the worst sort." She threw her cards down, as if in protest. "I fold."

Her just-one-game of Brag had turned out to be four games of Brag, during which her skill at Weaving had served her not at all; she had tried twice to cheat, and had iron pressed against her cards every single time. Her temper had darkened as the games went on, and Ashes could have sworn the space around her had become blacker as well.

The company's usual wager was chores written on slips of paper; whoever held the slip was exempt from the duty. Candlestick Jack held more than everyone else put together, and he was grinning like a guilty cat.

"It brings joy to my heart, seeing your optimism crumble like that," Jack said. "Soon you'll be a proper cynic, like Will and me."

"I am a pragmatist," William said haughtily. He looked at his cards, pressed his lips together, and gathered the few slips of chores he still had to his name. "For which reason I think I, too, will withdraw." He laid the cards down, clinging to his slips like a drowning man clutching a plank.

Jack's grin widened. "Can't bear to part with your exemption from buying meat, Will?"

"A butcher shop is no place for a respectable human being."

"Getting rather liberal with that term," Jack muttered.

William sniffed. "I *am* respectable."

"Wasn't what I meant. How about you, lad?" Jack turned bright eyes on his new student. "Seems there's a trend going around the table."

Ashes nodded thoughtfully, rubbing his thumb along the cards. "Never been much for trends, Jack."

"Lay your bet, then," said the Weaver.

"Never been much for playing the idiot, either."

The Artificer gave a bright and dangerous smile. "Then perhaps you'd best fold."

"Neh," Ashes said. "Can't do that, either, as I figure you've got some manner of Artifice on the cards just this moment."

"Then call for iron, lad. We don't have the whole night long."

Ashes smiled and shoved the last of his slips into the pot. "Twice your bet. I figure I'd like to see your cards, Mr. Rehl."

The Weaver matched his grin. "Pair royal. Duty, Wrath, and Judgment."

Ashes peered at them. "Those fake?"

"You're free to call for iron," Jack said. "If you're confident."

"I am," he said, and laid his cards down. Jack inspected them.

"Those look terribly like the Faces of Kindness, lad."

"That'd be because they are."

Jack set a handful of his slips into the pot. "Iron."

Ashes tilted his head. "You only need—"

"I'm calling for iron on all of them," Jack said. He pulled an optic out of his pocket, not content to wait for someone else to produce iron. He peered at Ashes's cards and scoffed. "Well. Damn. How did you manage that, I wonder."

Ashes grinned widely. "I've said I'm a lucky bloke, haven't I? I'm a lucky bloke."

"This is ridiculous," Synder said, standing. "I'm going to go clean some dishes. As I will be doing for the next two months, by the way, in case any of you ever wish to see me again." She shot a venomous look at Jack.

"Free will is meaningless without consequences, dear Synder," Jack said.

"I will retire as well, I think," said William, rising. "I am given to understand it is traditional to say it was a pleasure playing, but my culture frowns on lying. Good eventide, gentlemen."

Ashes frowned. "Aren't you coming—?"

"Good night, Will," Jack said, giving Ashes a sharp look. He shut his mouth until William was gone.

"He's not coming with us?" Ashes asked.

"Not tonight," Jack said, standing and leading Ashes out of the room. "Do you have your new face? Put that on, then. We'll want to be invisible tonight." Jack shifted something in his clothing, and a moment later was a different man. He looked vaguely Bärsi, with a thick, oily beard so dark it could have been blue.

"So I'm not actually doing anything tonight?"

"Not as such," Jack said. "No, this is more of what you could call . . . research."

Ashes looked at him in stunned disbelief. "You're *preparing* for something?"

"Is that so difficult to believe?"

"You're— Oh, bugger, how did Will say it? You're—encouragably temarious."

"Watch your mouth, lad," Jack said, smirking. "Properly pronounced, that might've been ten syllables altogether."

"He said it meant you were addicted to having no plan," Ashes said.

"Will struggles with the concept of improvisation," Jack said. "He's also not really happy if he's not complaining. I am not *totally* opposed to preparation."

The streets were utterly empty, except for the ever-present Lyonshire fog. It made Ashes's skin crawl, not that he would have admitted it to Jack. Burroughside was too far from the Lethe to experience much mist. Even if it had, Ashes was almost never out after sundown. It was a bad habit for Burroughsiders who liked the original arrangement of their intestines.

"So we're not terrible worried about the curfew, are we?" Ashes asked cautiously, not wanting to sound nervous.

"Not at all," Jack said. "Curfew's not such a concern for those with iron names."

"Um . . ." Ashes said, feeling a sudden urge to scan the darkness for police.

"Sorry, I ought to rephrase. It's not such a worry for anyone who *looks* like they have an iron name." He glanced at Ashes's clothes. "So long as you're wearing clothes that look reasonably clean, I doubt you'll have much to worry on. It's all about image, lad."

"Talking of." Ashes looked sidelong at Jack. "How long d'you think it'll take for Will and Synder to figure out you've been cheating at cards the old-fashioned way?"

"Those two? Decades, I imagine." Jack smiled wickedly. "You cottoned rather fast."

Ashes snorted. "You dealt every time. It's not *that* mysterious."

"And yet our resident geniuses have not caught on," Jack said.

That drew a smirk from him. After weeks of hearing William's passionless critiques of his Stitching, and the unending comments about Synder and how brilliant she was, it felt good to think that at least there was something they couldn't do. "Guess they're not as clever as all that."

"Perhaps," Jack said. "But even very clever people can be fooled when they're looking in the wrong place. Our house rules make it explicit that using Artifice is cheating, and they know me to be a cheater. They just look in the wrong places."

Ashes worked his mouth thoughtfully. "Seems almost like that sort of lying is . . . better than Artifice, almost. Sometimes."

"Losing faith in the magic, lad?" Jack glanced at him, vaguely amused. "Wondering if maybe you'd be better served with makeup and clever fingers?"

"It'd be easier," Ashes said. "Nobody could burn it away with iron. It wouldn't fizzle if you stepped over a stream. You wouldn't have to worry about someone seeing you with one of those stones."

"Don't let me forget you said that," Jack said. "You've just volunteered for another lesson."

"Not that it'd help overmuch," Ashes said, more than a trace of bitterness in his voice.

Jack looked sidelong at him. "Struggling with your education?"

Ashes clenched his jaw. "William hasn't told you?"

"I'm not talking to Will," Jack said. "I'm talking to you."

"Stitching's just a bit harder than I expected, is all," Ashes said evasively.

Jack gave him a look that, in the dark, Ashes couldn't quite decipher. "Feels a bit like you're wearing secondhand clothes, mm?"

"Seems it ought to be easier," said Ashes.

"Skill takes practice. Obscene amounts of practice." Jack clapped him on the shoulder. "Even Synder had space for improvement, back when Juliana found her."

"What about that watch? You said that was her application to study."

"It was, but we'd known about her a while before that," Jack said. "She couldn't apprentice until she was thirteen. So she was self-taught for most of her life, and then she brought the watch so she could . . ." Jack trailed off. "It's occurring to me that that information's not especially encouraging."

Ashes kicked at the stones beneath his feet, sending an eddy through the mist at his ankles. "What about you? Did it come easy to you?"

"I'm something of an odd case," Jack said. "And so are Will and Jewel—mm, bugger."

"None of you?" Ashes kept his voice steady, but only just.

"It doesn't mean you're not canted, lad," Jack said. "Just that you're young, and untrained. It'll come."

Ashes nodded, though he felt like he was lying. Not convincingly, either.

"There are other elements to it," Jack said, not unkindly. "Truth be told, now I've known you a little while, I'm rather shocked your gift is Stitching."

"How d'you mean?"

"Stitchers are subtle," Jack said with a shrug. "Most of them, at least. Quiet. *Deliberate*, really. They see details, and they lie when they have to." He grinned at Ashes. "You're more like me—incorrigibly temerarious. You don't lie for a purpose, you lie for the thrill of it. Stitchers *want* to be invisible. You, my boy . . ." The lamplight caught Jack's smile and amplified it against the dark. "You want that moment, minutes or days or years later, when someone thinks back and realizes they were fooled. You want them to know how clever you were. There's little room for that in Stitching."

Streetlamp light oozed around the air, thickened by the fog. Ashes guessed, from the look of the houses on either side, that they were in an Ivory neighborhood. Ivory neighborhoods meant police. He tensed.

"You'd want to do that after you've gotten away, though," Jack said thoughtfully.

"Right. Obviously."

"Since you're not an idiot."

"I try not to be."

"Have you wondered yet what we're doing?"

Ashes gave him a flat look. "You saying that's a question you'd answer?"

"I'm insulted. I answer questions all the time."

"But answer honestly, though?"

"I'll admit it's not something I'm fond of," Jack said with a grin. "Answering honestly tends to give one a reputation. But I'll answer honestly. This time."

"All right, then. What're we doing?"

Jack grinned. "Walking. But also, intermittently, talking, planning, and preparing."

Ashes scoffed. "I can't believe I fell for that. Ha bloody ha—"

"So that we can rob an Ivory Lord."

Ashes stopped. Jack did likewise. He wore an impish grin.

"Say that again," Ashes said.

"We're going to rob an Ivory Lord."

"You lying to me?"

"No lies between liars."

"Bloody—which one?" Ashes held up a hand. "Wait. No. What the actual *hell?*"

"Go on."

"You're robbing an Ivory Lord."

"*We* are robbing an Ivory Lord," Jack said. "And it's Lord Edgecombe, by the way."

"Why would you tell me that?" Ashes shook his head madly. "Wait. Don't answer that. Why would you rob an Ivory Lord?"

"Because they're the ones with the money, lad. Faces, that's hardly a question worthy of you."

"An Ivory *Lord*," Ashes said. "The ones that have legions of the police living in barracks on their front yards."

"Indeed."

"The ones that literally write the laws."

"The very same."

"The ones with the faces that go all shiny? Who're personally friends with the Queens?"

"You have assessed the situation adroitly," Jack said with a grin.

"You're *mad*."

"As incisive an observation as you have ever spoken."

"You're *mad*."

"So you've said." Jack was beginning to sound impatient now. "But my sanity's not the prime issue. Look."

They were standing at the gates of an Ivory manor. Now Ashes knew for certain they were in West Lyonshire; only the wealthiest of Teranis's governing class lived here. Beyond the gate, Ashes could see an absurdly massive garden, bright green even in the murk. The fog wouldn't let him see anything but the top of the manor, which had to be at least three stories up.

"This is the gate to Lord Edgecombe's home," Jack said. "And in three months, it will be flung wide open."

"How d'you know that?"

"Edgecombe's been absent from Lyonscourt for months now," Jack said. "And my sources have finally figured out why." He rested one hand on the heavy iron bars. "Lady Edgecombe is pregnant. The House will finally have a legitimate heir."

"I don't understand—"

"Lady Edgecombe's been childless for years," Jack said. "An Ivory Lord will throw parties for any reason he can find, but finally creating an heir for the family? It'll be a ball unlike anything this city's seen in years. Everyone who can rub a pair of crowns together will be invited."

Ashes nodded slowly. "And we're going to go. And rob him."

Jack smiled broadly. "We are going to do exactly that, my lad. Exactly that."

Ashes chewed his lip. "And I'm coming along?"

"Good help is hard to find these days, especially in my business."

"I was never a housebreaker," Ashes said dubiously.

"Who said I needed a housebreaker? *I'm* a housebreaker. *You're* a clever, watchful imp who can wriggle his way out of trouble at a moment's notice. It's a useful skill."

Ashes nodded absently. His thoughts were sluggish, drowned inside a fog of instinctive fear. Stealing from Ivories . . . no one was that stupid. The Lords of the city were too proud, too ferocious, and far, far too wealthy to evade for long.

But if anyone could get away with it . . .

"All right," Ashes said. "I'll do it."

Jack laughed softly and began walking south. "I'm glad to hear you're volunteering. Aren't I already paying you?"

"Where're you taking me now? This isn't the way back to the shop."

"Someplace familiar," Jack said, waving a hand carelessly. "You'll see soon enough." Ashes snorted, which made Jack laugh. "You sound a bit like Will when you do that."

"You make everybody sound like Will eventually," Ashes retorted.

"There's a disturbing thought," Jack said. "I think if I made people be like Will, I might be sad. He's not a particularly happy man."

"He's not a particularly anything man," Ashes said, but Jack shook his head.

"There are depths to Will that you've not seen, lad."

"If you say so," Ashes said, glancing around. They had left the posh neighborhoods of West Lyonshire behind. Ashes prided himself on knowing his way around the city, but it was far more difficult in the dark. Fog had swallowed up all his landmarks, leaving behind only the islands of streetlamp light. Here in the dark, all the distinguishing features of the city were erased: there were no signs over shops, no street names, no passersby to tell him what sort of road he'd found himself on. It unnerved him.

Jack said, "Tell me about the Ravagers, lad."

Ashes bristled. "What is it you want to know?"

"Anything, really," Jack said. "The police keep them out of the civilized districts, and I've not been to Burroughside in a dog's age. What are they like?"

"Terrifying," Ashes said. "You've seen cats, right?"

Jack nodded. "Ivories keep them as pets sometimes."

"And they're nice-looking, eh? You seen alley-cats? Patchy fur. Scratched up. Half a tail."

Jack nodded again.

"Wild cats'll keep themselves to themselves, but they'll fight if they need, if things get skittery. They're fierce, and they're cunning."

Jack glanced at him. "So Ravagers are like wild cats?"

Ashes shook his head. "*I'm* like a wild cat, Jack. A Ravager's what would happen if you took an alley-cat and skinned it, starved it, and drove it mad. They just want to . . . ruin things. They'll rip at you, if they can catch you, or at their own if they need." He breathed. "Or they tear at themselves, if there's nothing else they can find. They . . . just *hate*."

"They fear, too," Jack mused.

Ashes scoffed. "They avoid coppers like everybody else. But they'd fight one, no question. An animal'll run if it knows you could kill it. A Ravager wouldn't." Ashes shook himself, feeling suddenly skittish. "Why're you asking?"

"Idle curiosity," the man said.

Ashes looked askance at the man, but knew he wouldn't catch a hint to what he was thinking. Jack's face was a mask even without Artifice.

"I trust you won't tell our geniuses how I've been cheating," Jack said offhand.

"So long as you don't tell them how I won," Ashes said. "I know you know."

The Weaver chuckled. "You've got to get better at Cackle-witching. You fumble the cards at the very end, just a little."

"I'll keep it in mind," Ashes said.

He felt the street's texture change beneath his feet. He couldn't quite place it at first—wearing shoes rendered his feet nearly insensate—until he heard the squelching sound.

"Jack," he said softly. "Why the *hell* are we here?"

"I told you already," Jack said. "Object lesson. And the object in question can't be found anywhere else in Teranis."

Ashes's stomach opened up wide. "What?"

In answer, Jack let out a loud, wild scream. It sounded almost like—almost like the screech that answered him, somewhere off to the south.

Ashes snatched Jack's wrist. "What the Furied *hell* are you doing?"

Jack shook the boy's hand off and let out another wild cry. "Teaching," he said.

Ashes's mind raced. He could dash back to Lyonshire, but if one of the creatures saw him running, it would chase him for sure. And he couldn't leave Jack; the man had clearly lost his mind.

"We have to go, Jack!" Ashes grabbed his teacher's hand and tried to tug the man behind him. "We can still find somewhere to hide—"

"Why would we hide?" Jack met his eyes. He was perfectly lucid, perfectly calm. "We're Artificers, my young friend."

Ashes could hear the footsteps now, pounding toward them from everywhere. He could feel his heart in his throat. Could they hide? There *had* to be someplace safe. But if Jack wouldn't come with him—

*Save yourself.*

But his feet seemed bound to the street. He couldn't move. He could only watch as Jack stared up the street, and the first Ravagers came into view.

Two at first. Male and female, only distinguishable by the breadth of their shoulders. Then he saw three behind them, and another after those, the pack leader, burly and misshapen, and hands like claws.

"Jack!"

The man pulled something out of his coat, and the world became bright as the heart of a fire—

The next thing Ashes saw was flames surging from Jack's hand—not a single, small flame but a roaring, seething monster, many-headed and huge. It was soundless, but Ashes felt he could hear it crackling in his head, eager to blister flesh from bone.

The flames rushed against the Ravagers and struck two in the face, another in the gut, two more across their chests. Ashes had a fraction of a moment to think how silly it was to attack someone with illusory fire—and then the Ravagers started keening, and turned and ran away, clutching at themselves as if in terrible pain.

Two more leapt at Jack. The Artificer flung a shaft of light at them. It transformed into a barbed vine, and wrapped itself around their faces. There was no blood, but the creatures grasped at their eyes as if expecting something to pour out. They fell together in a tangle, the vine twining around their legs and arms and bellies.

Those Jack had struck with the illusions screeched and whined, sending a chill down Ashes's back. They sounded so terribly human, when they were in pain.

Seven Ravagers lay on the ground, crippled, but the rest of the pack advanced fearlessly. Jack gestured, ripping the image of a sword out of the air. He swept it effortlessly through a pair of Ravagers as they neared him. The ghostly sword passed through them, leaving no evidence of its passage except their pained cries and the looks of terror in their faces.

"Close your eyes," Jack snapped, and Ashes was too stunned to disobey. The burst of light that followed was so bright he felt its burn through his eyelids. Spots danced in his vision.

The screams died off gradually. Ashes heard the sound of many feet, running away at speed.

"Can I look?"

"You may."

What few Ravagers remained were on the ground. One or two writhed intermittently, still agonized by their phantom wounds. Ashes stared in abject disbelief.

"What did you do?"

"There will be no lasting damage."

"But—how?"

"Ravagers are . . . unique," Jack said. "Whatever it is that lets us disbelieve what we see, Ravagers do not have it. To them, there is no difference between what is *seen* and what *is*."

"You knew that already?"

Jack shrugged. Ashes noticed he was carrying a glass phial full of liquid light, which he had stoppered with one finger. The light within was witch-skin green, making everything around it look sickly and diseased.

He turned his attention to the Ravagers wriggling on the ground. They looked less terrifying now. Almost pitiful.

"You are half right, lad," Jack said thoughtfully. "Certainly there's a time for prestidigitation, for cleverness. There are advantages to being cunning. But never forget." He held the Artifice-light high, forming a great viridian circle around himself and Ashes and the groaning Ravagers. "Don't forget where your blood comes from, Ashes. Don't you dare."

# 19 Opportunity

"S IT up straight," Juliana said, not unkindly. "Everyone takes note of your posture, whether they realize it or no. We ought to start with that, I suppose. The first rule of being Ivorish: everyone is evaluating you, always."

Ashes swallowed. "Yes, ma'am."

Robbing an Ivory Lord was a fool's errand. Any Lord rich enough to steal from was rich enough to have a practical battalion of guards, servants, and police on retainer. Their iron locks were heavy and thick, almost impossible to bypass quickly. Their houses were infested with servants, all of whom knew each other by name and face and voice.

All of these details became insignificant, though, when a Lord opened his doors to invaders. In twenty years, House Edgecombe had produced only two heirs: one had died in the cradle, the other in a boating accident. Lady Edgecombe's pregnancy was cause for the greatest celebration the House had put on in decades. In three months, the Harcourt Lord would be welcoming hundreds of eligible, well-connected guests into his home, and the Rehl Company would be there—along with Ashes, who for the night would be Roger Dawkins, the progeny of Jack's estranged and folly-prone sister.

The son of a disgraced family member wouldn't need to seem *incredibly* Ivorish. But he would need to be far more Ivorish than Ashes was now, which meant even more lessons. Diction. Etiquette. Politics. Which houses were allied, which were subtly opposed, which were angling to establish themselves better in the endless parade of who's-in-charge-now. Altogether, Jack had promised, it would give Ashes an academy headache second only to the difficulty in learning to Weave.

"Denizen children start their lessons in decorum at age three," Juliana continued. "You are starting your education late, but we cannot afford to be lax. You will need to be convincing in this."

"Yes, ma'am." He had gotten used to her flawless speech by now. It sounded, sometimes, almost too precise to be real: like she was reading everything off a script held in her head. It seemed almost that Juliana didn't have conversations so much as leave pauses in her prepared speeches.

Juliana favored him with a slight smile. "I assume you have had no prior training in etiquette, presentation, or diction."

Ashes's thoughts darted to Blimey. "Just what I could pick up from folks, ma'am. But I'm a quick learner."

"You will have to be." She surveyed him with a cool glance. The stillness of her face reminded him of William, though subtly different. William's emotions, when they happened, were quiet and small. Juliana was different. Everything she said, or did, or thought—all of it was under her control. Her feelings could have been as powerful as a storming sea, but Ashes only ever saw them through clouded glass. "And Jack has told me you can read?"

Ashes grinned apologetically. "Not as quick learning that way, ma'am."

She sighed delicately—*How does she do that?*—and nodded. "I expected as much. Not to worry. We will conduct your education largely by way of example and oral teaching, I suppose. Sit up straight." She procured a massive book from her shelf and opened it on the table. No cloud of dust rose from the newly exposed pages, but it looked like there should have been one nonetheless. He could *smell* how old it was.

"Everyone is evaluating you," Juliana said, almost absently.

"Yes, ma'am," Ashes said. "You said that already."

"I want to make sure you understand it," Juliana said, eyes flicking over the dry pages of her book. "Even when you think no one is watching, behave as though everyone were. A moment of inattention can have vast repercussions."

"Is that true for regular Ivories? Or just me?"

"It's true for the regular Ivories as well." Juliana's eyes still hadn't left the text. Her mouth quirked downward, and she closed the book, swapping it for another. "All the families seek leverage over each other. The children need to be as impenetrable as their parents, or they risk staining the familial honor. Ivories are very proud. They move with precise steps. Everything must be done in proper order and with proper permissions and by the proper people. Every Ivory prays to the Face of Prudence foremost." Her fingers danced over the bindings of the other books, never resting on any of them longer than a moment. "But most of all, these proper people never, ever, *ever* betray what they are thinking."

Ashes looked at the woman's fine-featured face. *Never let them know what you're thinking. That sounds about right.*

"For Ivories, propriety is everything." She smiled faintly. "Do you remember what Jack said about glass rings?"

Ashes nodded. "About them being Artifice," he said. "Is it—it's propriety, for them to look that way?"

Juliana shook her head. "You're thinking about it like they do," she said. "The rings are laden, certainly. But it's not just that. Ivories are creatures of tradition. Of expectation. No Ivory has ever been seen without his glass ring, and that is why no Ivory *will* be seen without his ring."

Ashes peered at her. She laughed softly and waved a hand. "You will see, I think. You are a better listener than they are." She took a breath. "Politeness is next to serenity. There are many rules to Ivorish etiquette, but they all circle around respecting the hierarchy. If you can master that, you will be more than prepared for an Ivorish ball."

Ashes nodded, swallowing a lump in his throat. Polite and calm were not the *first* words someone might use to describe him.

"Most people will judge your mastery of etiquette by two things," Juliana said. "Presentation first—how well you are dressed, how you carry yourself, how you sit. After that it will be your diction: your vocabulary, your enunciation, your syntax. You must speak like one of us."

Ashes nodded. The idea, at least, was familiar to him. Looking and talking right were the foundation of every con.

"We will start with your speech. Your appearance we can change with Artifice and better dress." Her mouth quirked again, a flickering expression of distaste. No, not an expression—a communication. If Juliana hadn't wanted him to know she was annoyed, he would not have known. "I'm afraid your demeanor will take some time. Much of it is simply the practice of keeping one's face closed. The rest is memorizing rules." She let out another breath, this one sounding agitated. "*Copious* rules."

Ashes smiled. "I can talk with the best of folks, ma'am."

"You are certainly quick to speak," Juliana allowed, favoring him with another glance. "Jack has told me you have a deft touch with accents. That will serve you well, I think. We will start with vowels."

● ● ●

*Nearly four hours later,* Juliana let out a breath.

"I think it may be time for a respite," she said.

"Please, ma'am," Ashes said. "Yes, that'd be excellent."

His head was spinning. He'd never known how many ways there were to pronounce any given word, and even his gift for mimicry hadn't satisfied Juliana. They had slogged through the differences be-tween *ah, ay, ae, ai, ao, au,* and half a dozen other phonetic combina-tions. Four hours of one single letter. He thought he might explode.

It was all the worse for the fact that he wasn't really *doing* any-thing. It was all just practice, practice, practice. How did Ivories survive something so dreary? Their irritable idiosyncrasies made sense now. Anyone would become a maniac growing up under this sort of regime.

Juliana led him upstairs and brought bread and meat and cheese to the table, along with a bottle of brandy. Not nearly as lavish as the food he'd seen last night for supper, but even this was extravagant in comparison to how he used to eat.

Juliana set a glass of the brandy before him and nodded to it. "Drink."

Ashes looked at her, suddenly suspicious. Had she put some-thing in it? No—that would be silly. He took the glass.

"Hold it like this," Juliana said, demonstrating with her own. Ashes mirrored her, feeling self-conscious. "Only a sip at a time."

Ashes tipped the drink back. The alcohol brushed his lips, touched his tongue—

"Bugger all and brand me with a poker!" he cried, holding the wine as far away from him as possible. "It's fire!" The instinct to gag rose up, but he stopped at a look from Juliana.

"This is some of Yson's finest brandy," she said calmly. "From the distillery in Dorois. Only the Ivories and their relatives ever drink it. It is too expensive for any else."

"Don't waste too much on me," Ashes said, pushing the glass away.

"You need to drink it." Her eyes were trained on him, iron-hard. "And you will not react. If you cannot guard your face, you will draw attention, and that could be fatal. Entering a Lord's manor without an iron name could be the last mistake you're fortunate enough to make."

Ashes looked at the brandy. It didn't *look* like it was made of fire. Still, it made him anxious just thinking of letting it touch his lips again. He could smell it now, as acrid and acidic as William's cleaning supplies. It smelled faintly of cinnamon.

"I know it isn't pleasant," Juliana said. "But it may save your life one day."

Ashes didn't scowl, but he came close. He grabbed the glass and gestured to Juliana. "To fooling whoever believes me."

The Lady smiled and raised her own glass. "To fooling everyone else."

He tipped the brandy into his mouth and let it rest there for a moment, dreading the imminent sensation of flames in his throat. He kept his face perfectly still and gulped. He twitched, and his eyes watered and he wanted to spit all of it out. He resisted every instinct, and felt his ears grow hot.

"Good," Juliana said. "Good. That will do for now."

Ashes sucked in a breath and stuffed a fruit into his mouth. Juliana raised an eyebrow, but he couldn't bring himself to care.

"We will need to work on your table manners," she said.

"Yes, ma'am. Sorry, ma'am." He opened his mouth wide, hoping air might cool it. "Furies, that's a sharp thing."

Juliana's face instantly went cold and imperious. "I shall thank you *not* to reference the Queens in such a manner, Ashes," she said sharply.

Ashes drew back. "Sorry, ma'am," he said quickly. "I won't do it again."

"See that you do not," Juliana said.

Ashes grasped for a change of subject. "Do Ivories really like that stuff?"

Juliana's icy demeanor evaporated in a blink. "Not at all," she said calmly. "Many of the Lords keep Dorois brandy just to challenge everyone else to keep their composure at supper. It's a sort of game for them."

"Do they get used to it?"

"Never," Juliana said. "In twenty years it's gotten no better."

Ashes looked at her curiously. "How Ivorish are you, ma'am?"

"Quite," said the Lady. "I am two generations removed from Lord Raeben in East Lyonshire. My father is his nephew."

Ashes nodded. "So that's why you're the one teaching me how to be Ivorish?"

"Something like that. Jack would teach you, but he's far too busy, and he never needed to know Ivory etiquette very well anyway."

Ashes sipped at the brandy again, trying and failing to keep his face from betraying the pain. "How long you been married?"

"Eleven years," she said, looking faraway. "We married at sea."

Ashes's eyes widened. "You've been out to sea?"

Juliana nodded. "Jack was a sailor before he took up Artifice. He heard one of his old crewmates had gotten made captain of his own ship, and he convinced the man to let us use it for a time." She bent her head and smiled, as though what she recalled were still private to her. "It took me by surprise. I'd barely known him three months, but—well. I felt like I'd known him forever."

*Three months? I wonder what the Face of Prudence had to say about that.* "How'd you meet him?"

Juliana's eyebrows tilted toward each other, but only for a moment. "That is . . . a complicated story."

Ashes sensed a boundary, and decided not to press it. "So Jack was a sailor?"

Juliana nodded. "He worked for a . . . private merchant, shipping goods up the River Lethe and across the ocean. He speaks of it only rarely. Part of him misses it, I think. He loves Teranis too much to leave it, but, if he could . . . he would sail to the end of the world just to see what's out there. He wants to go where no one's ever gone before. Simple things bore him very quickly."

An image of Jack surrounded by green light and agonized Ravagers appeared in Ashes's mind. "He's an odd bloke," Ashes said. "I always get a feeling like he's not telling me something."

The Lady gave him an amused expression. "It's his way. Can you blame him? Robbing Ivories is hardly a safe career, nor one with much trust to spare. It's a testament to how fond of you he is that he's told you anything at all."

"Seems exhausting," Ashes said. "I could've turned him in already, if I were that sort. I owe him, though. Twice over."

"Even so," Juliana said. "Continue being trustworthy. He'll open up eventually. He's slow to trust. Surely you understand that."

Ashes nodded, staring at his plate.

"Oh, and now you're glum," Juliana said. "We can't be having that. Follow me."

She led him to a room on the second floor that he hadn't seen during Jack's tour. It was spacious, with windows large enough to let in the sunlight at any time of the day. It pleased Ashes to think that he'd noticed that detail; he would have missed it three weeks ago.

"Jack insisted I have a solarium," Juliana said as they entered. "I had one when I was younger, in my family's home. It was always my favorite place."

The back of the room was filled with canvases. Several were

blank, but more had paintings, done with realistic proportions and beautiful lighting. There was one painting of an old cathedral, one of a great ship, one of an Ivorish family with pale eyes and austere, gorgeous faces. He saw a portrait of Candlestick Jack, younger and intense, nestled behind a sketch of the Silver Tower.

"I've been tending to this as a sort of side project since you came to us," Juliana said, moving toward the wardrobe. "I expect it might be useful, given what Jack's grooming you for."

She produced a small cloak, dark blue as the deep night. Ashes could tell at once that it was tailored to exactly his size.

"Do put it on," she said.

Ashes obeyed, letting the Lady settle the cloak on his shoulders. It rested comfortably against his back. It was gently cool where it touched his skin, but the fabric was thick. It would keep him warm on cold nights, certainly, and even serve to keep him hidden if it was dark, and he stood very still.

"Do you like it?" she asked.

"It's beautiful, ma'am," Ashes said, running his fingers along the cloth. He thought he could feel something, a sort of vibration in the cloak, something familiar . . . "This is Weaving," he realized aloud. "What'd you put in it?"

Juliana smiled at his eagerness. "Pull up your hood."

Ashes obeyed, and felt the construct settle against his skin. His vision was not impeded—that was a difficult thing to do, he'd learned, unless you were very skilled or very careful—but he sensed that whatever was on his skin, it was not bright.

Juliana helpfully held a mirror out to him, letting him see his face. The sight made him smile wildly. The illusion lying over his face was one of near-total darkness. Not utter blackness—flat black was near as obvious as light clothing except in the deepest night—but dark enough to blend in with the shadows if they were long enough. It was almost gray.

"This is amazing," Ashes said in awe.

"I'm glad you like it," Juliana said. "It's yours, if you'll have it. Just something to keep you safe."

"Thank you, ma'am," he said, bowing. The cloak caught his bow and billowed, though not so dramatically as he would have liked. "I'll treasure it."

"You had best do so," Juliana said. She stepped closer and lifted his chin so he was looking in her face. For a moment, it seemed the veil she held around herself faltered, and he could see pain behind her eyes. Was the Lady about to cry?

The look vanished, and the refined, calm Ivory woman was standing before him once again. "It suits you," she said. "I'm delighted to see how well it fits." Her eyes darted away from him for a moment. "We'll continue your lesson tomorrow," she said. "Perhaps it's best you get some fresh air."

# 20 Secrets

**A**SHES walked through Lyonshire's merchant district wearing his Ivorish face and clean, proper Denizen clothes. He had adopted an expression to fit his Ivorish skin tone and posh clothing, and he walked with his hands out of his pockets, straight-backed and proud. It all made him uncomfortable and slow, but no one was leering at him suspiciously, and you couldn't overestimate the value of that.

It was strange how little notice he attracted—off-putting, even. Artifice wasn't a secret from the wide world. Everybody in Teranis knew that anyone with enough money could look however they wanted. Why did anyone trust what they saw? As long as there were Artificers, how could you know the beggar in front of you wasn't one of the Ladies? How could you know your friends were truly your friends, or your wife really your wife?

Maybe people just *couldn't* talk themselves out of believing what they saw. Artifice was more subtle than some coat of paint. It could be convincing even when you *knew* it was false. And, as Jack had said, the mind was a lazy instrument.

The glass shop front of a bookstore caught Ashes's eye. He hadn't set foot inside one in years; the first time he'd been daring enough to try, he'd lasted a grand total of thirty seconds before the shopkeeper threw him unceremoniously onto the streets. Gutter-rats were not welcome in shops; they cluttered up the atmosphere, scared off real customers, and only aimed to steal things.

He glanced at his face in the glass, and he smiled. Not a gutter-rat. Not as far as *they* knew, anyway.

A bell chimed over his head as he stepped inside. The shop within was inordinately full of books: thick, thin, tall, short, old, and new, and everything in between.

The man behind the counter, a large fellow with drooping jowls and a trimmed mustache, looked up at the sound of the door chime. Instantly, he became the picture of a delighted salesman: his face broke into a large grin and he clapped his hands together. The change in his attitude took Ashes by surprise. In the space of a moment he transformed from being simply fat to being jolly.

"Good afternoon, young master," he said. "What brings you to my humble place of business?"

For a moment, Ashes's mind felt gummed up. He wasn't sup-posed to be here, and he was wearing unfamiliar clothes and a face that wasn't his and, true to form, he meant to steal something here. The man ought to be grabbing him by the neck and forcing him out the door.

Then, all at once, his mouth started moving.

"Goodly evening," he said, forgoing Juliana's diction lessons for the instinctive command of the Lyonshire Denizen accent. "I'm looking for a book for my brother. It's his birthday tonight and I've gone and forgotten to get him something."

"Not a problem, sir!" the merchant said brightly. "What do you think your brother might be interested in?"

"He likes anything with words in," Ashes said. *Wait—that was wrong grammar, wasn't it? Damn!*

The shopkeeper hardly seemed to notice. "Well, I've got all manner of books with words in," he said, his grin growing even more. "How old might your brother be, if I may ask?"

Ashes bit his lip. "Coming up on thirteen, provided I've remembered properly." He manufactured an embarrassed smile. "As you've already guessed, I'm not so good with remembering things. My father never lets me forget it. Gods provide that I get into the priesthood, because if I end up taking over Da's shop, it might well ruin the whole family name."

The bookseller laughed. He had a huge, hearty laugh. "Well, if he's that age and he's fond of books, I believe I might have just the thing for him." He toddled around the counter, humming to himself as he approached the shelves. He ran his fingers over the spines lovingly, finally stopping on one. He took hardly a moment pulling it off the shelf before continuing down the shelf, picking more and more. He returned to the counter after a minute, bearing four large books.

"*Dreamcatcher's Spire*, *The Knotted City*, *Inandelia*, and Oeurmand's *Fables*," the man said, showing him each cover successively. "That last is probably best of the lot. The largest collection of fairy tales you'll find this side of the Vastness. Most of them your little brother'll know by heart already, although he'll love the illustrations if he's any sort of taste." He flipped open the cover, revealing a colorful sketch of an armored knight stabbing the heart of a many-headed beast. It was breathtakingly detailed. "The Moonsword Knight and the Beast of Trant. At risk of being a traditional salesman, young master, you will not find a prettier book."

Ashes's eyes widened. "How much for it?"

"A steal at twelve lumin," the man replied. "Were I a true businessman, it would be twenty, but I confess I'm just a book lover. I'll admit it's hardly a book I'd feel comfortable selling to someone very young. But if your brother is thirteen and asking for books instead of something inane like a horse or a short sword or a Glamour to make him look like Alavar Sunheart, I reckon he'd be ready for something like this."

Ashes's gut twisted. It was a beautiful book; Blimey would adore it. If anything could make up for putting Blimey in Batty Annie's basement, it would be this. But he didn't have nearly the money, and something about the way the bookseller caressed the pages made him reluctant to try stealing it.

*It probably isn't worth that much*, he thought desperately. *Probably isn't worth* half *that much. He's just doing his salesman bit, like all the merchants. He doesn't just want me to buy the book. He wants me to fall in love with it.*

Even so, it felt wrong. At least when he cheated arrogant Denizens at cards, they'd have the decency to try killing him for it. This fellow didn't have a clue.

*If I didn't look Ivorish, he'd be trying to pulp me*, Ashes thought. *He's just a merchant like all the rest.*

"I'll take it," he said aloud, then patted his side and adopted a stricken look. "Oh, Faces. I think I've forgotten my purse." He put a palm to his forehead. "Ah, of all the luck. I told you, didn't I? My brain's a thrice-cursed sieve. I'm so sorry to have wasted your time, sir. I'll just be on my way."

The bookseller's face fell. "Ah! But you could return to your home, could you not? I can hold it for you here, until you return with the money."

Ashes moved for the door, shaking his head. "I couldn't do that. I'm— It's too far, and I haven't a carriage. I doubt I'd get back in time. I'll get him something else, I suppose. Apologies for bothering you."

"Perhaps credit?" The bookseller held out the book. "A book lover should not go without his birthday present. Take the book today, and pay me for it tomorrow."

Ashes halted, looking longingly at the book. Blimey *would* love it . . . and Ashes was training to be an Artificer, after all. He would earn the money at some point, surely, and it wasn't as if he had any other expenses. He could get the money back to the man sometime in the future. It wasn't stealing, just . . . borrowing.

"Do you know why I sell books, young master?" The bookseller eyed him, as if waiting for a response. "They're one of very few things you can sell that isn't a commodity. I'm not selling food or dyes or clothes." He leaned forward and said, in conspiratorial tones, "I can't sell the same book twice, do you know? Books are too magical. They're meant for people." He tapped the book on the counter. "I see the way you look at this. You know that book's meant to go to your brother. You know how he'll love it and how he'll keep it to the end of his days, and pass it on to his son when he's old enough, who'll pass it on to his son when he's old enough. And by then the pages'll be torn and the ink'll have faded, but the book's even more magic then." The man proffered it to Ashes, almost like an offering. "Take it, young master. Pay me back for it tomorrow. I promise my store won't flounder and die for twelve overdue lumin."

Ashes took the book as reverently as he could. The bookseller smiled again. "You're good for it, I'm sure. Go on, now. You wouldn't want to be late."

On a sudden instinct, Ashes bowed his head to the man. "You're a real sort of gentleman, sir. I'll get you the money. You've got my word to it." And he meant it.

He left the shop with the book in hand, and got all of twenty feet when someone grabbed his arm.

*Furies!* He froze, immediately cataloguing escape routes and calculating how quick he could move. His legs had betrayed him too much recently to be trustworthy, but the book could slow them down—

"I suppose you think that was terribly clever of you." Synder was trying to sound grown-up, but even Artifice couldn't change her voice. She was wearing a new face, one that made her look about five years older and turned her hair platinum blonde. Her eyes hadn't changed.

"Afternoon, Syn," he muttered. "Something wrong?"

"You know exactly what's wrong," she whispered. "You should be ashamed, Ashes."

Ashes glared at her. "Why're you following me?"

"Don't change the subject." She leaned close and whispered harshly, "You stole that book!"

"Did not," Ashes whispered back. "I'm going to pay him back for it. I promised."

"You can't just take things from people!" The light around Synder's face turned dark, as though she'd just been obscured by a small cloud.

*She just gathered light without meaning to*, Ashes thought, looking at the shadows around her hands. He couldn't help but be impressed. "I didn't! He knows I have it. And he said I could pay him back for it later!"

The girl blinked. "A Lyonshire merchant just let you have something? On *credit*?"

"That's just what he said! On credit!"

"You're not lying to me?" She stared him in the eye, as if doing so would clue her in to his truthfulness.

"I swear it." Ashes held up his hands.

The terrible look around her passed, and the darkness with it. Sunlight struck her face again. She brushed a hair out of her eyes, still glaring at Ashes.

"Fine," she muttered. Her eyes flicked to the book. "Are you going to pay the man back?"

"Eventually." Ashes returned the gaze she shot at him. She sighed and rubbed her temple.

"That's not right, Ashes."

"Roger," he corrected. "I'm Roger out here."

"Whatever. You can't just take something and say you'll pay for it eventually. It's *wrong*. Why are you even taking it anyway?"

Ashes took another step back. "It's not any of your business."

Synder placed both hands on her hips. "Well, it is now." Her jaw was set. Gathered light formed a subtle halo around her face, making her look like an avenging angel.

*Furies.* "I'm going to resell it," he lied smoothly. "Make a bit of a turn off what it gives me, pay back the bookseller what I owe. You happy?"

Synder lifted an eyebrow. "Is that the best lie you can come up with?"

Ashes bristled. "It's not—"

"I wonder what Jack would think," she said slowly, "knowing that you're still a petty thief."

She stared at him flatly. Ashes ground his teeth together. The girl waited another moment, and then turned and began walking back toward the shop. She didn't look back. Either honest, or a far better bluffer than he'd thought. He swore colorfully under his breath.

"Okay, wait."

The girl stopped and tilted her head toward him.

"You have to promise," Ashes said, "that you won't tell anybody. No one ever, all right? It's the biggest secret I've ever kept. And if you tell then somebody could die, honest to Faces. You can't tell *ever*."

Synder faced him with a serious look. "I can keep a secret."

"Good." He exhaled, slowly, trying to keep his heartbeat down. "Okay. Follow me and I'll talk while we're going. Half a moment."

Ashes faced a wall and slipped off his ring, then dug his seeing-stone from his pocket and scanned the street furtively. None of the passersby looked any different, nor had they been paying attention to the boy whose face had just changed.

It had been foolish to leave the shop without looking behind him for someone wearing Artifice; he would have to be more careful in the future. Until he learned how to detect Artifice on his own, he'd need to consider the possibility of tails who could change their faces at a moment's notice.

Satisfied, he stowed the optic and swapped his face once more. "Come on, then."

"What was that all about?"

"Don't want anybody following us," Ashes said. "Especially not somebody wearing new faces all the time. I told you, this secret's important."

Synder nodded solemnly. Ashes started down the street, beckoning her to follow him.

"I got the book for a friend," he muttered, keeping his voice as low as he could. "Somebody from Burroughside."

"Why's that some big secret?"

"Because he's supposed to be dead," Ashes said.

Synder looked at him with concern. Ashes rubbed his forehead.

"Right," he said. "Look. A year ago, I lived with a crew, leader by the name of Mari. She was . . . decent. But that's not really a good thing in Burroughside. And we found this *rasa* wandering about. Had scars and bruises all over. Called himself Blimey. Mari thought we ought to take him in. Keep him safe. She did that sometimes."

Ashes's fists clenched. Even now the memory made his heart pound. "Anyway, we did. She was going to make him part of the crew, teach him to cheat cards or work with the pickpockets or something. Only . . . one of Mari's seconds was Saintly. He's a vicious bastard now, but back then he wasn't so bad. I didn't think he was, anyway." He blew out a breath. "Saintly—I don't know how, but he found out Ragged was looking for someone that sounded like Blimey."

"Who's Ragged?"

"Mr. Ragged," Ashes said. "You don't know who—? No, course

you wouldn't. Mr. Ragged's the—I dunno, the governor of Burroughside. None of the Ivories want to touch it, owing to how it's full of criminals and the like—"

"Well, they're not allowed to," Synder said.

"Eh?"

"Something in the city compact," Synder said, shrugging. "No Ivory's allowed to rule another district unless a majority from every neighboring district permits it. They can't even appoint somebody without approval. It's all very bureaucratic."

Ashes noted *bureaucratic* as some kind of synonym for *stupid* and moved on. "Anyway, Saintly found out Ragged wanted Blimey dead. Way he saw it, that meant Mari was hiding a fugitive. Breaking Ragged's law. So he killed her. He would've killed Blimey, too, if I hadn't got him out of there. Then I . . ."

Ashes took a breath. The memories burned in his brain. They were still so very, very vivid.

"There's a coroner down Finch Street. He'd got a dead kid that week, no name, no family, and he was about Blimey's size. I made it look like him, and I convinced everybody that was his body."

"I thought you didn't know how to use Artifice?"

"I didn't," Ashes said. "I just made sure the face wasn't nothing somebody'd recognize." He kept himself from shaking, but only just. The dead boy had been cold as winter's gut, and the blood had all congealed too much to spurt out. Even so, it had covered Ashes's hands and his clothes and the knife he'd used. He'd kept it near a sewer vent, where it was muggy and hot, so the blood would look wet. Ragged had been too disgusted by the rot-stench to look closely. That had been Ashes's salvation. He wondered now if, perhaps, he had Stitched it, just a little. Just enough.

Synder took a moment to understand exactly what he was implying. He could tell when the words clicked, because she swallowed. "Oh."

"That boy was already dead," Ashes said, keeping his voice level. "He'd been dead a while, and nobody knew about him. And I made sure he got a decent burial, too, 'cause he deserved it. He saved somebody else's life."

Synder nodded, though he could tell she was still horrified. "How long ago did you say this was?"

"Near a year now. I kept Blimey hid away, but I didn't want him going out of his mind. So I bring him books. He knows all sorts of Ivory words and things."

The girl's head cocked to one side and her face wrinkled in confusion. "Why not just bring him to the shop?"

"No!" Ashes's chest went tight. He took a deep breath. "No. I can't do that."

"Why ever not?"

"I just can't!" Ashes blew air out his nose. "I'm not gonna do that to him."

"Do *what*?"

"Stick him with anybody!" Ashes rounded on her, teeth clenched. "There's nobody I can trust but me, all right? I like Jack and all, and the rest of your crew. But I don't trust anybody with Blimey's life. Nobody but me, understand?"

Synder took a step back. "Okay. Right. Sorry I asked."

"Nobody else but me has any business in his life," Ashes snapped. "Soon as I've got the means, I'm going to put him where Ragged'll never touch him again."

"Very well," she said. "I'll keep it to myself, Ashes."

"Roger," he corrected sharply. "And you're not making a good case for how you can keep secrets."

Synder blushed furiously. "Right. Roger. Sorry." She looked away, trying to hide the red in her cheeks. "Lead on, then."

## 21 Discovery

**T**HEY halted down the street from Batty Annie's while Ashes examined the area. He didn't bother with the optic; it was better to keep his false face on while he was here, and he couldn't look through the stone without damaging the construct. Besides, if Ragged's boys had Artifice on their side, he might well be doomed already anyway.

He spotted no watchers outside Annie's. Thanking the Face of Cunning, and whatever other Faces must have started watching over him to grant this unparalleled run of luck, he took Synder's hand.

"From here to that doorway," he said, "we're a pair of Denizen teenagers who've gone to see a witch because, wouldn't you know it, you've missed your moon's blood and if your father finds out then we're both as rats in a cat's den. Got me?"

Synder's lip twitched and she nodded. "Got it."

He handed her the book. "Any chance you can hide this in

your petticoats somewhere?" The girl only smiled and vanished the book somewhere inside her construct. Faces, but she was good at this.

He led her forward, pulling on the identity of someone frightened for much more proper reasons than he was. He moved with an obviously unpracticed furtiveness, looking indiscreetly over both shoulders as he crossed the road.

He knocked on Batty Annie's door three times. The old door creaked open some moments later, and Batty Annie's face appeared behind the wood grain.

"Grandmother," Synder said, and her voice became, all at once, the perfect imitation of a proper young lady. "We're so desperately sorry to be bothering you. May we come in? It's *deplorably* urgent."

Annie eyed her skeptically, then looked at Ashes. The skeptical look intensified.

"I know your scent," Annie snarled, eyeing Ashes with profound distaste. "Wearing another—?"

"Please, grandmother," Ashes said sharply, slipping into an accent to match Synder. "It really is an errand of the utmost urgency. May we come in?"

Annie scowled and stepped aside. The moment the door closed, Ashes slipped off the ring.

"Sorry to be showing on your doorway with a false face, ma'am," he said, bowing. "I figured I ought to be extra careful."

The old woman fidgeted, looking annoyed. "Who's this one?" She looked intensely at Synder. "Discard that Glamour, girl-child, before I yank it off you."

Synder undid the thin scarf on her neck, and a moment later became half a foot shorter and a quarter as graceful and proper. She didn't take her eyes off Annie; Synder looked to be somewhere between fascination and wariness. "Do I know—?"

"Probably not," Annie replied sharply, giving Synder a cold look. "Carry on with you, then."

Ashes halted Synder at the steps to his room.

"Got to warn you before we go down." He looked her full in the face, intent on communicating how important this was. "Blimey don't look like most folk. He's got bruises and cuts and he weren't all that pretty to start with. You call him names, you leave. You get some horrified 'how could something like *that* happen if the gods really are good' expression, you leave. You call any attention to it, except that he mentions it, you *leave*, understand?"

She nodded.

"More'n likely he'll be skittish," Ashes went on. "He doesn't meet a lot of new people. So just stay calm and don't give him any reason to fright."

"I understand, Ashes. Calm down. I'll be gentle as a lady mouse, all right? Is that what you're looking for?"

"It'll serve."

He opened the door to the basement. The room beyond was lit by only two candles, casting faint and unreliable light on a well-appointed bed, an old desk with a thin stack of paper on it, and Blimey, sitting on the mattress with his book of words before him. His lips were moving silently as he read, noiselessly tasting every word as his eyes slipped over them.

"Blimes?"

The boy jerked away from his book and twisted. Joy filled his lumpy face. "You're back early. Tired of grand larceny yet?"

"Don't get smart with me, nonsenser. I've been off slaying dragons."

Blimey's eyes slipped past Ashes to the girl behind him. Ashes tensed, expecting Blimey to shrink back onto his bed. His friend was full of surprises, though: at the sight of Synder, Blimey slid off the bed, padded forward, took Synder's hand, and gave a deep bow.

"G-good evening," he said. "It is my—my pleasure to welcome a lady of your esteemed quality to my unworthy home."

Synder looked shocked, but she recovered quickly. "I am

blessed to visit so esteemed a home." The words were mechanical, a reflex: something Ivorish? Blimey's greeting must have had more to it than Ashes realized.

"My name is Nathaniel," Blimey said, still bowed. Ashes drew in a shallow breath; Blimey had never told him a birth name. *Rasa* remembered that much sometimes, but not often. *Which are you, Blimey? A rasa pretending to be a Denizen? Or the other way round?* "B-but you can call me Blimey, if you like. That's what most people say when they see me."

Synder grinned shyly, dipping a belated curtsy. "I'm Synder. It's a pleasure to meet you, Nathaniel."

Blimey straightened and pulled at the bottom of his shirt. He was wearing different clothes than he used to—had Annie found him new things? It looked as though he'd bathed recently, too.

"You're looking fit to be a princeling, mate," Ashes said.

Blimey's face went sunset-colored. "You're one to talk," he replied. "Since when'd you start wearing this fine stuff?"

"All part of the plan." He tipped Blimey a confident look, but doubted his friend even saw it. His eyes lingered on Synder. No surprise there; Blimey hadn't seen a girl in years, except for Mari. Judging by how he looked at Synder, Blimey was already layering every story he'd ever read about knights and fine ladies and noble heroes wedding princesses onto her; in his eyes she became King Cathar's wife and Lady Innevra and the Maiden of Gleaming, all rolled into one. And wearing trousers.

"I got you something, Blimes," Ashes said, holding up the book. If there was anything that could distract Blimey from the sudden intrusion of a girl, it would be a book. Even so, Blimey seemed reluctant to look away from Synder long enough to register what Ashes was carrying. His breath caught.

"Maker's love," Blimey whispered. "It's beautiful, Ashes." He held out his hands, taking the book reverently and setting it on the desk. He opened it the way a priest would open a holy text, his fingers lingering on the pages but only touching their edges, rather than dirtying the text with his fingerprints.

"Told you I'd bring you more books," Ashes said. "That's just the first, too."

Synder met Ashes's eyes, a warning in her gaze. She'd be watching over his shoulder now, whatever he did, and she was particularly squeamish about stealing. Inconvenient, but hardly a problem. He'd find a way around her eventually.

"How's things today?" Ashes asked. "You got one of Annie's books?"

"Good," Blimey said unconvincingly. "No, she, um . . . I finished the last history she gave me pretty quickly. She told me she'd get me a different one by week's end."

"Best that she does," Ashes said. "You're not bored waiting for her?"

"A . . . A little."

"I know a good cure for boredom," Synder said. She looked to Ashes as if asking permission to keep talking. "Do you know any good games, Blimey?"

Blimey closed the book with religious caution and faced Synder. He nodded. "I know some games, from a long while ago. And Ashes showed me a card game a few times, something he'd use to get Ivory money."

Synder shot Ashes an accusatory glance before turning back to Blimey. "You strike me as the sort of person who would *quite* enjoy chess. You heard of chess, Blimey?"

Ashes shook his head, but Blimey nodded enthusiastically. "Course I've heard of it!" he said. "It's the game Clever Tyru used to stop Gavin Brokenhand from going to war with—with someone, I can't remember if it was the Ladies or Rykar of the Steel. It's a sort of war game, isn't it?"

Synder nodded. "Sort of a war game, except with no killing. I need thirty-two pebbles, or bits of string, or any kind of useless bit of junk you can find. But it's got to be exactly thirty-two, all right?"

Blimey nodded and dove under his bed without further comment. Synder smiled, then turned to Ashes. "Got anything I can use?" Ashes shook his head. "Better start looking, then."

Five minutes later, Synder counted out thirty-two knickknacks and bits of litter, all collected from corners, pockets, and the drawers of the desk. When she had gathered them all, she separated them into two groups of sixteen, and pulled out a phial of aether.

Ashes caught his breath. Did natural Weavers just carry those things around all the time? It was such a cavalier way of doing things. Anybody could snatch it out of your pocket and you wouldn't even know it.

Synder looked around the room with a critical eye, chewing her bottom lip. "There's not much light in here. These might be a little dim." So saying, she stretched out a hand and gestured like she was coaxing a foal toward her. Ashes could just see a thin thread of light forming near her hand. The room grew dull as the thread thickened, pulsing larger with every passing moment. Synder gathered it all to herself unhurriedly, with a look of calm concentration.

Blimey's jaw had fallen open. Ashes, for his part, was deeply impressed. The light swarmed to her touch, eager to be molded; not a drop slipped away. Her focus must have been perfect. *This* was the genius Jack had talked about: a fourteen-year-old Ivorish girl who tugged on light as though it were real, who didn't let one strand diminish from her touch.

Both candles were being siphoned into Synder's grip now, plunging the room into ever-steadier darkness. The flames looked as tall and strong as ever. The only difference was a dullness, a sort of gray pallor falling over the fire.

Synder let out a satisfied breath and tugged sharply on the threads of light. What was left of them coiled into her hands, and though the operation was perfectly silent Ashes could almost hear the lines snap. The room became just a little brighter, and as the moments passed the light increased—as if the candles were gathering their strength back.

The girl sat with a pool of pale golden light in her open hands. It was so bright it hurt to look at, but somehow didn't illuminate anything but itself. Synder's face, so close to the gathered light, was no brighter than any other part of the room.

Wordlessly, she began to spin the light into miniature shapes, all of them cylindrical. She made eight identical constructs, each putting off a faint golden glow, and inserted a drop of aether in them before binding them to eight of the bits of junk at her feet. Another eight followed, pulsing faint silver, then eight golden figures with differing features, and their twins in silver.

Last of all, she pulled her handkerchief out of a pocket. It was a work of proper textile art—Ashes couldn't help but notice it was the sort a ragman would pay good money for. Shaking it out with one hand, she directed the light onto it with the other. The light fell in a pattern, alternating squares of light and dark—*formed* dark, like Juliana's cloak, not simply an absence of light but a yawning blackness set against the cloth. When she had formed the final space, she let the cloth drift to the ground, pulled it tight at the corners, and pressed her open palm against it. The construct went taut as she tipped a drop of aether onto the cloth. A faint sound came from it, like fat sizzling over fire, and when it passed she let her hand up. Finally satisfied, she sat back, letting out a long breath.

Thirty-three laden Anchors lay before her; the forming and binding had taken maybe five minutes. The pool of light in her lap had dwindled to nearly nothing, and her aether phial was half empty, but she wore a proud smile.

"There," she said. "Not even that bad, I'd wager." She glanced at the light still pulsing in her lap, and dipped one hand in. It obeyed her like sluggish water, slipping out of her hand in large, dripping trails. She let out a long breath, and the gathered light seeped away. Simultaneously, everything in the room became brighter—brighter than before she'd started working? Ashes couldn't tell. Maybe it only looked that way because of how dim she'd made it.

Blimey was sitting on the bed, staring at Synder with an unabashedly worshipful expression. Ashes held his admiration in better, but it was only slightly less than Blimey's. Blimey was only amazed at meeting an Artificer; he had no idea the level of skill he'd just witnessed. Ashes was educated enough to recognize that he'd just watched Synder produce a work of art, worth a minor fortune, in the dingy basement of a Burroughside madwoman. And she'd done it with *rocks*.

"Do you know how to play, Blimey? I can teach you, if you don't."

Blimey swallowed. "You're a— You're a Glamourist."

Synder gave him a shy smile. "More or less. Still just a journeyman, though. I only have my practicing license."

"You're *magic*," Blimey breathed, and turned to Ashes. "Did you see? She's *magic*!"

"Ashes has it, too," Synder said.

"Sure," Blimey said, "but he's never done something like that."

"Well, he's still learning." Synder beckoned Blimey to sit across from her. "Come on, then. Want to learn the game of kings?"

Blimey nodded enthusiastically.

"All right," Synder began. "We'll start from the outside in. This here is Tower, then Iron Knight, then Artificer, then Queen . . ."

● ● ●

*They left nearly two* hours later. Blimey bid them farewell cheerfully, failing to hide an eagerness to return to his new game. Synder had beaten him soundly three matches in a row, but each had been harder-fought than the last. Blimey stopped asking questions about what he was and wasn't allowed to do halfway through the first game, and by the end of the last he'd been matching Synder move for move. He would have won, too, were it not for Synder's clever gambit in the last few turns.

Synder warned him the pieces wouldn't last forever. The board would disappear whenever he folded up the handkerchief, but since the pieces didn't truly *fit* anywhere, they wouldn't stop glowing. No construct could keep its form forever; they would disappear eventually.

Blimey had nodded dutifully at her advice, but it was clear he didn't care much how long they lasted. What mattered was the game itself. Even when he didn't have the board out, Blimey would be playing in his head, imagining moves and strategies and traps. The illusions would be obsolete long before they faded away.

Finally, they found themselves on the road once more, headed north to Lyonshire and the shop. Synder walked confidently, immune to any worry of followers or malcontents. Ashes mimicked her walk, exuding the easy confidence of an Ivory who was both young and powerful, but he kept his eyes moving. He spotted no one keeping eyes on them, for which he was grateful. He didn't want to have to deal with a tail.

A block away from Annie's, Synder stopped abruptly and fixed him in a smoldering glare. "All right. Spill it. Why are you sulking?"

Ashes stared back. "I'm not."

"You are. I once sulked for three full months, I *know* what it looks like, and you're doing it. Why?"

Ashes looked around once again, evaluating if they were being watched, and let out a breath. "I feel like I keep getting deeper in debt with you, Syn." He leaned closer, dropping his voice. "Look, you don't know him, but I do. You giving him that set—that was incredible, what you did. He's going to have something to take his mind off things, and I can't tell you how great that is for someone with so much to think about. He's got something to *do* now, something that'll keep getting more interesting for him." He frowned, struggling for words. "Thanks."

Synder smiled. "It's no problem for me, really. I was happy to do it."

"You spent a lot of aether on that."

She tilted her head. "So? We're hardly short of the stuff."

Ashes looked the street up and down again. "Right. Anyway. I'm not sulking, just so's you're aware. It's just I haven't had to say thanks to someone so much before. You're a really decent person, Syn." He smiled awkwardly before shaking his head a little. "Right. We ought to get heading back." He stepped, and his foot hit a loose stone, sending him crashing into Synder. The girl let out a shocked gasp and grabbed his shoulder—and Ashes's nimble fingers slid inside her pocket and plucked out her aether, stowing it within his sleeve.

"Damn!" he muttered. "Sorry, Syn. It's that bloody witch-healing— you'd think my legs would've got their balance back by now."

"Don't worry about it," she said, helping him stand straight. "Witch-healing is useful, but hardly kind."

"You can say that again." The false face blushed furiously, but only because Ashes had made it do so.

*She didn't even feel it. Are all Ivories this easy to pickpocket?*

It was almost ridiculous how easy they were to distract. All he had to do was stumble, and he could pull things out of any pocket they cared to use.

"Come on," she said. "You can use my arm to stand, if you need it." She grinned. "You'd have to be walking on your own before we get back to the shop, though. If Juliana saw a man leaning on a woman for help she might actually die."

Ashes grinned. "Neh, I can walk on my own."

*She's an incredibly decent person,* some part of him said. He tried to quash the voice, but it kept going. *Making that chess set for Blimey. Helping you out. Keeping your secrets.*

*Looks like you're a bastard.*

Ashes looked over his shoulder. "Oh, Syn," he said, bending quickly. "I think you dropped this." He let the phial fall into his palm, then held it out to her.

Synder let out a shocked gasp. "Oh! Thanks." She stowed it back inside her construct, deeply perturbed. "Good thing you saw it. Goodness, can you imagine if someone picked this up?" She shuddered. "I'd have Hollowed someone."

Ashes blinked. That would not have been his first thought. That would not have been his twenty-first thought. "Yeah," he muttered. "Lucky."

Synder noticed something behind him. "Um." She pointed, not very subtly, and motioned for Ashes to stand up. "Ashes. Who's that?"

*Don't use that name here!* He turned, half expecting Saintly to be standing behind him.

"Furies and Kindness. Ben Roamer?"

The old madman was slumped against a wall, barely standing. His hair was even dirtier and mangier than the last time Ashes had seen him, nearly a month ago.

"'Lo," the old man said, looking at Ashes through a thicket of his coarse hair. "Who're . . . ?"

Roamer choked on his words and stumbled, going to his knees. His beard sank into the Burroughside muck.

"What the hell's gone on with you?" Ashes dropped to his knees, taking Roamer's face in his hands. The man's eyelids were swollen to nearly twice their usual size, and bruised deep purple. His skin was littered with small cuts, and Ashes caught the powerful stench of piss on him.

"Who is this?" Synder asked. "Do you know him?" She'd come closer, though Ashes doubted she'd stoop in this mire while she was wearing those nice Ivorish petticoats—

Synder's face was suddenly level with his. Ashes revised his opinion.

"Ben," he said, looking the man in the face. "Benjamin Roamer. You listening to me? You *here*?"

The old man met Ashes's gaze. There was no recognition there—no, of course there wouldn't be. Ashes yanked the ring off his finger. "You recognize me, Roamer?"

"Eshes." Ben's voice sounded like a creaking door. "You're sposa be dead, I thought."

"Can't nobody kill me, Ben," Ashes said. "I'm slippery as smoke."

Roamer laughed—thickly, wetly. There was some manner of fluid in his lungs.

"We ought to get him to hospital," Synder suggested.

"No!" Ben snapped. "No 'spittles!"

"Ben's afraid of them," Ashes said in a hushed voice. "Always figured they'd kill him if they got hands on him. He's got no iron name anyway, they wouldn't take him."

Synder's face was stricken. "What do we do?"

Ashes looked over the man. "He won't die from these," he said. "You have any money on you?"

"A little—"

"Anything over a crescent will do," Ashes said, and looked Ben in the eye again. "Ben Roamer, you listen to me right now. You're going to tell me which of Ragged's folks did this to you, and then you're going to take my money, you're going to find a dosser, all right? There's one on Regency Street. Rest for a week. Don't go walking about none, all right?"

Ben nodded weakly. "Figure I kin do that."

"Who did this to you?"

"Ashes, what does that *matter*—"

"Quiet, Syn."

Ben's eyes were wild and fearful, but Ashes wouldn't let him look away. "Broken Boys," he said at last.

Ashes nodded sharply. "Good. On with you, now."

The old fellow staggered from the alleyway, clutching the coin tightly in his fist. Ashes stared after him, mind racing, blood hot.

"What was that all about?"

Ashes hesitated. "There was something I've been waiting for," he said at last. "But now I don't think it's going to come."

"I don't understand."

"Nothing, Syn," he said. "Let's get back."

# 22

# *Broken*

THE workshop was empty. That was a stroke of luck.

Ashes strode inside, looking around nervously despite himself. Jack and William would be out for another hour or so, preparing in some form or another for the heist at Edgecombe House. Synder had gone home to her parents, and Juliana was upstairs. Ashes was alone.

Still, he couldn't keep himself calm. Somehow, this felt as perilous as picking a copper's pocket.

He moved swiftly to the cabinet at the end of the room. He let out a breath. *Stay calm*, he told himself. *Just get it done.*

He pulled a lock pick from his pocket, knelt, and set to work. Jack was no slouch in security; the lock was well made. Twice, Ashes got the catch nearly undone, only to be betrayed by his shaking fingers. The third time, he closed his eyes and bit his tongue. *Focus.*

The catch sprang. He eased the cabinet door open.

The cabinet was full of strange and interesting objects, most of which seemed to be unique Anchors: a sword hilt with no sword, a thin gold coronet, a silver watch with a broken face. He ignored these in favor of the phials of liquid light on the top shelf.

Heart still pounding feverishly against his chest, Ashes snatched three of the phials and stowed them in the pockets of his cloak. A quiet voice in the back of his head protested, but he had no other choice. He needed these, and he needed them now.

He was about to slam the cabinet shut when he saw the bottom shelf, and caught his breath. The shelf was entirely lined with phials of aether—it had to be nearly fifty in total. A fortune. *Ten* fortunes.

A stair creaked behind him. Quick as winking, Ashes closed the cabinet and clicked the lock, then dashed toward one of the shelves and snatched a random Anchor off of it. He held it close to his face, as if he were inspecting it.

"Oh! Ashes. You're here late."

Ashes looked up, feigning surprise. "Evening, Jack," he said.

"Inspecting the merchandise?" Jack asked. "You won't learn much from that. One of my earlier projects. Not my best work."

Ashes looked at the Anchor again, finally registering what he was holding. It was a tricorn hat, old and tatty. "What's inside?"

"A face," Jack said, smiling wickedly. "Not a very pleasant one, mind. Rather ghoulish, in fact."

"On purpose?"

"Very," Jack said, walking forward and taking the hat from Ashes. "I had an acquaintance some years ago who had a fondness for these. I swapped this out for his when he wasn't looking, and . . ." Jack set the hat on his head, and his face transformed into a grotesque parody of human features. The skin was yellowed, the eyes red and veiny, the nose overlarge and cocked to one side. Ashes burst out laughing.

"Not very mature of me, I'm afraid," Jack said, not sounding particularly regretful. He set the hat back on the shelf. "I'd have thought you'd be on your way home by now. Are you staying for supper?"

"Just got distracted, is all," Ashes said smoothly. "You're right, though, I ought to be on my way." He made to step past the Weaver, but Jack matched his move, blocking him.

"You certain you're all right?" Jack asked. "You look flushed."

"Eh," Ashes said. "I'm fine."

Jack's eyebrows bent inward. "You don't need to stay here?"

"I got nothing to fear out there, Jack," Ashes said.

● ● ●

*The sun was low,* the clouds dark. There was light, but not much of it, in the neighborhood near Barrister's coffee house. Jack would have noted that it was just bright enough to Weave, but, perhaps, not enough for just anyone to spot an illusion.

Ashes stood in the shadows not a hundred feet away from the coffee house, wearing the shadow-bound cloak. Its Woven darkness hid him well here in the twilight; no one looked twice at him.

He could see four Broken Boys inside Barrister's. He recognized them, by sight if not by name; brutes Saintly favored for his dirtier work. More than likely they'd been there for Ben's beating, even participated in it. Of Saintly himself there was no sign. Perhaps that was best; Ashes didn't intend to be recognizable, or even recognizably human, but if there was anyone who could mark Ashes by his voice alone, it would be Saintly.

The four Boys looked quite pleased with themselves. Barrister had brought them food and beer in abundance, though Ashes had not seen them give him a thin copper penny. Every other customer in the building was giving them a wide berth, no doubt leery of attracting their attention.

Ashes pulled the cloak tighter around himself and checked the stones hidden in his pockets. Artifice pulsed within them, faint and thready.

He tensed as he heard the door to Barrister's open. The Boys stepped out, chattering amongst themselves. Ashes set his jaw. He'd guessed right: they were coming this way. They would pass by him in a moment. He dug a wooden ring out of his pocket and slipped it on. Synder's voice echoed in his head: *It's actually quite good, if you were trying to make a gargoyle.*

"What a rush," said one of them. "D'you hear him whine when Tom kicked him?" The Boy pitched his voice into a stuttering croak. " 'Oh, no, no, please, don't 'urt me, ent done nothin'—' "

All four of them laughed; the storyteller laughed loudest. They were mere steps away now.

"Buggery little bastard," said another.

"Teach him to bother us."

"Saintly's right," said the first. "High time we started teaching these buggers proper respect."

Ashes let out a breath and stepped into the light, letting the vast cloak billow around him. He focused fiercely on an image of William the Wisp, and when he spoke, it was in the man's precise, unforgiving tone.

"Not that this isn't *scintillating* conversation, gents," he said, pulling a stone out of his pocket, "but I do believe we've business to attend to."

"The hell—?"

Ashes threw the rock to the ground and pulled the cloak against his eyes.

There was no sound, but it felt as if there should have been. A sun-bright flash lit up the street, burning Ashes's eyes even through the thick cloth. Without wasting a moment, he stepped away from the Broken Boys. All four were reeling, hands pressed against their faces.

"I do hope we haven't got off on the wrong foot," he said, stomping on the toes of his nearest opponent. The Boy let out a sudden yelp and snatched out to grab Ashes, but missed by several feet. "I think it's very important for you gentlemen to hear what I have to say." He smashed an open hand against another one's ear, hard enough to send the boy stumbling. Sensing the other two readying behind him, he whirled away, wanting more distance. He'd have much less of an advantage if anyone managed to get hold of him.

"Who the hell're—?"

"I'm Burroughside's vengeance, little Broken Boy, and I'm your worst bloody nightmare."

One of the Boys pulled out a vicious-looking knife and began to advance. He was blinking furiously, but clearly had enough of his sight back to be a threat.

Ashes swallowed, but his voice didn't waver. "That's rather small," he said. "Not the first time you've heard that, though, I expect."

The Boy grunted and slashed wildly. Ashes stepped back, and just as quick the Boy lunged forward. Off-balance, Ashes was forced to twist, throwing the cloak in front of his body to protect himself. The knife slid into the folds. Ashes grabbed the edge of the cloak and pulled it tight, wrapping the knife inside the cloth. The Boy jerked, but Ashes had the knife by the hilt.

"You seem to have lost your sticker," Ashes said.

"Didn't need it much," the Boy replied, and punched Ashes in the gut.

The breath *whooshed* out of Ashes. Another punch struck him in the ribs. He yelped.

"Not so brilliant now, are you?" The Boy snatched Ashes's hood and threw it back.

A warped, twisted face stared back at him, grinning like a demon.

"No, it's just the opposite," Ashes admitted cheerily, worming another stone out of a pocket. "I'm *quite* bright."

The stone struck the ground, producing another flash of fierce light. Ashes squeezed his eyes tightly shut and twisted away, though the light still struck him like a slap to the face. He hadn't expected them to be nearly so powerful.

The flash had taken three of the Boys by surprise, but the fourth—the angry one with the knife—had expected it. He approached Ashes slowly, as if his head was still spinning and the only thing keeping him on his feet was sheer force of will.

"You've got some fight to you," Ashes said, trying to exude that confidence again. "I've got to give you that."

"You a demon?" The Boy spit and made the sign of the Faces over his chest. "Or something?"

"Something," Ashes said. "Something you've not seen nor heard about."

The Boy smirked, but it was fragile; Ashes's monstrous face was getting to him. "Eh? And what'd that be?"

"I'm the vengeance Burroughside's been dreaming of since Hiram Ragged sat his arse on our home," Ashes said fiercely. "I'm the one that'll bring balance on the scales. That'll have an answer from Ragged for all the blood he's spilled, and all the blood he's let spill." Ashes took a step forward. There was fury in his belly. "I'm what'll stand between bastards like *you*," he spat, "and folks like Ben Roamer." He could see the fear in the Boy's eyes now, see it creeping up on him from within. "I'm slippery as smoke and angry as the gods, boy, and I don't mean to let you leave without some marks on you."

The Broken Boy's eyes were wide. Ashes took another step forward.

"You can tell Saintly that I'm coming for him next," Ashes said. "Him, and Ragged, and any else that'll dare beat on them who's weaker." He was only a few feet away from the Boy now. There was movement behind him, the others recovering from their dizzy spells.

The Boy saw Ashes's eyes flick, and his knife came up.

"Bloody *hell*," Ashes said, stepping back from the blade and flinging a stone at the Broken Boy's face. The Boy yanked himself away, eyes screwed up tight—

He tripped on a twisted cobblestone and fell hard, striking his head against the street.

"I didn't put bombs in *all* of them," Ashes said, turning away. The three others were back up, advancing cautiously, their arms up to shield from other blasts of light.

Ashes held his hands up. "That was the last of them, I'm afraid," he called, backing away. The Boys didn't let their arms down.

"Ah, well. Worth a shot."

Ashes dropped his hands and he threw the last three Anchored stones in quick succession, striking one of the boys in the neck and another in the fork of his legs. The last stone struck the street, inches away from his target's feet.

Three suns burst out of their cages simultaneously, and all went quiet.

Ashes's vision came back spottily, filled mostly with white. He seemed to be on all fours, and he didn't hear the Broken Boys anywhere. He blinked several times, hoping like hell that no one found him here, monstrous-faced and nearly blind.

He stood, shakily. His ears weren't ringing, but they certainly should have been.

The knife-wielder was on his back only a few feet away, groaning. He would be up in only a few minutes. Ashes glanced at the other three; they'd be up even sooner.

"I'm going to tell you something, Broken Boy," Ashes said softly, getting close enough for the Boy to hear him. "I could take your knife right now and skin you with it. Nobody'd stop me. Don't reckon I'd enjoy it, but I could try real hard." He paused, letting the Boy understand. "But I don't reckon I'm going to do that. Seems to me you're afraid, and that's good. You'll tell others how frighted they ought to be of me." Ashes felt the rage pounding in his head again, and something else, too. Something he'd only brushed against in the last four weeks, something he hadn't quite grasped until now. "But I think it's important you pay for what you done, too. Savvy?"

He pressed four fingers to the boy's temple. "This won't hurt a bit," he said, and drew his fingers diagonally along the boy's face. Bright red gashes appeared in the wake of his touch, as if he'd torn the boy's face apart. The Broken Boy shuddered, but didn't wail or groan or give any sign that Ashes had harmed him; the wounds were only Stitchery.

Moments later his work was done. Four livid scars stretched across the boy's face, twisting the skin. One crossed his eye, and Ashes knew without needing to check that when the Boy opened it, it would look utterly white.

*William would be proud*, he noted absently as he Anchored the image to the boy's eyebrows.

"I'm going to leave, now," Ashes said. "You make sure you tell Saintly for me, will you? Somebody's coming for him and Ragged both. Somebody powerful. Somebody *mad*."

My friend,

I have adopted a new strategy, one you may well consider foolish.
I have let the boy into my confidence.

Before you scold me, allow me to offer my evidence.

The boy has been following me. He is well trained; he managed to catch me during a transaction with one of the Gilders
who so generously subsidize my research. I'll admit this was
sloppy—I should have anticipated such a maneuver. The error
remains, and I am left to deal with its consequences.

Except there have been no consequences.

If the boy served one of the Gilders, I would by now have
been blackmailed. If he served the Guild Council, I would be
dead. Neither event has come to pass. In fact, he has ceased following me altogether, as if the first discovery was all he needed.
My business continues unmolested, and there are no indications
that this may change.

You may say I am being unreasonably optimistic, but in truth
I fear that my new recruit aims for a prize far more valuable than
merely my head.

Recognizing this, I have ceased hiding all but my most
dangerous secrets; if indeed he has been sent as an agent of an
enemy, he has enough rope to hang me with, and it seems foolish
to hoard the final inches. What truly matters is teasing out his
aims—what _exactly_ has this boy been sent to find?

I hope, for entirely selfish reasons, that your journey is a
smooth one. We must speak in person, and soon.

Jack

# PART 3

## *Smoke*

# 23

# Mischief

THE night was starless and murky, and the creature scuttling through Burroughside fit into it perfectly. Small and infernal it was, with a face of poisonous green and eyes that gleamed red, and skin like the skin of an insect. Its teeth, sharp and many, were filed into points, and its ears were long and narrow, like a bat's. Its arms were longer than they ought to have been, with an out-of-place joint beneath the elbow, and ended in spindly fingers like spider legs. It wore something dark along its body, something which appeared to be cloth but, if seen closer, certainly could not be. It blended too smoothly in the darkness. If it were to step beneath the light (and it would not, for it knew better), one might see the truth: this demon wore sewn-together shadow.

Altogether, Ashes felt rather proud of his costume. Perhaps he was no good at making pretty faces, but he didn't want pretty. He wanted horrific.

Two streets from Ragged House, he turned southward, and

circled the Beggar Lord's lair to come at it from the south. Three months ago, before he'd fallen in with the Rehl Company, this would have been more than a little stupid. Even Ravagers avoided Saintly's territory.

One of Saintly's scouts would see him, no doubt, but no reason to leave it to chance. "Ragged!" he screeched, in the hoarsest voice he could manage. "Ragged!" He snatched up a piece of rubble from the street and flung it at a wall. It produced a thunderous *crack*, and Ashes followed it with another screeching cry of *"Ragged!"*

That would do.

Ashes moved to the shadow of an alleyway and unwound the cloth strips around his head, arms, and legs, stowing them in the pack he carried. He felt the demon disappear, like a feathery weight being lifted from him. His true clothing was visible now: pants with no holes, a jacket that looked almost new. It was too clean to belong in Burroughside, but it was dark enough not to attract attention and covered up his skin. The added stealth was not nearly as valuable as the pockets: two on the inside of the jacket breast, two on the outside near his waist, and one on each hip. Each contained at least one Anchor. Including the Anchors in the pack he carried, he held perhaps one hundred crowns' worth of magic on his person.

With the demon-face gone, Ashes pulled up the hood of his shadow-bound cloak. Juliana's Weaving enveloped him in darkness. To anyone walking by, the alley would look empty.

He stood perfectly still. He did not have to wait long before he heard hurried footsteps. Saintly's boys were not a patient group.

Ashes knew the two Boys who came around the corner, though not well. Tom Wesel was nearly as small as Ashes, with a beady look to him. The other Boy, Reynard Bullface, was as brutish as the name suggested.

"Do you see it?" Tom muttered.

"Neh," said Bullface. "Nothing in here."

"It's a dead end," Tom said. "It can't have escaped."

"I ain't stupid, Tommy," said Bullface, cracking his knuckles.

Ashes stepped nearer, keeping his back pressed against the wall. He was nearly level with them now. Neither of them seemed to notice the floating blue cloak at their side.

"Well," Tom said. "Go on."

"Why?"

"'Cause whoever he is, he's in there somewhere, and it ain't gonna be me what finds him."

"You sure it ain't 'cause they said it was a demon?"

Ashes smiled. He could hear the light tremble in Reynard's voice. *Thank you, Face of Cunning, for superstitious folk.*

"I'm sure it ain't," Tom replied. He was a better liar than Reynard, but there was still a faint quaver to him. "And even if it is, better you against it than me."

"You're a yellow little bastard, Tom."

"And you're a big dumb ox what can punch through a demon's face in one go. Which of us you think *ought* to be going in to look for it?"

There was a knife on Tom's belt—or, more accurately, a strip of steel with rough edges and leather wrapped around one end. Ashes didn't like the look of it; better that Tom not have it, just in case. He reached out, trying to keep silent.

"Seems like a stupid idea. We could just *wait* for the thing."

"See, Bullface, that's why I'm the stupid one and you're the smart one." Tom slapped his own cheek and let out a sharp noise. "Oh, wait! *You're* the stupid one and *I'm* in charge. Go look into it."

Ashes's fingers could *just* reach the hilt . . .

Bullface growled, but obeyed. The large boy tromped into the dark. "Nothing here, Tommy."

"Keep looking. It's probably just some Ravager what fell in paint." Tom crossed his arms. "Or you're just too stupid to see it," he muttered, too low for Reynard to hear. He did not twitch as the knife lifted free of his belt. Ashes stepped, enshrouded, near the middle of the alley, just between Tom and Bullface.

"I'm telling you, ain't nothing here!"

"*Where,*" Ashes whispered, making his voice raspy as a serpent's hiss. "*Where.*"

"You hear that?" Tom asked. Terror flickered across his face, just the shadow of it. "Bullface! You hear that?"

"Didn't hear nothing."

"You're too damn—"

"*Where,*" Ashes rasped again, louder this time. "*Where is Ragged?*"

"I heard it, Tom!" Ashes was just close enough to distinguish Bullface's features. Bullface was frightened. *Good.*

"*Mr. Smoke has come for him.*"

"Show yourself!" Reynard demanded, putting up his fists. "Come out and fight, piss-face! I got something for you."

Ashes stepped behind Bullface and crouched, bringing out the knife. He slashed Bullface's side with it and threw himself against the wall just as the boy screamed.

"It cut me!" he shouted. "It cut me with its teeths!" He swung out madly with his fists, too high to hit Ashes even if he had been standing closer.

Ashes circled the brute. "*You are small, Reynard. Small and foolish.*"

"It's talking to me, Tom!" Ashes could smell the boy's sweat. Fear-sweat, sharp and acrid. "It knows my name!"

"*You're failing Ragged.*" Bullface punched at the noise again, but in the close space, Ashes's voice came from everywhere at once. "*You know what Ragged does to those that fail him, don't you? What happened to John Flint on Bruisemaker Eve?*"

"Tom!"

"Just kill it, Bullface!" Tom was standing at the edge of the alleyway now, clutching the side of the building.

"*You cannot kill me, Reynard.*" Ashes said. "*You cannot even touch me.*"

"Shut it, you!" Bullface whirled, trying and failing to find something he could punch.

*"You will fail him, Reynard. And he will punish you for it. He'll do more than just carve his name on you, Bullface. He'll make you . . . his."*

Reynard howled and struck out. His fist slammed against the wall—too close for Ashes's comfort. Time to terrify him. He dug one hand in the chest pocket of his jacket and slipped on the ring within. A construct settled on his face and he yanked the hood of the cloak back.

*"You're mine, Reynard!"* Ashes snapped, just as Bullface turned around. The boy let out a keening sound, whirled, and sprinted away. Tom was already gone.

Ashes slipped the ring off, and Ragged's face evaporated. Binding Ragged's old face to a new Anchor had been relatively simple. He hadn't managed the switch perfectly; the colors were harsher and the lines sharper than they ought to be. Even so, he was proud of it, even dared to think that William wouldn't be totally disapproving, if he ever saw it.

● ● ●

*No proper vendetta exists* without a spy network, and so Ashes had set to make one as quickly as he could. There was no shortage of gutter-rats who hated Ragged, and most of them had the skills necessary to trail after him without being seen. The critical factor was raw audacity. Not many people had the stones to follow after the Beggar Lord, even when they were being paid for it, and Ashes refused to hire a tail whose courage fluctuated with the size of his wallet.

Having set his standards high, Ashes had expected to spend weeks searching for a good shadow. He had found Jasin on the second day, and promptly stopped looking.

Jasin was maybe nine years old, and even smaller than her

peers. She was quick on her feet, she listened well, and she learned things with frightening speed. More importantly, she hated Ragged nearly as much as Ashes did. If Mr. Smoke hadn't entered the world, Jasin might well have started a little war of her own, given enough time.

Ashes had tasked her with following the Beggar Lord anytime he left Ragged House, and with spreading news about Mr. Smoke to the younger children and the crippled beggars. Anyone who needed to know Ragged wouldn't last forever. Jasin had taken to the task with a will. For the last two months, Jasin had kept watch over Ragged's habits.

She knew that when Ragged had fruit delivered, he was entertaining a guest. She knew that he sent mail by one postman, but that a second one came at dusk every month, and if Ragged gave him a letter, he would be gone the next night. And because Jasin knew these things, so did Mr. Smoke.

● ● ●

*Ashes reached Ragged House* without meeting another soul. He smiled despite himself. Apparently Tom and Bullface weren't the only Broken Boys afraid of Mr. Smoke. Still, it wouldn't do to dawdle. He had work to do.

There were no lights on in Ragged House. Ashes approached it warily all the same. Jasin claimed that Ragged and Carapace were both out for the evening, off on business somewhere in Boreas. Ashes didn't doubt she was right, but it would pay to be cautious.

He wore Ragged's face as he approached the house. The gate swung open at his touch. He walked through the bloodstained courtyard to the door and grasped the doorknob. It jiggled, but refused to turn.

Unsurprising. He produced a lock pick from his pocket and knelt before the door. The catch sprang in moments.

*Now you're in it.*

Quelling the instinct to run, he walked into Ragged House.

The house was dark and quiet, but he didn't dare trust that impression. Ragged wouldn't have announced the fact that the house was unoccupied—ruling over cutpurses and thieves for a decade had turned him from a cautious man to a paranoid one—but he would be just the sort to leave some nasty little trap, or a loyal watcher, to keep his home secure. So Ashes walked softly, and kept Ragged's face on.

At the best of times, Ragged House had a certain eeriness to it. Ashes half suspected that Ragged cultivated that, intending to unnerve anyone who set foot inside his home. This was Ragged's place of power. Anyone visiting was at an automatic disadvantage, even when it was inhabited.

In the dark, and in the silence, it went beyond eerie to genuinely unnerving. Ashes could almost feel the air crawling along his skin, recognizing him as an invader. *Go back*, it commanded. *You are not welcome here.*

He ignored it as best he could. He was well past superstition these days. Still, a little light wouldn't go amiss. He slipped a phial of liquid light out of a pocket, flicked the lip open, and covered the opening with his finger to feed it a tiny amount of his magic. The light inside the phial roiled, and a moment later turned bright enough to light his path.

*"Ragged,"* he whispered in his demon-voice. No sense trying for total stealth; if he could spook whoever was left behind, his job would be that much easier.

He kept walking, noticing no sounds or signs of life. Perhaps Ragged really had left the place empty for the evening. Ashes felt a thrill; he would only get this chance once, he suspected. Best to make the most of it.

He left the hallway to enter one of Ragged's sitting rooms. He took the place in at a glance: a bookcase along one wall, a cushioned chair in the corner, and two of those weird portraits Ragged favored on the opposing walls. He slung the pack off his shoulder, wondering what items would be best for his purposes. What sort of books would Ragged read often . . . ?

His thoughts were interrupted by the frantic sound of footsteps coming from the courtyard.

*Bugger and damn.*

Quick as winking, he dimmed his makeshift lamp and stowed it with his pack behind the bookcase. Next moment he'd flicked the room's lamp on, snatched a book off the shelf, and settled himself into the massive chair. He sank into it deeply, as if the cushions were trying to swallow him whole.

He heard the door slam open, and feet sprinting down the hallway. A moment later, Saintly burst into the sitting room, looking sweaty and panicked. Ashes, wearing Ragged's face, looked up slowly.

"Francis," he said, dropping his voice to a low, gravelly register.

Saintly's head twisted toward him. "My Lord," he muttered, bowing swiftly. "There's something out there, milord. A— My boys say it's a demon. Screaming for you."

*Faces, he really looks scared*, Ashes thought. This was quite an opportunity. What kind of confusion could he sow here? What story would fit? He could make Ragged seem fearful, or vulnerable, or weak . . . making the Beggar Lord look vulnerable to Saintly Francis was not a chance to pass up.

"I am aware of it," Ashes said slowly. "It's name is Smoke. It comes for me, on occasion."

"I think it aims to kill you."

"It would do so, if it could," Ashes said. "I am too sly for it." But he let his voice shake, just a little. Just enough that Saintly would notice.

Saintly's eyes flickered to the sides of the room. "Is it here, milord? Now?"

Ashes shook his head. "Even if it were, you would be of no use to me, boy. You cannot kill it. Your steel and fists would be insufficient even if you could see it."

"What *is* it, sir? Tom and Bullface looked fit to piss themselves. One of 'em *did*."

"A vengeful spirit," Ashes said, arranging his face into something dark and eerie. "The echoes of those I have killed, come back to haunt me."

"Is there a way to stop it?"

"If there were a way to stop it, Francis," Ashes said in dark tones, "do you not think I may have availed myself of those paths? Do you imply that I am *stupid*?"

Saintly's face paled. "No, Lord."

"There is nothing to be done except wait for its time to pass," Ashes said. "It can only come to me when the moon permits. But . . . this is the first time it has dared walk through Burroughside." He tipped the wine back, making sure to let Saintly see his hands tremble. "It is growing stronger, I fear."

"My Lord," Saintly said, taking a step closer, "there must be something I can do. You have my loyalty."

*You were always a good liar, Saints.* Ashes almost believed him.

"It fears nothing," Ashes said, feeling the shade of an idea cross his mind. "But it loathes the scent of gold. The treasures I keep prevent its laying hands on me. So long as I possess them, I am not in peril." Ashes let the thought hang in the air, unvoiced. *If you were to steal it, Saintly . . .*

"My boys'll keep some round," Saintly said, nodding sharply. "There anything else? Anything, my Lord."

"You repeat those words as though they mean something," Ashes said, injecting a low growl in his tone. "You cannot kill it, Francis. Conventional methods will not work: it does not bleed. It cannot be struck, burned, drowned, impaled, crushed, or captured." Ashes readjusted himself, moving slowly, to give the impression of a frail creature. "But I have other tasks for you, Francis. Something of the highest order of secrecy."

Saintly's eyes flickered. "Whatever you ask of me, Lord."

"It must stay between us," Ashes said. "When I have told you of it, do not speak of it again. And do not assign it to one of your small-minded creatures. I mean this task for you, and you alone." Ashes fixed Saintly in his gaze, mimicking Ragged's dead-eyed stare. "I have heard talk, in my ways, of a . . . hidden artifact. Something old, something powerful. Something I could use in further plans. Something even Bonnie the Lass would fear." He nodded to Saintly delicately. "It is a dangerous thing. I cannot send someone to fetch it for me whom I do not trust."

Ashes imagined he could see Saintly understanding the implications. *It's valuable. Powerful.* And, perhaps, if Saintly took it for himself . . .

Saintly's mouth pressed into a curious line. "Why not Carapace?"

Ashes leaned back, trying to capture the way that Ragged luxuriated. "He is wrong for this task. I need someone loyal *and* canny."

Saintly grinned dangerously. "Where can I find it?"

"The sewers," Ashes replied, maintaining a perfectly deadpan expression. "I am near certain it has been hidden somewhere beneath Bells Street, near the border of Lyonshire and Yson."

Saintly's face went pale. "It's powerful?" he asked. "Won't others be looking for it?"

"Not if we move swiftly," Ashes said. "And if we refrain from speaking on it henceforth. So far I have discouraged any from seeking it, but if any were to suspect I am not keeping to my word . . ."

"Right," Saintly said, nodding and tapping his nose. "Right, milord. I think I have the right of you. You want me to start now?"

"Stay here only long enough to appoint a leader in your absence, and then begin your search." Ashes wondered idly what path Saintly would choose there. If he picked someone canny and fierce, his own power was in danger . . . and if he picked some-one weak, the Broken Boys would be hamstrung. Either way it would harm Ragged's power. "You will know the thing when you see it. Find it for me, and you will be appropriately rewarded. And Saintly . . ." Ashes dropped his voice a little further, making it smoky and fearsome. "If you should speak of it again, understand it will be the last use of your tongue."

Saintly bowed and grinned. "Of course, sir."

"See to it, then."

Saintly whirled around and swept through the door. Ashes made a mental note to stow something down there. Next week, perhaps. It'd be a shame to let Saintly succeed too quickly.

He waited until he heard Saintly shut the door, and then waited another minute. Then another. When he felt certain he would no longer be interrupted, he exchanged the ring for his shadow-bound cloak, retrieved his pack, and set to creeping about Ragged House once more.

It boggled him to think that he had been here barely three months ago. The boy who had hidden in Ragged's closet felt so far away—he had been scared, desperate, powerless.

He had changed. Ashes wasn't cowering anymore. He was an Artificer's apprentice. He could wear a face as easily as a hat, be invisible when he needed to be. Ragged *should* fear him.

He stopped at one of the portraits of the old, sour-faced men. Grinning, he took a tiny pebble from his pack, held it in an open palm, and touched the painting with his free hand. His eyes closed, and he let out a breath. A close observer might have noticed some-thing faint and ghostly seep out of the stone, snake along Ashes's body, and settle on the portrait. But the only close observers were made of oils and canvas, and they saw nothing.

From time to time, as he walked through the house, he would repeat the process, taking something small out of his pack and transferring its Artifice to something in the house. Books, mirrors, table legs, armrests, silverware. Anything Ragged might touch personally, or breathe on, or be close to.

William would have called his constructs *evanescent*; nothing held them together but their Anchors. At a touch, the Anchor would release a fragile image, one that would vanish in an instant. They were rather costly to make for someone who could not manipulate raw light—Ashes had used up nearly six phials of aether-laced light. Jack would chide him, no doubt, when he discovered how much Ashes had used up for "practice."

It would be worth it, at any rate. He wasn't skilled enough to key the Anchors to Ragged specifically; they would release their illusions whenever a living person came close enough. Some would be wasted on Carapace, but Ragged would see dozens.

He'd started by crafting images of Ragged's death. Hanged, shot, stabbed, beaten, trampled by a horse, cut open, hobbled, beheaded, torn into dozens of pieces. It had taken him a long time to run out of ways to imagine Ragged's corpse. When he did, he made faces the Beggar Lord would recognize: Iames the Fool, broken and destroyed. Mari, lifeless under Saintly's wild knife. And Bonnie the Lass, living and furious. Her face was contorted, one hand outstretched. He liked to think she looked prepared to demand Ragged's death.

If Ashes was clever, and quite lucky, Ragged would still be finding these for weeks. Seeing his own death, seeing deaths he'd caused. If everything went reasonably well, Ragged would not sleep soundly after this week. If Ragged did not already see his victims in dreams, he would soon.

Ashes made his way upstairs. He had never visited this portion of Ragged House before, save the night he'd stolen Ragged's face. He would have expected it to be larger, perhaps grander. That was Ragged, though. People would see the first floor, so it had to be extraordinary. The only ones who saw the upstairs were him, Carapace, and—

He cut off that line of thought and made directly for Ragged's bedroom.

He held Tom's knife in one hand, ready to strike if anyone stood guard at the door. But he found no one within. Smiling, he set to work. He bound images to Ragged's bedroom with wild abandon, glorying in the thought of Ragged's reaction. He bound illusions to the mirror, the shaving razors, several of Ragged's jackets and vests and watches and spectacles . . .

In fifteen minutes, he had exhausted nearly all of his Anchors and all the obvious places to hide them. He looked around for something else to use, and spotted Ragged's bedside table. He recalled his last visit here, and felt a wicked smile play across his face.

Three more images of Ragged found their home in the magazines. Ashes entertained the thought of Stitching some of the pictures to resemble Ragged, but transferring two dozen constructs had him hovering on the edge of exhaustion.

He shut the drawer roughly, and heard something *clunk* inside it. He paused. There had been nothing but the magazines inside that drawer, he was sure of it. Had he dropped one of the pebbles inside?

He opened it again to make sure, holding his Artificer's lamp over the drawer to inspect it. He saw none of his erstwhile Anchors inside.

Something tickled at the back of his mind. He tried the third drawer, and found it locked as it had been before.

Any sensible housebreaker would pick the lock immediately, sensing important things hidden in the third drawer. Really, the first rule of robbing an unfamiliar place was to find the thing with the biggest, sturdiest lock and break it open. Nine times out of ten it held the most expensive items in the house.

But Ragged's mind was a strange, twisting, profoundly cautious thing. It had to be. He ruled a district of petty thieves and marauders. His direct superiors were Bonnie the Lass and the

Ivorish magistrates: he was surrounded by thieves, above and below and beside. If he had anything valuable, it would not be hidden behind locks . . .

Ashes scooped the magazines out of the drawer and set them carefully on the bed. Half expecting someone to burst through the door or for something venomous to snap at his hand, he explored the drawer with his fingers, searching for incongruities, for something out of place—

*Ah.*

He lifted the false panel from the bottom of the drawer and held his lamp closer, feeling deeply satisfied. Of *course* Ragged would keep valuables here. The locked drawer would have some sort of trap, no doubt.

Something sparkled at the bottom of the drawer. A ring, made of pure and perfect glass.

Ashes snatched it out of the drawer before he could think better of it. He turned it in the light, and caught its reflections dancing along the wall. He ran his fingers along the edges, feeling for the telltale energy of Artifice inside, and thought, just for a moment, that he felt something thrum within.

How could Ragged have one of these? He was powerful, certainly. He had authority over a full district, as the High Ivories did in Lyonshire, Boreas, Yson, and Ubärsid. But he was a mere Denizen. There was nothing Ivory in him, not in his bones. He dressed like one and spoke like one and pranced about pretending he had their blood, but the man was as mundane as the soles of his shoes. Had he stolen this? He had more than enough thieves at his disposal, even for something as audacious as robbing an Ivory Lord . . .

Another possibility pricked the edges of his mind. He pulled off his ring, not wanting to pollute the glass ring's construct. Then, with an odd sense of reverence, Ashes slid the ring over his finger and looked in the mirror.

And he laughed.

There ought to have been a brilliant face staring back at him. There ought to have been the subtle weight of a light-mask settled on his features. But the face looking back at him had none of those things: it was only his face, wearing a wild grin.

"Oh, Ragged," he muttered. "You pathetic old weasel."

Not a magic ring. There was no Artifice in it. It was only a mimicry, an affectation. Something for Ragged to put on when he wanted to feel important. Not to be worn outside his rooms, perhaps . . . not where anyone could see him wearing glass and looking just as plain as anyone. It was like the magazines, like his hat, like his house. *Oh, Faces.*

*Wanting is weakness.*

Hiram Ragged wanted to be Ivory. He wanted it so bad he kept a meaningless trinket hidden in the safest part of his house, so he could wear it in private, with no one knowing. Ashes hadn't realized just how deep that wanting went till now. Ragged wanted this. He ached for it in his bones.

Ashes almost laughed. There was no opportunity to gloat, though, not here. Not while he was still standing in Ragged's house. Ragged could kill him here, no matter how weak his wanting made him.

He slid the ring off. Part of him ached to steal it, just to make Ragged that much more afraid . . . but no, it wouldn't do. Better to be a ghost tonight, and let Ragged worry over his sanity these coming weeks. It was not the time for thieving.

He set the ring beneath the secret panel, and replaced the magazines just where they had been. And then he left, quick and quiet as a shadow.

# 24

# *Manners*

"ARE you sure you want to do that, Ashes?"

Ashes stared at the board. It had gone rather fuzzy and slanted. He found, now that he thought about it, that he wasn't sure which color he was playing. White or black?

"I think I am," he said.

"It's just that if you do that then I'll have you in check in two moves," Blimey said.

"I think I'm not," Ashes said, setting the Queen back down. He studied the board with what he hoped was an intent look, then picked up his Tower and shifted it to the right. "How's that?"

Blimey smiled ruefully. "You've earned yourself a stay of execution. It'd take me three moves now."

"Anything that'd buy me more than five?"

"Not at the moment," Blimey said. His eyes danced.

Ashes blinked wearily. "So . . . d'you reckon I ought to play it out, or'd you prefer I fold?"

"You can't fold," Blimey said reflexively. "You only fold in card games. In chess it's conceding."

"How do you even know that?"

"I think you should play it out," Blimey said, staring pointedly at the board.

"Is that 'cause I have a chance of winning, or 'cause your winning won't be as satisfying if I show my belly?"

"I *would* say both, but your record would make a liar of me," Blimey said, his wicked smirk twisting features that hardly needed more twisting. Beside him, on a sheet of paper they'd cribbed from a book Blimey had lost interest in, was the record of wins and losses. To his credit, Ashes had won four games. Four games was not bad. It looked rather less impressive against Blimey's thirty-seven.

Ashes blew out a breath and moved his Tower, trying to push through his wearied thoughts to get a better look at the present. It was hard to do; he'd gotten fewer than three hours of sleep last night. If it had been the only such night, he likely would have been just fine. He was, however, swiftly approaching the eighth night running on little or no sleep. Even a gutter-rat in the prime of his youth couldn't go forever.

Last night had been particularly difficult. He'd spent it binding Stitched messages to the walls of Barrister's coffee house and the surrounding environment. Nearly every beggar, borrower, and thief in Burroughside got their coffee and sundries from Barrister; putting messages there guaranteed they'd be seen. He'd Anchored them at his own eye level, where the younger ones would be sure to see them. Only a few could read, but they'd pass along the message quickly enough: *Ragged's Going Up In Smoke.*

Partly it was a threat. Saintly's boys would see it, for certain, and the word would spread from there. But he hoped it would do more. Faces knew the kids in Burroughside needed a bit of hope. The thought of someone working to take Ragged down would be a bright one to many of them. They needed to know there were things Ragged feared. That he was only a man.

Blimey was staring at him. Ashes looked at the board again, vision swimming. "Is it my turn?"

"Eh."

He moved his Tower again. Blimey captured it with business-like efficiency. The game lasted a scant three minutes longer, and half that time was Ashes staring at the black and white squares like someone undead.

"You all right, Ashes?" Blimey asked. "You seem . . . really tired."

Ashes had told Blimey nothing about Mr. Smoke. It would only have made the boy worry: thieving and begging were easy, but waging a secret war against Mr. Ragged was something else entirely. Blimey would know better than to try to stop Ashes, but it would eat away at the edges of his mind all the same. Ashes had no intention of letting that happen.

"Just waking up, still, is all," Ashes said. Blimey gave him a flat look, one that said with eloquence and perfect silence, *Still waking up at eleven in the morning?*

"Maybe you ought to sleep a bit," Blimey said. "Your boss's going to have you do something tonight, eh?"

Ashes nodded, slumping against the wall. A nap would be excellent; in fewer than eight hours he'd be helping Jack rob an Ivory Lord. He could use a bit of sleep before doing the impossible . . .

"Neh," he said bullishly, shaking his head to wake himself up. "I have to meet up with them in an hour anyway, to get ready. Want to play again?"

Blimey gave him a concerned look. "Are you really up to it? You could sleep if you wanted. I can wake you up."

Ashes eyed his bedroll on the floor. Faces, it was tempting. "You sure?"

"Eh," Blimey said, giving a brave smile. "Probably best that way. I have better games with myself."

Ashes lay down, stretching out as languidly as a cat. "How's that, now?"

Blimey folded up Synder's chess set with great care and set it under the bed. He leaned against the wall and closed his eyes. "Don't need the board anymore," he said, more than a hint of pride in his voice. He tapped his temple. "I do it all in my head now, when I'm bored. Pretend I'm two people and play against myself. I usually win." His smile was big and delighted and would, perhaps, have looked charming on someone else. Smiling made Blimey look like a gargoyle preparing to eat someone.

"That's dead clever, Blimes," Ashes said. "I'm impressed. Really."

"I thought I should probably get good at it," Blimey said. Ashes noticed an errant note in his voice, something wistful. It wasn't far removed from the way he talked about being a gallant knight, or saving princesses. Ashes had learned to mistrust that sound.

"Sounds like you're talking about more than just passing the time," he said warily.

Blimey didn't respond for several moments. Then he said, "You remember how you used to play games with Ivories?" He paused—not waiting for a response, but steeling himself. "You said there's some kind of thing you do with them, when you want to take them for some money."

"Conning," Ashes said. "Eh."

"Well, I thought maybe I could try some of that," Blimey said. He was very pointedly not looking in Ashes's direction. "You know. Start to do a little bit more around here. I figure I could probably make a fair turn at it, you give me enough time. And if you make Glamours for me . . ."

"No," Ashes said. "No, Blimes, I don't figure that's a good idea."

Blimey gave a tight-lipped smile. "No. Yes. I guess not." He chewed on his bottom lip. "Why's it not a good idea?"

"'Cause I got the tar kicked out of me more often than I

didn't," Ashes said flatly. "Folks hate getting scammed. It insults them, y'know. It's not just you could beat them—you could beat them so easy you played around, like a cat messing with a mouse. Folk don't much like feeling they've just got played for fools by somebody that don't even have beard hairs yet."

"I wouldn't be *obvious* about it," Blimey said. "I could make it look convincing. Like I just won by a fluke."

"You got to be a good bluffer to do that sort of thing, mate."

"I could be clever," Blimey said, sounding faintly hurt. "You know I'm clever."

Ashes squirmed. *But you're just a kid, Blimey.* "It's a different kind of clever, that's all. I figure you're a damn good chess-player, but that's different from being good at cons. You gotta be able to read folks."

"Huh," Blimey said. "Eh. I guess you're right."

"Course I'm right," Ashes said, pitching his voice into something cheerful. "Blimey, you know you're clever, *I* know you're clever. It's just a whole different sort out there, you know? It's not about knowing words or playing chess. It's playing people."

"Eh." Blimey looked at him, finally. "If you say so." He was not convinced.

Ashes rolled onto his side, intending to go to sleep. He could practically hear Blimey thinking of arguments, but didn't press him. It wasn't a fight that Ashes particularly wanted to have at the moment. Better to sleep, if he could.

"Ashes." Blimey's voice wasn't confrontational. It sounded curious. It also sounded rehearsed. "Why are we still here?"

"What are you on about now?" Ashes said, more bitingly than he'd meant to.

"Just that it's been months," Blimey said hesitantly. "And—and I thought you were going to be looking for other places we could stay. Somewhere out of Burroughside, I thought. We can't stay with Annie much longer."

"I have been," Ashes said.

He could hear Blimey let out a breath. "No you haven't, or we'd *be* there by now."

Ashes stiffened. "The ruddy hell you mean by that?"

"I mean I've seen you *focused*, Ashes." Blimey was biting the ends off the words now, trying not to sound angry and failing. "I've seen how you are when you want something done. And . . . well, when you really want to make something happen, it does. Seems like you're not as focused right now."

"It's not like it's easy," Ashes snapped. "The Ivories have us trussed up good and tight. I can't get anything without an iron name—"

"Which you could've gotten," Blimey said softly. "You're clever enough for that, Ashes, don't say you're not."

"I just haven't—"

"And it's not like those are the only places in the world," Blimey went on, as if Ashes hadn't spoken. "Why aren't we staying with that Artificer? Your teacher?"

"'Cause I don't trust them," Ashes said reflexively. He wasn't lying; he liked Jack and his company well enough. He could at least say that Synder had kept her promise. But two months hadn't changed the truth: he wasn't part of the Rehl Company. He was hired help. Jack still hadn't even bothered to tell him what they'd be stealing from Lord Edgecombe. At first Ashes had suspected it was Jack's compulsion to improvise, but the Weaver had planned every other detail of the heist so carefully, down to what they'd wear and what doors they'd use to get in and out. Jack already knew what they'd be stealing. Probably Will did, too, and Synder and Juliana. Ashes was being kept in the dark deliberately. They didn't trust *him*, either.

"But you trust Annie?" Blimey challenged. "How d'you figure she's any better?"

"I don't!" The words came out louder than he'd meant them to, but he couldn't stop himself now. "Look, Blimes. I can't trust anyone with you but me, all right? And I don't trust Annie, but I know she hates Ragged as much as we do. I can't—I don't know the same about those Artificers."

"You mean you can't control things with the Artificers," Blimey said quietly.

"Yeah, maybe I do." Ashes huffed. "Look, Blimey, I just— I'm not going to let you get hurt because I made the wrong decision. I'm not going to do that over again."

"But why's it have to be your . . ." Blimey stopped. After a minute, Ashes turned to face him. The younger boy's mouth was tightly shut, his knees pressed against his chest. He looked so small. Fragile.

"I've just remembered," Ashes said, rising, "I think they actually need me there now."

"Best go, then."

Ashes moved to the stairs, and paused. "I *am* going to fix things, Blimey."

"If you say so, mate." Blimey was no liar, even when he wanted to be. He didn't believe Ashes at all.

Ashes's chest went tight. "And I'll think about what you said," he promised. "Might be we can get you out of here without needing those damned iron names. Trust me." It wouldn't be long before Ashes found a way to bring Ragged down for good. And with the Beggar Lord and his pet monsters gone, Blimey wouldn't need to hide anymore.

Blimey said nothing, and Ashes left.

● ● ●

*"I absolutely will not!"*

"You most certainly *shall*, young lady!"

"What about me makes you think that's a valid term? Am I not communicating effectively? Do I need to be more *explicit*? I have some thoughts on ladyship, your Ladyship—"

"Syndia Wellingham—"

"Faces' *sake!*"

Synder rounded the corner, light swirling in a wild maelstrom around her, and nearly crashed into Ashes. Her furious gaze landed on him, and just as quickly galvanized into the most affected parody of submissiveness Ashes had ever seen.

"*Pardon* me, sir, I fear I did not see you coming," she said, loudly enough to carry to the room she'd just left. "I worry that my teeny-tiny lady brain lacks the necessary *function* to identify my superior. Alas! But at least I'm pretty, and that will never ever *ever* change, and as we all know that's what bloody *counts!*" She stepped adroitly around Ashes, bumping him with her shoulder. She didn't seem to notice.

"Ware that tongue, Syndia!" Juliana's voice was as clipped and precise as ever. Albeit rather strained. Ashes realized, on balance, that perhaps he had come a little earlier than was entirely wise. He tried sneaking past the door, but Juliana's voice stopped him inches away from safety. "Roger! Do come in, I need to make certain this will fit you."

Ashes obeyed, looking around in astonishment at the state of the walls. Light played along them, shifting and twisting every moment. The swirling was strongest around Mrs. Rehl, who was holding his suit for the evening. He gave it a suspicious glance, then took it behind a temporary changing station in the corner.

"You've arrived rather early," Juliana said as he changed. "Nervous?"

"Bit jumpy," Ashes said, stifling a yawn.

"Tired?" Juliana gave him an inquisitive look.

"Floor's not particular soft, where I'm sleeping."

"Particular*ly,*" Juliana said. "We are attending an Ivory Lord's ball, Roger. It will not do to forget our manners."

"Right," he said. "Sorry. Is Syn all right?"

"Syndia seems to think her attire is a matter of distinct

moral importance," Juliana said. Ashes couldn't see her face, but he would have bet anything her mouth had gotten that pinched look it had when she was keeping her irritation under control. "Or perhaps she simply finds a great deal of purpose in iconoclasm."

Ashes paused in the act of buttoning a cuff. "She don't—sorry, *doesn't* like the clothes you picked out for her?"

The light on the wall swirled violently for just a moment. "Are you quite finished?" Juliana asked, as if he hadn't asked anything.

That was a boundary if ever he'd seen one. "Just one more button, ma'am." He stepped out from behind the screen wearing the miniature version of an Ivory's formal clothing. The suit felt like it had been made specifically to keep people from moving their arms, which made Ashes more than a little nervous. At the same time, though, they gave him a heady confidence, like being just a little drunk. He could tell without needing to look in a mirror that these clothes, and perhaps a little confident bluffing, made him nearly as much a Denizen as the next fellow.

*The next fellow*, he thought. *That's right. Not the next bloke, not when I'm wearing this. The next fellow.*

Juliana looked at him appraisingly. "Nearly there, I think," she said. "I'll need to hem it a little."

"If you say so, ma'am." He rolled his shoulders. "Feels like it fits just fine at the moment."

"You're going to an Ivory party, Roger," she said, giving him a gentle smile. "'Just fine' won't suffice."

He changed back into his old clothes, feeling all the more comfortable after the stiffness of the Ivorish clothing. He noticed, as he fixed the shadow-bound cloak around his neck, that Juliana was eyeing him strangely.

"Everything all right, ma'am?"

"It fits you well," she said. "That's all. Jack will want you in the laboratory, I imagine."

"Yes, ma'am."

"If you find Syndia there, tell her there is more to our work than idealism and moral stances, will you?" The Lady smiled sweetly. "And remind her that Ivorish women have a patron Face."

"Erm—yeah, I'll do that," he said, sidling out of the room.

It would be a lie to say he was surprised to see Synder and Juliana at odds. The Rehl Company's two women stood as far apart as light and dark. Synder spoke her mind, laughed easily, and had decided with almost no hesitation that she preferred trousers to dresses. Juliana could have held up the whole weight of Ivorish tradition on her own. The tension between them rarely did more than simmer—Synder's preferred method of expressing anger was biting sarcasm, a form of attack that barely grazed Juliana's emotional armor. Still, he'd seen a fair number of tiny fights between the pair in the last three months.

Jack and William were laboring intently over the table when Ashes stepped through the false wall. "You're rather early," Jack said, though his back was turned to the entrance.

"Didn't have much else to do," Ashes said absently. "Is Synder's real name Syndia?"

"I expect so," Jack said. "Will? It's been a while since I've used her full name, to be honest."

"Syndia Amalee Wellingham," William supplied without looking up. His face-mask turned his voice muffled and tinny. "Weaver, I need more aether."

"How've I been working with you a quarter of a year and never heard that name?"

"Perhaps you're not a particularly good listener? Here you are, then, Will," he said, passing a thin phial to the man.

"And who's the patron Face of Ivorish women?"

"Duty, I think," Jack said, leaning back from his project and looking at Ashes. "Something on your mind?"

"Syn and Juliana are going at it," Ashes said. "Looks to be one for the history books. Juliana's kicking up a whirlstorm in the other room."

"Mm," Jack said. "They've picked a fine time."

"Weaver, another dram—"

"*How* do you not have enough yet? Hold it there." Jack stood, wiping his hands on a cloth and moving to the cabinet.

Ashes followed him. "You haven't seen Syn, then?"

"We'd have noticed," Jack said. "Probably would have warped our construct all to hell if she'd visited. No, odds are good she's just off on a walk. She'll be back in an hour. A little calmer, if we're lucky." Over his shoulder, he said, "I'm only getting you a phial, you know."

"Bring two," William said.

Jack rolled his eyes as he slipped the key out of a pocket. "Satisfying folks is a fool's game, Ashes. Don't ever get tied up in it." He opened the aether cabinet, angling his shoulders to keep Ashes from seeing inside. Ashes felt a flicker of discomfort, but didn't show it.

"Juliana said you wanted to see me?"

"I did. I do," Jack said, handing William a single phial of aether. "I wanted to talk about your role tonight."

William stopped and stared at the phial. "This is only one."

"It's all you're getting." Jack leveled a warning finger at him. "I'll know if you take more. Just because I'm capable of interacting with humans doesn't mean I'm unable to do basic sums."

Ashes squirmed at that—he had used more than a few phials for his excursions into Ragged's territory—but Jack didn't seem to notice his disquiet. He steered Ashes from the library by his shoulder, then led him out of the shop.

"How're you feeling, lad?" Jack asked.

"Well enough," Ashes said, though at the moment he was

feeling rather nervous. It had nothing to do with the heist; did Jack know about the aether Ashes had been using? "A bit jumpy."

"That's to be expected," Jack said, not unkindly. "It's your first real heist, you're robbing an Ivory Lord, and you're doing it with a gang of magicians-cum-criminals you've only known for two months. If you didn't feel a little wobbly I'd worry for your sanity."

"Seems everyone's on edge," Ashes noted.

"You mean Syn and Jewel?" The Weaver chuckled softly. "I can see why you'd think that, but you're a little wrong. Our thievery isn't the cause of their argument so much as an opportunity to continue an old one, so to speak."

Ashes gave him a questioning look.

"Juliana and Synder are the most Ivorish people in my company," Jack said. "Will's as foreign as a spider in a teacup. Me, I was born so far down the ladder I had to stretch my neck to get spat on." He smiled ruefully at Ashes. "You know how that is, I'm sure. But Juliana and Synder come from the more dignified stock of humankind."

Ashes snorted, earning a wry smirk from the Weaver. "Odd thought, isn't it? Our genius is many things, and conventional is not one of them. It's always been a bit of a sticking point between her and Juliana."

"Why, though?" Ashes asked. "So she wears trousers. It doesn't seem that important."

"Trousers are the least of Juliana's concerns," Jack said. "She's far more annoyed with Synder's attitude."

Ashes looked at him, lost. "I don't understand."

"Hardly surprising." Jack's mouth twisted as he thought. He held out his right hand, as if presenting something. "Consider Syndia Amalee Wellingham. Outspoken, yes. Sarcastic, also yes. Brazen and bullish and headstrong, not particularly careful how she speaks. The girl's got very few boundaries."

*Damned right about that*, Ashes thought.

"Consider, on the other hand, my lady wife." Jack held out the other hand, and Ashes saw Juliana's face in it for just a moment. "Juliana is *very* Ivory. She's . . ." Jack paused thoughtfully. "Let me put it to you this way. When Juliana was very young, her grandfather was her favorite person in the world. Kept her company during her family's parties. Visited every week. When her pet cat ran away, he carved a new one for her out of wood, with his own hands.

"Her grandfather caught the wasting flu when she was eight. He didn't linger long. She cried at his funeral—not loudly, I think. Jewel's never been the sort to wail in agony. She did it quietly, so she wouldn't disturb anyone, but she cried. So her parents locked her in the closet. No food, no water. They let her out after two days."

Ashes's stomach turned. "Oh."

"She learned her lesson, all the same," Jack said bitterly. "Iron-clad composure, she has. No one will ever see her cry."

Ashes swallowed. "Wow."

"You're starting to see why Synder's outbursts are not her favorite thing," Jack said.

"Wow," Ashes said again.

"Don't focus on it overmuch, lad," Jack said. "This's not the worst fight they've had. It's not the worst fight they *will* have. For now the best thing you can do for anyone is stand out of their way. They work together when it counts."

"So they'll be fine tonight?"

"I have no doubts. They will play their parts as admirably as ever."

"You still haven't told me what we're lifting," Ashes said pointedly.

Jack laughed. "Would you like to know why?"

Ashes looked at him. He already *knew* why, didn't he? The Weaver didn't trust him. Ashes wasn't particularly angry about it; refusing to trust anyone was the first rule of survival. Besides,

Ashes *wasn't* trustworthy. He hadn't turned Jack in to the police or the Guild of Artificers, admittedly, but he'd used up a small fortune of the man's aether for his own purposes. Still, it would be churlish to reject the man's offer outright. He said, "Sure."

"I was a little worried you'd refuse to do it if I told you," Jack admitted.

Ashes narrowed his eyes. "Why's that?"

"It's just that it's rather important," Jack said. "My contact told me that Edgecombe keeps it hidden in the basement of his manor, locked up good and tight and surrounded by guards who can't be fooled by Artifice."

"The Iron Knights?" Ashes asked.

"Without doubt. Edgecombe could afford a fair few, I wouldn't wonder."

"What's so important he's got to—?" Ashes stopped. "You telling me what I think you're telling me?"

"It's interesting to note," Jack said, not looking at him, "that every Ivory family has a very specific number of them. And everyone knows exactly how many, too. It's a matter of historical record, for instance, that Lord Tyr's family have five. That the St. John's Woods have eight. And House Edgecombe, according to every record I've found, has three." His eyes twinkled. "Did you know no one's *ever* managed to steal one? People say they're cursed with witch-magic. Anyone who takes one without permission is driven irrevocably mad by the touch."

Ashes shook his head in wonder. "You're safe, then. Witch-magic couldn't drive you any madder if it tried."

"The mad ones have more fun."

"So, tonight . . . we're really going to . . ."

"Say it out loud, lad. Think about just how much fun it'll be to steal a magical glass ring from Lord Edgecombe *himself!*"

# 25 Conjuring

THERE was a fine line separating mansions from palaces, and Lord Edgecombe's home skirted the line with the boldness of an Ysonne whore. It could have swallowed Jack's house whole and still been hungry afterward. It was fully three stories high, with wings bursting out to the east and west, and gilt pillars and fabulously decorated stained-glass windows as wide and high as a carriage. The grounds over which the manor presided were themselves large enough to be a municipal park. One section was a grove of tall trees, dark and heavy as if they had been carved of stone. Another was a vast garden bursting with every color that could grow from the ground, and several that couldn't: where botany faltered, Artifice soared. Deep in the center of the garden-maze, a clock had been built into the ground, so large you could walk atop its face. At the start of each hour, the petals surrounding the clock changed colors, shifting from violet to red or from blue to green.

A clever Artificer would deduce that a dozen constructs had been cunningly bound to the clock's gears. A cleverer one would realize how much time, energy, and aether was required for what was, essentially, a party trick, and then make his services available to Lord Edgecombe with all speed.

On the night of Lord Edgecombe's celebratory ball, there were some thirty such Artificers in attendance, and each in turn made their begrudging way through the garden of shifting flowers. They shared the same bitter thoughts. Any contract with an Ivory was a high prize. But Edgecombe was one of the Lyonscourt, commander of nearly a fifth of the Lyonshire police, burdened with a dozen dozen mercantile contacts who all ached to please him, and a fortune to rival any ten merchants'. An Artificer who could claim Edgecombe's patronage was secure for the rest of his days. None of the Artificers who passed the gardens had been so favored. Their looks of envy could have scorched iron.

The sights within the house were, if anything, even more impressive. Edgecombe had gone thirty years without an heir—a true-born one, at least, if the rumors were to be believed. Thirty years of pent-up excitement had been released all at once, and it had aged like fine wine.

Each of the high Ivory families had been invited, as well as the Denizens who had climbed high enough on the ladder to lick the boots above them. Everyone was arrayed in their finest, and in Teranis, one's finest was a high bar indeed. People had come wearing masks like noble beasts, and dresses that glittered as if they contained the midnight sky, and billowing cloaks with Woven darkness in their folds. Violet-eyed gentlemen danced with platinum-haired ladies. There was not a single face in the crowd that could not be called elegantly beautiful.

Not wanting the party to die in its infancy, Edgecombe had made a formal request to the police that the curfew be suspended for the night. It meant very little—the greater Denizens and the

Ivories obeyed the curfew by accident more often than by intent—but it sent a clear message that the Harcourt Lord intended for his revel to be one his peers remembered. And it would *certainly* be that.

Relaxing the curfew, opening his house to anyone, forbidding the use of iron by any of the staff: Lord Edgecombe may just as well have hung a sign on his door that said *Rob me, please.*

And Jack's company was eager to please indeed.

**● ● ●**

*Ashes felt stupid.* Worse than stupid, noticeable. There was nothing worse for a thief than being noticeable.

He rubbed the bottom of his shirt for the fifth time, sharing an aggrieved look with Synder. Juliana had seen to their costuming for the evening. Ashes was dressed in the most appropriate of Ivory fashions: a dark-gray vest over a white shirt, with a bow tie over his throat that felt like a perpetual, gentle strangling, a tightly fitted suit jacket, and pants that were stiff enough they felt they ought to creak. Worst of all were the shoes, which sloped upward in the middle so that they dug into the meat of his foot, and produced an irritating *clack* when they touched the ground.

Synder had it worse. Juliana had trussed her in more garments than Ashes could readily name, along with what Synder had taken to calling her "painted doll face," a Stitching that William had bound to a pin she held in her hair. It made her look far more Ivorish than normal, softening her harsher features and widening her eyes. She loathed it. Out in public, she was managing to keep a stiff upper lip, exhibiting the Ivorish talent for swallowing one's own opinions. That had not been the case back at the shop. Her response to Juliana's wardrobe selection had been thunderous, but the doll face turned her downright volcanic.

Jack and Juliana, true to form, looked like minor gods. Jack strode around in his stiff finery—the adult version of Ashes's outfit, though it looked far sleeker on Jack—as smoothly as if he'd been born to it. Juliana looked radiant as ever, gliding through the party in a dress as blue as the sea in summer. William would likely have been just as uncomfortable as the children, had he been present. The Wisp had been tasked with watching over the shop.

"How d'you figure he does it?" Ashes muttered as they left the garden, aimed for the ballroom inside. "Jack?"

"Do *what*?" Synder asked in low tones.

"Look like he belongs here." Ashes inclined his head at the man.

"He's a good liar," Synder whispered with a shrug. She went abruptly rigid, and muttered, "Watch out."

"Mr. Beauchamp!" Jack said gregariously. The man approaching was large, almost ridiculously so: six and a half feet tall, at least, with broad shoulders and a slight paunch. He had a soldierly look in his bearing, though it was much decayed. "Always a delight to see you."

Mr. Beauchamp eyed Jack with what Ashes had come to recognize as Ivorish scorn. The look was polite—Denizens were always *polite* to their equals—but behind his eyes Ashes could see derision, annoyance.

"Mr. Rehl," Beauchamp said, shifting. Ashes caught a flash on the man's breast, a burning spark wrought in deep gold. "What a surprise to see you here. I would have thought you busy with other pursuits."

"When an Ivory Lord opens his doors, there are no other pursuits," Jack said with a dangerous grin. "I don't believe you've met my little cohort here. This is Roger Dawkins, my nephew"—he gestured at Ashes—"and Syndia Wellingham, my prize pupil. And you've met Juliana, of course."

If Synder's warning hadn't set Ashes on edge, the man's response would have. He made a tiny, deliberate shift in his stance, so that Juliana was not even in his line of sight. He inclined his head toward Synder and Ashes.

"A pleasure, I'm sure," he said. "I had no idea you had family, Mr. Rehl."

"I'm a man of many secrets," Jack said. Something in his voice had changed; there was less of the smooth confidence and bravado. He sounded blustery and hollow. "Best of evenings to you, Mr. Beauchamp."

Ashes stared daggers at the man as he walked away. "Who the bloody hell does he think—?"

"*Language*, Roger," Jack said sharply, setting a hand on Ashes's shoulder. "Best not to worry about it for now."

Lord Edgecombe's ballroom was vast as a church inside. Tables lined the edges of the room, leaving a great space in the center for dancing, though at the moment it was filled mainly by Denizens talking. Jack led the company to seats at the edge of the room, deftly avoiding any further conversations. Less than a minute after they sat, a snappily dressed server brought them trays of food, then flickered back into the crowd.

"So what was that?" Ashes demanded in a low whisper. "With that Ivory?"

"Not an Ivory," Jack said softly. "Artificer, and quite an important one, too."

Ashes looked at Synder in confusion. She indicated the golden pin over her heart. It resembled Beauchamp's pin vaguely, though the circle in its center was larger. "It's the pins," she muttered. "Apprentices have suns, journeymen have stars, and so on. Beauchamp has a spark—the only higher Artificers are the Guild Council."

"Right, but what sort of bastard is he?" Ashes asked. "Snubbing Juliana like that."

Jack and his wife shared a secretive glance, and Juliana smiled. "You've picked up more Ivorish than I thought, Mr. Dawkins."

"Mr. Beauchamp is Juliana's—oh, bugger, sixth cousin? Eighth?"

"Language, Jack," Juliana said softly.

"But which one?"

"Mr. Beauchamp is my third cousin," Juliana chided.

"So what's he doing snubbing you?" Ashes demanded.

"My family and I have had . . . disagreements," Juliana said. "It's complicated. Mr. Beauchamp is firmly allied with my parents in our dispute."

"And it's not polite to pry," Jack said, tipping Ashes a warning glance.

Ashes bit down on the questions bubbling to his mouth and directed his attention to the party. He had seen crowds of Denizens before, but never quite like this. It wasn't simply that they were finely dressed. They looked *different*. Wilder, stranger. Their cheek-bones were sharper, their eyes brighter. No one had come tonight without some form of Artifice to make them more alluring.

Some were not simply beautiful. He saw one woman with a face like a cat's, small and delicate with a predator's eyes. A man sitting at a nearby table reminded him, inexplicably, of a stag; Ashes had to check twice to make sure he did not have antlers. He saw a trio of women with flashing violet eyes, and crimson streaks in their hair. He guessed they were meant to evoke a coven of witches, though they were far more glamorous than the witches in the stories he'd heard.

"Ah, Mr. Bloom," Jack said beside him. "So delightful to see you here."

"Likewise a pleasure, Mr. Rehl," said Elleander Bloom. "Have you room? It would do a man good to rest his feet."

"Please," Jack said.

Ashes turned away from the party, keeping his face carefully under control. Elleander Bloom sat across from him, wearing an expression of cultivated boredom.

"I wouldn't have expected you here tonight, Mr. Bloom," Jack said politely. "Lord Tyr has your patronage neatly sewn up, does he not?"

"He does," Mr. Bloom said, making a study of his fingernails. "As such, I am relieved of the need to fawn and prostrate myself before the Lord Edgecombe Almighty. Milord Tyr is a friend to him, though, and thus . . ." He gestured grandly at himself. "Here I sit."

"The woes of the terminally employed, Mr. Bloom," Jack said, lifting a glass. "There are worse problems to have."

"Is that what brings you here?" Bloom's gaze flicked over Ashes and Synder, lingering just a moment longer on Synder's golden pin. "It's a shame for Artificers to grovel, Mr. Rehl."

"But a greater shame for Artificers to starve," Jack said, smiling gently. Ashes swallowed a laugh; the toothless sycophant Jack had suddenly turned into was as unlike his teacher as anything could be. It was like seeing a dragon transform into a tabby cat. "And, as I've recently been confronted with another mouth to feed . . ."

Bloom's stare landed heavily on Ashes. "Who are you, boy?"

"Roger Dawkins, sir," Ashes said, summoning his best humble demeanor. "Mr. Rehl's my uncle, sir, and I'm staying with—"

"Are you teaching him?" Bloom said abruptly, turning back to Jack. "I hadn't heard you were taking another student." His eyes glinted.

"Not at all," Jack said. "I hold out hope that he'll carry on the family business one day, but I'm afraid he missed the registration deadline. It was a near thing."

"Tragic," Bloom said with a brittle smile. He glanced over his shoulder and rose dramatically. "I find I must be going. Best of luck to you in the groveling and prostrating, Mr. Rehl. If you manage to find a job, keep your valuables trussed up tightly. I heard tell of a pickpocket chasing Artificers. *I've* not been foolish enough to be robbed, but forewarned is forearmed. Wouldn't want your little family here to starve." His eyes flickered toward Ashes.

"I appreciate it, Mr. Bloom," Jack said. "Do enjoy the party."

Bloom grunted something vaguely affirmative and vanished into the crowd.

Ashes waited until the man was out of earshot before he muttered, "I think he might've recognized me."

"Not terribly likely," Jack said. "Bloom's not canted. You can usually tell with those types—if they *did* have the cant, the whole world would know about it."

Ashes nodded, though he didn't feel particularly reassured. "What was that about me missing registration?"

"Jack has to register new students with the Guild when he takes them on," Synder said. "So they can test them for aptitude."

"And so they can keep tabs on everyone," Jack said. "The Guild keeps records on all their Artificers. Iron names, true faces, whether they're canted or not. It's all very formal and annoying. You wouldn't have liked it."

"The Guild administers a trial at the New Year," Juliana said. "Those who pass continue their apprenticeship. Those who don't are hobbled."

"You *really* wouldn't have liked it," Jack said. He perked up. "Ah. I do believe this party's about to get started properly."

"Attention!" a loud voice called. A chamberlain stood on a raised platform near the bottom of the stairs, looking proud as a priest on Chiming Day. "The Lord and Lady Edgecombe."

An Ivory Lord and Lady stood at the top of the stairs, arm in arm, their faces outshining the lamps. The Lord was easily six feet tall, and looked like he could have walked out of a portrait. The Lady was similarly gorgeous, and quite pregnant.

As one, the party guests faced the Lord and Lady and bent the knee. As the Ivories descended the steps, some of the crowd bowed even lower, pressing their faces against the ground or lying entirely prostrate. Ashes watched in bafflement. Even those who had stayed on one knee looked . . . *rapt*. They were awed. Some had tears welling in their eyes. What on earth?

He turned to Jack, wanting to ask what was going on, but

paused. Jack wore the same adoring, reverent expression as everyone else. It was the same with Synder and Juliana.

"Jack?" Ashes asked, trying not to sound worried. The Weaver didn't respond. "Syn?"

No sound from either of them. Ashes's heart thudded harder in his chest. Everyone in the room was transfixed but him. Why? What was going on? He would have to find out later. For now, he faced the Ivories and numbed his expression, trying to look as soft and mindless as the other guests.

Lord and Lady Edgecombe descended with ritual slowness. Halfway to the bottom, they halted, and Lord Edgecombe lifted a hand.

"Esteemed guests," he said. He did not speak loudly, but he didn't need to; there were no other sounds except rapturous breathing. "I am—so honored, to see you all here this evening. It means a great deal to see so august an assembly, and for something as dear to us as the arrival of an heir. I am—so very, very deeply touched."

Ashes's ears pricked. The man's speech was not unlike that of Elleander Bloom: polite on the surface, but brittle and fake. Bloom was by far the better actor, though. Edgecombe spoke about being deeply touched with all the earnestness of a decrepit priest—but no one seemed to care. Whatever enchantment lay over the room, it wasn't just drawing attention to Lord Edgecombe. It made his stilted speech convincing, too.

The Lord and Lady reached the bottom of the stairs, and on cue the doors at the end of the hall opened. The chamberlain produced a long list of names and began announcing the new guests as they entered: "Lord and Lady Tyr. Lord and Lady Duvale. Lord and Lady Lefevre . . ." They were all Ivories, though they didn't shine as brightly as the Edgecombes.

Ashes's attention wandered as the chamberlain recited the names, but Jack, Juliana, and Synder were still staring raptly forward, as if there were nothing else in the world but the beautiful people coming through the door. What had come over them? He nudged Jack's foot, but the Weaver didn't notice, or if he did he gave no sign of it.

There was nothing for it but to keep imitating them. If it was a sign of respect and deference, he didn't want to embarrass Jack's company. And if it was some sort of magic—a thought that became increasingly heavy as time passed and Jack continued to make no sound—then it could be very bad indeed if Ashes was the only one in the room whom it didn't affect. And why was that anyway?

The chamberlain reached the end of the list, and the crowd palpably shifted—like someone waking from a light sleep. Ashes, watching the Ivories' faces, saw the light dim a little. The music started up, and just like that the spell over the room was broken.

"Well," Jack said, as if nothing strange had happened. "I hope you're all quite ready for the next bit. We'll be moving in no time at all."

"Wait a moment," Ashes said. "You're not going to tell me what just happened?"

"Roger, you're family," Jack said jovially, "but you really must learn to control your questions."

"What just happened to you?" Ashes said in a low voice. "What happened to everyone?"

Jack looked at him, puzzled. "You've not seen an Ivory in person before?"

"I've seen them," Ashes said. "I just haven't seen folk drooling all over themselves at the sight of one, not that I can remember."

Jack laughed, low in his throat. "Interesting. But I'll tell you this, lad: there's a very good reason people say it's impossible not to love an Ivory. While you're looking at one, at least."

"I don't understand."

"We've better things to be worrying on, lad," Jack said with a broad smile. "Jewel, I have a sense that we ought to dance while there's dancing to be done, don't you? You two, be ready for my signal." With that, he took his wife's hand and whirled onto the floor. It was already teeming with Denizens, engaged in a slow, deliberate waltz.

Ashes looked at Synder. "Was he telling the truth? Ivories and people loving them and that?"

Synder's mouth quirked. "There's a law in the Teranis charter," she mused, "about how anyone who refuses to bow for a passing Ivory was to be seized, tried before the Queens, and then hanged publicly."

"That's a buggery law," Ashes said acidly.

"It's very silly, for certain," Synder said, still reflective. "I remember when I read it, I thought it was like someone writing a law that any rock that didn't fall to the ground was to be sentenced to death. Why make a law like that, when it happens anyway?" She shrugged eloquently. "I mean, people can't help themselves. When a Lord walks into the room, they're sort of the only thing there, aren't they? Everything else gets kind of . . . gray."

Ashes shrugged. "You read that?"

"When I was eight," Synder said. "I wanted to be a solicitor. I was very precocious."

Ashes blinked at her, but the girl didn't blush. She was staring at the dancers with something bordering on longing.

"It's not magic, though. Not Artifice," he said, mostly for something to say.

Synder shrugged and tucked an errant strand of hair behind her ear. "Silly assumption. Artifice is all about changing the way people see things. What the Ivories do could be an application we haven't really studied."

Ashes scoffed, though not loudly; something in the atmosphere, in the ballroom and the music and the dancing, made him want to be quiet. "How much is there left to study? It's shaping light."

Synder smiled mysteriously at him. "You sound terribly confident."

"Why not? That's what it is."

"Then why are Stitchers different from Weavers?"

"Eh?"

"Stitching and Weaving shouldn't be particularly separated," Synder said. "If they're both just moving light around, that is. But they're different breeds entirely. Stitching looks different to a seeing-stone. Stitching can manipulate solid aether, but Weaving can only affect it when it's liquid. They *seem* to affect the same substance, but they don't, not really." She flexed her fingers, as if preparing to snatch light out of thin air, and then thought better of it. "Weaving puts a mask on the world. Stitching convinces the world to change."

"That's almost how Jack said it. Stitchers treat the world as a canvas."

"He's full of little quips," Synder said. "Artifice is about more than manipulating light. It deals with *perception*. And Ivories do that." She shrugged. "Or maybe it's witch-magic and I'm talking stuff and nonsense. Who's to say, really?"

Ashes nodded. Silence stretched out between them, filled with stringy music and the rhythmic *shush-shush-shush* of footfalls. "Do you want to dance?"

Synder turned to him, horrified. *"What?"*

"Dancing," Ashes said, gesturing toward the swirling mass of Denizens on the ballroom floor.

"I—" Synder closed her mouth and then turned away. "No. Sorry. I keep forgetting what you don't know."

"What're you on about?"

"Me dancing," Synder said. "It'd be . . . inappropriate."

Ashes stared at her. "You wear trousers."

"More inappropriate than usual," Synder said. "Girls my age aren't allowed to dance. It would be a step past wearing trousers or wanting to study law. Several steps. Juliana would rip all the light out of the room herself."

"If you say so," Ashes said.

The dance continued, transitioning to a slow and elegant waltz. Jack and Juliana were lost among the crowd. Everywhere Ashes looked he saw illusory faces—strange and wonderful and gorgeous. When the song ended, he shook himself, embarrassed at how hypnotized he'd been.

"How's Nathaniel?" Synder asked.

"You know that's not his real name," Ashes said. "He got that out of a book somewhere." *Probably.*

"It's what he likes being called," Synder said. "There's no harm in it."

Ashes shook his head. There *was* harm in it, though not for any reason Ashes could properly articulate. He had his doubts about Blimey being *rasa*; always had. The boy knew too many things. It followed, then, that Blimey was only pretending, either because he did not want to be found or because he wanted to forget what lay behind him. Calling him Nathaniel could only dredge up memories best left buried.

"Dead silence from you, Roger? I think I must have said something really brilliant."

"You don't understand," Ashes said.

"I understand just fine," Synder snapped. "I understand you've got him imprisoned because you think it's for his own good. And I understand—"

"You don't understand *at all.*" Ashes's voice had gone low and dangerous. "You don't know him, all right? You don't know hardly a thing about him. Stay out of my business."

"Why is it only *your* business?" Synder said.

Ashes opened his mouth to reply, and paused. "Say that again."

"I said, why is it only *your* business?"

The tone was right, he thought. And the words were nearly the same.

"You've been visiting him," he realized aloud, feeling his chest constrict. "You *have* been visiting him, haven't you?"

Synder flushed. "What? No! Of course not." But her eyes shifted, just enough.

"You—" Ashes's jaw snapped shut. "No. You know? Never mind. That's spectacular. *You've* been visiting him. You've probably been telling him things, too, haven't you? Like that he could come and stay with Jack and the company and that it's not right he's stuck in someplace so small. *Haven't you?*"

"Well—he shouldn't!" Synder said, eyes flashing. "He shouldn't be trapped there just because you think it's the only safe place!"

"*I'm* the one that's responsible for him—"

"*He's* the one that's responsible for him—"

"Ugh!" Ashes leapt to his feet. He rounded on Synder, feeling the anger in his chest burst out to flood his veins, to thrum in his bones. "That wasn't yours to do, Syn. Furies! All you Denizens, you think you can swoop in and fix everything, don't you? Gods, but you meddle. I'm sick to death of it." He turned and stalked away, snapping over his shoulder, "You'll stay away from him, understand?"

"Roger—"

Ashes did not respond. It was a tiny bit of fortune, he thought, that he was not a powerful Weaver like Synder and Juliana. Lord Edgecombe wouldn't look too kindly on someone mucking with the light in his ballroom.

The music had stopped. The dancers were vacating the center of the room. Lord Edgecombe strode into the emptied space, and Ashes felt a hush fall over the crowd again. It was magical, he was almost certain: anyone who laid eyes on the Lord went abnormally still. Their eyes dulled. They were aware of nothing and no one but Edgecombe, and the center of the room may as well have been the core of the world.

But it couldn't be Artifice, could it? The illusion over the Lord's face was obviously Woven. But making everyone in the room go slack . . . that was nothing like the light-magic Jack had shown him. Was it witch-magic? Jack had told him the Ivories received all their glass rings from the Queens; when one was lost or destroyed, the Lords petitioned the Ladies for a new one. It kept the Kindly Ones firmly in control. No Ivory had ever re-created the rings on their own; it seemed unlikely that it was for lack of trying. Why did the proud, power-hungry Ivory Lords bow to the Queens? Because without the Queens, no one would bow to the Lords.

Ashes stopped moving as well, trying to imitate the stiff posture of Edgecombe's admirers. He was angry with Synder, but not so much that he would ignore her counsel. He had no desire to be hanged, publicly or otherwise.

"It is my great pleasure," Edgecombe said—and he only had to raise his voice a little for it to carry through the whole room; no one else was even whispering—"to provide you with tonight's entertainment. My friends, the Lords Tyr and Sivern, have arranged for a *truly* prodigious display this evening. Both have been blessed by the Faces with true Artificers for sons. Today, for your enjoyment, they will present a Conjurer's Duel!" He lifted his hands. The people sensed an unspoken signal, and began to applaud as two young men strode into the middle of the room.

The duelists were pure-blooded Ivory by their clothing, which was velvety soft and reeking of money. The crowd surrounded them, forming an empty circle nearly fifty feet in diameter. The boy in Lord Sivern's green-and-black was built like a general, dark eyed, dark haired, with the cultivated paleness of someone who rarely worked beneath the sun. His opponent, wearing a stylish cape in Lord Tyr's colors, reminded Ashes powerfully of Saintly. He had the same effortless good looks—though who knew how much of that was Artifice—and the same confident, deceptive smile. He moved like a dancer, all lithe grace and precise steps.

An older gentleman stepped into the middle and held out small gold badges to the two Ivories. They pinned the badges to their chests, and the young Tyr passed one hand over his. A moment later it was bloodred and glittering, a bit of spontaneous Stitching that would have impressed even William.

Sivern scoffed as he Stitched his badge to match, then moved to the edge of the circle.

The space went dim as Sivern drew in a breath, gathering light to his fists. In a moment he was swathed in a bubble of shade, his hands shining like streetlamps in the fog. Across from him, Tyr smiled good-naturedly and turned so that his shoulder faced his opponent.

"Come on, then," he said, laughing.

Sivern drew still more light to himself, and in moments it looked as if he'd been eclipsed by a storm cloud. Ashes could see him laboring for breath, sweat beading on his forehead.

"You're going to pull a muscle," Tyr taunted.

Sivern threw the light. It changed as he threw it, shifting in color from pure gold to a raw, hungry red. It was fire, Ashes realized, just as it engulfed Tyr.

Soft cries came from the crowd. But the fire was an illusion, and dissipated to reveal a seemingly solid wall of ice surrounding Tyr. He was smiling broadly.

"You'll need to try harder, I think," he said loudly. Several people in the crowd laughed.

*He must've conjured that in a breath,* Ashes realized. He hadn't even seen him gather the light.

Sivern chuckled, too, but did not seem amused. He snatched a bit of light from the air, and threw a tiny burst of fire. Tyr stepped to the side. He plucked the meteor from the air, and in his hands it became a bolt of white-hot lightning. It surged back at Sivern, who crushed it in one massive fist.

"It's quite beautiful, isn't it?" someone said at Ashes's shoulder.

He whirled, startled, but the speaker caught him by the shoulder. "Relax, young Mr. Dawkins. I'm more friend than I'm foe."

"Who the ruddy hell—?"

"Oh, Juliana mentioned you had a bit of mouth to you," the man said. "Best that we keep a mind to propriety, young master."

Ashes turned around, slowly. The man behind him was not very small, but he seemed like it. His shoulders were turned inward, as if to add another layer of protection should someone try to attack him. He was clean-shaven from the bottom of his neck to the top of his head, and his eyes were bright.

"Who're you?" Ashes asked.

"A friend of your uncle's," the man said, winking so quickly Ashes almost missed it. "Desiderius Tullenedaram. You may call me Tuln, if it's easier. I was Jack's teacher when he was younger."

"Jack sent you to keep an eye on me?" Ashes asked.

"I think he must have suspected you'd get yourself in trouble if you separated from Ms. Wellingham. I'm sure I couldn't imagine why."

Ashes turned back to the Conjurer's Duel. Sivern was in a rhythm now, not bothering to see if one shot landed before gathering light for another one. He'd left long, shadowy trails in his wake as he moved about the edge of the circle, trying to land a hit on Tyr.

"What do you think of the Conjurer's Duel?" Tuln asked.

"I don't understand it," Ashes said honestly. "I mean, I get that it's supposed to be—well, it's like the Artisans, right? Our ancestors."

"Quite correct."

"What're the badges for?"

"A necessary concession," Tuln said, tugging a handkerchief from his jacket and coughing into it. "The Stitching is neither Anchored nor solidified with aether—it can be affected by other Artifice. An illusion striking the Stitching may damage or destroy it, at which point the duel is over."

"You sound sort of annoyed, sir."

Tuln nodded, looking absent. "Not annoyed, young man. Disappointed. To see a proud race aped like this . . . it almost wounds the soul, to think how far we have fallen from our ancestors."

"Is it true they could make things?" Ashes asked. "Real things?"

"Not all of them, no. The Conjurers could, as easily as our Weavers make illusions now. The Shapers, like the Stitchers, could change the world, but they changed it truly, not superficially. The Vanishers—well, but of course they are less relevant today."

"The Glamourists?" Ashes asked. "What did they do?"

"Strange things," Tuln said. "Very strange. Glamourist is a very modern term for them—in the histories they were called the Unmakers."

"They destroyed things?" That seemed to fit well enough. Weavers made, Stitchers changed; there was a certain symmetry to the Glamourists having the power to undo it all.

"It is difficult to say for sure," Tuln said. "The Conjurers and the Shapers had very straightforward magic: creation, manipulation. The Glamourists were . . . different. Their magic changes from story to story. In some they render themselves invisible. In others they turn away whole armies with a wave of their hands, leaving no deaths, spilling no blood." Tuln paled. "They could be . . . fiercely proud. They once wiped out a city for daring to ask them for help in a war. *Truly* wiped them out, mind. They were very thorough."

Ashes blanched. He looked back to the duel, though its details didn't register in his mind. A whole city gone?

"They had a great deal of political power, when they wanted it," Tuln said. "Religious, as well. At least one of the churches in Yson began as a shrine to them." Tuln shrugged. "One of the mysteries of our art, I'm afraid, and unlikely ever to be solved. The Glamourists are long destroyed."

"Shouldn't they have dissidents?" Ashes asked. "Like the other ones did?"

Tuln looked at him oddly. "Descendants?"

"Eh, that."

"They might have," Tuln allowed, "but the Glamourists were wiped out. None have been seen since the Chiming War."

Ashes met this statement with a blank look.

Tuln sighed heavily. "Someday Jack will appreciate the importance of passing on history. The Chiming War was the event that destroyed the Artisans, when the Kindly Ones took power. . . ."

Ashes's eyes wandered, and then abruptly stopped. Tuln kept speaking, but the boy could hardly hear him.

A cluster of Ivorish folk had formed at the edge of the room. They each had the haughty, reserved look of someone terrifically important. One of them was—

Ashes's thoughts jerked, at once very fast and unbearably slow. What was *he* doing here? He did not belong here. He ought to be in Burroughside, cowering in his bedroom, not at a party with a drink in his hand . . .

But it was certainly Ragged. His face was subtly different from the one Ashes remembered; he must have needed a new Artificer to render it from daguerrotype after killing Mr. Tremaine. The nose was longer. The eyes were darker.

How *dare* he? How could Ragged have the nerve to set foot outside his kingdom? He did not deserve to be careless. He didn't deserve to be calm.

No matter. Ashes would remedy it.

"I'm sorry, sir," Ashes said to Tuln. He wasn't certain if he'd interrupted the man. "I've just realized there's something I ought to do."

He gave a half-embarrassed smile and shook Tuln's hand. "It's been a real pleasure talking with you, sir," Ashes said as his free

hand found Tuln's handkerchief and teased it out of the man's
pocket. "I learned an awful lot."

"You're quite welcome—"

Ashes's head was pounding as he orbited closer to Ragged.
He felt his magic rise to him, burning like a fire in his chest. He
clenched the handkerchief in his fist and willed words onto it,
words as red as blood—

*Did you think you were safe?*

# 26 Vanishing

CANDLESTICK Jack watched. He was uncommonly good at watching, better than some might expect. From the dance floor, he could see nearly everything.

He saw an irritated Lord Edgecombe in muttering conference with his butler. He saw Synder sulking in the corner. He saw in glimpses, from the next room over, Tuln enticing Ashes with a history lesson.

And he saw, to his dismay, the moment when Ashes left Tuln.

*I'll owe Tuln a new handkerchief,* Jack thought.

Jack watched as Ashes came close to a group of minor Denizen politickers. He watched as the boy stepped close, terribly close, to one man on the edge of the circle, and carefully slipped something inside his pocket. The man did not seem to notice. No one, in fact, could have seen it if they were not watching closely.

Jack watched closely, and his heart sank.

"The boy's found his employer," Jack muttered to Juliana.

There was a flicker of worry in his wife's eyes. "It may not be that—"

"We can't risk otherwise," Jack said. "We have to shift our footing. We'll rearrange. You'll go with Synder. *I'll* keep watch over our little informant."

● ● ●

*Jack's signal flashed in* Ashes's eyes mere moments after he'd slipped the Stitched handkerchief into Ragged's pocket. Not a moment too soon. Ashes grinned wildly. Ragged would *fear* tonight. But he had to get moving.

Jack had expressed several times how deeply he hated *planning* his heists. Things had a spice to them when there was a genuine chance you'd be captured, imprisoned, and tortured to death. Even so, when the Weaver *did* plan things, he did not skimp.

In the last two months, Jack and Ashes had visited Edgecombe House in a variety of inventive disguises, all of which had been put together with ink and glue and false hair—risking the whole operation on a disguise that might fail at the touch of an iron doorknob would have been profoundly stupid. They had walked the space a dozen times, mapped it out in exhaustive detail, and memorized every corner they'd been able to reach. There were several blank spots on the map, but Ashes still could have gotten to the rendezvous point blind.

He undid his tie and unbuttoned his vest the moment he'd escaped the Ivories and their extravagant party. Furies, but it felt good to be able to breathe properly again. At the first opportunity, he stopped in a dark side corridor and stripped the rest of the fancy clothing off. Underneath he wore the clothes of a low serving boy, with Lord Edgecombe's sigil Stitched on the breast. He shoved the clothes into a corner, Stitched them to blend into the darkness, and was on his way again in mere moments.

It was difficult to keep from shaking with excitement as he hurried down the corridors, occasionally rubbing his face to set a layer of Stitching over his features. He stopped one corridor away from the kitchen, forcing himself to keep his breath steady. This was where the rest of the company would meet him, so that they could break into Lord Edgecombe's personal suite together by way of a hidden passage connecting the kitchens to the wing of bedrooms. If Jack's nameless informant was correct, it would only take a few picked locks before the Rehl Company went on their merry way.

He waited in the dark for several minutes before he heard hurried footsteps. He sequestered himself deeper into the shadow, making himself small and unnoticeable, until he saw the person rounding the corner. It took him a moment to recognize her; Synder was always harder to spot through her constructs than Jack.

"Here," he muttered. The girl turned, peering into the blackness, and stepped closer.

"You do a good job hiding," she said under her breath. Like him, she wore the uniform of Edgecombe's servants. Her disguise was far more intricate than Ashes's, though. She'd changed her hair to blonde on the way, and given herself a rather doughy, unimpressive look. It was a profoundly bland face, one that nobody would look at twice. Even at a time like this, her Weaving was as good as anything he'd seen.

"Are the others coming?"

"They'll meet us on the way, I think," Synder said. "Jack made some adjustments."

"I thought he wanted to plan this one!"

Synder shrugged helplessly. "A comforting lie, I'd guess. He does those sometimes. He and Juliana are staying for a few more dances and then they'll meet us at the doors to the wing."

"Fine," Ashes said. "Let's move."

Synder followed him wordlessly. Probably stewing on their

argument, although she didn't seem the type to stew. Even so, it would be a distraction.

"Oi," he said, looking at her. "There anything you need to say to me? Before we get started?"

She looked at him, and her mouth went tight. "No. Anything you'd like to say to me?"

"Just that I'd rather we not get hanged because we got stupid," he said honestly.

"I'm fine, Ashes." She sounded annoyed. He could hardly see her face in the gloom. "And I'll thank you to remember that this isn't my first time out of the shop."

"Fine," he said. "But I'm sorry for snapping at you, back there. I wasn't thinking straight."

"If you say so."

Ashes swallowed an angry retort and stepped around the corner, entering Edgecombe's kitchens. The great room was busier and far more frantic than the ballroom upstairs; he had trouble getting a sense of just how many chefs and waiters were running to and fro, carrying plates piled high with food and drink. All of them had the harried look of someone working very hard at not mucking things up.

Synder made an uncomfortable noise. "This is a lot of people," she whispered.

"The better for us," Ashes said. "Watch."

Ashes eyed the tables, seeking a likely prop, and snatched up a large plate full of food. Eyes forward, he moved directly for the passageway to the bedrooms. He heard Synder come up behind him, carrying another plate. He could sense her nervousness.

"Look right ahead," he muttered to her out of the corner of his mouth. "Look like you belong."

"Not my strongest suit," she whispered back, but he sensed her straighten. He felt a few eyes land on them, but so long as they kept their confidence, no one would challenge—

A cook stepped in front of them. Rather, a cook's belly obstructed them, and was shortly thereafter followed by its owner.

"Who might you be, then?" he said. It was not overtly hostile, but certainly suspicious.

"We're new," Synder said, voice shaking only a little.

"We're with Lady Edgecombe," Ashes said confidently. "She's got us bringing food to her rooms for after the party."

The cook surveyed the items they carried with deep distrust. "What on earth would the Lady Edgecombe want with a plate of pickled herring? And a chicken soup?"

"You ever met a pregnant lady, sir?" Ashes said flatly. "Lady Edgecombe wants pickled herring and chicken soup, she's ruddy well going to *get* pickled herring and chicken soup."

"Why was I not informed of this?" the cook demanded.

"She only just now realized she wanted them, sir," Synder said. Her voice was far steadier; it had been fifteen seconds and the cook hadn't figured out they were thieves, so she must have felt more assured. "You know how these things go. May we get on, sir?"

"Very well," the cook said. "See that you hurry."

"Certainly, sir!" Synder said, cheerful. She pressed Ashes forward, leading him swiftly to the servants' passage in the back of the room. "That was exhilarating!" she said under her breath.

"I thought you'd done this before."

"Only once or twice," she admitted. "But that's more than you!"

The passage curled to meet a staircase, which led them to a dimly lit hallway. They stepped quickly, abandoning the pickled herring and chicken soup at the first opportunity.

"Did he say which door to use?" Ashes asked.

"The southeast wing," Synder said. "I'm not sure—"

"I know where it is," Ashes snapped, then bit his tongue. "Sorry, Syn. This is getting ridiculous."

"Don't look at me," she said. "Jack's the crazed mastermind here."

Ashes checked around the corner before he turned. "I just don't understand why he's being so stupid about it. We all could've gone together—"

"What?"

"Back! Someone's coming!"

"Ivories?" she whispered.

"Not important, get to the stairs—"

"Wait, I can—"

She took his hand and yanked him toward the wall. Ashes found himself compelled to follow—the girl was surprisingly strong. She pressed herself against the wall and motioned for Ashes to do the same. He looked at her, trying to communicate his skepticism without speaking, but the girl's stare was firm and confident. He huddled next to her.

Two sets of footsteps came down the hall, moving slowly. Ashes could hear a man speaking, but his voice was muffled and quiet. His words were indistinct. His tone wasn't. The man was displeased, not quite angry but close to it.

Beside Ashes, Synder uncorked a phial of aether and made several swift motions. Something dark and nebulous formed in the air, floating above their heads. After a series of sharp, economic gestures, the cloud stiffened and straightened, becoming almost a wall. Ashes looked at her, questioning, but the girl didn't even notice his attention.

"You can't ask me to do this," said one of the people down the hall. This one was a woman, young and distraught. "It's not right. It's not *decent*."

"I wouldn't ask if it weren't of the highest importance," the man said with forced dispassion. "And you're overreacting anyway."

Ashes looked at Synder again, eyes wide. They would be coming to the corner soon. If she was going to do something, she would have to do it now—

"How can you say that to me!" the woman demanded, voice quavering on the edge of fury. "After—after . . . *gods!*"

"It's just that it's not as important as you think it is."

"Cleary *you* think it's important."

"No, you— I'm sorry, you just don't understand."

"You're an ass, is what I understand."

The sound of the slap echoed all down the hall. "Don't you *dare* speak to me that way, woman. Remember who I am."

Ashes felt Synder's fingers lock around his wrist, and heard the girl draw a sharp breath. The dark thing in front of them rushed forward, and vanished.

"It's not me, anyway," the man said after several quiet moments. "My father would never allow it. He's forbidden it, to tell the truth."

"Gods know we wouldn't want to disappoint your father," the woman said softly. Her fury was concentrated now, crushed to form a poison that laced her words.

"Very few can afford to." The footsteps halted. "Look. I'm sorry to ask it of you. Really, I am. But you knew how this would go. I never lied to you about that. These were always the rules."

"It's awful that you can be so . . . calculating about it," said the woman. "Didn't it ever mean anything?"

"It meant a great deal," the man said, with so little conviction that Ashes was not sure who he was trying to convince, the woman or himself. "I think, perhaps, that when this is over—"

"Don't say it. Don't you dare say it. Whatever *this* is, whatever has passed between us, I'm done with it tonight. This very moment. I've no interest in sharing a bed with someone so cold."

They stopped walking, mere inches from the corner. "Very well. I suppose I could not expect much better of you."

"Pity. I expected better of you."

There was a sharp intake of breath, but the slap Ashes had expected didn't fall. "Those words were ill-chosen, Bessie," the man said, very softly. "Very ill-chosen. You will not speak to me that way again. You will not speak to me ever again. Your employment here is over."

"You can't—"

"I can do whatever I damn well please, you foolish girl! Be silent!" The man paused, drawing a heavy breath. "I cannot abide your disrespect, but I do not hate you. You may return to your rooms. Take those things of yours that you can carry. I will instruct the chamberlain to furnish you with severance. And Bessie—I can persuade him to be generous. If you do the right thing."

"And if I don't?"

"Then I am truly sorry to say that I can be of no further help to you." He sounded about as genuine as a wooden leg. "Good night to you, Bess."

The man came around the corner, sparing not a glance for Synder and Ashes behind their shadowy curtain. He had the severe features of the Ivorish, but his clothes were a butler's. Ashes eyed him as he walked, looking for details as Jack had taught him to. Well-groomed hair, trimmed fingernails, clean-shaven . . .

Something wasn't right, though. Ashes couldn't put his finger on it. There were no obviously incorrect details, but somehow the man's face looked fake—and, at the same time, hauntingly familiar. Ashes hadn't met him before, had he? Perhaps on one of the reconnaissance trips he'd taken with Jack? No, it wasn't that. Wherever he recognized this fellow from, it wasn't here in Lord Edgecombe's mansion.

There was no time to dwell on it. A moment later, a pretty, somewhat plump girl came into sight. She stared after the butler for several long moments, looking like she was reining in the impulse to shout something after him. Ashes couldn't tell if she was crying. Finally, she turned on her heel and walked briskly down another branch of the tunnel.

"Come on," Ashes said when they were long gone. "I don't hear anyone else."

Synder dispelled the illusion, sweeping the light back into her phial with a single motion. Her hair was damp with sweat.

"You all right?" he asked.

"Brilliant," she muttered. "Come on. Jack and Juliana will be waiting."

● ● ●

*The lock on the* door sprang after only a few moments of dedicated effort, and Jack swept through before the thing was open.

"Less than exemplary timing," he whispered as Juliana followed, shutting the door behind her. "The two of you weren't ki—"

"*No!*" Synder snapped in a harsh whisper. "Sorry. We got held up."

"Keep your voice down," Juliana said coolly. "No harm done yet."

"What's the plan?" Synder asked.

"There's a *new* plan?" Ashes demanded. "I thought we were all—"

"No time for that right now, lad," Jack said. "Syn, you and Juliana will take the cellar. Ashes and I will take milord's bedroom." Synder gave Juliana a look too complicated for Ashes to understand, particularly when his head was already spinning.

"Cellar?" he asked.

"I've just said we have no time for questions, haven't I?" Jack gave him a sharp look. "Love, you have your equipment? Exceptional. We'll meet you back in the ballroom in an hour, not a *minute* more, and if we're not there get back to the shop. Step lively."

Juliana nodded. She and Synder exchanged a glance and then set off together, making for a staircase to a lower floor.

"Jack, what in all hell?"

"Quickly, lad, we're losing time. We can talk as we go."

"What's happening?"

"I had to make some adjustments to the plan."

"Why?"

"Because my contact said that Edgecombe has one ring he doesn't use, which he keeps in a locked room deep in the heart of his mansion," Jack said. "And my other, rather more secretive contact has said that Edgecombe keeps the ring his son will wear tucked safely in a hidden room near where he sleeps. His family have only the three rings—there's almost no doubt on that score. What's that say to you?"

"Seems . . ." Ashes paused, chewing his tongue. "Seems like one's got bad information. Or both of them."

"Agreed," Jack said. "And I've no way of figuring just which it is. Nor do I fancy the thought of passing up such an absurdly valuable take because of conflicting information. Thus, I split our little group."

"But why send Juliana and Syn together? They're hopping mad at each other."

"Doesn't worry me overmuch, for three reasons. First, Juliana and Synder are professionals. They won't let their standing irritation interfere with their goal. In point of fact, I wouldn't be surprised if being forced together for this doesn't quell things a little bit. Spring this door for me, will you?"

Ashes bent to get a look at the keyhole. "What did you do with locked doors before you hired me?"

"Mostly I wept at being foiled by mere strips of metal. It's really discouraging, as a master thief, to be confounded by something so small and insignificant." Jack grinned widely. "I'm joking. I walked through the walls. Sometimes I blew things up."

Ashes sighed. "Whatever."

"Secondly, I can't in good conscience send you and Synder together into the belly of the beast. Juliana's very passionate about propriety. I can't let the two of you cavort around darkened spaces without a chaperone."

"What's the third reason?"

"Third? I said two reasons. You ought to listen better."

The lock released with a soft *click*, and the door swung open. Beyond was an expansive sitting room, with a grand table to one side, and several ornate, comfortable chairs. One wall boasted an assortment of wine bottles, any one of which no doubt cost more than Jack's home.

Jack scoffed softly. "Huh. Lad, if I didn't know any better, I'd suspect this is where the vaunted Lord Edgecombe plays cards with his friends. Or whatever Ivories play when they're bored, I suppose. How about that?"

Ashes tried to imagine a group of Ivories sitting at this table, their faces shining fit to light up a cavern. Though, of course, they wouldn't wear their glass rings in private, would they? It would be so irritating, trying to speak to someone when you had to squint to look at them.

"Card games or skulduggery," Jack amended, moving across the room to the far wall. He tapped it lightly with a fist. "Mm. See? This wall is Woven. A handy little secret entrance for someone to enter through when they didn't want to be seen, I'd wager anything."

Ashes pulled his seeing-stone out of a hidden pocket. As Jack had said, the wall was false; the optic revealed a small door. There was a strange little hole in the corner as well, half as tall as Ashes. A trash chute of some kind, perhaps?

"Come along, lad," Jack said, moving away from the illusion-clad wall to the exit. "Time's wasting. Let's nab that ring, shall we?"

They entered a short hallway, which opened into a great bedroom. As they approached, Jack motioned for Ashes to wait, and buried his hand in a pocket. A moment later his face and clothing darkened, blending into the blackness around. A shadow-bound construct of some kind, and an impressive one, too. Ashes heard the Weaver's quiet footsteps, but could barely see him as he slipped inside Lord Edgecombe's bedroom.

Thirty seconds passed, then sixty. Nervousness started worming inside Ashes's belly. Were there guards inside? Edgecombe couldn't be *that* paranoid, could he? If they were Knights of Iron—

Ashes took one step forward, breath coming short, and just then Jack reappeared in the threshold.

"Just us in this cozy little space," he said. "Come along, lad. Another pair of eyes would do us good."

Jack lit up an Artificer's lamp as Ashes stepped inside. At this point, Ashes fancied himself pretty much immune to Ivorish opulence; he'd seen so much of it in the last few months, and more just in the last night. Even so, Edgecombe's bedroom made him want to stop and marvel. The bed alone was large enough for three or four people to sleep in it comfortably.

"Stones, lad," Jack said, lifting one to his face. Ashes did likewise, and they began their search.

Fifteen minutes later, after fruitlessly investigating every likely- and unlikely-looking cabinet, drawer, nook, and cubby, Jack scoffed and pocketed his optic. "We're not getting much of anywhere, lad. Time to get along."

Ashes looked up from the clothes he was rifling through. "We haven't searched everything yet."

"We've searched everything that matters," Jack replied. "No Ivory in Teranis would hide his only other glass ring in the pocket of a suit anyway. Know your enemy, lad. Ivories are like peacocks. Edgecombe couldn't bear to hide his magical ring anywhere mundane, and there's not a single Weaving in this whole damn room. Come along."

"Ja—"

Jack motioned sharply, cutting Ashes off. "No names, my young friend, not even when we're alone. Walls have ears."

"But what if it *is* here?"

"Then Edgecombe can keep it," Jack said. "He's outfoxed me."

Ashes followed Jack to the door, then paused. He took one final look around the room, his optic over one eye.

"Lad, we've got to—"

"Wait just a minute," Ashes said, darting to a stretch of wall just to the right of the vanity where Lord Edgecombe got dressed every morning. He reached above his head—just about where Edgecombe's eye level would be, he guessed—and closed his eyes, pressing his fingers against the grain of the wood.

"What are you doing?"

"Shh!"

*There.* Just a tiny flaw in the wood. Not worth noticing for most folk, but if you looked at it just right, it almost looked like a button. Ashes pressed it, and felt a square of the wood slide inward. There was a moment of increased pressure from the false wood, as if its back were pressed against a tiny spring. A moment later, the hidden drawer glided outward, just above Ashes's head.

"What in all the rotted hells?" Jack was standing next to him, watching in fascination. "How'd you figure that, my lad?"

"An Ivory couldn't bear to hide something valuable in a mundane space," Ashes said. "And, if I was Lord Edgecombe, I'd want to be able to check on my extra ring every day. I'd want to make sure it's there."

"Clever," the Weaver said, leaning forward to look inside the drawer. There was a sound like perfume being sprayed, and Jack recoiled like he'd been bitten.

"Jack!"

"Furies and hell!" Jack's eyes were screwed tightly shut. He pressed a hand against them, as if trying hard to concentrate. "Keep names to yourself!"

"Sorry. What happened?"

"Damn thing sprayed in my face," Jack said. "Gah! *Furies,* that burns!" He reached a hand out. "Get me to water. This is misery itself."

Ashes led the man to Edgecombe's sink in the adjoining bathroom, where Jack proceeded to splash water onto his face for nearly a minute. The Weaver's face was drenched when he finally stood straight, blinking furiously.

"Furied damn," he muttered.

"That was a very weird trap," Ashes mused.

"You're not wrong," Jack said. "My gods. I'll bet my eyes are red as a demon's. I'll need you to Stitch me up a bit, before we go back out to the party. You can handle that?"

Ashes nodded.

"Brilliant," Jack said. Out of nowhere, he broke into a wild grin. "Let's give that little drawer a more thorough once-over, eh? All in all, I feel that could have gone much worse. I'd have bet on Edgecombe to devise something a little more sinister than spraying me with perfume."

"It's not poison?" Ashes asked.

"None that I've any familiarity with," Jack said as they reentered the main room. "You'd think someone with Lord Edgecombe's money might put more effort toward protecting his . . ." He looked inside the hidden drawer and said, "Ah. Well. Bugger and damn."

"What?"

"Looks as though the jury's still out on whether Lord Edgecombe would divert more resources to protect his glass ring," Jack said grimly, motioning for Ashes to come closer. "As the little perfume-trap was not, in fact, guarding it." Jack pushed the drawer back into the wall with a disgusted noise. "Furies blast it all!"

Ashes's heart sank. "Damn."

Jack patted his shoulder. "Don't worry yourself, lad. It was very good thinking. Turns out that Lord Edgecombe considers his taste in cologne to be very privileged information, that's all. Any other drawers like this one in here, do you think?"

Ashes shook his head. "If he's using it for that, he's not using one for his ring."

"Fair point. Let's be on our way, then."

They left by the same hall they'd come in, moving silently. Ashes refused to let himself hang his head. Jack had been right; it *had* been a good thought. He reassured himself that in any other self-respecting Ivory's stronghold, it would have been a stroke of genius. It seemed Edgecombe was simply more concerned with personal hygiene than he'd anticipated.

They came again to Edgecombe's comfortable sitting room, and made swiftly for the door. Jack grabbed the handle, twisted it, and then swore softly.

"What is it?" Ashes asked.

"Locked," Jack said. "That's . . . rather odd."

Ashes heard something low and rumbling behind them. He turned.

At the far end of the room were three vicious-looking hounds, half as tall as Ashes. Their teeth were bared, slaver dribbling down from their lips, steel-gray hackles raised. They faced the door. Their muscular bodies were coiled, prepared to pounce.

"Jack . . ."

"Bugger," the Weaver said, yanking a handful of light to him. "Cover your—"

Ashes shook his head and pointed at the beasts' eyes—or rather, at the dark holes where their eyes ought to have been. The hounds were blind.

Jack swore softly and released the light. "If we're quiet . . ." he muttered. The hounds' ears twitched, and one growled again, low enough that it seemed to rumble inside Ashes's chest as well.

Ashes took a soft step to the left, careful to make no noise at all. The hounds inched forward, and Jack moved to the right, gesturing toward the secret door. Ashes nodded, heart in his chest, and took another step. The hounds' noses twitched again, and they turned toward Jack almost as one.

Jack met Ashes's eyes as they realized, together, just why Lord Edgecombe had hidden a bottle of potent perfume where there should have been something valuable.

"Run!" Jack snapped, just as the hounds leapt forward. The

Weaver jumped to one side, barely dodging two of them. The third crashed against his chest, knocking both of them against the wall. Jack and the animal cried out. The Weaver got to his feet first, got a solid kick into the beast's side, and dodged backward, only to find his back pressing against a wall. Two of the hounds edged forward, wary but vengeful.

"Get out!" Jack snapped. "They'll still be hungry when they're finished with me, I expect—gah!"

One of the hounds had dashed forward and leapt toward the sound of Jack's voice. The Weaver's reflexes were good, however, and the animal found itself with teeth lodged in the man's arm. Jack swore loudly as the second hound surged forward, getting its teeth into Jack's calf.

"Ashes—!"

"No names, sir," Ashes said as he snatched two bottles of Dorois brandy off the shelf. He sprinted forward. He swung with one bottle, striking the hound on Jack's leg; the animal yelped and fell backward, dazed. Jack screamed as the hound on his arm ripped and worried at it. Ashes swung the second bottle with all his might, striking the beast in the ribs. Glass shattered. The hound yelped and released Jack's arm.

An instant later, Ashes's nostrils filled with a potent, vile stink, strong enough to singe his nose hairs. All three hounds yelped and moaned piteously. He looked to Jack, and found the Weaver on his feet already. Ashes sucked in a breath. He could see bone poking through the mangled, red flesh. The Weaver limped toward him, and jerked his head at the hidden door in the wall.

"I think that perhaps we ought to skip the rest of the party," he said.

# 27     *Loss*

**K**EEP quiet," Jack said.

"What'd you think I was doing?"

Candlestick Jack grunted, but made no further reply as he and Ashes crept through the gardens of House Edgecombe. Grunts, in fact, were nearly all that Jack felt capable of making. Every step sent fire up his leg. He had spent years developing the focus he needed for Weaving, and it took every ounce of his mental strength not to cry out in agony every time his foot struck the ground.

*This'll need witch-healing,* Jack thought grimly. *Tonight, if I don't want to explain toothmarks to the Guild . . .*

"Lean on me," Ashes said.

"Damn fool thing to do, lad," Jack muttered. "We'll only end up on the ground."

"I'm stronger'n I look," Ashes replied, taking the Artificer's undamaged arm and setting it along his shoulders. The boy wasn't lying. With an effort, he held Jack upright, and they hobbled toward the edge of the estate with all the grace and coordination of a four-legged gargoyle.

"Buggery thing to have happened," Ashes opined as they walked. "What kind of Ivory keeps *hounds* for guards?"

"One who's worried about thieves who account for Iron Knights, I suspect," Jack said. "That was quite good thinking, though. The brandy."

"Figured it'd bother them at least as much as it bothers me," Ashes said. "It was lucky, really."

"Not at all," Jack said, biting back a gasp. "Quite clever. You saved my life."

"Don't go soft on me," Ashes said, smiling at him. "Just makes us even. Almost."

*Who is this boy?* Every time Jack thought he'd solved him, Ashes did something unexpected. It made no sense. He followed Jack into the sewers, tailed him to clandestine meetings, spent long hours scurrying around Burroughside to no discernible purpose—surely he *had* to be a spy. Surely.

Then why was he so loyal? Why did Jack feel such a powerful confidence that Ashes, whatever else might be said of him, would never think of betraying the company?

He didn't dare trust his intuition. Not with this boy, not if his guess was right.

"You falling asleep, Jack?" Ashes asked. "Only you haven't cracked wise for near a minute. You're breathing, eh?"

"Breathing, lad," Jack said with a soft laugh.

Mercifully, they reached the edge of the garden without incident. Jack was glad of the respite. He had no confidence in his ability to outrun or outfox a guard just now. Hidden deep beneath the foliage was a tiny entrance, presumably for the gardener to come and go as he pleased. It had no locks. Ashes and Jack hobbled through it to a Lyonshire thoroughfare not far from Harrod Park.

"We'll get a carriage," Ashes said.

"Not on your life," Jack replied immediately.

"You can barely walk!"

"I'll manage," Jack said. "We just have to get back to the shop. I can send for a witch from there. Being seen by a cabbie is the very last thing I'd like to do just now."

Ashes grimaced but didn't argue. *Good lad,* Jack thought. *Unless you're not.*

The walk to Redchapel Street was easier than Jack had expected. Rather, Jack found that when they finally stopped, he had no memory of the intervening time. It was blotted out, erased. His head felt weirdly empty, as if he'd been smoking opium.

"Come on," Ashes ordered, dragging Jack to the back of the shop. "Caution first, Jack, remember?"

"Of course," Jack said blearily. Had he blacked out? Or . . .

Ashes tripped the switch of the hidden door in the back and pulled Jack into the shop with grim determination. Jack found that he could not look away from the boy.

He had to speak with Tuln. Tuln would help him think about this matter clearly.

"Sit," Ashes ordered as they passed through the false door to the dining room. Jack obeyed wordlessly. "I'm going to get some bandages from William's surgery," the boy said. "*Don't* move."

"I'll be fine," Jack protested. "There's a witch—"

"And while we're waiting for her, I've no mind to let you get blood all over her Ladyship's chairs," Ashes said, sprinting through the door.

Jack waited, and while he waited, he thought.

*He may be true. He may be as loyal as he seems. He may be exactly what we need . . .*

The wiser voice, the one that always warned him when he had been too reckless or gone too far, disagreed. *This is all a ploy. He cannot possibly be what he seems.*

The thing that bothered him most deeply was that Ashes had more than enough information to see Jack hanged, if that was his goal. But the boy didn't seem concerned with Jack's misdemeanors. And if he was a plant for the Ivory Lords, and had betrayed them to Edgecombe, why would he save Jack from the hounds?

Too many conflicting stories. Too many possible conclusions. And Jack didn't dare trust what his gut told him.

Ashes returned with his arms full of bandages. Jack cringed to think of how annoyed Will would be, but Ashes seemed to have no concern for that. He began wrapping them around Jack's arm.

"Pull it tighter," Jack advised. Ashes obeyed, intent on the work.

Ashes couldn't be a spy for the Guild. It seemed he was not a spy for Lord Edgecombe and his cabal of intriguers. That left only a handful of possibilities, all of them frightening, and in every one of them Jack's next move was clear. In for a penny, in for a crown.

"Ashes . . ." Jack said slowly. "I do want to thank you. I'd be very dead if it weren't for you."

Ashes shrugged. "Can't learn Artifice from you if you're dead, Jack."

"Still," the Weaver said thoughtfully. "It was appreciated, lad. I try to overvalue it when someone saves my life. Keeps people inclined to do it more often."

"You saved mine. We're even."

"Very well. But you ought to know—the next time I give you an order, I expect you to follow it." He paused. "Obedience counts for a lot, when you're a member of my company."

Ashes looked at him, eyes wide. "What're you saying?"

"Nothing definite yet, lad. I wouldn't consider it a formal job offer. More like . . . probation. I've only known you a handful of months, so it's not as if I'd throw the doors wide for you, but . . ." He shrugged with his good arm. "You're still much too eager to gamble when you don't hold the cards. You still want to be clever when you ought to be smart. But folk can grow out of their flaws. There's a chance I could use someone of your talents on a more permanent basis."

Ashes caught his smile before it got out of hand. Jack stifled a laugh. The boy was so determined to hide himself.

"I'd have to think about it," he said.

"Of course, of course," Jack replied. "Sleep on it all you want."

The front door banged open. Jack and Ashes exchanged a worried look.

"Police?" Ashes whispered.

"I don't—"

"Jack!" came Juliana's voice. Jack relaxed.

"In the dining room, love," he called out.

Juliana and Synder appeared in the doorway a moment later. They were both short of breath, though it showed more in Synder. Juliana had already managed to collect herself. The composure shattered when she saw Jack's arm.

"What happened?" she demanded, sweeping forward. Ashes darted out of her way as she advanced on Jack. "Who did this?"

"A run-in with some mangy animals, love, nothing serious," Jack said. "What are you doing here so early? Why'd you leave the party?"

Synder gave him a confused look. "It's nearly midnight," she said. "We left with the crowd."

"Is it already?" Jack looked at the clock. "By the Faces. Right, then." He shifted in his seat and couldn't keep a pained scowl off his face. "What news do you have for me?" he demanded. "Do you have what we came for?"

Juliana and Synder exchanged a worried glance. "There were Iron Knights guarding the door," Synder said.

"And you—"

"We got around them," Juliana replied. "There was another way in."

Confusion flickered across Ashes's face. "And?" Jack pressed, eager to move on before Ashes asked the question on his mind.

"And there was nothing inside the room," Synder finished. "We looked all over, seeing-stones and everything. Nothing."

"There might've been some clever ones," Ashes said. "There was one that was Artificed to look like the hidden panel behind it, so even through an optic—"

"Juliana would've found it," Jack and Synder said together.

"Synder, take Ashes and send for a witch," Juliana commanded. "I must tend to my husband."

Synder pulled Ashes into the hall. Juliana picked up the bandages on the table.

"No gauze?" she asked.

"He's not a very experienced medic," Jack said.

"You found nothing?"

"Mad hounds and some truly pungent brandy," Jack said, wincing as his wife began to wrap the bandages around his leg. "Ashes saved my life."

"Such loyalty," Juliana said gently.

Jack's jaw clenched. "In any case," he said. "You found nothing. Ashes and I found nothing. And Will—"

"My timing, as ever, appears to be impeccable." William entered at the back of the room.

"You'd better have some good news for me, Will," Jack said. "I am in no mood for your wit, either. What'd you hear?"

William sat across from him. "I bring a mixture of good and bad news," he said. "The Lyonshire police have no evidence pointing to our company. There remain no indications that the Ivories have discovered our endeavors."

"Barring the mad hounds and the distinct absence of anything worth stealing, you mean."

Will inclined his head. "Barring those. But it seems that, as yet, you are not betrayed. Not by the boy, nor by your conflicting contacts."

"It bothers me to know that you haven't gotten to the bad news yet," Jack said.

"A message went out from Edgecombe House after you left," Will said. "It passed through quite discreet channels. I had to be quite cautious to catch a glimpse of it."

"And?"

"It seems that someone accomplished your goal first," Will said. "Lord Edgecombe has issued a warrant for the thief who stole his heir's glass ring."

"Which means—" Jack paused. "Damn. Which means we planned for three months, snuck inside an Ivory Lord's house, and I got my leg damn near ripped off for nothing." Jack let out a breath. "*Shit.*"

## 28 | Lass

THE night after Lord Edgecombe's ball, Southern Boreas lay in a deep dark, and even deeper fog. Light shone from the windows of the Court of the Lass. The mist gave them solidity, turning them from bright, distant stars into beams. You could almost reach out and grab them.

Within the warehouse, the Lass sat at her high table, surrounded by her counselors. Most looked dangerous, and those who did not were the deadliest of all. Her guards stood at the doors, armed and watchful. Her gun sat comfortably in her hand, even while she ate her supper. It fit her grip flawlessly.

Something small and glittering rolled along the floor. One of the guards spotted it, and cried out. He was not fast enough. The glass marble struck the leg of a chair, and the room exploded in a brilliant white flash.

Moments later, when everyone realized they had not, in fact, died, the room erupted into an organized panic. The big man seated at the edge of the table leapt to his feet, drawing a gun with the quickness of a serpent. No fewer than three of the Lass's personal bodyguards had short, wickedly sharp knives in their hands, poised to be thrown at the first obvious target. The guards at the door had both drawn their pistols and were shouting madly, orders like, "Get down, miss!" and "Stay where you are!"

There were only two people in the room who did not betray any sort of shock or anxiety. One was the cloaked man who had appeared in the center of the room, drenched in unnatural shadow. The other was Bonnie the Lass. Her gun had been trained on his heart for the last several seconds, well before any of her subjects had recovered enough to make certain their limbs were in the correct places.

"Am I expecting you?" Bonnie gestured eloquently with her gun. Her subjects had recovered entirely. Any of the twenty people in the room could shoot the man dead in a blinking, even if he blinded them again. All it would take was a word from the Lass, and he would look, suddenly, like a sieve.

"I sent no word, ma'am," the man admitted. "But I don't think I'm unexpected."

"Smoke."

"The same, miss." The cloaked man swept his hood back, and the unnatural darkness surrounding him evaporated—no, it was drawn back, buried within the cloak. The face it revealed was young, perhaps twenty years old, and hard-eyed.

Ashes swallowed, but not noticeably, as he looked at the Lass's supper guests. He recognized a few, but only dimly: folk Bonnie had brought along to Burroughside when she collected her Tithe. Thugs, they looked like, but the Lass wouldn't take someone just because they could make someone eat his own teeth. There was a sly look to them, too. He would need to step very carefully.

"You'll see I brought no weapons," he said, sweeping the cloak back.

"That some manner of joke?" The man at the end of the table lifted an eyebrow. "You're an Artificer."

"You've got my word, then," Ashes said smoothly. "Which is worth a good deal more."

The large man let out a barking laugh, and swallowed it swiftly when Bonnie gave him a withering glance. She turned to Ashes.

"I don't have much trust for them as can't show their own faces," she said darkly. "Where's your iron?"

"My wearing iron wouldn't be worth much to you, miss," Ashes said honestly. "I'm here to do business."

"I'll do business with no one as wears a false face," Bonnie said firmly.

Ashes laughed. "That's a lie—"

Five pistols clicked. The big man at the end of the table eyed Ashes furiously. "Have a care what you say, small man."

"You've done business with Hiram Ragged, miss." Ashes met her eyes, wondering if even she had known. "And he's been faking his face for years now. But if it means so much to you . . ." Ashes slipped a thin bar of wood out of his pocket. The Stitching he'd put on it earlier made it gleam darkly, like iron. He pressed it against his face and held it there, meeting Bonnie's eyes. "Satisfied?"

"Just what is it you're here to discuss?"

"The bastard you've let rule Burroughside," Ashes replied firmly. "And what we can do about it."

The Lass lifted an eyebrow. It was the first time he'd seen her look surprised. "Do I look the sort of person to have a duty to Burroughside?"

"Not a matter of what you owe," Ashes said. "It's about what you're already doing."

Bonnie looked at her lieutenants, as if searching for some manner of signal. "And what might that be?"

"Losing money," Ashes said. "And being played for a fool while you're at it." Bonnie's look darkened, but Ashes plunged ahead.

"Hiram Ragged owes you a Tithe every year. Any ten Burrough-siders you choose, isn't it? He's been cheating you. Probably been cheating you for years. Crewleaders who'd serve you well are slaughtered before year's end. And that's not everything." Ashes slipped an envelope out of his cloak: a souvenir from his last trip to Ragged House. "Seems he's been writing letters to police. Mentioning little details about where your poppies come and go. Enough details to put a strain on your purse."

"How am I to know that's not a fake?"

"I've got an honest face, don't I?"

Bonnie looked over his shoulder. "Take him," she said.

Ashes spun, palming one of the glass marbles to aid his escape. He could distract the two guards, easily—

There were five of them. One struck him on the head, the marble fell from his hand, and everything went white before it went black.

● ● ●

*Water splashed against his* face. He gasped and sputtered, and heard someone say, "I recognize him. Asked after some redheaded girl—"

Bonnie said, "Leave us."

This raised a number of softly spoken protests, all of which went silent at once.

"What manner of untried girl do you take me for?" Bonnie snapped. "Go."

When the world came back into focus, he found himself in a dimly lit room. Bonnie sat across from him, holding her pistol as casually as ever.

"Morning," he muttered, more drowsily than he felt. His hands weren't bound, nor were his feet. That had been foolish of them. Now there was nothing between him and escape but . . . ah. Nothing but Bonnie the Lass. The absence of restraints was an insult, not an oversight.

"Not nearly," Bonnie said drily. "You've been asleep an hour, if that. My men were very gentle."

A line of water crawled down his face. Soaked as he was, he couldn't feel the weight of his construct against his skin, but he still wore its Anchor. Had Bonnie burned it away with iron while he'd been asleep? Probably it wouldn't matter; the Lass had him good and true, regardless what face he was wearing. "We've got some different opinions on that word, miss."

"You did not deserve gentle," the Lass went on. "They could have killed you. They have done as much for people who enter my house, unwelcome and unannounced."

"I wasn't *quite* unannounced."

Bonnie gave him a deadly look. "You did a very stupid thing. As you can tell, no doubt."

"What makes you think this isn't right where I want to be?"

"You have no weapons," Bonnie said reasonably. "My men have your Artificing tools and your Anchors. Even if you are canted, there is not enough light in this room for you to blind me, dazzle me, or distract me. And you are weak."

"But *very* charming," Ashes added.

"You have no power here, boy," Bonnie said. "I want you to be clear on that point, so you don't try anything stupid. I quite like this floor. I'd hate to soil it with your innards."

Ashes swallowed. In most things, he had learned, there was a winning move: some gambit or scheme he could use to wriggle his way out of whatever he'd gotten into. But in some rare cases—those when a copper had you, or an Ivory had decided you were worth the time he'd spend ruining you—the only winning move was to lose.

"Understood, miss."

"If we're to do any sort of business, you and I, you should be aware that it will be almost entirely one-sided. I am a queen. You are a bandit, and a prisoner." She inclined her head, as if to say *Understand?*

"Yes, miss."

"You came here some time ago," she said. "Asking about a girl. Describe her for me." The Lass resumed her casual, calm posture, but Ashes heard something in her voice. Something more invested than meager curiosity.

"She had red hair," he said immediately. "Fiery, like, not that dull coppery nonsense you see on an Ysonne Ivory. It was really red. And she had bright eyes. A little taller than me, maybe, but not by much. She had freckles, too." Ashes frowned, grasping at the details. He'd met the girl well before Jack had taught him how to remember faces accurately. "I can't remember how many, or where. I think she had them, though."

"How and when did you meet her?"

"Four months ago, near. In Burroughside, ma'am. She was running from the Broken Boys, only she'd gotten shot. Right here." Ashes pressed his finger against his abdomen, imagining as he did the pain the girl would have experienced. Belly wounds were fearsome things. A slow, agonizing death if you couldn't get to help. "I helped her get away."

"Why?"

"Frustrating the Boys is its own reward, miss," Ashes said honestly. "And she said she worked for you. I thought it couldn't hurt to do a favor for someone with important friends. I got her to Boreas." He swallowed. "I hoped she would make it."

"She did not," the Lass mused, looking away.

Ashes figured this would be a very good time for him to stay quiet.

"Adrianne was a dear friend," Bonnie mused. "Not one of my lieutenants, not publicly. Someone in my position needs agents who are not obvious. She was very . . . eager to please."

"You didn't send her to Ragged," Ashes realized aloud. "She went on her own."

"I thought the police had found her," Bonnie admitted. "It is a common hazard, in our work. I assumed she had taken residence somewhere under the Lethe." Her voice had a forced kind of flatness. She had to be cynical about this, to keep from being inconsolable. "And you say she was stealing from Ragged."

"Trying to," Ashes said. "They got her before she could. She was trying to steal his face for you." Then, sensing an opportunity, he said, "Ragged killed her, miss."

"*Don't* speak to me that way," Bonnie snapped. "Don't you *dare* try to manipulate me, facechanger." She gestured with her gun once more. "Remember you have no power here. No authority. No leverage."

"I've got something," Ashes said. "I've got Hiram Ragged's face."

"I have no need of Ragged's false face," Bonnie said.

*Damn. Why did Adrianne want it, then?* "Then I'm offering my services. I can help you hurt Ragged. He killed Adrianne—"

"*Quiet,* boy."

Ashes shut his mouth so fast he bit his tongue. Bonnie's eyebrows had drawn together in a sharp peak. Her eyes bored into him.

"I can't trust a word from you," Bonnie said. "You're set against Ragged. Who's to say you didn't find my—that you didn't kill Adrianne, to put words into her mouth she couldn't refute?"

"You said yourself she's not known to work with you," Ashes said quickly. "She was your ghost. Someone that could do things for you without being noticed."

"Ghosts have been noticed before."

"Ghosts that work for the Queen of Thieves?"

Bonnie's jaw worked. "Still. It's terribly convenient for you. Someone I trust telling me, from beyond the grave, that I ought to help you in your mad little vendetta." She stared at him fiercely. "Convenient enough to make me look at you sideways."

"Maybe," Ashes allowed. "But it's the truth."

Bonnie was deep in thought. Her look was distant. The pistol was still trained on Ashes, her finger tight against the trigger.

"You've brought me intriguing news," Bonnie said slowly. "Certainly I'd be a fool to ignore you. But I'd be a fool to take you at your word, too."

Ashes nodded. Suspicion was a required skill for important folk in Teranis. And also folk who wanted to see their next sunrise.

"I won't aid you against Ragged," she said heavily. "But neither will I oppose you. If you're telling me the truth, it would be a shame to kill someone who was kind to my friend. If you are lying . . . well, I can respect someone who recognizes my authority. And I would weep not at all if Hiram Ragged passed from my world." She stood, letting her pistol point away from Ashes. He let out a heavier breath than he'd expected. "I will be alert for signs of betrayal. From Ragged, and from you." The delicate stress she put on *alert* said *more alert than usual.*

Which had to be pretty damn alert, in Ashes's humble opinion.

## 29 Burning

**T**HE moon was high when Ashes left Bonnie's lair. The Ravagers were roaming, letting out their hunting cries, but Ashes felt no need to run back to Batty Annie's.

That fact made him smile. A handful of months ago he would have sprinted this stretch, heart in his throat, wondering if he would see another sunrise. Tonight, he was near invisible in his shadow-bound cloak. If they came near, his Artificer's lamp could scare them off. And if that still didn't suffice, he was a far quicker hand at Stitching now. Close enough to bite him was close enough to get blinded or worse at his hands.

It was intoxicating.

It had been a good month. An *excellent* month. His visit to Bonnie had gone well—not as well as it could have, perhaps, but he had walked away from it. Very few people managed to do that after entering the Thief Queen's own house, false-faced and uninvited. And he'd put a hole in the peace between Ragged and the

Lass. As soon as Bonnie reckoned there was a real problem in Burroughside, Ragged would have hell to pay.

The real question was how to force Ragged into betraying himself. What would Bonnie consider evidence of treason? Not Ragged's face—why had Adrianne wanted it in the first place? Why didn't Bonnie want it now?

Perhaps the specific details didn't matter so much. Ragged was keeping all sorts of secrets, and he'd have a much harder time keeping them quiet if Mr. Smoke was taking up all of his thoughts. Bonnie would find *something* before the end of the year, and he and Blimey would be free of Ragged's influence forever.

A good month. A very good month indeed.

He entered Annie's house by the back door. The house was as utterly quiet as ever, lacking even the hushed scurryings of illicit vermin. Annie even scared rats away.

Blimey was awake and reading by the lamp when Ashes entered their room at the bottom of the stairs. Ashes pulled his cloak off and rolled it into a bundle, waiting for Blimey to pull himself out of the book of his own accord. Interrupting him while he read would do more harm than good anyway. Even if Blimey looked away from the text, he'd be effectively useless until he could return to it.

Besides that, Ashes wasn't eager to talk to Blimey. Things had been odd since their argument a week ago. It wasn't anything objectively noticeable; all their actions were the same. They played chess occasionally, and Blimey told Ashes about the new words and ideas he'd read in Batty Annie's books, and often Blimey smuggled away food from Annie's table, in case Ashes hadn't eaten while he was out. The difference was quiet and slippery, difficult to tie down with words.

Blimey didn't laugh as easily. He chewed his thoughts more carefully before he spoke them. Sometimes he looked as if he wanted to say something, but couldn't figure out how to do it, and so said something else instead. He was like someone who'd gotten too close to the fire, and now kept his distance and a wary eye, afraid of burning himself again.

He would get over it eventually, Ashes was sure. Blimey was good at enduring things, so long as he had his books. It was difficult just now, certainly. But Blimey would survive. That was all that mattered.

Blimey closed the book so carefully it made hardly any noise at all and turned around in his chair. He rubbed his eyes and grinned.

"Who'd you rob tonight?"

"No idea," Ashes lied. "Jack doesn't tell me their names much. Says it'd be a breach in security."

"Anything good?"

"Just bits of paper today," Ashes said. "Lots of it, though. Whole books of the stuff. These Ivorish, I swear they write everything down." He grinned, though Blimey didn't seem to find it very funny. "What're you reading tonight?"

"History," Blimey said absently. "I'm in the late Reconstruction right now."

"Any new words?"

"Nothing very interesting, unless you ever try to swindle a scholar," Blimey said. "How's Synder?"

"Eh?" Ashes felt himself tense. It took a conscious effort to relax. "Fine. We haven't talked much. It's been busy."

Blimey nodded, but his smile had faded. "Eh. You have been real busy."

"Care for a game?" Ashes asked, nodding toward the Artificial chess set.

Blimey shook his head. "I'm tired. Reckon I'd rather go to bed."

"I'll count that as a forfeit, then," Ashes said with a forced smile. "Seems about the only way I'll get a win these days."

"I'll make sure I note it," Blimey said woodenly. He climbed onto his bed and lay on his back, kicking his legs up against the wall. Ashes busied himself making his own bed, a nest of dirty cloths not unlike the one he'd slept in back at the Fortress.

"Ashes."

"Eh, mate?"

"Have you thought any more about my idea?" Blimey's voice didn't tremble, but it was a near thing. Whatever foundations of courage it stood on were perilously fragile.

Ashes tensed. Of *course* Blimey would get up the gumption to talk about something that frightened him on a night when Ashes was already exhausted and busy. But Ashes owed him a hearing at least. Whatever Blimey or Synder thought, Ashes wasn't a jailor.

He kept his voice level, not wanting to scare the boy. "Which idea'd that be?"

"About me trying what you do," Blimey said. "Hustling. Confidence games. Those things. With chess."

Ashes bit his lip. "Eh. I've been thinking about it. I think— probably not yet, Blimey."

Blimey's face took on a serious cast. "I've been practicing," he said. "I could play it off like it was just a fluke, I'm *sure* of it."

"It's not just about that," Ashes said, hating himself. "There's other things you'd need to worry about, mate."

Blimey set his jaw. "Like what? You keep telling me that. But you never say what I've got to be so worried about."

"Like that if you got caught, you'd be stuck in an *actual* prison," Ashes said, trying to keep cool. "No books. No way out. And prison's your best hope, too. If they throw you back into Burroughside like they do with most of the gutter-rats . . ." *Ragged would find you. And you'd be dead for true this time.*

"I've kept my face out of Burroughside half a year already," Blimey said. "Ragged wouldn't off me just like that for mucking up once—"

"He damn well *would*," Ashes said sharply, feeling his neck get hot. "Ragged *would* kill you if he saw you."

Blimey's eyes darted down, searching for an answer. "Maybe we could increase our dues to him?" he suggested. "I could be like one of his thieves."

"No again," Ashes said.

"Why not try, though?" Blimey asked, nearly begging now. "Ragged's not a fool. I'm more useful to him if I'm bringing in coin."

"He won't care. You're forbidden to be seen in Burroughside," Ashes said firmly. "That's the deal we made. We break it, he kills us both."

"But it's a stupid promise to make," Blimey said. "Especially when I haven't *done* anything to him!"

"You think you know Ragged better than me, mate?" Ashes said quietly. "If you're ever seen, we're dead. If we ask for different terms, we're dead. If we ever try to do it differently than he wants, we're dead."

"You're so pessimistic," Blimey said, with almost enough humor to make it a joke.

"That's the way it is," Ashes said. "So long as Ragged's in charge of anything, we've got no other move. We have to keep you hidden or get away from Burroughside for good. It's the only way for you to be safe."

Blimey shifted to a seated position, resting his back against the wall. "I lived half a year in that tower trying to stay safe," he said, looking into space. "And I've lived two whole months here under the ground. And I'm tired of it. I'm tired of hiding in holes and crannies. Ragged's left me alone all this time, hasn't he? What's he going to mind if I leave Burroughside for good?"

"Blimey, *stop*."

"No," Blimey said. "I want to leave. I want to be away from here. Ragged—"

"He's left you alone because he thinks you're *dead*!" Ashes snapped. "You've got to stay here because if he found out you were alive—if anybody saw you, just in the street, if you slipped out of the disguise for a *second*—he'd kill you. The only reason he stopped looking for you is that he thought I killed you."

Blimey stared wordlessly at the opposite wall. "I thought you said Ragged was going to let me go so long as I never bothered him."

"I had to tell you that, didn't I? So that you'd not feel scared all the time."

"No, Ashes. You really didn't."

Silence stretched between them, a miserable and uncomfortable thing. Finally, Blimey said, "Ashes, I'm just tired of being here. I want to see the city. I want to meet people." He chuckled softly. "I never thought I'd say that. I used to hate meeting people."

Ashes felt like his insides were being wrung out. "I know it's awful," he said. "But we've got to just endure it. It's what's best."

Blimey looked at him, jaw bulging. "What did you say to Synder?"

The question caught him off guard. "What're you talking about?"

"She came by today," Blimey said. "While you were out. Told me she's sorry, but she can't visit anymore. She said things have gotten all sorts of busy, and she won't be able to come by much. Maybe at all. So what'd you say to her?"

Ashes faltered. Was there anything Blimey would believe? *No*, he thought. *Not now he's seen me stop to think.* "I told her she should stop filling your head with talk about leaving here," he said.

"Because you don't mean for me ever to leave?" Blimey asked flatly.

"Not yet," Ashes said lamely. "It's not safe."

"I'm starting to wonder if that even matters," Blimey said. He looked away from Ashes and chewed on his tongue. "You probably ought to leave."

Ashes grinned weakly, though he knew it wouldn't do any good. "It's time for bed, mate. I'm going to sleep."

"I know you're not really going to sleep," Blimey said. "Did you think I hadn't noticed? You always make a big fuss about fixing your bed and then an hour later you slip outside again. I'm not stupid, Ashes."

Ashes clenched his jaw. "I didn't want you to worry."

"There's a lot of things you don't want me to do."

"I wasn't trying to keep secrets," Ashes said lamely.

"You don't really need to *try*, do you?"

"I've been working on a way to get you out of here," Ashes admitted. "I'm trying to get rid of Ragged. I didn't want to tell you, because—"

"Because it's too much for my fragile little heart," Blimey said bitterly. "I'm glad you've got yourself a good way to fill the time up, Ashes. Best get to it. Don't let me hold you up."

"Stop being an idiot," Ashes said sharply.

Blimey threw the thin blanket over his head and lay down. "I'll work on it. You should get going, Mr. Smoke. I'd hate to slow you down."

• • •

*Ashes stalked through Burroughside* in his shadow-bound cloak, paying no attention at all to his route or his surroundings. Nearly invisible and habitually noiseless, he had little to fear from Burroughside anymore.

He couldn't focus. He felt his head ought to have been spinning, but everything was horridly, painfully clear. Blimey wanted to be free. He wanted to escape. And he didn't care in the slightest that Ashes was working on *just that*. So far as his friend was concerned, Ashes was nothing but a jailor, keeping him confined simply to—what, to appease some protective impulse?

Why couldn't Blimey understand that Ashes was doing everything he could? Ragged was the thing preventing Blimey's freedom, the only one that mattered: once he was removed from power, everything else would be all right. Ashes had a treaty with Bonnie the Lass. He'd sent Saintly scrabbling under the sewers. He was *doing* things! It wasn't as if he was sitting on his backside all day long, opining how much better things would be if Ragged would hurry up and leave already. Ashes had made progress. Ragged's power base was crumbling. If Blimey could only see those things . . .

Fuming, he slipped into a deeper shadow at the passing of a group of Ravagers. This was all Synder's fault. Blimey had been fine until she showed up, telling him he ought to leave, telling him he could live with Jack's company. *Ashes* didn't even live with Jack's company! It was absurd!

*Furies, what a mess*, he thought, stepping under the eave of a dilapidated building. He rested his back against the wall. His forehead pounded. He could feel his heartbeat in his ears.

Whatever else happened, he couldn't lose focus: that much, at least, he'd learned from Jack. He was set against Ragged. Everything else was a distraction. He could still make this work. Blimey would hate him for a few weeks, perhaps a few months, but he trusted Ashes enough to stay in Annie's basement until the work was done. Soon Bonnie would find real evidence of Ragged's treachery, and she'd sweep through Burroughside like a summer storm. Ragged would be gone. Saintly would be gone. Everything would be all right again.

He heard voices around the corner, and jerked up. People moving about at this hour of the night in Burroughside? Either mad, under orders, or stupidly confident. He stood, adjusting the shadow-bound cloak to make sure the construct would hide him in the darkness.

A trio of men came down the street, bearing a sickly-green light: the same color Jack had used to frighten away the Ravagers. Ashes's eyes widened as he realized who held it: gullible, feeble-hearted Reynard Bullface. The two enormous boys walking beside him weren't familiar to Ashes, but they moved with the kind of confidence that came with the ability to kill whatever annoyed you.

"I'm just saying," Bullface muttered, "you two don't really understand what we've got into. *I* hope we don't find him."

"You've the stomach of a little gull," said his partner to the left, in a thick Ysonne accent.

"It's *girl*," said the other. "You got the stomach of a *girl*, Bullface."

"Say what you want," Bullface grumbled. "But *I've* met him. He makes your bones go soupy, he does. He knows what you're thinking. Knows what you're afraid of. He can get in and out of your head like *that*."

Ashes smiled viciously and dug around in his pocket.

"I *shall* say what I like," said the Ysonne. "Getting inside *your* head cannot be deeficult. It is like log. Thick outside, but naseenk inside it."

"Gods above, you're unbearable—"

"Pardon me, gentlemen," Ashes said, stepping into their path and sweeping back his hood. He wore his demon face, and his smile must have cut Reynard Bullface's spirits in half. He'd made a number of improvements to the construct in the last few weeks, he looked nearly six feet tall and brutish. "But you wouldn't be looking for *me*, would you?"

"Smoke!"

"Get him!"

"I—uh—"

Ashes stepped forward, putting himself inside the circle of larger boys. He had barely a moment to move, if that, but he wasn't worried. Adrenaline burned in his bloodstream. Time was crawling.

*No need to worry about Reynard*, said part of his mind. *Too busy pissing himself. The Ysonne is too close by half, but that's nothing to worry about. His arms are too long to be much use this nearby, and he'll aim too high anyway. That leaves you, Mr. On-the-Right . . .*

Ashes punched upward, striking the boy on the right in the nose. He felt a satisfying crunch, and then a warm spurt of liquid on his hand. He laughed aloud as the boy stumbled backward, a laugh he'd practiced alone for hours. It was high and wild, crazed enough to put a chill to the bones.

A punch whistled over his head, passing through the illusion of his head and missing its true target by several convenient inches. Ashes whirled, kicked the Ysonne in the shin, and then again in the knee. The boy stumbled backward, yelping. Ashes took a quick step forward, placing the bulk of his weight on the Ysonne's foot, and drove a flat palm into the boy's throat. The Ysonne gagged and fell to the ground in a heap.

Ashes spun to strike at Reynard, letting the cloak flare out dramatically, but Bullface had retreated nearly ten feet. He was shaking, visibly sweating. Ashes took a menacing step forward and then saw the pistol in Reynard's hands.

"You've nothing to scare me with, boy," Ashes bluffed, eyeing where the boy was aiming. This was a difficult thing to assess: Reynard was shaking so badly that the gun's snout kept moving in a jerky circle. Most of that circle, though, was Ashes. Reynard was aiming at Mr. Smoke's heart, and Ashes was just tall enough that a bullet aimed there could cause him significant discomfort.

"Y-you look scared," Reynard said bravely. "You're stopped, aren't you?"

"Fire that gun and I'll take it as a personal insult," Ashes said, taking a careful step. He glanced over his shoulder; the other two boys were getting to their feet, scowling, but moving gingerly from their injuries. "I'm stopped because you don't seem the sort that would survive me feeling personally insulted."

"Don't take another step."

"Shoot him, Bullface!" said Righty.

"Do not be an eediot!"

"Don't be a fool, Reynard," Ashes said, taking one more step forward. Reynard clicked the hammer back, but it was too late. Ashes dropped the glass marble, and a burning light exploded in the street. This time, the light was accompanied by an appropriately ear-bursting noise, as Reynard, surprised, clenched the trigger. Ashes dropped to the ground and thought he felt the wind as the bullet sped over him.

He heard the Ysonne screaming, but he had no moments to waste on interpreting his cries. He sprinted forward and took Reynard by the collar. Bullface was blinking helplessly, moaning, "I'm blind, I've gone blind, he's taken my eyes—"

"Not your eyes today, Reynard," Ashes snapped, and pressed his hands against the boy's face, covering as much as he could. He felt the magic surge inside him, fueled by his rage, his frustration, his fear, and when he ripped his hands away Reynard was screaming. His face looked burned and blackened, as if someone had branded him with hot iron in the shape of hands.

"My face!" the boy cried. "My face, what'd you do to my face!"

*Idiot*, Ashes thought. *If you stopped whimpering for ten seconds you'd realize it doesn't even* hurt.

Ashes whirled, seeking a new target. The Ysonne was on the ground, whimpering and surrounded by something wet and red, but Righty was on his feet, squinting, his hands raised in readiness to fight.

"Stop fighting," Ashes offered, "and you won't suffer my anger."

The boy's grim look faltered. Ashes leveled Reynard's gun at him.

"I surrender," the boy said, throwing his hands up.

"Drop your weapons," Ashes said. "And recognize that any little voice in your head saying *You can outsmart him* is gonna get you killed. I'll know if you keep even one of them hid."

The boy produced a makeshift knife and another gun, setting

them on the ground before getting to his feet and holding his hands over his head.

*Two guns for three of them?* Ashes wondered. *Is Ragged arming them? Where does he get the money?*

The Ysonne was whimpering again, clutching his shoulder. Ashes realized where Reynard's bullet must have gone. Reynard was sobbing.

"Get on your belly," Ashes commanded Righty. The boy obeyed, spreading his limbs out obligingly. Ashes put a foot between his shoulders, keeping the gun aimed at him.

"Furies!" Reynard screamed. "Gods, my face!"

"You going to kill me?" the boy asked. He did not sound frightened; he was almost resigned.

"Don't intend to, boy," Ashes said, kneeling. He put a hand against the boy's cheek, summoned the magic still roiling inside him, and Stitched. Another burned face, like Reynard's, to tell Ragged this really was the work of Mr. Smoke—

The boy screamed.

Ashes jerked back, shocked, and then realized it must have been a trick, the boy would throw him off in just a moment. Ashes leveled the gun at him again, preparing for the attack—

But nothing came. The boy remained under Ashes's knee, panting, eyes rolling wildly.

"Bastard," Righty snapped at him, venom in his voice. "You're as bad as Ragged."

Ashes jumped away from him and ran.

# 30 Breaking

**P**ERHAPS an hour passed. Perhaps less. Ashes didn't remember it at all.

He'd thrown the gun away somewhere—he couldn't remember where. Now that he thought about it, leaving something like that in an alleyway somewhere in Burroughside had been a damned stupid thing to do. There was nothing for it now. He didn't even remember getting rid of it.

He felt exhausted in every way it was possible to be. His breath was coming hard, burning in his chest. His head spun, all his focus stripped away and left to smolder on the roadside. His head had not ached this badly since he'd started studying Artifice.

The only thoughts he could manage were *What* and *the* and *hell*.

He had Stitched the boy's face. He had Stitched people's faces before. They hadn't been real, had they?

*Stupid*, he thought. *You can figure this out for yourself.*

He grabbed his own wrist, and found that he was shaking. He

gritted his teeth, told himself not to be a coward, and Stitched. His head throbbed violently. He felt the magic gutter and shake, like a candle flame beneath a breeze. He grasped at it, trying to force the illusion through his fingertips, and felt the magic slip out of his hands.

He looked at his arm and grimaced. He hadn't even changed the color of the skin. It had been weeks since he'd failed so thoroughly. *Focus*, he ordered himself.

He laid his hand over the skin again, took a breath, closed his eyes. *Do not command the light*, William said in his head. *Coax it.*

The magic bloomed in him again, slender and frail as a sprouting flower. He took another breath, gathering his strength, and Stitched.

When he opened his eyes, the skin of his right arm was blackened and flaky, looking like it had been burned to a crisp. He let out a breath. There had been no pain.

What had the boy been doing, then, when he screamed? Was it just a trick, something to get into Ashes's head? He had certainly succeeded there. It seemed silly, though, for him to expect Mr. Smoke—legendary terrorist, the ghost that haunted Burroughside, the enemy of Mr. Ragged himself—to be affected by his screams. He had been *right*, admittedly, but still . . .

Ashes shook himself. He had to get back in control of himself. He was, after all, Mr. Smoke, legendary terrorist, etc. The boy he'd Stitched had gotten into his head. He couldn't let that happen again, not with so much at stake. What if he'd hesitated like that and the Ysonne had managed to capture him? Ashes would be dead. The war on Ragged would be over.

He would get better. He was just off-balance tonight. Off-balance and exhausted and scared. He wrapped the shadowbound cloak tighter around himself, as if to protect against a chill.

There was more to do tonight. Gods, he wanted to sleep, but he couldn't stop. Not just yet.

● ● ●

*Ashes crept toward the* ramshackle building where he had been meeting Jasin for the last several months. The shadows here were deep, covering a hole too small for a full-grown Ravager to enter. Ashes had to get on his knees and crawl to enter the basement, miraculously untouched by whatever had leveled the aboveground floors, where Jasin would already be waiting.

Before he pushed himself the last few feet into the small room, he exchanged the demon-face for another version of Mr. Smoke: slightly closer to his size, with a fierce, but otherwise normal, adult face, suited for meeting people he wanted to impress but not terrify. Jasin was young still, and he had no interest in giving her nightmares.

He emerged from the tight hole and pulled out his Artificer's lamp, willing it to light up the small room. Jasin was asleep on the floor, waking slowly as the light invaded her dreams.

"I'm not paying you to sleep," Ashes said, not unkindly. The girl jerked, scrambled to her feet, and gave him a stubborn look.

"You were late," she said. "I'm not sure by how much, but you were *definitely* late this time."

"Other priorities demanded my attention," Ashes said. "What word did I give you last time?"

"*Peaches*, sir." Jasin smiled broadly, proud of herself for remembering. Ashes felt more than a little proud as well. He was getting to be as paranoid as Jack.

"Good girl. You have news for me?"

"Juicy things," the girl said with a ruthless and gap-toothed smile. "Mr. Ragged's issued a bounty on you, sir."

Ashes blinked. "What?"

"Heard it with my own ears, sir," Jasin said. "Bounty on Mr. Smoke. Five hundred crowns, living or dead."

"That's—that's a lot of money," Ashes muttered, still shocked.

"Not enough to make me turn on you, sir," Jasin said.

Five hundred crowns for Mr. Smoke? Ashes could hardly believe it. Where was Ragged getting that sort of money?

His shock was quickly superseded by elation. *Five hundred crowns.* Ragged really *was* scared. Ashes's message must have spooked him.

"Anything else?"

"Ragged went somewhere last night," Jasin said. "Some carriage came and picked him up. *Big* carriage. There were guards on it an' all."

"Did they see you?"

"Course not," Jasin said, her eyes flicking away from him. "I'm too good, sir."

He gave her a hard look, tugging his magic to himself once more. He willed the eyes of the false face to turn violet for just a moment, and felt the energy slither out of him, but he couldn't have said if it worked. He kept his expression hard and wise, though, just in case. "You oughtn't lie to me, Jasin. I know when I'm lied to."

Jasin's cheeks paled, but only briefly. "Eh, one saw me. He didn't catch my face, though, I'm damn *sure* of that."

"Only promise me you'll be more careful in the future," Ashes commanded, trying to imitate Jack's air of authority. "You'd be much less use against Ragged if you're captured."

"Sir," Jasin said, inclining her head. She looked him in the eye and smiled widely. "And I've got something else for you, too, sir."

"What'd that be?"

"I think I probably ought to show you, sir," she said, making for the tunnel out. "Do you trust me?"

Ashes paused. His default answer to that question was *no*. "I don't trust many folk."

"You can be invisible for it," she offered. "If you want. But I really think you ought to see it for yourself. It'll mean more."

He grimaced. He didn't have time to indulge this girl's whims. He was exhausted, all the way down to the bone.

"All right," he said. "Fine."

There was no trap awaiting them outside their secluded meeting-place, which did a lot to soothe Ashes's suspicions. He had certain surprises prepared in case someone found the meeting-place, but such contingencies seemed more fragile when they were the only thing standing between you and a determined fighter.

He put up the hood and traveled alongside Jasin as they flitted from shadow to shadow. Jasin was as adept at moving stealthily as anyone Ashes had ever met; he had to work to keep up with her. He noticed, also, that the girl moved with the caution of someone trying to avoid being followed. She certainly wasn't behaving like someone who didn't want to be seen at all, which was what any sane Burroughsider would be doing this late at night.

"You're not worried about Ravagers," he noted.

"Not tonight," she said, looking in his direction with something like faith. "I don't worry about them at all when I go to meet you."

Ashes frowned, but let it pass. Jasin was an odd girl.

She led him for fewer than five minutes before she stopped outside one of the larger buildings. He recognized it as the headquarters of the Motleys—at least, that had been the case when he left Burroughside. Real estate changed hands quickly here.

"What're we doing here?" he asked.

"Wait and see, sir," she said.

He tried again to make his eyes flash, and again couldn't have said whether it worked. "Jasin. I need you to understand. If you're leading me to a trap, or if you're trying to gain some advantage over me, it will not go well for you. I'll come for you when my business with Ragged is finished."

"You got nothing to worry about, sir," she said. "Nothing at all, not from me. I wouldn't turn you in to Ragged ever. I wouldn't turn you over to nobody." She said it with a profound seriousness that bordered on reverence.

"All the same," he said, "I think I shall stay invisible until I'm convinced."

"You do that, sir. Just through here. Would you like to go first or second?"

"Second," Ashes said, stepping through the empty doorway ahead of her. He held the folds of his cloak in his fists to muffle the noise. Being nigh invisible wasn't much use if you could be heard by a deaf idiot.

"As you say, sir." Jasin walked calmly through the entryway and made a grand gesture, as if she were presenting something. "How'd you like to meet your crew?"

Ashes peered at the girl, searching her for some indication that she was lying. The girl's face was perfectly sincere. They came around a corner into a large, open room that murmured with the soft breaths of sleeping people. *Many* sleeping people . . .

"Not a lot of 'em awake just now, I'd bet anything," she muttered. "But I've been telling people about you, sir, just like you asked."

Ashes looked at her, confused, as understanding began to creep through his head. His confusion turned to shock, then to disbelief, and then to frustration.

"No," he said softly. "No, this wasn't . . ."

"There's about thirty of us now," the girl said softly. She hadn't heard him. "Ever since I started telling folks, they've all wanted to meet you."

"Jasin?" said someone. A form split away from the darkness, baring a sharp knife. "What the hell? How'd you get in here?"

"Rafe!" Jasin's voice went low and urgent. "Don't be an idiot!

You have to ask me what the password is!" Her eyes flicked around, searching for Mr. Smoke's silhouette, no doubt. She made an exaggeratedly frustrated face, but she couldn't hide her nervousness.

"What's the password, then?"

"*Criminey crickets,*" she said proudly.

"How the hell'd you get in here?" Rafe demanded. "We've got patrols going—"

"I'm good at this!" Jasin said, beaming. "But you'd better make sure your patrols get sharper. We've got a visitor tonight." She leaned forward, trying to whisper. "We'll want to impress him." The girl inclined her head suggestively.

Rafe's eyes went wide enough to be noticeable, even in the gloomy dark. "*He's* coming?"

"He's here," she said. "He might have moved already. Are you there, sir?"

Ashes did not reply. He had barely even heard her. His head was full of one single fact: there were more than thirty people sleeping here, and they wanted to see *him.*

*This wasn't what I meant,* he thought, staring wordlessly at nothing. *I never wanted something like this to happen.*

Jasin had called it a *crew.* That was a heavy word in Burroughside. A crewleader was as much of a father as some of the gutter-rats ever had. Your crew decided your loyalties, where you slept, how well you ate. If your crewleader was angry at someone, you were angry at them. If your crewleader fought someone, you fought them.

When the leader moved, the crew followed. Unthinking. Unquestioning. No hesitation.

*This isn't what I wanted.*

She was only supposed to bring them hope. She wasn't supposed to be recruiting an army. Ashes fought alone. That was his way. Letting someone else get involved was dangerous. They might fail him. Worse, he might fail them.

"Must be among them," Jasin said reverently. "He's invisible when he wants to be."

"I'm here." Ashes said, keeping his voice as level as he could. He watched Rafe carefully, wondering if the Motley boy would recognize his voice. He pulled down the hood of his shadow-bound cloak, letting Mr. Smoke appear. "Jasin, what've you done?"

"Just like you told me, sir," she said. The girl couldn't hear the fear and frustration in Ashes's voice; she was far too pleased at how well she'd done. "I told them about you. Told them about Ragged and how he's going to fall. I told them *everything*."

"And who are you, then?" Ashes turned to look at Rafe, and pulled on Jack's confident tone as easily as a ring.

"Slippery Rafe, sir." Rafe gave a short bow. "The Motleys are yours, sir, if you want them. We've been waiting for you ever since Jasin told us. We'll be ready when the time comes."

Ashes eyed the boy. Rafe was older than him by a pair of years. Seeing the Motley bow to him made him feel distinctly false.

"Jasin," he said slowly, "I think we must've misunderstood each other."

"How're you meaning that, sir?"

"I don't want a crew," Ashes said heavily. "I'm not a crewleader. I don't want— I'm not here to start an actual war."

Jasin's mouth opened, then shut. "Sir, I . . ."

"It's all right," he said. "I'm not angry with you. But I meant something different when I told you to spread the word. I wanted . . ." He looked at the sleeping Burroughsiders. "I just wanted them to know. They don't need to fight. This is something I have to do."

The girl's face fell. "I didn't realize. Yes, sir, of course—"

"Hang on just a moment," Rafe said. "You're saying you don't want us?"

"I don't want you *hurt*," Ashes said firmly. "Right now the fight's between Ragged and me, and he can't touch me. But if you're involved . . ." He took a breath. "Ragged can hit any of you, anytime he wants. It's safer for everyone if it's just me."

Jasin grabbed Rafe's arm. "If that's the way he wants it . . ." she said.

"No," Rafe replied. "Bugger that and bleed on it, too. You think this is just between the two of you?" He scoffed, loudly enough that some of the sleepers began to stir. "It hasn't been that way. Ever. The Motleys've been looking for our chance at payback ever since Ragged gutted Iames the Fool. And ever since *you* showed up, *sir*, Ragged's been bleeding us dry. Two taxing days every month, and he expects just as much every time. We can barely feed our own, he's taken so much out of us, and we're one of the best crews in Burroughside. Half of them've disbanded already. Couldn't keep themselves together."

"Rafe, look—"

"No *you* look," Rafe said hotly. "Iames won't be the last of us he takes. Whether you take him down or not, he'll have blood from us. And damn it if I'm going to take that showing my belly." Rafe glared at him fiercely. "This hasn't ever been just *your* war. We're in it just as much. And we'll see Ragged cut. Mark me."

Ashes was stricken. There was nothing he could do but nod.

"Good," Rafe said, letting out a breath. "Look. You don't have to lead us. We can handle ourselves. But we damn well are going to help you, whether you want it or not, so you'd best let me know how we can do it without mucking up whatever you've got going on." He paused. "And you ought to show these folks your face. Talk to them. You owe them that much."

Ashes nodded. He did owe them something. They were here for him.

"Is there a place I can stand?" he asked. "Where everyone could see me?"

Rafe gave him an odd look. "You realize it's nighttime, don't you?"

"Let me worry about the light. Where would you go if you wanted to talk to everyone at once?"

Rafe led him to a small raised platform in the back of the room. "Iames used it," the boy said, almost tonelessly. "Back when he was here. I've not set foot on it."

"I don't think Iames would mind our using it tonight," Ashes said. "Wake them all up for me, will you? You're right. I *do* owe them some things."

## 31 Savior

**T**HIRTY half-awake Burroughsiders surrounded him. Most looked displeased at being woken, but the irritation melted off their faces as the word spread around. *Mr. Smoke. Mr. Smoke's here.*

*Don't muck this up.*

Ashes let the whispers swell for a moment, then turned the light of his Artificer's lamp pure white and let it expand until it illuminated every face around him. He stepped onto the platform and set the lamp at his feet.

"I think most of you know who I am," he said softly. The whispers ceased. "I've been calling myself Mr. Smoke. It's good to meet you all."

He scanned the audience. Many had adopted the same expression Jasin had when she spoke to him. Respect. Awe. Almost worship.

*I could've swindled a lot more money if I'd known how to make everybody like this.* Was this what an Ivory felt, when everyone in the room looked at them like a god who'd set foot on earth?

"I've been told you're all here as my crew," Ashes said, raising his voice. Surely he should have been nervous, but he couldn't feel it just now. There was a crowd. He was lying to them. He was home. "That you're here to serve me. The bad news is I don't want a crew."

He paused again, let his eyes go hard.

"What I really need is an army."

He pressed his shoe lightly against the Artificer's lamp and tinted the room red.

"We're at war with Ragged," he said loudly. "It's always been that way, even if we didn't know it. Mostly he's won. He's bled us of our money. He keeps us sleeping in holes, quaking in fear of the Ravagers. He lets the Broken Boys run over Burroughside like a pack of wolves. You all know it. There's a war on, and he's been winning. We're going to change that." The red tint deepened. "We're going to change that *tonight.*"

He fished around in his pocket and met Jasin's eyes, motioning for her to join him onstage. "I've known what it's like to be under Ragged's thumb. He looks invincible, doesn't he? Dozens of burglars and thieves, and not one of us has gotten in his house. He's practically Ivory."

Jasin stood beside him. He slipped a ring into her hand. "There are some things need clearing up. First of all, none of you's ever seen Ragged's face." He nodded to Jasin, who cautiously slid the ring over her finger. "Not his real face, anyway."

The crowd gasped as they saw Ragged's face on the stage. One or two cried out, and Ashes stepped in front of Jasin before anyone could throw a knife.

"Mr. Ragged wears a false face," he declared, letting them glimpse Jasin again. "I know because I snuck in his house and I stole it, right out from under him."

Their attention was riveted to him. He could almost feel it, like a million tiny hooks lodged in their minds, with strings connecting them to his fingers.

"Ragged's been hiding his face from you for years," Ashes said. "You know why that is, Burroughside? You know why Hiram Ragged's afraid you'll know the truth about him?" He stared out, and Stitched his eyes as bright as they could go. He felt the magic take this time. "Because he fears you.

"You outnumber him and his boys twenty to one. You're small but you're fierce, and of course you are. You're the gutter-rats, the Motleys, the strays and outcasts. Every scrap of bread you've ever tasted, you fought for. Mr. Ragged, though? He wears a face he didn't earn, in a house he can't defend, in a district that won't have him any longer!"

It was the moment to cheer, and everyone in the room caught their cue. A shout went up from them.

"Ragged's afraid of you!" Ashes shouted above the din. "And he damn well *should be!*"

They screamed again, louder this time. Ashes raised his fist, and felt something twinge in the back of his head. Something was wrong, someone was behaving weirdly, a hand that had gone up but stopped at shoulder level, and something was pointed at him—

No time to think—

Ashes jerked away reflexively, but the platform was too small. His foot struck empty air. He stumbled backward.

The gunshot cut through the shouting, and turned the cheering into screams.

Ashes's head spun. His ears rang. A line of fire seared along his shoulder.

Someone was shouting. *Many* someones were shouting. Screaming, in fact—chaotic, terrorized screams. So loud and disorganized he could hardly think.

"They killed him! He's dead!"

"Mr. Smoke!"

*Have I died?*

He decided he was probably not dead. He had been here before, in a fuzzy stasis between awake and permanently asleep, and it was not death. Not quite.

The pieces came together swiftly, but not without effort. *Someone shot me. I fell back. They think I've died, and nobody's bothered to check yet . . .*

It was at this point that he got a very audacious idea. A manipulative, cunning, truly bastard-born idea. He thought briefly of the Burroughsiders screaming on the other side of the stage, and how they trusted him. Then he thought about what Jack would say if he ever found out about this: *Good thing you didn't hesitate.*

He put his hand over his heart and grasped for his magic. He wouldn't need much; just a little would do. It would be more theatrical like that anyway.

There was a bullet wound high on his shoulder. The shot had practically grazed him. That made twice he'd gotten inordinately lucky against a gunman in a single night. Someone was looking out for him. He prayed to the Face of Cunning for strength as he put his fingers over the wound and made one final Stitching. This one would have to last. His magic was more exhausted than his body. For good measure, he spread some of the blood around on his shirt, just over his heart.

His focus slackened, and the screams filled his head once again. He stood.

The noises stopped.

"Where is he?" Ashes demanded. "Did we catch him?"

The crowd parted, revealing a burly, familiar boy. Ashes approached him, and heard the whispers start up as he passed. Everyone within ten feet of him could see the ghastly bullet hole in his chest. If they looked closely, they would see the hole slowly shrinking. Any canted Artificer would spot the magic in a moment;

weak Stitchings couldn't hold for long. The subject's true image would reassert itself. But there were no Artificers in the crowd. After tonight, everyone in Burroughside would hear about Mr. Smoke, the man who disregarded a bullet through the heart.

"What's your name, boy?" *Because I can't keep calling you Righty.*

"I'm telling you nothing," he spat.

Ashes had to admire his pluck. He'd left Reynard and the Ysonne behind to creep into enemy territory and kill Mr. Smoke. Even surrounded by enemies, he refused to back down. It was a pity he belonged so wholly to Ragged.

"You followed me?" Ashes watched Righty's face, but there was no flicker of weakness in him. "No. Course not. You keep your ear to the ground, eh? Heard about it all on your own, and figured you'd be Mr. Ragged's new best friend. Saintly wouldn't have looked on you too kindly for that, my friend."

"Bugger off!"

"Tie him up," Ashes commanded. The illusory bullet wound in his chest was gone entirely. Only a little blood remained. "Wouldn't do to have him running ahead of us."

Slippery Rafe gave him a questioning look. "Ahead of us?"

"Ahead of us," Ashes said heavily. "I figure it's time we paid Mr. Ragged a visit, mates. Don't you?"

## 32  Shivers

IT was past midnight in Burroughside, and a small army of children who had never before set foot outside after dark were surging down the street. There was a demon at their head, and he carried a bar of sickly green light in one hand, illuminating their way. Grim and silent they were, and some were shivering. Winter had begun creeping into Teranis, and the grasp of the fog had grown colder.

There was a pit in Ashes's stomach. His legs deeply wanted to shake, but he would not let them. There were thirty people behind him, most of them children. To them, he was Mr. Smoke. Mr. Smoke was never afraid. Mr. Smoke could not be killed. Mr. Smoke was the one who would take Ragged down.

It did not matter that Ashes was doing his best to keep from pissing himself. In this, as in Artifice, all that mattered was what people *thought* was true. He glanced over his shoulder to check on the children behind him. On his command, they walked in a tight formation, keeping the smallest of them in the center. No doubt some of them thought the group would serve as protection from the Ravagers. There were others who thought it was Mr. Smoke's presence keeping the monsters at bay. They were nearer to the truth; he kept them in a tight circle because the light from his lamp only extended so far.

Slippery Rafe came up beside him. "What exactly are we going to do with Mr. Ragged, sir? When we've caught him?"

Ashes let out a breath. It was encouraging to hear the Motley leader express his faith so casually. Ashes had been thinking in terms of *if*.

"I'm not ready to spread that information about just yet," Ashes said, pretending he was Candlestick Jack. The Weaver had a knack for seeming totally sure of himself no matter what was going on. Part of it was that Jack never admitted that he didn't know what to do. There were never any unanswerable questions; only answers Jack hadn't chosen to share with the wide world yet. "Rest assured I've got plans for him."

Bonnie the Lass would certainly suffice to get rid of Ragged. She might execute him or imprison him, depending on whether she'd decided he was a traitor, but she certainly wouldn't let him keep Burroughside when he'd been so thoroughly rejected by its population. A coward couldn't control the district.

"We going to kill him?" Rafe asked in a low voice.

Ashes blinked. "No," he said quickly. "Definitely not that."

Rafe eyed him, suspicious. "You don't have to lie to me, sir. I've been the crew's leader a while. They might be green, but I'm not."

"We won't kill him," Ashes said, trying to make his voice firm. "I'll tell you that honest. We kill him, the Ivories'll come down on Burroughside like you've never seen. They'll kill us outright, no question."

That, and Ashes could still remember the sticky feeling of blood on his hands. The Lass might kill Ragged. Ashes certainly wouldn't. Nor would the children behind him. Ashes couldn't permit that.

They were two streets away from Ragged House now. Ashes could almost feel the children shaking. He stopped and turned around, holding the sickly green light over his head.

"I don't want you to be afraid," he said, knowing they would believe it. His voice thrummed with confidence, with power and strength. "You've no reason to be. Ragged fears you, just like he ought to, and he won't see us coming. We're going to capture him, tonight, and take him where he won't harm us or ours ever again. You can trust to that, eh?" He met as many eyes as he could in a quick scan, willing them to believe in him. He needed them to be confident, assured. If Ragged didn't come along willingly, they'd need to force him, and Ashes didn't know how little it would take for the police to fall on them like a sack of stones. Everything would be well if Ragged came willingly, and their best shot at that was to convince him he had thirty-some desperate, hungry Burroughsiders standing at his door, prepared to do whatever it took to remove him.

It would work, though. It had to work. Ragged had no protections save Carapace and his alliances. Neither of those would save him here, in the dead of night . . .

Ashes stopped. It would be good to check.

He gave the Artificer's lamp to Rafe and slipped his cloak on. "Hold on to that for me," he commanded. "And don't any of you move. I'll be back in a moment."

Rafe looked at him oddly, but a moment later Ashes was swathed in darkness. The Motley blinked.

Ashes came around the corner noiselessly. Ragged House loomed before him, surrounded by the ruthless, bloodthirsty fence. His eyes drifted to the gate. Under his breath he said, "Bollocks."

He appeared in the midst of his army a moment later, face grim.

"What's on?" Rafe asked.

"Broken Boys," Ashes told them in a low voice. "Half a dozen. And they've got pistols."

He heard two or three stifled cries of alarm. "I understand you're frightened," he told them. "I've been on the other end of the Boys and their fists." At this, Rafe gave him another odd look. *Idiot*, Ashes chastised himself, but kept going. "I wouldn't blame you if you wanted to turn back just now. You all know bullets don't bother me overmuch, but they'd mean a hell of a lot to you. If you want to go back, I won't stop you."

The children stared back at him, plainly frightened.

"Can you protect us?"

"Can't promise it," he said. "But you have my word I'll do everything in my power to keep you safe."

Jasin scoffed. "Don't be daft, you all," she said fiercely. "You know who you're looking at? This is *Mr. Smoke*. We go in with him, we'll all be just fine."

Ashes gave her a sharp look. "I can't promise that," he said.

"You have got some sort of plan, though?" she challenged.

"Some sort."

He looked out at the children, held their gaze for a moment. None of them wavered, and he smiled broadly.

"All right, then."

● ● ●

*Ten minutes later, Ashes* came within sight of Ragged House. The hood of his cloak was down and he held the Artificer-light high. Jasin and Rafe walked beside him, while he resisted the impulse to keep looking at them anxiously. He had not wanted anyone with him for this part; both had flatly refused to obey him. The plan functioned better with two or three people than only with one, Jasin argued. Ashes could have convinced Rafe, if the Motley had argued alone, but Jasin had enough fire for both of them. Ashes hated to admit it, but she'd probably been right. With his Artifice exhausted, he needed every diversion he could get his hands on. And Rafe and Jasin were more than competent in their way. So long as they kept their heads, everything would go well.

Even so, Ashes couldn't banish the knots tying in his belly.

"Remember," he muttered. "Hit the ground straightaway."

"We'll remember," Jasin whispered back.

"They're not trained, I don't think," Ashes continued. "There's gonna be bullets everywhere. Get to shelter quick as you can. Behind a wall or something."

"We got it, sir," Rafe said. "Not to worry. It'll all be over before you know it."

"You there!"

The Broken Boys had their guns up, though Ashes noted that they looked just as awkward and untrained as Reynard's miniature gang had been. Ashes stopped and held up his hands, motioning for Jasin and Rafe to do the same. They were nearly fifty feet away from Ragged House and the Broken Boys—too far to close quickly. If it came to gunshots, there would be no contest.

"Don't none of you move," said one who stood at the center; Ashes recognized the voice of Tom Wesel. His pistol was aimed at Mr. Smoke. "Not a one, else we'll put you out like lights."

"What're you doing here?" another one demanded.

Slippery Rafe took one bold step forward and stopped as two guns swiveled to point at his heart. "Sir?" he asked.

"I'd recommend that we become very, very obedient, Rafe," Ashes said steadily. "Best strategy when you're staring down an iron barrel, in my experience."

"Who the hell're you?" one of the Boys asked.

"No one of any particular importance," Ashes said, in the tones of someone who is of very particular importance.

"Best tell us," Tom Wesel said coolly, "else I think I'll start putting holes in you."

Jasin let out a harsh, barking laugh. "You don't know who's looking at you?" she snapped. "You'd think even somebody stupid as the Broken Boys ought to recognize Mr. Smoke!"

Ashes saw two quickly cover up looks of shock and fear, but the others held steady. The guns bolstered their courage.

"He dies just as easy as anyone, you put a bullet to him," one said.

"Shows what *you* know—"

"*Jasin,*" Ashes said, grabbing the girl by the shoulder. "Stay *quiet.*"

"What're you doing here, then?"

Ashes gave the Broken Boy a look of profoundest disbelief. "You really asking that?"

But Ashes didn't wait for the Boy to reply before he pulled Candlestick Jack's confidence over himself.

"I'm Mr. bloody *Smoke,*" he said. "I've been all over Burroughside telling you what I'm going to do for the last month. You've not been paying attention?" He let out a theatrical laugh. "Oh, bollocks, you're stupid. All right, then. I'm here to sack Ragged House, incapacitate Carapace, and drag Ragged out of Burroughside by whatever body part seems most available at the time. What the hell did you *think* I was doing here?"

Two of the Broken Boys exchanged frightened looks, but Ashes had no intention of letting them get their feet under them. "That was the plan, leastwise. I admit that finding you and your adorable little crutches here puts a bit of a kink in my plans, so maybe I'll just be on my way."

That got to them. "You bloody well won't!" one said.

"Please, gentlemen," Ashes said smoothly. "This isn't something to get upset over. Seems to me this is the sort of disagreement we could solve if we all performed some judicious pretending and forgetting. I'll say that we seem to have gotten lost on our way somewhere, and you don't have to shoot anyone tonight. The plan's bloody foolproof."

"That so," Tom Wesel said flatly.

"No reason it has to come to any sort of unpleasantness, gentlemen," Ashes said. "We can all be very civil about this."

"Sir?" Jasin demanded in a hoarse whisper, just loud enough it would carry to the Broken Boys. "What are you doing? Their guns don't mean anything to you."

"They mean a hell of a lot to you, though," Ashes said back. "That's enough for right now, Jasin." Ashes turned back to the Broken Boys, and realized Saintly was unaccounted for. The thought made him feel more than a little anxious.

"Now, then, Tom—"

"No!" the boy snapped. "Don't talk. Don't you say a damn word to me. Everything you say's poison, eh? I seen what you did to Reynard, too. You speak another thing to me or any of my boys, I'll shoot your head off, eh? Then I'll shoot whoever else I get to, if you take too long to lay still."

Ashes searched the boy's eyes. They were deadly cold, and serious as stone. He nodded wordlessly.

*Faces, let them all be ready*, Ashes thought.

"Sir?" Slippery Rafe asked, looking at Mr. Smoke.

Ashes did not answer, except to let the Artificer's lamp go out.

"Down!" he roared, as the Broken Boys shouted in alarm, and the bullets started flying. He rolled to one side, bumping against Rafe, and then surged forward with his belly against the ground. Bullets whizzed over him. One struck the street only a few inches from his hands. Ashes cried out, but kept moving. He had to keep moving.

"Don't shoot, stupid!" Wesel snapped. "You'll waste all your shot! Don't shoo—"

Then came further cries of alarm, and savage noises from the

Broken Boys—and from the swollen ranks of Mr. Smoke's Motleys. Ashes, hidden behind the corner of a building, had no hope at seeing everything. But he could hear the battle shouts coming from all sides. Six against thirty was no real fight, even when the thirty were mostly young and small. Those who couldn't make their punches felt would make up for it with their teeth and their stature, from which they struck the most tender of targets.

It was ended in a few moments, punctuated with short, frustrated shouts. Ashes stood, not wanting to be seen cowering behind a wall when the Motleys told him everything was safe.

"We got 'em!"

Ashes came out from hiding, but didn't light his lamp until he was in the middle of the street. Three of the young Motleys were holding guns they had taken from the Broken Boys, who were currently on the ground, moaning and cussing.

"They threw away some of the guns," one of the Motleys said apologetically. "So that we couldn't have them." He looked profoundly irritated.

"Wouldn't fuss about it much," Ashes said. "The fewer guns around Burroughside, the better. Anyone hurt?"

The boy jerked a thumb over his shoulder. "Ell and Maisie got punched in the teef. There's maybe three of us got knocked out. Everybody else is good."

Ashes grimaced, but this news was far better than it might've been. "We have anything to tie them up with?"

The Motleys exchanged thoughtful glances, but no one volunteered a solution. Ashes made a note of that: it would be good to have some rope handy next time.

*Next time. Gods, I hope not.* Better to end Ragged's time as governor of Burroughside right here. Tonight. There would be no next time.

"You three," Ashes said, indicating those who had procured a weapon. "You stay here with the Boys. Keep your aim steady, stay a few feet back. If they move, shoot them somewhere painful." He suppressed a shudder. Guns were a street fighter's worst nightmare. In crews, you could fight to decide who was in charge, and you took whatever dirty advantage you could get, and in the end you both walked (or limped, or crawled) away. Guns evened the playing field, at the expense of putting both fighters on the edge of a cliff. "Some of you stay with them. *Don't* let them get those guns back."

He moved to stand over Tom Wesel and stared him fiercely in the eye. "And mark me, here. If any of you bastards *touches* these kids, I will have it out from you in blood. Folk won't even *remember* what I did to Reynard 'cause they'll be so horrified at what I've done to you."

Wesel's eyes widened in terror, and he nodded eagerly. Ashes could feel the fear pouring off him in waves.

"Good, then," Ashes said. He straightened. "The rest of you, let's go talk to Mr.—"

The door to Ragged House opened. Light poured out from it, blocked only by Carapace's tall, bulky shadow. The butler took one step forward, surveyed the Motleys, and then stood aside. Mr. Ragged followed.

"Mr. Smoke, I take it," the Beggar Lord said. He did not sound frightened. He didn't even sound wary.

*His mistake*, Ashes thought.

"That's right," he said. "Mr. Smoke and the Motleys, to be precise. Seems you've got a problem with your doormen." Ashes gestured brazenly to the Broken Boys.

Ragged stepped down off the porch. He looked out at the small army Ashes had gathered. "They weren't doormen," Ragged said, sounding mildly annoyed.

"You going to come out, then?" Ashes demanded. "Or am I going to have to bust down your little gate and drag you away?"

"By all means, use the gate," Ragged said. "It's not locked. Carapace, you didn't lock it, did you?"

It was at this point that Ashes realized he should be frightened. Ragged's attitude did not match that of a man with a mob on his doorstep. He was too calm, too disinterested. He barely sounded annoyed.

Ashes looked at the children around him. His instincts were screeching at him that this had to be a trap of some kind. The children wouldn't turn back now, though, not when victory was so close. What could Ragged *do*, anyway? It was only him and Carapace in that house, just like always; they'd had no warning that Mr. Smoke was coming. Maybe it was a bluff?

*Don't be daft!* everything in him screamed. *Get them out of here.*

He turned to the children. "Listen," he said, "we ought to—"

"Let's get him!" Jasin shouted, yanking the gate open. The children cheered behind her, and they flowed in a swift tide into Ragged's courtyard. Ashes found himself being pushed forward against his will, but there was no way to stop them now. Whatever gambit Ragged had, Ashes would have to play it out.

*"All right!"* He held out his hands, trying to take command back. "Nobody touch him!"

The children bristled at this, but Mr. Smoke's reputation was powerful enough to drag them to a stop. They formed up in a loose semicircle around Ragged, with Ashes at the center. The Beggar Lord only looked bored, his hands clasped neatly behind his back. Carapace, motionless on the porch, matched his master's expression.

Ragged lifted an eyebrow. "Something wrong, Mr. Smoke? You are here to take me by force, are you not?"

"If you don't come willingly." Ashes tried to sound threatening and powerful, but he couldn't quite manage it.

"Oh, fear not," Ragged said with a faint grin. "I will not be doing that."

"Then this is going to get ugly."

"I expect it might." Ragged's faint grin got a little wider. "Are we going to begin, then?"

This was all wrong. It wasn't how he'd expected things to go. Ragged should be frightened, shouldn't he? Why was he not *afraid*?

"Take him," Ashes commanded, and then felt the air shift.

The little ones felt it first; you could tell because they started wailing, as if they'd been badly burned. It took the older ones only a moment more: Ashes heard Slippery Rafe's knees strike the ground beside him. Jasin fell to the ground in a heap, unconscious.

It seemed to strike Ashes last. A cloud seemed to wrap around his mind, dark and red. His vision narrowed, his breath came short. He stood under open air, and that was far, far, *far too small, he was trapped in a tunnel and there were monsters down here—*

He looked at Mr. Ragged, and felt an overwhelming need to beg for mercy.

"That's better," the Beggar Lord said placidly. "Everyone in the appropriate positions. It would seem that I am not so vulnerable as you think, am I, Mr. Smoke?"

Ashes's throat constricted. The air was too heavy, pressing in on him from all sides. His eyes stung, and tears streamed down his cheeks. He could feel sweat tingling on his forehead and his palms.

"What've you . . . What've you done?"

"I think you ought to take your constructs off, Mr. Smoke," Ragged suggested. "Else I will have to kill you."

*My face—*

*He'll know my face—*

*He's going to kill me—*

Ashes turned and ran. The children were packed together tightly in the small space, but he had found something even more frightening than being confined, and it was standing right behind him.

"Damn," he heard Ragged say. "Carapace, fetch him."

Ashes pushed through the press of the Motleys to see his guards standing over the Broken Boys. The guns were all on the ground.

The young Motleys looked stricken and pale, dead eyes staring forward. They turned to see Ashes as he burst, frenzied, through the gate. He heard Carapace's relentless footsteps behind him.

"Time to go," said a soft voice in his ear. A column of blackest smoke burst into existence around him; the monster had caught up. He screamed.

"That won't do, either."

Something struck the back of his head, and the world melted into black.

# 33 Failure

**A**SHES woke in a room that smelled sharp and clean and empty. The smell burned, forced its way up his nostrils and rooted around in there, setting fires on the edges of his brain . . .

He had not died, then.

He sat up. The world wanted to spin, but he was an Artificer's apprentice. He focused, and the spinning stopped. What had happened?

He'd been shot. He'd gathered up an army to storm Ragged House. They had dispatched the Broken Boys. They'd taken the guns. Mr. Ragged had come out . . .

And then horror. Fright like he had never felt before. A certainty that he was going to die, be crushed to death or eaten or consumed entirely, body and soul and mind, by the dark. Ragged's face was carved inside his brain, and even remembering what had happened made him want to vomit.

He heard footsteps. He knew it was Jack before the Artificer even entered the room.

"Oh," Jack said as he came around the corner. "You're awake."

"How long've I been out?"

"A pair of days," Jack said tonelessly. "I doubt I've ever seen you so lazy."

*Two days?!* "Blimey!" Ashes said. Two days without seeing or hearing from Ashes except their last argument—what would Blimey think? What would he have done? "Oh, bugger bugger *bugger.*"

"Missed teatime with the Queens?" Jack asked drily.

"I need to leave." Ashes swung his legs off the table and was pleased that both landed adroitly; Jack hadn't taken him to a witch. That was good. He would need to get back to Burroughside quickly. "What time is it? Bugger, I can't even— Where's my cloak?"

"In the sitting room." Jack's voice was patient and calm, and something about it made Ashes pause.

He looked at the Weaver. "How the hell'd I get here?"

Jack smiled, but there was pain in it. "Got there at last."

"Jack, what's going on? I remember— How've I been asleep for two days?"

"Exhausted your magic," Jack said. "Your body, too. You're still quite young to be doing so much Artifice so quickly."

Ashes peered at him. "You followed me?"

Jack nodded. "I've been keeping tabs for a little while."

"Where d'you get off doing that?"

The Weaver shrugged. "Try not to sound quite so indignant, boy. It saved your damn life. As for where I get off, it's likely the same place you get off using my Anchors and my aether to enact your little vendetta." His gaze bored into Ashes, unrelenting.

The boy froze. "I dunno what you're talking about," he said, but much too fast.

"Don't you," Jack said tonelessly. "Well, that's very interesting, because it would mean that someone *else* has been nicking my materials for some nefarious purpose. I was really hoping it was you. Better the petty thief you know than the petty thief you don't, and all that."

"I . . ." Ashes bit his cheek. "Look, Jack, you don't understand."

"What don't I understand, Ashes?" Jack asked. His voice had the deceptive calm of a lake in the winter, layered in ice as thin and frail as paper.

"I was going to pay you back."

"Were you indeed." Not a question. There was irony twined in the words.

"And I needed them," Ashes said. "For something important."

"I would never doubt that." The Weaver gave him a flat stare.

Ashes felt his stomach twist. "Jack, look, I—"

"It seems that the polite thing," Jack mused, "when you have something important to do, and you need someone else's resources to do it, is to ask that person if you can borrow them."

"I couldn't ask you," Ashes pleaded. "You'd have said no in a heartbeat!"

"Then why the *bloody buggery* have you been robbing me, lad?" Jack said, the mask breaking for just a moment. His eyes went perilously bright, and Ashes noticed the light in the room flicker. His heart juddered. Jack was so angry he was approaching calm from the other way round.

"It was important—"

"So you've mentioned!" Jack snapped. "It was important, was it, to get all those homeless children to believe you were some kind of magic man? It was important to muck around with the governor of Burroughside? It was *important* to sneak around, night after night, using *my* Anchors and *my* aether and *my* training, so you could—what, get revenge? So you could establish who could piss further between you and that bastard?"

"It's not like that!" Ashes said, nearly shouting.

"Running around in that cloak, no less!" Jack threw up his

hands. "You've no idea, do you, how worried Juliana would be if she knew what you were doing?"

"That's none of her business!"

"The ruddy hell it's not her business!" Jack leveled a finger at him dangerously. "You've eaten food from our table. You've shared our secrets, our dangers, our time together. We've sewn you up and let you sleep under our roof. She cares about you, even if you won't acknowledge that."

"I don't need someone to care—"

"Oh, of course you don't," Jack interrupted, and the lights flickered again. "Since you're so bloody cautious, aren't you? Running about in the dead of night, getting shot at from every direction." Jack rubbed his forehead. "I get the exhausting sense that we've had this conversation before, lad, haven't we? Wherein I tell you that it's better to be invisible until you're holding all the cards you need? Or have I only dreamed those?"

"You don't understand, Jack," Ashes said again.

"Enlighten me, then, little liar," Jack said softly. "Test my understanding."

Ashes opened his mouth, and snapped it shut. He tried again to speak, and failed.

"I'm listening," Jack said. His voice was just above a whisper.

"He's *evil*, Jack," Ashes said. "You don't know, you've never had to live under something like that." He searched for words. How could Jack not understand this? Ragged was a stain on the world, he *needed* to be removed . . . "He's merciless and cruel and vile, and he's not scared of *anything*, Jack. And it's not right that someone that awful can do whatever he wants, it's not *fair*." Bright spots of pain lit up in his palms, where his fingernails dug into his skin. "No one in Burroughside can do anything about it. They're too scared. But me . . ." He felt something shift in his chest; the light around him flickered, just a little. "I've got magic in me. What's the use of having it if all I ever do is make pretty faces for rich folks?" His jaw locked.

"Every time Saintly knifes somebody. Every time Ragged buggers some kid. That's on *me*, if I could do something, and I just stand by."

Jack's eyes fell to his lap, but he did not speak.

"I've stood by before," Ashes said, "'cause I was scared. Mari died 'cause of that. Iames died 'cause of that." He swallowed. "I won't do it again."

The Artificer's silence stretched on. Ashes chewed his tongue, and finally said, "I shouldn't've stolen your Anchors—"

"You're damn *right* you shouldn't have stolen my Anchors," Jack said in biting tones. "*Or* my aether. My company functions on trust, Ashes!"

"Oh, does it?" Ashes said. "I wouldn't've known, really. You couldn't bother to trust me with the *actual* plan when we were robbing Edgecombe."

"And the evidence certainly seems to back me up, doesn't it?" Jack gave him a hard stare. "I was right not to trust you. You've been picking my pocket since we first met."

"I was going to pay you back!"

"Stop *lying* to me, Ashes!" The light around him warped violently, making it look as if the room were shaking. "No lies here. Keep your secrets if they're precious—I won't hold that against you. But don't you *dare* lie to me. I took you in. I taught you my craft. You saved my life. Don't sully that."

Ashes realized his fists were shaking. He gripped the edge of the table. "Fine, then. I needed the Anchors. I needed the aether. I figured I'd find a way to pay you back eventually. But I also figured that if you never noticed, then it couldn't be that important to you."

Jack's look was heavy. "You couldn't think of any other reason, lad?"

Ashes ignored the question. "I don't have time to argue about it with you just now. There's things I got to do." *Like talk to Blimey*, he thought. *And find out— Oh, Faces, what did Ragged do to the Motleys?*

"So if you're gonna throw me out, fine. Do it. Don't threaten about it. Play me straight. No lies between the liars, right?"

Jack set his jaw. "I need to think about that, lad. I'd hate to do something stupid because I'm mad at you."

"Fine," Ashes said. "Then I've got to go. Let me know when you've got something figured."

Jack stepped in front of him, blocking his path. The man met his eyes. "I'm disappointed in you, lad," Jack said. "In many ways. Angry, too. But I'll tell you something." He grinned weakly. "I'm *appalled* that you're waging this little war of yours for free." The Artificer shrugged. "If Ragged's half the dirty bastard you seem to think he is, he must have wealthy enemies *somewhere*. You want my advice? Get yourself an investor, boy."

● ● ●

*Ashes stepped out of* the Rehl Company into a dark thick enough to wear for a winter coat. He could hardly believe it wasn't only a few hours ago that he'd set out to drag Ragged away from his precious fort.

His head spun as he hurried toward Burroughside. Everything had gone wrong somehow, hadn't it? When he'd taken those first phials of aether, he hadn't cared much if Jack found out. He was just another Denizen, after all, albeit one who'd done him a good turn. Back then, the Artificer had been just . . . a means, really. Someone who could guide Ashes from being a Burroughside gutter-rat to another version of himself, one with a future, one with a way out. Ashes hadn't worried himself over what Jack would think if he found out.

But now . . .

When had it shifted? When had he started caring what Jack thought of him? It was absurd. Faces' sake, Jack was a *Denizen*. Ashes robbed people like him all the time. Robbing Denizens was how Ashes found food!

Yet Ashes's belly felt shrunken. His neck was hot. He felt shamed. He'd let Jack down. Even now the Artificer was sitting in the shop, considering Ashes's future. And Ashes cared what the man decided. He cared quite a lot. He hadn't been part of a family in years. The Rehl Company had accepted him with hardly a question. He belonged there.

And, in the end, Jack hadn't been the one doing the betraying.

*Blood and bones*, Ashes thought. This really was his fault, wasn't it? Jack had trusted him—not entirely, not with everything, but who would expect that? He'd confessed things to Ashes that could've gotten him thrown in jail. He'd taught Ashes to use magic. He'd given him a future.

*Damn.*

It was strange, looking back. For the last few months, Ashes had been watching the Rehl Company, wondering—though not always consciously—if perhaps he could bring Blimey to them. If the two of them would be safe in Jack's shop. If, maybe, they'd found a Denizen who wouldn't throw them to the police. He'd wanted to know if they could be trusted. He shouldn't have worried. It hadn't mattered anyway.

It was his fault. He and Blimey *could* have stayed with the Rehl Company; of course they could have. If he'd been more willing to trust them, if he'd told Jack the truth from the very beginning . . .

And it was too late now, wasn't it?

He stopped beneath a streetlamp and ran his hands beneath the light. He could feel the weight of it against his skin. In perhaps a year, he'd be strong enough to draw it out of thin air. If he wanted to change the lamppost's iron-gray to a glossy gold, he could. That was within his power.

Jack's doing. He wouldn't have any of it if it weren't for Jack.

*Bugger.*

Ashes turned back toward the shop.

## Faith

**34**

CANDLESTICK Jack, who had not been born Jacob Rehl but preferred that fiction to the truth, checked the time and rubbed his eyes. Gods, he was tired. All the time now, he was tired. It hadn't been that way when he was young.

He forced himself out of the sitting room chair and made for the laboratory. They would be expecting him.

Past that false wall next to the fireplace, into the peaceful, quiet space where he'd worked for the last ten years. He let his eyes linger on some of his favorite projects, but not too long. He had an appointment.

In the back of the room was a magnificent old grandfather clock. It was a masterwork of carving, made of dark, rich wood with a heavy golden pendulum swinging eternally back and forth. Jack was not a man of rigid routine, but he maintained this clock with a fervor that bordered on the religious. The first thing he did every morning was wind the springs in the back, to keep the pendulum swinging.

Jack pulled away the panel on the side, revealing an intricate system of gears. He hummed an old sailing song to himself as he slipped a thin metal rod into the mechanism, forcing the pendulum to stop. He reached deep inside it and plucked out a gear of dull, aged gold.

A space beside the clock, which had previously been a blank stretch of wall, became the opening to a tunnel. Jack smiled despite himself. He was world-weary and cynical, certainly, but even he hadn't yet grown used to this. The passage was hidden in a manner that no Artificer would ever duplicate, and no seeing-stone or Iron Knight could pierce. He'd used it for a decade and he couldn't take it for granted.

He knocked heavily, three times, on the side of the tunnel, and then sat on the bench.

"He'll be up in a minute," Jack called absently.

The illusion that separated the workshop from the Wisp's study parted. The pale man entered with his customary dourness and sat opposite Jack.

"Has your pupil recovered?"

"As much my student as yours, Will," Jack said.

Will made a soft noise low in his throat, one Jack had learned long ago meant *dismissal*. "He is not of my folk, Weaver."

"Hardly one of mine, either," Jack mused. "Ergo, we have equal claim to him. It's not as if he's the worst student you've ever had."

"Mmm." It was as noncommittal a sound as Will had ever made.

"Talking about poor students, are we?"

The man who came from the tunnel was clean-shaven from the bottom of his neck to the top of his head, and was not as small as he looked.

"Evening, Tuln," Jack said.

"*I've* had poor students. I have stories that would make your hair curl," Tuln said mischievously. He winked at Jack. "Not yours, of course, since you star in most of them. But I'd wager I can make the pale one chuckle a bit."

"You manage that and I will give you every last ounce of aether I have in this shop," Jack said. "Every drop."

"There's an audacious bet."

"You don't understand who you're dealing with," Jack said.

Will gave them both a blank look. "I assume this passes for being very clever," he said.

"Exceedingly," Jack said. "Can I get you anything, Tuln?"

The older man waved a hand as he sat. "Nothing tonight. Rude of me—I imagine you haven't stopped celebrating since the ball, have you? The whole city's buzzing about your escapade."

Jack and Will shared an uneasy glance. "We have bad news," Jack said.

"It would appear we were not the only ones interested in Lord Edgecombe's artifact," Will said.

"Someone else stole it?" Tuln asked, incredulous. "Out from under *you*?"

Jack's jaw clenched at the thought. "That, or something subtler," he said. "I used a pair of informants on this. Both were wrong. One led me into a trap. I'll admit it's possible someone else saw Edgecombe's party as an opportunity. The other possibility I see here is that someone anticipated my visit. Edgecombe *wanted* me there—either to capture me, or as an opportunity to tell the Queens his glass ring has been stolen."

Tuln nodded thoughtfully. "Giving him a fourth, is that it?"

Will's mouth drew into a thinner line than usual. "There is no question that House Edgecombe longs to gather more glass. And it would be quite a cunning ploy, if such things were not a matter of public record."

"High-interest public record, too," Jack added. "The sort of thing everyone would notice very quickly."

Tuln's brow furrowed. "Making it quite an ineffective scheme."

"Or quite an effective one," Jack said, "with a goal we can't discern just yet. I don't particularly like either idea."

"The Weaver leaves one line of reasoning untouched," Will noted. Jack shot him a disapproving glance, but Tuln was clearly intrigued.

"What might that be, Jack?"

"There's also the possibility we were sabotaged from the inside," Jack muttered.

Tuln's eyes narrowed. "The boy?"

"The boy," Jack said heavily.

"You're playing your hand very recklessly here, Jack," Tuln chided. "If you are so suspicious, why keep him?"

"He's useful," Jack said. "And damn if he isn't clever. I'd rather have ten of him than any hundred Guild graduates. *Two* hundred. He's fierce."

"But not trustworthy?"

"I'm not sure," Jack admitted. "He's far too convenient. He's compulsively secretive. He doesn't trust me a whit."

"Is *that* why you had me delivering that impromptu history lesson?" Tuln shook his head sadly. "Still manipulating your students, Jack . . ."

"If I didn't, everything would take much longer and be much harder."

"There's so much to be said for traditional teaching methods. There's no subterfuge, for one. Nor stolen handkerchiefs."

"You haven't met this boy, Tuln. He sees traps everywhere. If *I* told him about the Artisans, he'd start to think I'm setting him up somehow."

Tuln's eyebrows dipped down harshly. "So to keep him from feeling manipulated, you are, in fact, manipulating him."

"It's complicated, Tuln." Jack ground his teeth together. "He sees through glass."

Tuln's eyes widened. He leaned forward hungrily. "You're certain?"

"We *think* so," Jack said.

"It is the soundest explanation," Will said. "The boy is no canted Stitcher. Nor is he a Weaver. What comes naturally to either cant, he achieves only with great effort and at great cost. It is possible he simply lacks the focus necessary to master the magic—"

Jack laughed once, harshly.

"Though we find that unlikely," Will finished.

"He saw an Ivory Lord for the first time at Lord Edgecombe's ball," Jack said. "He asked me afterward why we were all so enraptured. He didn't understand."

Tuln's eyes were wide and bright. "That is . . . suggestive."

"It's not all, either. I've been following him a while now," Jack said. "Two nights ago he beat the stuffing out of a little gang of rough-and-tumbles, all on his own. And when he had them on the ground, he started punishing them. Stitching their faces to look like they'd been burned half to death. Except they started screaming when he did it. As if it were real."

Tuln put a hand to his chin. "Odd. Very odd."

"Bloody exceptional, is what it is," Jack said. "I've been suspicious since before he walked through our door. What's like an Artificer, but not quite, Tuln? That's your favorite question, if I remember right."

"These things are not conclusive," Tuln warned. "Not in themselves."

"I'm aware. I meant to confirm it when we robbed Edgecombe, but the opportunity got away from us."

"But you're convinced it's true?"

"I'm convinced it's *possible*," Jack said. "I'm playing cautious at the moment."

"And you also think he may be a spy."

"I think he has to be," Jack said. "Like I said, it's far too bloody convenient. What're the odds, you think, that we would find a canted Artificer with no previous loyalties tangling him up? No debts to High Lords, no family, no record that he exists at all. A ghost with everything I could possibly want."

"A trap laid around treasure," Tuln concluded.

"Exactly so," Jack said. "He *might* be a gods-blessed coincidence, clever and fierce and, most noticeably, canted in ways we haven't seen before. He *might* be exactly what I've been looking for. Or, on the other and *incredibly more likely* hand, he's a trap. Whoever set us up with him is twice as clever as me and playing a game deeper than I can tell."

"Thus the surveillance."

"Thus the surveillance," Jack said. "Most of his free time he spends on some personal vendetta against Governor Ragged, down in Burroughside, which is good. It doesn't leave him much room to do anything else. But—"

"Perhaps it is a smokescreen," Tuln said thoughtfully.

Jack laughed softly to himself. "Yes. A smokescreen. Appropriate." He rubbed his face, exhausted. "Thing is, even if he is a spy, there's more than a slim chance we can sway him to join us."

Tuln looked at him incredulously. "That seems uncharacteristically optimistic of you, Jacob. Have you been drinking?" He turned to Will. "Has he been drinking?"

"It's not optimism," Jack said. "You haven't seen the way he looks at us, Tuln. At supper, or when we sit to talk at the table. Whatever this boy is, we're the closest thing to family he's seen in a long time . . . Maybe our mastermind is clever, but not wise. Ashes's skills—whatever we may think them to be—are not nearly as important, I think, as his loyalties."

# 35 Ugly

**"** . . . are not nearly as important, I think, as his loyalties."

Jack continued to speak, but Ashes could no longer hear him. He stepped away from the false wall where he had been listening for the past quarter of an hour, and clutched his head, and resisted the urge to scream.

*No lies between liars, Ashes. Don't play me for a fool, Ashes. My company functions on* trust, *Ashes.*

Jack hadn't trusted him. Jack had never trusted him. To him, Ashes was a spy, just someone to be manipulated into doing and thinking things so Jack would benefit. Ashes had been played.

*Still manipulating your students, Jack . . .*

*He sees traps everywhere.*

Jack had been playing him ever since they met in Yson. Everything he'd done—every supper, every bloody card game, even that damn heist in Edgecombe's mansion—it had all been calculated. A scheme to win Ashes's trust from the "mastermind" Jack imagined pulling Ashes's strings. It had all been fake. Had he ordered Juliana to give him the cloak, too? Had Synder followed Ashes to Batty Annie's under Jack's command?

Ashes clutched the back of the chair, feeling abruptly queasy. Even their argument had been staged, hadn't it? Ashes had felt like a traitor, just like Jack wanted. He'd thought the lock on the aether cabinet sprang too easily . . .

Faces, he'd been such a fool.

*Whatever this boy is, we're the closest thing to family he's seen in a long time.*

Bloody right, they'd been. Ashes had been looking for someone to be a new Mari. He'd wanted a family so bad it made him stupid. Jack had seen that. He'd seen it and exploited it. No hesitation, no mercy. Wanting is weakness indeed.

Ashes walked briskly out of the room and down the hall. His head was spinning. He could hardly think. He'd been so foolish.

He flung open the door to the staircase and nearly crashed into the person coming up the steps. He paused. Synder.

"Oh! Ashes!" she said. "I—"

"No," Ashes said harshly. "Don't you dare say another word to me."

Synder recoiled from him. "I didn't—"

"Haven't you said enough?" he snapped. "Get out of my way."

"Ashes, I have something—" She brandished a bit of paper, but Ashes couldn't find it in him to care what she was saying.

"I don't want to hear it." He stepped sharply around her and hurried down the stairs.

Ashes flung the door open and burst onto the street, breathing hard. He could hardly think straight, but one thing was sure. This would be the last time he ever left the Rehl Company Shop. Jack wanted him to play into his hands? Jack could stuff it. Ashes wouldn't be coming back. His education was finished. He was done learning from Jack; he had everything he needed now.

*Get yourself an investor, boy.*

● ● ●

*Lord Horatio Edgecombe, arbiter* of Lyonscourt, Minister of Harcourt, came out of his room in the middle of the night for a drink. His face did not gleam, and his eyes did not shine, but he was recognizable instantly. Even without the luster covering his face, he looked crafted. The work of an artist.

It was more than a little gratifying to see the man's eyes widen as he turned away from his wine to find Mr. Smoke sitting in his chair.

"Bloody *hell*," he said.

"Good to know," Ashes said. He wore the appropriate-for-meetings face, rather than the demon, tonight. He would prefer to gain Edgecombe's trust quickly, and for that he needed to look adult, confident, and not monstrous. "I'd sort of wondered if Ivories knew those words."

"Who are you? What are you doing here?" Edgecombe rose to his full, imposing height. "I should warn you that I have guards standing just outside the door."

"Does that threat work, typically?" Ashes tilted his head. "Think about it. If they're outside the door, they'll come as soon as you scream. Thing is, if someone's breaking into your house to do you harm, how much good is that going to do you? *You'd* already be dead, sir."

The Ivory peered at him. "They're very swift. Are you here to kill me?"

"Not much for me to gain by that, sir," Ashes said honestly. "There's a few things I'd like you to do for me."

Edgecombe still looked like a started cat, ready to tear away at the first sign of danger. "That's a no, then?"

"I'm called Mr. Smoke," Ashes said calmly. "And I'm more your friend than I'm your foe."

The Lord scoffed. "I've heard those words before. You're looking for a favor."

"In a manner of speaking, sir." Ashes smiled winningly. "It's more that I think we can be of service to each other."

The Lord approached the table, eyes fixed on Ashes. "I don't typically negotiate with people who break into my home."

"I don't typically break into homes, sir. Desperate times." Ashes shrugged. "If I'd shown up on your doorstep, your chamberlain or whoever else you've got on the door would've got rid of me without even hearing what I have to say. And that'd be a loss for you, sir. I thought I'd go right to the one in charge of the operations."

Edgecombe sat. *Good*, Ashes thought. *He's curious, at least.*

"Well?" Edgecombe said impatiently. "I'm a busy man. What is it you'd like to tell me?"

"I've found out where your glass ring is, sir," Ashes said.

Edgecombe smiled. Ashes couldn't tell if it was dangerous or simply frightening. "I cannot help but notice that you did *not* say that you have it with you, and are prepared to bargain for me to have it back."

"Quite correct, sir. Didn't say that."

"You intend to sell me the information, then. Very well. How much would you like? Money is hardly an obstacle."

Ashes spread his hands gregariously. "Now, that's hardly much of a deal, sir, is it? You give me all the money I could ever want just in exchange for, what, maybe a sentence's worth of information? You're not a dab hand at buying things, are you, sir?"

"Typically I command that things be done and then wait," Edgecombe said. "I could, for instance, shout for my guard and wring the information out of you. It's a messy process, though. Not good for one's reputation in the informant community."

"Very wise of you, sir, very wise." Ashes searched the man's face, trying to read him the way he used to read card players. "Here's what I'm proposing, sir. The man what's got your ring is a bit of a cunning bastard. Makes it difficult to pick his pockets, you understand. And I'd not be doing my duty to the city if I set an Ivory to do his own muck-digging."

"I'm honored," Edgecombe said drily.

"What I'm proposing, sir, is that you give me a modest bit of cash. Maybe you let me—maybe, say, borrow a few of your little guards. I go, I storm the place, I bring you back your ring all nice and cleanly."

Edgecombe gave him a flat stare. "You cannot possibly think I am that stupid."

"Not stupid, sir," Ashes said with a grin. "Efficient. *I'm* the one knows who's got your ring. *I* would dearly like to kick his teeth in myself, hence my willingness to do your dirtier work."

"And then steal my ring yourself," Edgecombe said. "Using *my* money."

"Got to be honest, sir, I've not the littlest interest in taking your ring," Ashes said. "Send along somebody to keep me company and make sure I don't bugger off with the thing, if you like. All I care about is getting to take the bastard down myself."

Edgecombe stared at him for several quiet seconds. Ashes stared back. Neither blinked.

"I think I may be persuaded," Edgecombe said finally. "But I demand you tell me who the thief is beforehand. And how you know."

Ashes smiled. "I reckon that's easy enough. Shake on it, sir? Gentleman's agreement?"

"You are no gentleman," Edgecombe said, extending his hand.

"Keep good company, though," Ashes said, shaking Edge-combe's hand firmly.

Edgecombe's brow furrowed for a moment. "Who is it, then?"

"Hiram Ragged, sir," Ashes said. "Governor of Burroughside and all-around horrid human being. I've been known to throw that term around, though, *human being*. Might be a bit too generous."

Edgecombe's eyes narrowed. "And how have you reached this conclusion?"

"I'm sure you've heard, sir, about the little tiff Mr. Ragged and I have going on at the moment? It's given me cause to inspect his quarters on a few occasions. Mr. Ragged's more than a little obsessed with your folk, sir. Keeps a little glass ring hid in his room, which I reckon he wears sometimes when he wants to feel important."

"What of it?"

"A pair of nights ago, I saw Ragged reduce a whole crowd of children to screams and tears," Ashes said. "Burroughside children, mind. Tougher blighters have not been born. He made them all weep, and he didn't even *move*." Ashes shrugged. "I know what you Ivories do to people. I know that whatever it is, you keep it tied up in your rings. Your face's not shining and I'm not presently bowing, sir, on account of how you're not wearing your ring." Ashes gestured aimlessly. "More pertinent, sir, is the fact that Ragged's got a whole damn legion of housebreakers, lock-pickers, chimney-climbers, and window-slippers. If there's anybody could mount an operation to pilfer your little trinket, sir, it's him. He's been wanting to replace his toy with the real thing for a while, I reckon."

Edgecombe stared at him, blank-faced. Again, Ashes returned the look. The Ivory broke their stare first.

"Ah, me," he said. "Did you know the gods favor the Ivories? It's a very significant point of doctrine in some of the churches. Guards!"

Ashes leapt to his feet as two men walked through the door. They could have been brothers: both were hairless and blank-faced, their mouths set in identical grim lines. Their eyes were as white as the moon. Iron Knights.

"Take him," Edgecombe said wearily. Ashes dashed toward the secret exit, but he hardly moved more than a foot before a hand grasped his wrist. The grip was iron-hard; Ashes cried out as he felt his shoulder strain. The Knight who had caught him didn't let him move an inch. He stank of something like old milk.

"What's going on?" Ashes demanded. "What're you doing? We agreed!"

Edgecombe tutted softly. "Why on earth would I honor a bargain with a terrorist?"

"I can help you!" Ashes said. "I know Ragged, I can get the ring back for you, I don't even want it—"

"I don't think you'll be procuring the ring for me, boy," Edgecombe said, moving to the wine rack and reaching through the bottles. He pulled a dark-colored knife from the shadows. "I daresay your vendetta against Hiram is finished as well."

"Don't—"

"Silence him." Another hand, cold and solid as stone, clamped around his mouth. Edgecombe moved closer and brought the knife close to Ashes's face. Ashes felt the construct around him quiver; the blade was solid iron. "It was very dangerous of you to come here tonight, Mr. Smoke. I can only assume you were desperate, now that Hiram has so thoroughly removed that *ugly* friend of yours."

Ashes's eyes widened. *Blimey? Blimey, oh gods—*

"I confess, you had me genuinely worried," Edgecombe continued, pressing the knife's edge against Ashes's forehead. The construct started dissipating, revealing Ashes's face. The Lord flicked the blade across Ashes's scalp, opening a line of fire on his skin. "Hiram told me he had taken all but one of the children who saw him use the ring. That wouldn't do. Where would we find you? How would we keep you silent?" He laughed softly. "Hiram knew better. He said you wouldn't wait to throw yourself against the next trap you could find. I will have to congratulate him. He was so reckless as a boy. It does a father proud to see him improving."

**PART 4**

*Flame*

## 36 Dangerous

"IMMOBILIZE him," the Harcourt Lord commanded. "Not permanently. Hiram would be discouraged if I took away his fun."

The hand covering his mouth moved, just long enough for Ashes to gasp out, "You're his *fa—ugh—*"

A single strike beneath his ribcage drove the breath out of him, so forcefully he thought for a moment his lungs had collapsed entirely. Another blow followed, this to the back of his neck, and he crumpled like paper. Edgecombe's guards were absurdly strong; each punch hurt like another bullet wound.

"A little more thoroughly," Edgecombe commanded. Ashes felt something strike his leg, but his mind had retreated somewhere away from his body, ensconcing itself away from the pain. He heard, rather than felt, the solid thump of the guard's boot against the bone of his leg. Mercifully, he heard nothing snap—although what would it matter if his leg broke now anyway?

"Send for a squadron of four guards," Edgecombe said. "Have

them escort him to one of the lower rooms. And rouse one of the messengers. Hiram will be delighted to hear this, and I'd hate to deny him something he'd so enjoy."

The Ivory Lord left. Ashes, curled in a heap on the stone floor, was just dimly aware of the sound of footsteps, of a door opening and closing, and then voices, slurred and incomprehensible. Ashes didn't have the strength, physically or mentally, to keep up with whatever was happening outside of his head. The thoughts within were too loud. All-consuming.

*Blimey's dead. Ragged is the son of an Ivory Lord. Blimey is dead. They've got me, they're going to take me downstairs and then when Ragged gets here he'll kill me himself and* Blimey is dead. *All the Motleys are either dead or captured, and that's all my fault, and Blimey is dead. Ragged killed him.*

Ashes was on his feet now, being shoved out the door and down the hall. His vision swam, nothing made sense, they were giving him orders but he couldn't hear them, much less understand them—

*Blimey is dead and that's my fault.*

They were on cold stone steps now. Ashes felt something warm and wet trickling down his cheek. Blood, no doubt, from the Ivory Lord's knife. Ashes stumbled down them drunkenly.

*Ragged killed him and that's my fault.*

The hallway was lit by expensive-looking lamps, powered by some kind of Artifice. Ashes looked at them, dully, and blinked as the light they produced suddenly went out.

*The Motleys are doomed and that's my fault, too. I should've been more careful, should've thought further ahead. I never should have involved the Motleys, of course I shouldn't have, I knew it was stupid. I should have told Jasin she'd made a mistake, and just left. Should've been smarter, should've been better. If I hadn't been such a fool . . .*

Muttered curses all around him. "What's on with the lights?"

"What in Furies?"

"Someone go get a torch—"

"Gentlemen."

The voice was soft, confident. A deep and reassuring voice, laced with power.

"Who's there?!"

*I should've been better.*

"I have a friend who's very fond of riddles," the voice said. "He's not here at the moment, but I think he'd appreciate this one. When is the single most dangerous man in the room even *more* dangerous?"

"Who the ruddy hell—?"

"When there are *several* of him."

The lights came back on, and Ashes looked up. All five guardsmen now wore the face of Candlestick Jack.

To their credit, they did not *immediately* panic. Two of them pulled out clubs, and another went for a gun. The lights flickered again, and one of the men staggered backward, clutching his eyes.

"He got me!" the man cried. "The bastard got me!" He pointed wildly. "There! I saw him!"

"Take the boy back!" the one with the pistol said, leveling it at the end of the hallway. The two with clubs arranged themselves back to back. The fourth pulled Ashes away from the group, back toward Lord Edgecombe's room, and tripped when the one on the ground lunged forward and caught him by the heel.

"You gentlemen aren't very good at counting, are you?" the guard said. The lights went out once more, and Ashes heard several sharp, wet *smacks* of fist against yielding flesh. At least two people were shouting, before one of them shouted, "Quiet!"

Silence came after that, and then a guttural *"Argh!"*

Some base instinct, unaffected by the roil in Ashes's head, took command of his legs and pushed him down the hallway, as far from the action as he could get. When the lights came back on, the three armed guards stood only a few feet from each other, all poised to fight and wary as cats. Two men were on the ground, unconscious, both wearing Jack's face.

The gun-wielder recovered first, staggering backward and aiming the pistol at each of his comrades in turn.

"Names!" he snapped. "Say your names! And you *bloody well* be convincing!"

"Reid—"

"Wesson—"

"Good enough," the leader said. "Where'd the lad go?"

"Wait, what's your name?"

"Wrong question," the man said. He flicked his wrist, and blindingly bright light streamed from his fingers to the man's face. The guard clutched his eyes, while the other lunged at Jack. The Weaver aimed the pistol at him, hesitated, and then stepped adroitly aside as the guard passed him. He smashed the pistol against the man's temple, and the guard fell in an instant doze.

The blinded guard had fallen to the floor, helplessly rubbing his eyes. Jack approached him calmly, dissipating the illusion over his face with a wave of his hand.

"Know anything interesting you want to tell me?" he asked. "Anything you'd count on to save your life?"

"I don't—"

"Very good, then." Jack smashed the gun against his head, and the man fell asleep. The Weaver straightened, grimacing. "You'll all be having very nasty headaches in the morning, I'd wager. Pity you don't have better taste in employment." He held out an open palm, and the illusions of his face streamed away from the guards, gathering over his hand. Jack held the makeshift lamp toward the end of the hallway. "Lad? Are you all right?"

Ashes trudged out of the darkness, peering at Jack bewilderedly. *Blimey's dead and it's my fault, my fault, my bloody, bloody fault.*

"Come here, lad," Jack said, bending so he was on Ashes's eye level. "We must be getting on."

Ashes approached Jack with the skittish caution of an alley cat. The Weaver looked him in the eye, steady and calm, and held out a hand. "Come on, then, lad. We haven't very much time before someone comes down here."

"How did you find me?"

"Followed you," Jack said simply. "I've gotten rather good at it."

"You—did you hear—?" Ashes trembled, and even though he screamed at himself inwardly for being a cowardly, stupid little child, he couldn't stop himself. *"He killed Blimey."*

"I'm not sure what you're talking about, Ashes," Jack said earnestly, "but we *must* get *away*. Come along."

Ashes took the Weaver's hand, and followed him out as quickly as he could.

The hallways rushed past. Ashes clutched tightly to Jack's hand, fearing that if he let go, he would never find his way out. The Weaver, who had memorized Edgecombe's halls just as well as Ashes had, led them unerringly toward the servants' entrance, and then out into the cold, wet Teranis night.

"Breathe deeply, lad," Jack said. "Keep moving. Don't stop."

Ashes stumbled along behind him, insensate except for the knowledge that he had to keep moving and Blimey was—

*STOP IT.*

He had to get control of himself. He had to be stronger. It didn't matter if Blimey was—was— *It didn't matter* right now, he had to focus again, had to keep his head.

"Just keep breathing, Ashes," Jack said. "Don't you dare pass out on me. It's been a while since I carried you out of those damned sewers. I've gotten old and you've gotten fat ever since you started eating Juliana's cooking." Jack glanced at him. "What, no laugh? Not even an aggrieved grin?"

*Blimey is—*

He stopped the thought, bundled it up in rags, and shoved it to the back of his mind. There was no time for that right now. He had to survive. He had to get out of here and plan his next move. He had to—he had to—

"This should do just fine," Jack said. They had stopped under the eave of some ancient, dusty church. Jack slumped against the wall and took several long breaths. "Are you hurt, lad? There's a witch down the way—"

"*No,*" Ashes said, though as he did he was acutely aware of the purpled bruises that were decorating his hip and his ribs and the back of his neck. A witch-healing would only make him clumsy and sluggish and thickheaded, and he couldn't afford that just now. Swiftly, he took a mental tally of his injuries, trying to guess how quickly he could move.

*Blimey is dead.*

"Very well," Jack said, wary. "Though I think it would be wi—Ashes, where the hell are you going?"

The boy did not respond except to run even faster toward Burroughside.

## 37 Despair

"ANNIE!" Ashes shouted, banging a fist against her door. "Annie!"

He heard Jack's voice behind him, calling his name, and paid the man no mind. He was not important just now.

"Annie!" He smashed a closed fist against the door again and again and again. There was no sound from within. "Open this bloody door!"

There was no answer on the other side. He felt a dull heat in his knuckles, knew that they had split open. He couldn't feel it.

He thrashed wildly, unsure what he was thinking, and felt Jack catch his wrists. Without thinking he whirled on the man.

"She's not here!" he cried in panic. "She's *always* there!"

"Breathe, boy. We need to think—"

"We need to get in there!"

Jack looked him in the eye. Ashes couldn't have said what the man saw there, but it convinced him in the space of a breath.

"Stand back."

Ashes obeyed, and the Weaver kicked the door at the handle. The thing creaked and moaned, but did not give way.

"Damn," he said. "Stay back another minute or so, Ashes. I can get past, I just need you to be quiet for a moment. Understand?"

Ashes nodded, and he stood away from Jack as he bent and began to pick the lock. Ashes's stomach twisted and tied itself in knots over and over again, there was a frenzy in his head. He had gone mad, a little.

"Breathe deeply, lad," Jack said. "I need you to do that for me. I can't focus if I'm worried you're going to pass out over there."

"You don't understand—"

"Help me understand, lad," Jack said. "Talk slowly. Pretend I'm dumb."

"Edgecombe is Ragged's father!"

"I sussed that," Jack said calmly. "What's got you so worked up *now*, though? Talk me through it."

Ashes stared at him, his panic cramping up. How could Jack not understand?

"I need to find Blimey," Ashes said.

"Friend of yours, I take it?"

Jack didn't know. Of course Jack didn't know. Ashes had been keeping Blimey a secret because . . . because . . .

*Why* couldn't he think straight? He needed to find Blimey. Everything else was insignificant. Blimey mattered. Nothing else had that distinction.

"Yes," Ashes admitted.

"Can you tell me—?"

"No, Jack, I bloody well *can't* tell you," Ashes said, feeling the same ruthless survival instinct taking over his brain. Anger superseded panic, just for a moment. "Can't tell you much of anything, can I? I'm just a game to you. A mark."

The Weaver paused and looked at Ashes, dour-faced. "How much did you hear?"

"Enough," Ashes said.

"All of it, then?" The Weaver pressed the lock-pick carefully forward, generating a soft *click* inside the mechanism. "You need to understand, I had good reasons—"

Ashes had no interest in hearing them. He slipped past the man, through the door, straight to the stairs. He took the stairs downward three at a time, and burst through the door to the cellar room—

The room was empty. Blimey was gone.

He heard Jack come down the stairs, but didn't turn as the man entered the room.

"Make sure you keep breathing," the Weaver said, stepping past Ashes to get a better look at the place. He took the room in at a glance. "Your friend lived down here?"

"Yes," Ashes said shortly. He was leaning against the door-frame; he was suddenly unsure if he'd be able to stand without it. "He wasn't a spy for anybody, either, just in case you were wondering."

"I wasn't."

"*Good.*"

"Ashes, you need—"

"Go away, Jack."

Jack paused, frowned. He moved away from Ashes, toward the bed. "Not ready to do that just yet, I'm afraid." He lifted the thin blanket, revealing a set of knickknacks that glimmered faintly with degraded Artifice. "Hmm. I'll need to have a little chat with Synder about keeping secrets, too."

"No lies among liars, right?" Ashes said bitterly.

"No lies among liars," Jack said softly. He scanned the room with an air of calm concern, then looked at Ashes. "I—"

"Shut up, Jack." Ashes met the man's eyes, and tried to access the anger that lay buried underneath his grief and his guilt. "You can stop pretending to be some sort of bloody father figure for me now, all right? Your game's up. I heard all about how you're trying to make me—make me feel like I *belong*, eh? You can stop lying to me now, too."

"It wasn't all an act, lad," Jack said. "You think I'd have come if it was? You think I'd have followed you to Lord Edgecombe's home, hoping that you had some other reason to visit than telling your boss your cover was working brilliantly, and you had the stupid Rehl Company all sewed up?"

"I was never a spy," Ashes said.

"I've more or less figured that part out by this point," Jack admitted. "Shame it took me so long. It's been a real pain tiptoeing around you every moment."

"Serves you right," Ashes said. He set his back against the frame and slid to the floor, hanging his head between his knees. He felt—not exhausted, not spent. *Hollowed.* Like someone had dug around in his chest and removed parts of it with a spoon.

"Serves us both right, I imagine." Jack blew out a long breath. "I'm sorry, for what it's worth. You understand what it's like to live a second life as a fugitive. Everyone is suspect. Everything is a trap."

"Can you *stop* for a moment?" Ashes demanded. "Just for a moment, could this not be about *you*? My friend is dead. Ragged didn't even need his stupid father to tell him who I am—he had me figured two nights ago. Everything I've been working for in Burroughside is gone." He laughed harshly. "Up in bloody smoke."

Jack glanced at him, then returned to his investigation of the room. "You're certain he was taken? He's not just out for—?"

"Blimey wouldn't leave this place," Ashes said. "He wanted to. He couldn't. And I wouldn't let him."

"I'll assume you have your reasons for that," Jack said.

"Annie should be here, too," Ashes said. "That's way out of place. She's *never* gone from here."

Jack made a noncommittal noise in his throat and turned to face Ashes. He didn't say anything.

"You done making jokes, then?" Ashes asked.

"I was under the impression you're not in the mood."

"I'm not."

Jack crossed his arms. "This your plan, lad? Sit in the doorway feeling sorry for yourself?"

"That's about the aim at the moment, yeah," Ashes said.

"Hmph," Jack said. "I'm learning all sorts of things about *you* tonight. I wouldn't have guessed you were the type to turn pathetic when you lost."

"Go to hell," Ashes said. "Swallow a brick on your way."

"You disagree?" the Weaver challenged. "Is this, perhaps, the first move in a grand scheme? Oh—you're formulating some daring master plan, but it helps you to weep about things while you do it? Lubricates the engine, as it were?"

"You're a bastard."

"I'm a pragmatist, Ashes, and right now you are being *distinctly* useless, which I'm not particularly accustomed to seeing."

"Leave me alone! I don't want you here!"

"Perhaps not," Jack said. "But you certainly *need* me here, on account of how deeply you're in need of a swift kick in the ass."

Ashes surged to his feet, clenching his fists. "My friend is dead!" he said, nearly shouting. "Ragged knows who I am. I've burned two bloody months trying to help Burroughside, and I have *mucked every portion of that.* Now leave me alone!"

The lights shivered, taking Ashes aback. Had that been him? Or was Jack far more involved in this argument than he looked?

"And all of that is a convincing case for just giving up now, is it?" Jack demanded. "Furies. Edgecombe was much cleverer than I thought."

Ashes looked at him, confused.

"Seems he managed to throw me off," the man went on. "I *was* looking for my apprentice. You might've seen him, before Edgecombe put his face on you? About your size, only ornery? And with a noticeable will to live?"

"Stop being such an ass!"

"You *first*, boy!" Jack snapped, and the light in the room seemed to warp again. "Your friend's gone. Your enemy knows your name. So bloody what? The boy I've been teaching wouldn't fall down and weep about how badly he's failed. The thief who conned me in Yson, the one who got threatened with the police and *kept on playing*, would not be doing this. Gods—if this is who you've been underneath, I'm ashamed. I was so worried I had someone dangerous studying under my roof, and all along you were *this*. I shouldn't have been so fussed."

Ashes set his jaw. "Stop. I did my best."

"Horseshit," Jack said. "Your best? Ragged's been grinding your face in the dirt as long as you can remember, and now he takes your friend, and *this* is what you do? This is your best? No." Jack advanced on him, eyes burning. "I won't hear it. He hurts you, you *hurt him back*. You owe your friend that."

Ashes punched him in the jaw. Jack flinched backward, swore colorfully, and rubbed his face.

"Feel any better?" the man asked.

"You'd be *stunned*."

"Glad to see you're still capable of getting angry."

"Hitting you is easy," Ashes said. "Hitting Ragged *isn't*. You saw what he did to us in the courtyard."

"I didn't, actually," Jack admitted. "My view was a little impeded. I figured it out once you mentioned it to Edgecombe."

"Ragged's got nothing to fear from me," Ashes said miserably. "Not so long as he has that ring with him."

Jack blinked, surprised. When Ashes offered no further comment, he said, "So figure out how to get it away from him. Force him into a bad move. Make him look the other way. Stop pretend-ing you're not *good* at this."

Ashes hesitated. "There's no point," he said. "Blimey's dead. Bringing Ragged down wouldn't bring him back."

Jack lifted an eyebrow. "You're wrong on that count, lad. This kid—Blimey—he's smart, eh? *You're* certainly not the one reading"—he glanced at one of the book covers—"*The Fall of the . . . Ymrani Hegemon*, so unless you've got some other roommate you're not telling me about . . . ?"

Ashes shook his head.

"Then he was smart enough to get taken as a hostage rather than make a fight of it with whoever came to bundle him up," Jack said. "There's no sign of a struggle here."

"There wouldn't be," Ashes said reflexively. "Blimey's helpless in a fight."

"They didn't have much reason to rough him up, then," Jack said. "And Edgecombe said Ragged expected you on his door any day now. That's either him expecting you to be very stupid, or . . ."

"Or he's got something he knows I'll bust through doors to get back," Ashes said softly. "Blimey."

"Just so." Jack tapped his cheek, thoughtful. "Which means your best move is to regroup. Set a trap, make a plan. Ragged and Edgecombe know who *you* are, maybe, but they don't know a bloody *thing* about me or the Rehl Company. You can lie low with us, get prepared—"

"No," Ashes said. "Absolutely not."

Jack sighed. "I *am* sorry I've been manipulating you, Ashes."

"It's not that," Ashes said, meeting his eyes. "That's not even— That's not important right now. What's important is that if you're right, then Blimey is at Ragged House *right now*. And Edgecombe sent a runner—"

"Saying that he had Mr. Smoke in his basement," Jack said. "You think he'd leave him unguarded?"

Ashes shook his head. "Not a chance in hell."

"Ragged might not have left yet," Jack said doubtfully.

"Doesn't matter," Ashes said. "I don't have time to wait. If there's even a chance."

Jack nodded slowly. "Best not waste time, then."

"Good-bye, Jack," Ashes said, moving for the door.

"The hell are you talking about, lad?" Jack asked, following him. "You didn't think I'd let you go *alone*, did you?"

# 38 Invasion

IT was the Witches' Hour, just before dawn when the darkness was thick and grasping. Fog had uncoiled all throughout the city, like a relaxed predator stretching its legs. Clouds had swarmed the moon, wrapped their wispy fingers around it, and strangled it to nothing. The strongest light came from lamps, and even that was scattered, distended by the mist.

Two Artificers approached Ragged House, and when the Broken Boys standing outside noticed them, the oldest Artificer made a swift, ruthless motion with one hand, like he was flinging something at them. Three of the Boys yelped, and grasped their eyes. The rest lifted their guns, preparing to aim them. By the time they had lifted their hands, two more were struck blind.

"Stop!" said one of the Boys.

"They're not very well trained," said Candlestick Jack. "I'd guess not one in eight of their bullets would even hit us."

"Just takes one bullet to ruin your whole day, Jack."

"*Very* salient point. Gentlemen?"

"If you so much as twitch your little finger—" said one of the Boys.

"Did you think that was necessary?" Jack plunged his hands in his pockets. "That's *adorable*."

The lights shining from Ragged House warped and bent. Threads broke away from it, twisting and wringing themselves until they turned black as pitch. The ribbons of darkness streamed toward the Broken Boys and lashed to their heads. The two Artificers stepped smartly away from where they'd stood, just as a chorus of gunshots rang out, and a set of bullets streaked near their last positions.

"Best stop now," Ashes warned.

"Blind as you are, I expect you're more likely to hit a friend than us," said Jack. "Drop the guns."

Two of the Broken Boys ignored the suggestion, preferring instead to take one more shot. Ashes got close enough to one to grab his wrist and strike him in the elbow before his finger clenched the trigger. He wasn't nearly strong enough to break the Broken Boy's arm, but it would keep him occupied. A few feet away, the other Boy sent a bullet into the wall of a building before Jack snatched the pistol out of his hand.

"Now, then," Jack said. "It seems we've established which of our groups is more threatening."

"We're onto you!" one said brazenly. "We know you can't blind us forever!"

"Well, no. Not without considerable trouble on my part," Jack said absently. "And a significant *mess* as well. I've no fondness for the practice. Guns on the *ground*, please."

The Boys obeyed.

"Now," Jack said. "I think it's only sporting if I let you know that in a few minutes, a whole horde of tiny, angry children—what're they called, the Motleys?—they'll be pouring out those gates, and I suspect they're going to be *powerfully annoyed* with Mr. Ragged, along with anybody who happens to be his affiliate."

"So you'd best be getting along," Ashes added. "Your chances are dead even at the best of times. Blind, weaponless—well, they could take you all for whatever they wanted, couldn't they? So you all just shamble off to the right—that's in the direction of the hand you piss with, by the way, for those of you who was slow to catch on—and make yourselves content hiding in some gutters, savvy?"

"There's Ravagers out there!"

"What a shame. Jack, is that gate unlocked?"

● ● ●

*The Motleys will be* in the cellar," Ashes said. "He wouldn't be able to fit them anywhere else, and it's where he keeps anyone clever enough to charm a lock."

"We go there first?"

"They'll be helpful," Ashes said. "They might know where he's keeping Blimey, and they can warn us if Ragged starts back."

"Lead on, young master."

Ashes nearly sprinted through the house, not bothering to check around corners. He knew its layout nearly as well as he knew Edgecombe's manse, after all his raids.

*I'm coming, Blimey. Just be all right.*

He crashed against the cellar door wildly and checked the knob. "Locked," he said to Jack. It was a good sign; Ragged wouldn't bother to keep it locked if no one was down there.

"Can you spring it?"

"Do the priests shit in the river?"

Jack thought for a moment. "Yes?"

"Half a moment."

The bolt was heavy and well made—bought with Lord Edge-combe's money, no doubt. Ashes worked at it for nearly a minute before it clicked open.

"Impressive lock," Jack said. "Twenty seconds over your nor-mal time."

Ashes straightened. "See if there's anybody in these other rooms," he said. "You see anything that looks important . . ."

"I'll get imaginative," Jack said, tilting his head in a shallow bow. "Your show, lad."

Ashes smiled grimly and raced down, pulling one of Jack's spare lamps out of his pocket as he reached the end of the stairs. The ghostly light illuminated a large, dank room, previously light-less, with spiders crawling along the walls and the chittering of unseen rats coming from the corner. The floor was decorated with sleeping Motleys. Ashes learned everything he needed to know with a glance and a brief, abortive sniff. Most of the children had livid, multicolored bruises along their faces and shoulders. The stench was tremendous, even after a pair of days; there was abun-dant evidence that Ragged didn't particularly care what his prison-ers used for a privy.

"Motleys," he said, trying to sound confident, trying to bury the thoughts that reminded him just how they'd ended up here. "Motleys. Wake up."

Some of them stirred reluctantly, but were too tired to get up. One or two of them looked at the stairs. He recognized them only vaguely; they looked horrid.

*Two days*, he thought, aghast. *Two days under Ragged, and this is what happens to them. I ought to die.*

"Who're you?"

Ashes blinked. Didn't they recognize Mr. Sm— No, of course not; his Mr. Smoke face had been dissolved in Edgecombe's parlor. There was nothing left of it but flecks of light.

"Name's Ashes," he said. "Mr. Smoke sent me."

"Ashes?"

Slippery Rafe crawled into view. Ashes caught his breath. The Motley leader's face was a mess of cuts and welts. One eye was swollen entirely shut. On the other side of his head, where his left ear ought to have been, there was only a bloody stump.

"What're you doing here?" Rafe asked. His voice was scratchy and dry, entirely drained of the strength it had had. Ashes's stomach churned.

"I'm here to get you lot out," he said.

Rafe's one open eye landed on him heavily. "To do *what*, exactly?"

Ashes stopped. "You won't be here," he said. "I can get you away from Ragged."

"So he can capture us again?" Rafe demanded. "So he can be even *angrier* at us? The *hell* do you think you are?"

"Mr. Smoke sent—"

"Mr. Smoke can shove a pistol up his arse, for all we care," Rafe snapped. "*He's* the one got us into this in the first place! Saying we could take Ragged out, saying we could make Burroughside better. It's his fault we're in this mess. All of it is his fault."

"He's right," one of the Motleys said. "Mr. Smoke did this to us."

"That's right. It's him what led us up a chimbly and left when the fire lit."

"Bastard."

"Turncoat."

"Him's the one that let Ragged take little Jasin!"

Ashes jerked toward the last voice. "Jasin? Where's she?"

"Ragged took her up to his study, didn't he?" the Motley shouted back. "After he took Rafe up there yesterday. Killed her, like as not. We've not seen her since we've been here."

Ashes felt a powerful need to be sick. "I need to find her, then." He looked out among the Motleys. The horrid, hollow feeling had returned to his chest. "I'm sorry for what Mr. Smoke did to you," he said. "Gods, I'm— I *know* he's sorry, too."

"Sorry enough to send someone *else* in his place," someone cried.

"Sorry enough he abandoned us the second Ragged came out," said another.

"Led us right into a trap," Rafe said viciously. "Filthy son-of-a-whore, Mr. Smoke is. No wonder he sent you, instead of coming himself. Probably smart enough to know what we'd do to him, if we saw him." He looked around at his beaten, helpless crew. "You're a decent sort, Ashes, but take it from me: get away from the bastard quick as you can. If you see Smoke again, let him know from me just how bloody *thankful* we are that he bothered to remember us."

Ashes's cheeks burned. "I'll— I'll let him know," he muttered. "Make sure you get out quick. There are some Broken Boys out in front of the yard, but you—you can probably take them, if you're quick."

"Eh," Rafe said. "Motleys! To me!"

The crew of thieves surged up the stairs behind Ashes, whose eyes were stinging fiercely. They poured out from the cellar door just behind him and made swiftly for the exit. Rafe slapped him on the shoulder, not unkindly, and he was gone.

He found Jack in Ragged's office, watching in satisfaction as a stack of papers burned on the desk. He turned as Ashes entered, and his expression softened immediately.

"Everything all right, lad?"

*Turncoat. His fault we're in here. Filthy son-of-a-whore.* "All's well so far," Ashes lied, smooth as ever. "You brought matches?"

"Matches are for mortals," Jack said with a smirk. "I think I've gotten most of Ragged's more important documents. And I got a little larcenous with some of his personal correspondence." Jack patted his side. "Your Beggar Lord has *several* dirty secrets of the sort policemen find deeply intriguing."

"Good," Ashes said. "We ought to move—Blimey's got to be upstairs. And there's another one with him, too, I think."

They moved briskly to the staircase, just as the last of the Motleys limped out the front door. Ashes stared after them for a long moment, heart wrenching. Rafe and his crew would never forgive him, but that was . . . fair. He deserved that. He deserved much worse.

"No time for dallying, lad," Jack said. "We're for it once Ragged figures out you're not at dear old Dad's."

Ashes nodded and followed the man to the upstairs hallway. The old men in the portraits glared down at them, as if they knew the Artificers shouldn't have been there.

"Creepy," Jack muttered.

Ashes grimaced and nodded. A familiar scent tickled his nose. He paused, frowned. Something like sour milk—

"I do not recall inviting you into milord's home."

Carapace stood at the midpoint of the hallway, standing perturbingly still. His hands were clasped behind his back, his posture perfect, just as a butler ought to be.

His eyes were fixed on Ashes, and they were dark and pitiless and wild.

"We're not much for invitations," Jack said.

Carapace's gaze shifted to the Weaver. For a moment, he looked puzzled. "I recognize the gamin," he said. "Who are you, sir?"

Jack straightened his back and tilted his head just so, a subtle shift like the ones he had taught Ashes to use. The man appeared, suddenly, more heroic and dashing, brazen and impressive.

"I think you'd know me as Mr. Smoke," he said.

"Oh," Carapace said. "Of course."

There was a rush of air as Carapace moved; in a bare heartbeat, he was standing in front of them, his serene face contorted in rage, his lips drawn back to reveal his teeth, his eyes open so wide

Ashes could see the veins running through them. He drew his hand back to strike Jack—

The Weaver was just as fast. He flicked his fingers, and the room went dull. Brilliant light burst in front of Carapace's eyes—

The butler's fist landed on Jack's chest. The Weaver gasped and flew backward, as if held aloft by some massive, invisible hand that deposited him unceremoniously on the ground, nearly ten feet away. Jack coughed, and flecks of blood flew from his lips.

"Bollocks," he muttered.

*Get away.*

Ashes jerked to the side, trying to get out of reach of Carapace's spindly arms, but the butler was too quick. He grabbed Ashes by the throat and flung him forward, to land in a heap beside Jack.

"You might've mentioned Ragged kept a bloody *stonebreed* in his damn house," Jack snarled.

"What?"

"The poor man's Iron Knight," Jack growled. "Slower, weaker, not quite as difficult to kill. But a Knight of Iron in every other respect. That bastard doesn't even know I tried to blind him just now."

Carapace proceeded calmly toward them, folding his hands behind his back again. His madness wasn't gone; it had only slithered under an old, comfortable mask. Ashes felt a yawning emptiness in his stomach. Carapace had seen through his illusions. How else could Ragged have discovered Mr. Smoke's real identity?

"So do we run?" Ashes asked.

"What? Do I look like the kind of idiot who'd pass up this kind of opportunity?" Jack flashed a wicked grin. "I've been dreaming how I'd fight one of these things for *ages*." The man rolled to his feet and spread his arms. "Come on, then, sir, if you think you have it in you!"

Carapace paused, looking wary for a moment. "You intend to work some sort of trickery," he said.

"Damn right," said the Weaver. Ashes noticed the hallway lights seeming to shrink, the shadows growing grayer, the color leaching out of the world. "You ever fought an Artificer before, my friend? A *real* one?"

"I have not had the pleasure," Carapace said.

"Then that makes two of us who're fresh to the field," Jack said with a wide grin. "I'll try to be gentle."

He thrust his arms down. All the light in the room swirled to his fingers, leaving minuscule white pinpricks in Ragged's alchemical lamps. Ashes heard him grunt with exertion. The Weaver's hands shone like stoked fires, light spurting wildly from his fingertips and oozing from his palms. But it was Woven now, and radiated only a little; despite the absurd quantity of light painted on Jack's hands, Ashes couldn't see past the man's knees. The floor was drowned in darkness.

Carapace chuckled. "I suppose you think yourself terrifically clever."

"I suppose I do."

Jack met Ashes's eyes and jerked his head urgently. Ashes nodded, understanding; Jack would distract Carapace while Ashes moved through the hallway. Without another glance, the Weaver laid a hand on Ashes's shoulder, loosely binding the light to Ashes's skin. The boy took control of it, holding it tightly to himself to preserve Jack's fragile advantage. The floor creaked as Carapace approached. Ashes, carefully, moved forward into the darkness.

"You were very foolish to come here tonight," Carapace said. "It would have been wiser to continue working through your agents, if you intended to survive this scheme."

"Not known for my wisd— Oh, *bugger*—"

The sound that followed was like a minor explosion; Carapace had punched the wall.

"Very good try, friend," Jack taunted. Ashes glanced back; Jack was moving swiftly from one side of the hall to the other, binding the light to the portraits on the wall. It would lighten the burden on his magic, but only by a little; without any aether to act as a solvent, Jack would need to keep the light tied there with his mind.

Apparently, the mental burden didn't concern the Weaver, for as Ashes watched, he stopped, turned, and raised his hands. Light streamed from his fingers, twining through the hallway in a luminous helix. Carapace's silhouette appeared, starkly outlined.

"Gods," Jack said confidently, "it would seem that I'm an experienced, highly skilled natural Artificer and you're a menial handservant. Perhaps you'll need to move a bit *faster*."

Ashes jerked away, hearing Jack's hint for what it was. He peered into the grasping darkness of the hallway, and felt a brief dizziness swim through his head. It was like being underground again, with the aetherlings—

*Stop that*, he told himself. It *wasn't* like that. He had light now.

He had to move faster. Where would Ragged be keeping Jasin and Blimey?

*Bedroom*, he thought immediately. It was the first place Ragged hid everything he thought valuable, as well as the most easily guarded room in the house if the window-locks held. Behind him, he heard Carapace grunt. It was followed by Jack gasping, and then, "Is that really the *best* you have?"

Ashes entered Ragged's room and released the light, letting it burst into the room like a firework. The flash illuminated everything for the barest space of a moment—enough time for Ashes to see Jasin huddled in the corner. He rushed unthinkingly to her side.

"Jasin." The girl stirred, opened her eyes a fraction of an inch. Ashes produced his Artificer's lamp and let the light pour out of it, shading it a soft red—half to wake her gently, and half so that he would not see the colors of her cheeks. "Wake up. We've got to get you out of here."

"Hrr yeh?" the girl slurred. Her voice came mostly from her throat, as if she couldn't bear to part her lips.

"Mr. Smoke sent me," he said, smiling as reassuringly as he could. "Mr. Smoke, Jasin. Get up. We've got to get you out of here while Ragged's away. And I need your help finding my friend."

"S-Smoke?" the girl asked.

*Furies*, Ashes thought. She sounded *raw*, like someone who had screamed too long and too loudly. "That's right," he said gently. "Come on, then, Jasin. The Motleys are outside."

The girl didn't respond. Her eyes were closed. Ashes's heart skipped, but she was still breathing. She had only passed out.

*This is my fault.*

"Don't you worry, Jasin," he said to her. "We'll get you out of here. Ragged won't even know what hit him."

The door to the bathroom opened. Ashes whirled around, feeling his heart leap into his throat.

The man who stepped out was the portrait of a young Lord Edgecombe. He had the same eyes, the same cheekbones, the same smooth dark hair. The cruel cast of his face was one Ashes knew well. It had been burned in his brain for months.

"Just how confident are you of that?" Mr. Ragged asked. "Exactly?"

# 39

# *Invincible*

**A**SHES lunged forward, but Ragged was faster. Ragged slid the glass ring over his finger, and Ashes felt his mind *twist*. Screams erupted in the back of his mind; Ashes felt as if the ceiling were swooping down on him, the walls folding inward to crush him to dust. Ragged stood only a few feet away, but it may as well have been miles for all that it mattered now. The screams in Ashes's head intensified, and he realized they were coming from him.

"Quiet, boy," Ragged said. "Gratifying as it is, I am tired of hearing it."

Ashes's mouth clamped shut, as surely and tightly as if he'd been muzzled. He stared at the Beggar Lord, felt his insides quivering, heard the blood thundering in his ears.

Ragged came close. Ashes flinched away, dreading the man's touch, but not quickly enough. Ragged took his chin in one hand, forced him to look up. The man inspected him dispassionately, like he intended to bring Ashes to a market.

"I'll admit I'm impressed," Ragged said softly. "I thought you'd died some time ago."

Ashes gritted his teeth, trying to force them to stop chattering. "D-didn't take."

"Francis pranced around Burroughside for weeks afterward. He would be so thrilled to see you here now."

*Would be?*

"What did you do to him?" Ragged demanded.

"N-nothing."

"Liar," Ragged said, striking Ashes across the face with a closed fist. His head rang like a struck bell; Ragged had a cosh hidden under his fingers. "What did you do to him?"

"Nothing!" Ashes protested. His head was marvelously clear for just a moment, trading his terror of Ragged for the far less oppressive cloud of pain. "Look, if you're going to kill me—"

"Don't interrupt," Ragged said, unconcerned. "And make no mistake, I *will* kill you. I intend to take my time about it. You did nothing to Francis?"

Ashes shook his head. Ragged leaned close, so they were eye to eye. The pain from Ragged's punch evaporated, crushed to nothing under the weight of Ashes's fear. Ragged searched his eyes, then stepped back.

"Pity," Ragged said. "It seems he was simply stupid, then." He clapped his hands briskly, taking a seat on the bed. "Now then. A brief interrogation is in order today, I think. Is that Mr. Smoke outside?"

"No," Ashes confessed. "I'm him."

"Fascinating." Ragged looked at him with disturbingly bright eyes. "Utterly fascinating."

"W-what've you done—to Blimey? Where is he?"

Ragged raised an eyebrow. "Safely tucked away. I must say, your little . . . agent proved to be a *fountain* of information. It was so generous of you to loan her to me. She had such fascinating thoughts." Ragged strode to his bedside table and unlocked the third drawer. Ashes heard the clinking of bottles. Ragged withdrew a thin phial of frosted glass; Ashes couldn't have guessed what was within it. "She seemed to be under the impression that Mr. Smoke had maneuvered me into the most elegant of traps, and I was imminently doomed. Her theory about my alliance with Bonnie the Lass was *most* intriguing." Ragged smiled wickedly. "I'll admit you won that little battle. I'd wanted to let Bonnie putter around a few more months, but you forced my hand. I imagine it's something of a comfort to think that your little mischiefs have inconvenienced me." Ragged smiled coldly. "Have you visited the crater yet, where the ugly bitch used to live? I burned it down to nothing, because of you. *Well* done."

There was a crash outside, and Jack's voice screaming exultantly, "Didn't expect *that*, did you, you bastard?"

Hardly a moment later light streamed through the crack at the bottom of the door. Something slammed against it once, twice, and on the third time the door crashed open. Jack stepped through, awash in Artifice, light streaming from his palms and his eyes. His magic oozed off him like heat from a fire.

"It wasn't locked," Ragged said calmly, not looking at him.

"I've always gotten a sort of perverse pleasure in kicking doors down," Jack said. "It's so much more dram— Oh, *bugger*."

The Weaver fell to his knees as Ragged faced him. The Beggar Lord smiled.

"Again—I'm impressed," Ragged said. "You did well for yourself, boy. Turning a fully licensed Artificer into your personal bodyguard must have taken quite some time."

"Holy . . . *damn*," Jack gasped.

Ashes shook violently, feeling tears well up in his throat. There was no way out. No one knew they were here. Their Artifice did them as much good as pebbles thrown at a knight.

"Present from my father," Ragged said proudly, letting the

glass ring flash in the light from the hallway. "Whom you've both met by this point, I'm sure. He seemed to think you were in his custody, Ashes."

Ashes gritted his teeth. "I'm flattered," he spat, feeling a tiny burst of control come back. Mocking Ragged combatted the fear, just a little. If his mind were a carriage, at least he had a grip on the reins, even if the horses had gone mad.

"Bold words." The Beggar Lord turned on one of the lamps, suffusing the room in a soft glow. "You, Artificer. What did you do to my butler?"

"Sent him home pissing himself," Jack snarled. "With all due respect."

"Mm," Ragged said. "That cannot have come without cost."

Jack let out a harsh, forced laugh. "I took some blood out of him, too."

"How droll," Ragged said. He nudged Ashes's ribs with a toe. "Hear that, boy? You've damaged *two* of my servants. That's an accomplishment. You should be very proud. You've made the most of quite a short life."

Ragged swirled the liquid in the phial, holding it so the light streamed through it. The liquid inside seemed to swallow the light entirely, leaving nothing to escape to the other side. "I'll admit, Ashes, that you've proved a more engaging diversion than I could ever have imagined. It's a poor precedent to set, killing your entertainment, but . . ." He shrugged. "Cost of doing business, I suppose."

Jack met Ashes's eyes. The boy shivered. The look in Jack's eyes was as unsettling as Ragged's magic; Candlestick Jack was *scared*. Not broken, not yet. But it would not be long. The light he had wrapped around himself had all but dissipated, leaving him mundane and unremarkable. Candlestick Jack, laid low.

*Traitor. Failure. Fraud.*

Jack's eyes narrowed slightly—a look not of mistrust but

fascination. He searched Ashes's face, pressed his teeth together, and forced out a laugh.

Ragged looked at the man, politely confused. "That is an uncommon reaction," the man said.

"Not surprised," Jack said. "Do you know, Mr. Ragged, I think you might've overestimated yourself. My friend here's got something of a talent for misdirection. You ask me, he's not the one who's walked into a trap."

Ashes stared at Jack, dumbfounded. Had he lost his wits already—broken under the mental strain? It was all Ashes could do to keep himself from screaming. But Jack had always seemed so strong . . .

"I think that if he wanted to," Jack went on, "Ashes could take this absurd little charade—this illusion of yours, and he could make it disappear. *Poof*. Isn't that right, lad?"

Ragged glanced at Ashes, a faint wariness playing behind his eyes. Ashes felt his insides quiver. It was the look he'd sworn to see on Ragged's face again, one that said he didn't know everything, that there were events outside his control. Ashes should have felt triumph. There ought to have been an exultant surge, some feeling that he'd snatched the advantage away . . .

"He does it all the time with cards," Jack said, sounding more desperate with every word. "Cheating bastard, him. He can look at something and make it vanish."

The word tickled something buried in his memory. The word Tuln had used for the last breed of Artisans. The Unmakers. The *Vanishers*.

*Their magic changes from story to story. In some they render themselves invisible . . . They turn away armies with a wave of their hands. They once wiped out a city for daring to ask their help in a war.*

"You've truly gone mad," Ragged said, sounding both fascinated and deeply amused. "What a delightful little surprise. You'll be great fun, I think."

*Anyone who refuses to bow for a passing Ivory was to be hanged pub-*
*licly. I thought it was like someone writing a law that any rock that didn't*
*fall to the ground was to be sentenced to death . . .*

"Now for you, Ashes." Ragged unstoppered the phial and
sniffed the liquid inside. "Given your new taste in company, I'm
sure you're familiar with the properties of aether."

*That boy is no canted Stitcher.*

*What is like an Artificer, but not? He sees through glass.*

"Lie down, Ashes. And open your mouth. I expect this will
hurt."

The room lightened a shade; it was dawn. The glass ring caught
the light coming in from the window, and it turned briefly into a
circle of pale flame. Looking at it filled him with dread and revul-
sion, a total certainty of his own helplessness. Ragged was holding
all the cards here, and Ashes had nothing to play—

*He asked me why we were all so enraptured. He didn't understand.*

*Artifice is about more than manipulating light. Artifice deals with*
perception. *And Ivories do that.*

Ashes looked at the ring again. A charade. An illusion.

"Glamour," he whispered.

Ragged twitched. "What did you say, boy?"

*It's all the same magic. Making people love you and making them fear*
*you, it's all the same, it's all changing perception. And I—I—*

"I can see through glass."

Ragged stared at him. His expression shifted to one of profound disappointment. "Damn it all," he muttered. "You're *much*
less interesting with your sanity gone."

*I could see through Lord Edgecombe's glass ring at his party. Why*
*can't I see through this?*

He knew the answer at once. *Because Ragged makes me afraid.*

He wasn't willing to bow to an Ivory. Ragged was another
story altogether. He feared Ragged. He always had. The ring's
magic found a foothold in him because he was *willing* to be afraid.

"That's ridiculous," Ashes said aloud.

"I'll have to make do," Ragged said. "Get on your *back*, boy."

"No," Ashes said, looking at the man. He felt the pull of the ring at every side of his mind, felt the overwhelming pressure to submit. He refused. "No, Ragged. I won't."

He stood, slowly, fighting the Glamour every moment. He felt its weight on his shoulders, and he pushed back.

"What the *hell* are you doing, boy?"

"Changing the game," Ashes said. "See, you need me to be afraid of you. And I'm not. I've got no reason to be."

Ragged chuckled. "You're a good liar." He flourished the knife, still wet with Ashes's blood. "Get on the floor and you have my word it'll be quick." He smirked. "Or at least *quicker*."

"You're not understanding me, Hiram," Ashes told him, his voice strengthening with every word. "I'm a gutter-rat of Burroughside. I'm *fearless*."

There was a faintest shadow of uncertainty in Ragged's eyes. Ashes smiled viciously. *Now I've seen that from you twice in a night.*

The Beggar Lord's confidence came back all at once, and he lunged with the knife. Ragged was relatively young and in good health, but Ashes could see in a glimpse that the man had never really fought. He slashed with elegant precision, expecting Ashes to flinch back. It would give Ragged a slender advantage, enough for him to slide the steel between Ashes's ribs.

Ashes read the move in the twitch of the man's muscles. He was quick enough to get away, probably, but even now the glass ring made his body treacherous. He didn't dare trust it. And knives were useless at a distance. Ragged would have to get very *close*—

It all went through his head in a flicker. Ashes leaned forward and twisted at the waist, and Ragged's knife went through his shoulder. The metal bit into him, pain bright and sharp as a lit match in a lightless room. The cloud around his mind broke for just a moment.

"I am Mr. bloody *Smoke*," he snarled, and lunged forward. He caught Ragged's hand with both of his and, unthinking, shoved the man's fingers into his mouth. He felt the cool glass against his teeth, and clenched his jaw.

Ragged screamed. Warm blood burst into Ashes's mouth, and shards of glass. The jagged edges cut his mouth, his tongue. Ragged yanked his hand back, howling, swearing: a wretched gash lay across his ring finger, halfway through to the bone. Ashes spat a bloody glob on the floor and smiled widely, letting the dawn light dance over his red smile.

"Am I still entertaining?"

"I'll *kill you*—"

Jack rose up behind the man, grabbed him by the throat, and threw him to the ground. Ragged thrashed briefly, and the Weaver lay a foot heavily on his chest.

"You know it's possible," Jack said in a low growl, "to kick someone's skull hard enough that their brain *bursts*? Like an overripe plum. So I'm going to recommend that you act very, *very* nice to me."

"I will see you gutted like a *pig*," Ragged swore.

Jack looked at him judiciously, then pulled a clear glass phial from within his jacket. This he dropped to the ground, where the glass shattered. Clear liquid splashed on Ragged's face. The man started screaming again, clawing at Jack's leg with both his hands, heedless of the bloody mess his finger had become.

"That *wasn't* very nice," Jack said levelly.

Ragged stopped thrashing. He lay perfectly still.

"Face of Kindness," Ashes said. "You killed him."

Jack laughed harshly. "I doubt it, unless he's got quite an obscure allergy. Very swift, very *localized* anesthetic. He'll wake in a few hours with perhaps the most terrific headache of his life."

Ashes nodded woozily. With the haze of Ragged's ring gone, he was becoming much more aware of the blood seeping out of his shoulder, and the bruises and cuts he'd earned tonight.

"Glad you cottoned to those clues I was throwing out," Jack said. "Took your bloody time about it, though."

"You couldn't have just *told* me?"

"You wouldn't have believed me," Jack said plainly. "Hell, you'd've seen some kind of trap and run off."

Ashes scowled, and failed to find a counterargument; most of his mental processes seemed to be rusting over with every passing moment. "What'll we do with him?" he asked.

"Lord Trevilian's police will be *delighted* to take him under their roof, I expect," Jack said, nudging Ragged's unconscious body to make certain the man was asleep. "Particularly since he'll have so many letters recommending him so highly. His father's will bear quite a lot of weight."

Ashes looked at him quizzically. Jack gave a wicked smile. "The Ivory Lords are expressly forbidden from interfering in the business of other districts. Installing your son as governor in the next neighborhood over would be frowned upon. Severely."

Ashes looked at the sleeping form of Mr. Ragged, and imagined him spending the rest of his days in a cell. He nodded, unsmiling. "Good."

● ● ●

*They left Ragged House* an hour later. Jasin hobbled along beside them. She was hardly recognizable, covered as she was in bruises, cuts, and burns. The most noticeable difference was in her demeanor. She moved slowly, but her eyes never stopped flicking from side to side. The brazen girl who'd defied Mr. Ragged was long gone. Ragged had removed her, with almost surgical skill, in less than two days' time.

Mr. Ragged was even more unrecognizable. Ashes had colored the man's face a thick shade of brown, torn and shredded his fine clothing, and Stitched horrendous-looking scars and welts over

every visible portion of his body. It was a necessary lie; he didn't
dare let Burroughside see Ragged helpless. They would kill him,
and the Ivories would not take the offense lightly. Better to avoid
the whole thing.

That was how Ashes found himself helping Jack carry Ragged
through the streets like a tragic martyr, with Mr. Smoke's most
vocal supporter limping quietly beside him. Ashes couldn't focus
on either fact. He couldn't even bring himself to care about the
merciless flashes of pain that accompanied his every step.

Blimey had not been in Ragged House. They had searched it
twice over, looked in every room, opened every door and cabinet
and closet. Jack had looked it over with his seeing-stone, and found
no hidden passages or false walls. He had admitted, too, that the
architecture of Ragged House didn't lend itself to the intricacies
his shop made use of.

It hadn't come as a surprise. The truth had struck Ashes well
before they'd found Jasin: Ragged hadn't known Mr. Smoke's real
identity until Ashes arrived on his doorstep. He hadn't tracked
Blimey down, or captured him. His friend was simply gone.

*Vanished*, he thought bitterly.

It was a small comfort to think that Ragged would rot in a
prison cell for the rest of his life. Even Lord Edgecombe's funds
couldn't prevent that, so long as Lord Trevilian found out about
it first. The Lord Premier's judgment would take priority. Courtesy of the documents Jack had tucked in his coat pocket, Ragged's
secret would soon see him to the inside of a tightly barred cell.
Ashes could feel pride, once he stopped feeling ashamed.

They were halfway to Lyonshire when Jasin stopped and looked
at them. "I'll be going now." Her voice was raw and cracked.

Ashes nodded. "Mr. Smoke told me he's—he's sorry for what
happened to you," Ashes told her. "Really sorry."

Jasin met his eyes and smiled weakly. "Course he is. He's sorry for lots of things, I reckon. Sorry he involved us. Sorry we got caught. Sorry some of us got hurt."

"All those things," Ashes said. "I think he—he wishes he could've done it different. Better."

"Everybody does, eventually." Jasin shrugged. "I'm sure he'll blub awhile. But . . . well, there's nothing comes for free, is there? Tell him that. When you see him." She stepped forward and gave him an awkward, unexpected hug. Surprised, Ashes hugged her back. After a moment, she released him, and limped away without looking back.

"You found yourself quite a disciple, Ashes," Jack said.

Ashes rounded on him, something monstrous rising up in his chest. "Don't," he snarled. "Don't joke about her."

"I wasn't."

"Well—good," Ashes said. The girl had already disappeared into the twisting, slimy maze of ruinous streets. Burroughside had taken her back. "She deserved better."

Jack shrugged. "Perhaps. But she didn't seem disappointed to me."

● ● ●

*The Weaver and his* apprentice brought Hiram Ragged to the Lyonshire police and left him there, after explaining how they'd found him drunk and babbling in the gutters that morning on the way to their work. The police had no reason to disbelieve, and wouldn't, until the construct they had foisted on him dissipated—revealing the face of Burroughside's governor and a pile of solicitations, debts, blackmail, and incriminating documents in his pockets, all marked with Lord Edgecombe's personal seal. They must have thought themselves very clever.

Their construct did not fool the woman standing across the

street. Lord Edgecombe had sent her the moment he realized the whelp had escaped. As insurance, he had said. A precaution.

She had not needed to clarify his meaning.

When the Artificer and the boy were out of sight, she approached the watch-house boldly and entered by the front door. The man at the desk inside recognized her immediately.

"Madam," he said, leaping to his feet and snapping out a hasty salute. "Is there anything—?"

"No," she said curtly. "Be about your business."

The man obeyed with admirable swiftness. She did not smile—though it was tempting—and strode briskly toward the holding cells.

Hiram Ragged, the most significant in a long string of her master's youthful indiscretions, lay motionless on the stone floor of a cell. She did not have the patience to let him wake gently. She reached through the bars and slapped him.

Ragged's eyes opened slowly. He sat up.

"So he sent you," he said.

"Your father is a man of his word," she murmured. "These days, at least."

"My efforts did not sway him, then."

"Is your memory clouded, Hiram? I seem to recall him saying the only way to atone for your brothers' blood was to succeed in this."

"I needed more time," Hiram said. "Better resources. Better opportunities."

"Luxuries," the woman spat. "Advantages you did not earn."

"I earned them!"

"Slaughtering your kin when they are hardly old enough to walk does not constitute *earning*, Hiram," she said venomously. "Would that one of them had lived, instead of you."

"They were nothing," Ragged snarled, his eyes going wild. "*I* should have grown up in that house. I proved it. I even fooled *you*."

"No longer," she said. "You cost milord two heirs. I will not pretend to be disappointed that this task fell to me."

She left a minute later, her lord's letters stowed safely in her coat. Ragged screamed and swore at her from his cell, though she paid him no mind. His screams stopped all at once. By the time she reached the door, Hiram Ragged was dead.

# 40

# Lineage

"O H. Hello."

"Hello, Syn," Ashes said, settling onto the bench beside her.

She gave no further response, but the construct in front of her—a delicate crystalline swan the size of Ashes's hand—began to flux brighter, and the light around Synder took on a gray tinge.

"Syn," Ashes began, "look, I don't know how to start this, but I'm sorry. I shouldn't've snapped at you."

The miniature swan flickered, turning briefly red. "You're not wrong," Synder said, voice tight.

"I was just . . ." Ashes swallowed. "Look, I don't have a good excuse. And I'm sorry."

Synder said nothing as she Wove more light into the construct. Ashes bit his tongue, uncertain if he should press on.

A minute passed. Two. The swan under Synder's fingers became more defined and detailed.

Synder felt no burden to continue the conversation, then. "I need to ask you something," Ashes said.

"I thought you might," Synder said softly.

"It's about Blimey. He's gone."

"Yes."

"You don't seem surprised."

"That's because I'm not," Synder said. "He told me."

Anger ignited in Ashes's chest. "And you didn't think to tell me?" he said, voice tight.

"I came to tell you right away," Synder said coolly. "But, if I recall, you didn't want me to say another word. I'd said enough, apparently."

The hot anger went out in an instant, replaced with the feeling of ice in his belly. "You were trying to tell me then."

"Correct," Synder said.

"Did you try to stop him?"

"He was already gone by the time I found out," Synder said. "I went to Annie's that night to talk to him. About what you'd said, about what I'd said. I didn't want to get between you."

"Then how—"

"He left a note," Synder went on, sliding a folded slip of paper out of her pocket. "Two of them, actually. One for me, one for you."

She handed it to him. It was torn at the edges. Blimey must have ripped it out of one of his books. Ashes's hunched over it as he laid it flat against the table. He mouthed the words silently to himself.

*Ashes,*

*I'm sorry to tell you this way, but I didn't think I'd be able to do it in person. I'm leaving.*

*I don't want you to think it's because I'm angry. I'm not— well, I am a little. But that's not why. I've discovered something about myself. Something important, I think. I want to learn more about it, and I can't do that here.*

*You kept me safe when no one else could, or would. Thank you for that.*

Blimey

Ashes bit his lip.

"Have you read this?" he asked.

"Of course not," Synder said. "It's private."

"Did he tell you anything? Why he left?"

"Nothing at all specific," Synder said, pursing her lips. "That he'd found something out and wanted to know more."

"I've got to—"

"No, you haven't got to do anything," Synder said firmly. She set the construct on the worktable and bound it to one of the temporary Anchors. "I don't think he wants to be followed, Ashes. He's clever enough to cover his tracks, too. Annie didn't even know that he'd left." She looked at him ruefully. "And Teranis isn't small."

Ashes's jaw clenched. "He should've stayed. Should've talked with me about it."

"I don't think that's true," Synder said. "You don't know him like you think you do, Ashes."

Ashes's cheeks grew hot. "I—"

"I'm not trying to insult you," she said wearily. "I'm not even trying to say that you mistreated him. You sacrificed for Nathaniel. You were his friend when he needed it. But—I think he was tired of being told he wasn't allowed to *do* anything. You weren't the only ambitious one living in Annie's basement, you know?"

"So you're saying you think he should've left," Ashes said. His words were clipped, curt.

"No," she said. "Not necessarily. I think he's in danger outside. I think there's a chance he could get hurt. But . . . I understand why he left. I understand why he would want to test himself without you being there to catch him."

Ashes looked away from her. He felt betrayed. Misunderstood.

Blimey *couldn't* survive out in the world; that was why Ashes took him in in the first place.

"He's more capable than you give him credit for," Synder said gently. "You'll be surprised."

*No I won't*, Ashes thought, but instead he nodded. "Eh," he said. "Maybe I will be."

They both looked up at the sound of footsteps on the stairs, and a moment later Candlestick Jack swept into the workshop, looking as handsome and confident as ever. He showed no sign of having fought off a stonebreed. The first stop he and Ashes had made on the way home had been to a witch on Rasping Way, whom Jack had visited before. The crone's fees had been just as absurd as Jack predicted, but the Weaver paid it without blinking. Ashes's shoulder itched fiercely, and his legs searched eagerly for ways to betray him, but that was the worst of it.

"Evening, Jack," Synder said brightly. "I hear you've been having adventures without me. I'm pretty sure that's a breach of contract."

Jack lifted an eyebrow. "I'm sure we'll find time to address that later. Aren't you behind deadline for that little bird?"

"I would be if I Wove as slowly as you do."

"Ha very ha," Jack said. His eyes fell on Ashes. In the months Ashes had known him, the Artificer had never looked so solemn. "Ashes, I think I owe you a drink. A drink and a long talk."

● ● ●

*"If you have questions,* now's the time." Jack set two beers at the table, then seated himself directly opposite Ashes. He looked remarkably relaxed. Ashes, for his part, felt remarkably small here, surrounded by surly men whose primary mode of communication seemed to be subvocal grunts. The Iron Barrel was sparsely populated at this hour of the night, and the people sitting here seemed more than content to keep themselves to themselves.

"When did you figure it out?" Ashes asked. "About me. And the . . . what I can do."

"Wrong question," Jack said. "I figured it out when you told Ragged to go to hell and near bit his finger off. But I've suspected it ever since you beat me at cards."

Ashes stared at him flatly. "You figured I had magic that hasn't been seen in centuries because I *beat you* at *cards*?" he asked quietly.

"I've never really struggled with self-esteem," Jack said with a wink. "Nothing short of eldritch power can keep me off my game."

Ashes's brow furrowed. "But I could Stitch without being—" He paused. "You bastard. You tuned me that first day, didn't you? You Stitched my face and it tuned me."

"Guilty," Jack admitted. "Sloppy of me, if I wanted to make certain you were a Glamourist, but I couldn't afford to let you think I'd swindled you somehow. You needed to believe you were an Artificer."

"Why'd you keep it a secret from me?"

Jack took a slow drink. "Before I answer that, there're things you've got to understand about Artifice. About the Artisans." Jack gazed into his cup for a moment, as if staring into a magic mirror. At last, he said, "Glamour's old magic, lad. Older and more powerful than what I can do on my best day. But it's also . . . mysterious. Tricky. It's difficult to nail down, because—"

"Because it's mind magic," Ashes interrupted.

Jack's eyebrow peaked. "Have you been cheating?"

"It was something Synder said a while ago," Ashes said. "Artifice isn't just about light. Elsewise, why would Stitchers and Weavers be any different? They don't just change light. They're changing how people see the world. Weaving's the obvious one, just putting light in different places so it looks changed. Like putting a mask on. Stitching changes—I think Stitching changes *you*, only it's not real. It just looks like you're manipulating the light." Ashes bit his lip. "And the only other way I could think to change the way something looks is to change the way people see it."

Jack looked at him for several moments. "That's quite a leap."

"It was the only thing that made sense," Ashes said, shrugging. "Tuln told me the Glamourists had weird magic. That they did lots of different things, like turn whole armies away and turn invisible and destroy a whole city. But it didn't make sense if they just . . . *unmade* things. And—and I thought that sounded like a card trick."

"Blood and bone," Jack said, laughing. "Of *course* you'd think it's like cards."

Ashes stuck his tongue out at the man. "It is! You can make someone believe anything if you know where they're looking. If you wanted to turn a whole army away, or be invisible, or destroy a city that asked for your help, you could do it all with the same trick. You make the army believe there's no reason to go to war. You make the people around you believe you're not really there. And the city." He grinned, excited despite himself. "If a city asked your help beating invaders, you make the invaders believe the city's not there anymore. You don't leave any trace it existed in the first place."

"Damn," Jack said, leaning back. "You cottoned to that rather fast."

"Course I did," Ashes said. "You set me up to."

Jack nodded ruefully. "In my defense, *I* had to find the relevant information all on my own. When I was younger, Tuln and I spent quite a bit of time researching the old powers. He's wanted to know more about them for *years*. But all the best books are squirreled away in one fat Ivory's basement or another, and few of them are book-lenders, so . . . ."

"So you found ways around that," Ashes said.

"The Artisans had . . . power. Real, inescapable magic. Their magic made them gods. And their descendants—Will and me, and the other canted Stitchers and Weavers like us—do just what they did. Only it's weakened. Imaginary. They made real things out of nothing, and we make unreal things out of light. We figured that if the Glamourists still existed—"

"They'd do what the Vanishers could do, only illusionary," Ashes said. "But the Glamourists already used illusions. Just a different kind. So . . . what happens to the illusion magic when all the magic becomes an illusion?"

"That's where I ran into problems," Jack said. He grabbed a handful of light reflexively, looked around, and let the light disperse. "If I had to guess, it didn't change their magic much at all, and that's the reason the Queens had almost all the Glamourists slaughtered after the Chiming War. They had no other way to keep them under control."

"*Almost* all the Glamourists?" Ashes asked.

"Oh, come, now, lad," Jack said. "Those glass rings are packed full of Glamour-magic. And I can guarantee you're not the first to destroy one." He grinned. "Although you might be the first to have done it with your teeth."

"They're making new ones," Ashes realized aloud. "They have a Glamourist imprisoned with them."

"My thoughts precisely," Jack said. "A whole line of Glamourists, more than likely. No doubt they've been breeding them to keep their supply constant." Jack looked into his mug. "The magic you have, Ashes, is remarkable. Unprecedented, maybe. You're the first of your kind we've seen in generations." He still did not meet Ashes's eyes, as though he could find answers swirling in his drink. "But I do know this: Glamour could well be the strongest magic still living in Teranis. But it's incredibly volatile. Fragile in some cases, explosive in others. I feared that if I took too much of a hand in developing your gifts, I might render them useless. That, and I didn't dare frighten you away."

It was Ashes's turn to start examining the insides of his cup. "You were right about that," he said eventually. "I think I would have thought it was a trap."

"I'm not proud of doing it," Jack said. He sounded sincere. "But I can guarantee you it was necessary. Keeping you nearby, and keeping you safe . . . that could have very far-reaching consequences. You could change the course of this city."

"Sounds like you don't want me to struggle with self-esteem, either," Ashes said.

"I'm being quite serious, lad," Jack said. He leaned forward. "You're *rasa*. You woke up in Lyonshire one day with soot all over your face and no memory of who you were, where you came from. And now we come to find out you wield one of Teranis's oldest magics. You're an important mystery, and one I mean to solve."

Ashes stared at him skeptically. "You're making this sound very important, Jack," he said. "Last I checked, we're just thieves."

"Artificers, too."

"So really *good* thieves."

Jack smiled wearily. "I'll try not to overdramatize, then," he said. "I think, between the two of us, we could turn this city upside-down. More than just stealing from Ivories. I think we could change the course of history."

"You're overdramatizing," Ashes said.

"I'm really not," Jack said. "I can't think of anyone better suited to accomplish something extraordinary. I want you to join my company."

"Jack, I—"

"I know you're worried about your friend. We'll help you look for him, of course. But after that—I want to work together. I want to be there when you change the world." He thrust out a hand. "What do you say, lad? Do we have a deal?"

Ashes hesitated. Then he smiled and shook the Artificer's hand once, firmly. "Eh. I think we do."

# Acknowledgments

O**H, WOW.**

I've read a fair quantity of acknowledgments pages, and it seems like every author starts off with, "There are so many people to thank!" and that always came off as disingenuous to me—like they were just covering their backs to make sure no one cropped up later to demand gratitude.

And wow, was I wrong. There are, in fact, way more people deserving of thanks than would fit in this space. And it'd just look like a really long list, anyway.

Thanks to Kelsey, without whom there would be no book. She has endured long stretches of me being not-particularly-husbandly so I could finish this project. She was *the* support system when I didn't think I could finish. It's terribly cliché to say these things, but that does not make them any less true.

Thanks to my parents, without whom there would be no me. There would certainly be no me-who-could-write. They were the ones who indulged my arty habits, so my career as a writer is mostly their fault.

Thanks to Sophia, who put up with something like thirteen missed deadlines and still believed in *The Facefaker's Game*, and in me.

Thanks to Amanda, who knows all the weird details about publishing and keeps me from making stupid decisions.

Now we've come to the really huge list of names. Thanks to every one of the beta readers (Nathan, Amy, Chelsea, Meredith, and Kyle), who have been thoughtful and gentle and more helpful than they can possibly imagine, though they have very big imaginations. Thanks to the many teachers who have sharpened me as a person and a writer. Thanks in particular to Aaron, who would, I think, hate having his whole title written out here (despite it being an impressive title).

Thanks to Mrs. Hoffarth. I wish I'd finished this in time for you to read it.

There are more, and I'll feel very silly in a few months when I remember all their names. Thank you, anonymous crowd of benefactors, for the many ways you've changed, shaped, and taught me.

Here's to fooling everyone who'll believe us, and fooling everyone else.

# About the Author

Chandler J. Birch grew up ignoring the Rocky Mountains in favor of Middle Earth, Narnia, and Temerant. He lives in Colorado Springs with his wife, Kelsey, and their two dogs, Winter and Bandit. This is his first novel.